Butcher Bird

Other books by Richard Kadrey:

Angel Scene
Kamikaze L'Amour
Metrophage
The Covert Culture Sourcebook, Volumes 1 & 2
From Myst to Riven

NIGHT SHADE BOOKS
SAN FRANCISCO

Second Printing

ISBN 978-1-59780-086-0

Night Shade Books
Please visit us on the web at
http://www.nightshadebooks.com

For N, with love

"This whole world's wild at heart and weird on top."
— Barry Gifford, *Wild at Heart*

ONE
AUTO-DA-FÉ

"They say that when your head gets chopped off, it can still see and hear for a few seconds, so I'll have to go with beheading," said Spyder Lee to Lulu Garou.

Spyder Lee was drinking shots of Patrón Añejo tequila with Lulu, his business partner, at the Bardo Lounge just off Market Street in San Francisco.

Lulu looked into her empty glass and thought for some time, took a drag off her Marlboro Light and winked at the woman tending bar. "Being beaten to death," said Lulu. "Badly. I don't mean like with a baseball bat or rebar so you're out cold, but something small." She crushed out her Marlboro in the ashtray the bartender slid in front of her. "An eight ball in a sweat sock. That'd give your killer a good workout."

"Not if the guy hit you in the head right off," said Spyder.

"My mama was pretty free with her hands. I'm a faster ducker," Lulu replied. She grinned. Spyder could tell she was unimpressed with his argument.

"Burning at the stake," he said.

"Drawn and quartered," Lulu countered.

Rubi, the bartender, took their empty glasses away. "Exactly what are you two rattling about?"

"Worst ways to die," said Spyder. "Being covered in honey and staked out on a red ant hill."

"Dying of thirst. Like right now," said Lulu.

Rubi slid her hand across the bar and took hold of Lulu's left pinkie. "You parched, baby?"

"I'm drier than Candy Darling's cunt."

"Candy Darling was a man," said Spyder.

"Exactly."

Rubi leaned forward and kissed Lulu's pinkie. "I'll get you both another round. On me." As she left to make their drinks, Lulu called after her, "That ain't all that's gonna be on you tonight." Rubi stuck her tongue out at Lulu.

"Being crucified. That's supposed to be horrible," said Spyder.

"You're only saying that 'cause that's how they talk about it in movies. You ever known anyone who was crucified? Or even heard of one? Hell no. Maybe being crucified is great. Maybe it's a fucking hoot. Maybe it's a blow job and ice cream on your birthday." Lulu took out another Marlboro Light and lit it with a pink fur Zippo. "Know what would really suck? Being force fed a bucket full of black widows."

Spyder made a face, half frown and half smile. "Jesus, girl," he said. "You're upping the ante on me."

It was the end of another day at the tattoo studio and piercing parlor Spyder and Lulu ran together. Spyder did the ink while Lulu handled the metal. It was a pleasant business. It let them both pretend to be artists while making money and getting a lot of tail on the side. Rubi, for instance, had been one of Lulu's earliest and most regular customers.

"She's got about five pounds of me on her at all times," Lulu liked to tell friends.

Rubi brought back their drinks and set them on the bar. "What time you getting off tonight?" asked Lulu.

"Early," said Rubi. "'Bout an hour."

"Sweet."

"Being eaten alive, *Night of the Living Dead*-style," said Spyder.

Lulu turned to him. "You mind? We're having a moment here."

"Wait, better than that," Spyder went on. "Being starved to death, but given topical anesthetic and surgical equipment, so the only way you could stay alive'd be to amputate your own limbs and eat them."

Rubi said, "You two ought to get married. Move into the Bates Motel." She went down the bar to serve other customers.

"Now you ruined our surprise," Spyder called after her.

Lulu took a long pull on her tequila. "Flayed alive and drowned in pickle brine."

Spyder looked at his hands. The back of one was covered in an intricate black tribal snake pattern while the other hand sported a cartoon red sacred heart. MANS RUIN was tattooed across the knuckles of both hands. He'd gotten the letters while doing a year in reform school for car theft. They were bullshit tats. Kid stuff. But they marked a period of his life, so he never bothered to have them lasered off. From his neck to the tops of his feet, Spyder Lee was an explosion of images and pigments.

He'd never felt normal until he'd been tattooed for the first time. The ink felt like some kind of magic armor. His tattoos, even the stupid ones, made him feel bulletproof.

He was one of those lanky Texas boys you see working on cars in oil-stained driveways, a cooler full of Coors, his only concession to the summer heat. A perpetually messy mop of black hair and long arms covered in grease working on the transmission of a vintage Mustang of questionable ownership.

"Split open, your organs torn out with hooks and replaced with red hot coals," he said.

Lulu leaned in close. "Strapped to the front of a burning boat and driven through a mile and a half of electrified razorwire in a Tabasco sauce hurricane."

They both broke up in drunken laughter, spitting and slamming their hands on the bar.

"You're both wrong," said a woman sitting to Spyder's right. He and Lulu turned to look at the woman. She was small, with fine features and the smooth grace of a dancer. The woman was drinking red wine and wearing sunglasses. In her right hand she held a white cane, the sort used by the blind.

Lulu called over Spyder's shoulder, "Okay Ray Charles, what's the worst way to die?"

The woman finished her wine and stood up. "To be betrayed by the one you love."

She turned on her heels and, swinging her cane in small arcs in front of her, pushed her way through the crowd and out of the bar.

Spyder watched the door as it closed behind the woman. Lulu took a drag off her Marlboro. "Stupid bitch," she said, and dropped the butt into the woman's empty wine glass.

TWO
THE GREAT DIVIDE

The Earth was born in a furnace. When the world grew strong enough, it crawled into the dark void to cool and heal itself. Soon, however, it grew too cold and shivered with ice.

The Earth looked around and found a small star to warm it up. Deciding it liked the neighborhood and the climate, there the Earth stayed.

Life appeared across the Earth, splashed in the water and glided on thermals through the sky. It didn't take life long to grow so abundant that it began preying on itself.

Crows, bats and eagles, the lords of the air, scooped up fish from the seas and dumped them in the desert until the dry lands were piled high with their bones. These carcasses became the Earth's first mountains.

Other animals learned to climb the trees and attack the birds as they hunted for food. The land dwellers decorated the bare trees with the birds' feathers and painted the ground with their blood. The gray earth suddenly had color.

Every creature who lived in the sea—the fish, the whales, the seals, the crabs, the squids and the rays—met in the South Seas and beat their fins, claws and tentacles, and raised an enormous tidal wave. The wall of water shot across the earth, drowning millions of the land and air beasts. This is how the many rivers and oceans of the world were born.

After an eon or two of mass murder, when the surface of the Earth was a stinking slaughterhouse, the lords of the different realms of life met at the ancient human city of Thulamela to see if they could end the butchery. This wasn't all that simple, since the many different creatures of the Earth were going to have to live on the same planet, but give each other plenty of room.

They divided the world into three Spheres, with each Sphere being invisible and out of the reach of the others. Humans and the most numerous animals of the land, sea and air were given one Sphere.

4

A Second Sphere was home to the rarest creatures—the phoenix, selkies, vampires, barbegazi, corrigans, tengus, lamias, rompos, sylphs, gorgons, volkhs, wyverns, trolls and other exotic beasts.

The last realm was left to the most glorious and dangerous inhabitants of the planet: angels and demons.

So it was that each of these groups lived and grew old and died in its own Sphere, inhabiting the same time and space as all the other Spheres, but rarely touching—unless a creature was powerful or clever enough to learn the spells of crossing over. Because the town meeting that divided the world had taken place in a human city, cities became the places where the creatures who moved from Sphere to Sphere would meet up to talk, joke, eat, exchange spells and news, make love or commit the occasional genocide.

Over the next few thousand centuries, the creatures who dwelled in the second and Third Spheres struck a kind of détente. Unfortunately for the beasts in the First Sphere (which included ninety-nine percent of humanity), they forgot about the other Spheres completely and only glimpsed them in their dreams.

Or so they thought.

THREE

STRANGE ATTRACTORS

Later, Spyder went out the back and into the alley behind the Bardo Lounge for a quick piss.

It wasn't Spyder's habit to urinate in public, but at the best of times the Lounge's toilets were questionable. Sometime during the day, Rubi told him, they had committed hara-kiri. "One summer during college I was trekking in Nepal," Rubi said. "First night out we came to this little village and I asked this lady who ran the local teahouse where the toilets were. In Nepali she said, essentially, 'Anywhere but here,' and pointed to an open field."

As Spyder unzipped in the alley, he considered the club's name and wondered if the real afterlife would be at all like this. A tab at your favorite bar. Pretty girls to chat up. The occasional piss in an alley next to God's own dumpster. It didn't seem like the afterlife would be too bad a place. Spyder wondered who the bouncer in the Bardo Realm would be. The Black Bhairab, he decided. Shiva's most wrathful form. The six-armed, crown-of-skulls-wearing Mad Max of the afterlife.

Spyder zipped up and turned to reenter the club. Like a bad dream, the Black Bhairab was right there beside him. Something big enough, strong enough and wild enough to be the Black Bhairab, though Spyder knew that these qualities were also present in many of your dedicated crackheads. This particular crackhead grabbed Spyder by the front of his shirt and lifted him off him feet, tossing him into the trashcans and empty liquor boxes at the back of the alley.

Stunned, Spyder reached for his cash, hoping this would get the guy to back off. The mugger came up and slammed his boot into Spyder's midsection, then kept kicking, even after he'd snatched the money from Spyder's hand. Spyder didn't even get a decent look at the guy and that really bothered him. He wanted to see the face of the man who was about to kill him.

As if the mugger had heard Spyder's thoughts, he felt himself being pulled up by his collar until he was standing upright. Then Spyder's feet lifted from the dirty alley floor and he hung limp in the air at the end of the mugger's arm. "You know how to whistle don't you? Just put your lips together and blow," Spyder croaked as he hung there. He punched the crackhead as hard as he could. The guy's face gave as if there were no bones in there, just a lot of flesh-colored pudding.

The mugger's face began to change. His skin crawled in the jittery sodium light from a streetlamp. The mugger's eyes swelled and burst from their sockets, black and glittering with facets. His lips seemed to melt, drawing down into a long, twitching tube. Cracked, curved horns burst from the sides of his head. The mugger exhaled a fetid cloud of steaming breath. Spyder's brain was on overload. The adrenaline rush and oxygen deprivation had him flashing on a frantic stream of schizophrenic data. Snakes. Insects. Wolves. Angels. The mugger had a smell. Overwhelmingly sweet. Vanilla roses. Rotting fish. The perfume of dead schoolgirls. Spyder thought of his room in high school. He'd had a poster on the wall, a parody of the kind of out-of-date Civil Defense instructions they used to give kids in case of nuclear attack. The last line had read: *Put your head between your legs and kiss your ass goodbye.*

Spyder vomited on the mugger's arm. The puke seemed to have some kind of mysterious juju power because at that moment the mugger's head sheered off and rolled to the alley floor. His body, which still had a solid grip on Spyder's collar, followed a second or two later.

When he could open his eyes, Spyder saw a pair of shiny vinyl boots in front of his face. He closed his eyes again, ready for this new intruder to finish him off.

"Get up," came a woman's voice.

Spyder looked up and saw the blind dancer he and Lulu had spoken to in the bar earlier that night. She was holding a long and bloody sword in her hands.

"I'm tapped out. The dead guy got all my money," said Spyder.

"I'm not mugging you, fool. I'm saving you. Not that you deserve it." The blind woman reached down for Spyder's arm and helped him to his feet.

"Thanks. What the fuck just happened?"

"A Bitru demon attacked you. I killed it."

"I don't believe in demons."

The woman nodded. "All right. It was a junkie with the head of an insect and possessing superhuman strength."

"Okay," Spyder croaked.

Spyder looked at the body at his feet. He hadn't been hallucinating. The body wasn't even vaguely human.

"What the fuck... Why would a demon want me?"

"A Bitru doesn't just drop by for blood and crumpets. He doesn't come unless he's called."

"I did not call any goddam bug monster thing to kick my ass. I wouldn't even know how."

"You must have his mark on your body. Near your heart," said the woman. She ran both sides of her sword across the demon's body, cleaning the blood from the blade. Planting the tip of the sword on the ground, she gave it a hard shake. The sword blurred and when she stopped shaking, it had transformed into the white cane she'd had earlier.

"Damn." Spyder opened his shirt and looked at his chest. "I have a lot of ink on me. Geometrics. Tribal work. Religious geegaws."

"Any runes or symbols?"

"A shitload."

"And do you know the meanings of all those runes?"

"'Course. Some. In a Trivial Pursuit kind of way. They're just designs."

"So says the man covered in demon blood." The woman moved closer to Spyder. "Did it ever occur to you that those symbols have meaning and power?"

"Where? How? I've done a thousand tattoos like that on people."

"Some of them are probably going to have a dream date like the one you just had." She laid her hand over his heart. "You don't believe in demons, but you believe in magnetism, right? These symbols you put on your body, like the Bitru's sigil, these are a kind of magnetism. You don't have to understand how they work. The demons do."

"What can I do?"

"Take it off. Change it. All the signs and symbols that you don't know."

"What's your name?" asked Spyder.

The woman took her hand from his chest. "Most people just call me Shrike."

"Thank you, Shrike."

She ran a hand lightly over Spyder's cheeks and jaw. "Good thing you're pretty. You're not the quickest little pony on the track, are you?"

"You underestimate me," said Spyder. "This was all my clever plan to meet you. I think it went pretty well."

"Take care of yourself," Shrike said, moving back toward the mouth of the alley.

"My name is Spyder," he called to her.

"Take care of yourself, Spyder." She waved without turning around.

"Wait. Do you have a phone number or email or something? I owe you."

"You don't owe me anything."

"But I'm madly in love with you and stuff."

She turned gracefully and continued walking backwards, never breaking stride. "Not the quickest pony at all."

She was gone. Spyder started after her, but when he tried to take a step, his legs shook so much that he fell against the alley wall. A few minutes later, Lulu came outside looking for him and helped him back into the Bardo Lounge. Spyder noticed that Lulu didn't seem to see the large dead demon lying nearby in the alley. Together, Spyder and Lulu got very, very drunk.

FOUR
TRAFFIC JAM

It was light out when Spyder woke up, but his eyes refused to focus, so he couldn't read the time on the Badtz-Maru clock radio near the bed.

His head felt as if someone had scooped out his brains and filled his skull with broken glass and thumbtacks. When he tried to sit up, every part of his body ached. He rose slowly to his feet and walked stiffly to the bathroom. Spyder's shoulder throbbed and when he switched on the bathroom light he saw why.

There was a long gash running across his shoulder and down his chest. He had a black eye, a swollen lip and his arms and ribs were spotted in livid purple bruises. Spyder remembered the scene in the alley. It wasn't a dream. He had been mugged.

Blood from the gash had dried on his skin, gluing part of his white wife-beater to his chest. Spyder stood under the hot shower until the blood softened and the water soothed his knotted muscles.

When he stepped out of the shower, he left the wet shirt draped across the towel rack beneath the framed *Lady from Shanghai* poster that Jenny hated. The gash on his shoulder burned and his headache was coming on strong behind his eyes. Spyder slapped on some gauze squares and taped them down with white medical tape.

Christ, he thought, I was supposed to call Jenny last night and tell her I was going to be late. She must be pissed. Then it hit him, as it had hit him almost every morning for weeks: Jenny was gone. She'd packed up and moved the last of her stuff to LA. That's why he'd gotten so drunk with Lulu. It was the one-month anniversary of her desertion.

No fucking way I can put ink on anyone today, he thought. It was already after one in the afternoon. Spyder didn't want to go to the studio, but he needed to call his clients and reschedule. He dressed quickly into battered black jeans, steel-toed Docs and the largest, loosest gray Dickies shirt he could find in his closet. A pile of Jenny's abandoned textbooks were stacked at the back, *The Gnostic Gospels, Heaven and Hell in the Western Tradition, An Encyclopedia of Fallen Angels.* Spyder slammed the closet door.

The warehouse Spyder rented was across town from the tattoo studio. He usually rode the Dead Man's Ducati—the bike he'd bought cheap from a meth dealer he knew down in Tijuana; the previous owner had gone missing and did Spyder want first dibs?—but he felt too shaky for two wheels today. He called a cab and waited by the curb in the warm afternoon sun.

"Do you have the time?"

Spyder was so out of it, he hadn't seen the tall man in the gray business suit approach him. The man was bald, but tanned and healthy-looking, with deep wind and sunburn creases on his cheeks. It took Spyder a second to answer.

"Uh, no. Sorry."

"No worries," the man said with a slight shrimp-on-the-barbie accent. "Lovely day."

"Yeah. Great," said Spyder

"You all right, mate?"

"Just a little hungover's all."

The businessman laughed. "That's how you know you had a good time," he said, and clapped Spyder on his sore shoulder. "Cheers."

As the man walked away, Spyder saw something attached to his back. It was sort of apelike, but its head was soft, like a slug's. It had its teeth sunk into the man's neck and was clinging onto his back by its twisted childlike limbs. Spyder wanted to call out to the man, but his throat was locked tight in fear and disgust. The parasite's head throbbed as it slurped something from the businessman's spine.

Spyder took a step back and his shoulder touched a rough wooden pole planted in the ground through a section of shattered pavement. Pigeons and gray doves were nailed up and down the pole. Animal heads were staked around the top. An alligator. A Rottweiler. A horse. Other more freakish animals Spyder couldn't identify. Each head was decorated with flower garlands and its eye sockets and mouth stuffed with incense and gold coins, like offerings.

Across the street, a griffin, its leathery wings twitching, was lazily chewing on the carcass of a fat, gray sewer rat. Emerald spiders the size of a child's hand ran around the griffin's legs, grabbing stray scraps of meat that fell from the beast's jaws. The spiders scrambled up and down the griffin's hindquarters. Gray stingray-like things flapped overhead, like a flock of knurled vultures. A coral snake lazily wrapping itself around the sacrifice pole stopped its climb long enough to call Spyder by name.

Spyder's head spun. He stepped into the street, flashing on the demon in the alley the night before. The mugging had been real. Had the monster part been real, too? He leaned his head back. Spinning in the sky overhead were angels with the wings of eagles. Higher still crawled vast airships. Their soft balloon bodies glowed in the bright sun, presenting Spyder with profiles of fierce mythological birds of prey and gigantic lotuses.

A cab turned the corner onto Harrison Street and Spyder frantically flagged it down. "Haight and Masonic," he said to the driver, trying not to sound as deranged as he felt. Spyder slid into the backseat and as the driver pulled away, he peered out the cab's rear window. The businessman was on the corner, talking to three pale men in matching black suits. Their clothes and general formality reminded Spyder of bankers in an old movie.

One of the bankers stepped forward, reached into the businessman's chest and pulled out his heart. Turning stiffly, he dropped the organ into an attaché case held up by another of the trio. That done, the third banker used a knife to carefully peel the businessman's face off. The cab turned the corner and Spyder lost sight of them.

FIVE
COMMUNICATION BREAKDOWN

"How you voting on Prop 18?"

Spyder looked up. The cabbie looked exhausted, Spyder thought. One of those guys in his forties with eyes that make him look ten years older. His skin hung loosely on a gray, unshaven face.

"The companies make it sound like it'll put more cabs on the street, but really it's just going to screw up the medallion system even worse and give all the power to the big cab companies. We aren't employees, you know. All us cabbies are freelance. I owe money the moment I take my cab out. The moment I touch it. A cab driver has the job security of a crack whore. Worse than slaves, even. We're up at the big house begging the master for more cotton to pick."

"I'm sorry, said Spyder. "I don't know anything about Prop 18. I don't vote…ever."

The driver shook his head. His black hair stuck out at odd angles, as if he'd been sleeping on it just a few minutes earlier. "Voting's not a right, you know. It's not a privilege. It's your duty. My daddy died in the war so you could vote."

"Hey driver, uh," Spyder looked at the name on the man's taxi license, "Barry. Do you want to play a game?"

"I don't think so."

"There's a $20 tip in it for you. "

"Are you a cop?"

"No."

"Fag?"

"No."

"You from the cab company?"

"No, Barry."

"What kind of game?"

"Don't rush getting me to the Haight," Spyder said. He leaned his head

13

against the window. It was cool on his forehead. "Take your time. Let the meter run. As we hit each corner, you're going to tell me what you see.

"What's on the corners you mean? Like buildings and people?"

"Exactly. Big or small. Whatever strikes your fancy."

"Give me a for instance," said Barry. "Like this corner."

"Okay," said Spyder leaning forward to peer out the windshield. "That semi up ahead. The blonde eating a taco in front of a bodega. The mailbox painted like a Mexican flag. That blimp shaped like Garuda."

"What's a Garuda?"

"A bird-beaked messenger deity from Thailand."

"I don't see nothing like that."

"Tell me what you see."

Barry breathed deeply and craned his head on the end of his long, doughy neck. "Some bums with shopping carts. Some hookers. Mexican or Asian, maybe. Can't tell from here. They got on high heels and the littlest goddam skirts. You can see all the way to Bangkok when they bend over."

"Keep going," said Spyder.

"Just stuff?"

"Just stuff."

"A Goodwill. A closed down porn theater. Cholos drinking forty-ouncers by a low-rider. A cop car stopping near 'em…" Barry fell into a singsong pattern, reciting as they drove. "A mom with her kid in a stroller. A couple a dogs fucking. Get some, boy! Some dope dealers. Bunch of teenyboppers cutting school. Little shits. Don't learn to read and we end up paying their welfare so they can have babies." Barry glanced into the rearview mirror at Spyder. "This is kind of a stupid game, buddy. When is it your turn?"

"My turn?" Spyder lit a cigarette, his first of the morning. "Everything you saw, I saw. But there were other things, too.

"Dazzle me."

"A winged horse. A lion turning into a golden bird, then into smoke. An angel sharing a cigarette with a horned girl whose skin's blue and hard, like topaz."

"Jesus fuck, man," said Barry. Spyder saw the driver's eyes widen in the mirror. "Are you on drugs or do you need drugs?"

"There's a naked, burned man walking down the street. No, not burned. Cooked. Glazed and cooked like a ham. There's a swarm of little sort of bat things flying around him taking bites. He doesn't seem to mind."

"I'm letting you out at the corner, guy."

"Keep going or you don't get your tip."

Barry shook his head. "Keep it. Getting stabbed by some psycho fuck isn't worth twenty dollars."

"Do I seem like a psycho to you, Barry?" asked Spyder.

"I dunno. Sure talk like one."

"I understand. This is weird for me, too."

"Then maybe you just want to be quiet and not talk about it anymore," Barry said. "Anyway, we're almost to your drop."

"Do you see that building on the corner? I can't tell what it's made of. It's like pink quartz, but the walls are shifting like the whole thing is liquid," said Spyder.

"It's a vacant lot, man."

"Maybe I'm just dreaming."

"If it's a dream, you can give me a fifty-dollar tip instead of twenty."

Spyder smiled. "Or I could stab you in the head, suck out your eyes and skull fuck you. I mean, if this is just a dream."

The cab screeched to a stop. "Get out."

"Let me get my money," said Spyder.

Barry turned around to face him. He had a lime green windbreaker draped over his arm to hide the old Browning .45 automatic he was holding. "Get the fuck out."

"Jesus, Barry. Tell me that's not your daddy's gun," said Spyder. "Pretty Freudian, don't you think?" The cabbie's eyes narrowed. "I'm kidding, man. I'm just having a weird day. Let me give you some money."

"Keep your hands where I can see them and get out. I'll shoot you and tell the cops you tried to rob me. When they find all the dope in your blood, they'll believe me."

"Sorry I scared you."

"You didn't scare me, you pissed me off," said Barry. "Can't you tell the difference?"

Spyder got out of the cab and leaned in the front passenger window. Barry kept the gun pointed at him. "Funny, my ex said something like that when she split."

Barry gave Spyder the finger, gunned his engine and shot straight down Haight Street before being caught at the next corner by a half-dozen jaywalking punks.

That guy was going to shoot me, thought Spyder. He considered that as he walked the last half block to the studio. Maybe it wasn't such a bad option. The hallucinations weren't letting up. Maybe being shot was what he needed to kick his brain out of the peculiar abyss into which it had fallen. Spyder had the feeling that the day wasn't going to get any better.

SIX

A TRICK OF THE LIGHT

Spyder walked with his head down, not allowing himself to look around no matter how odd or enticing the visions: black hooves, crows chatting with rats, the suddenly sinister insect-silhouettes of panhandlers he'd seen a thousand times before.

He smelled musk and ambergris, cook fires and sewage. It reminded him of the Moroccan souks, but he was very far away from Morocco. In fact, very far away from anything familiar right now.

A sense of relief came over Spyder when he entered the tattoo studio and closed the door behind him. A couple of college girls were inspecting the flash designs on the walls and giggling nervously to each other. They didn't have wings or horns or extra eyes. They were a beautiful sight. Spyder could hear Lulu in the back with one of her piercing customers. "You'll feel some pressure, then a slight sting," she said. "Just like popping your cherry."

Hungry for a normal moment he spoke to the college girls. "If you have any questions about the tattoo work, that's what I do around here, so you can ask me."

The girls looked at him and the taller one, a café-au-lait brunette with bright green eyes, said, "How much for the black panther? That's a real traditional one, right?"

"Yeah. All the pieces on that wall go way back. And we charge by the hour, so the price depends on how big and where you want it. We have a hundred-dollar minimum."

The girls whispered to each other, then turned to Spyder. "We're going to think about it. Do you have a card?"

Spyder went behind the counter and found one of the studio's cards. He felt self-conscious handing it to the brunette. The card had a symbol on it. Spyder knew it was something Celtic, but he had no idea what it meant.

"Thanks," said the dark-haired girl, letting her fingertips brush against Spyder's as she accepted the card. Under normal circumstances, Spyder would have taken that as a signal to go into his charming act, complete with self-effacing patter and a certain calculated awkwardness that gave him the look of someone who might need just a little looking after. Today, however, all he could muster was a tired smile. "Any time," he said, and turned away from the girls, looking for his appointment book so he could cancel everyone set for that day. Maybe for the rest of the week, he thought.

His head and body ached and his hands shook a little as he leafed through the appointments. "Every rabbit hole has a bottom," he said quietly, remembering something that Sara Durango had told him after giving him his first hit of acid when he was fourteen.

Lulu and her female client were coming out of the back room when Spyder settled on the numbers he needed to call. He didn't look up, not ready to deal with the world, much less make eye contact with Lulu or the girl.

"Remember," said Lulu, "you're going to want to soak in a sea salt bath and use that antibiotic cream every day."

"Every day," said the other woman. Spyder heard the little bell over the door ring as she left.

Spyder had to concentrate to make his fingers punch the right numbers into the phone. It rang a few times then gave a subtle click as it switched over to voice mail. "Hi. This is Spyder Lee over at Route 666 Tattoos. Sorry, but I have to cancel our appointment for this afternoon." He settled back in his seat, giving Lulu a pained smile. "I'm not feeling that well and...holy shit...."

Spyder set down the receiver and stood up, coming around the counter. Something was terribly wrong. He took Lulu gently by the arm. "Goddam," said Spyder leading her to a chair. "What happened to you?"

Lulu looked at him, puzzled. "Nothing happened to me. You're the one who got stomped, 'member sugar?" She laid her hand on his cheek. The hand was cold and the skin was stiff, like dried-out leather.

"What happened to you?" Spyder repeated more insistently.

Lulu kept smiling. She had to. She had no lips. All the flesh from the lower part of her face had been cut neatly away, leaving her with a permanent leer. She wore a T-shirt cut low from the neck, and her dry white skin was crisscrossed with old scars and stained stitching. Spyder thought of the cheap boots and vests he'd bought on teenage road trips to Juarez, across the border from El Paso. Bad leather sewn together crudely and carelessly. Worst of all were Lulu's eyes. They were gone. Over her empty sockets torn scraps of paper were taped in place, each with a smeared, childlike drawing of an eye.

"What the fuck happened to you?"

The exposed muscles around Lulu's mouth twitched a little. She reflexively pulled away from Spyder and covered her face with her hands, then quickly lowered them. "Oh my god, " she said. "You really had your brains rearranged last night."

"Tell me I'm fucked up," Spyder said. "I've been seeing the most horrible shit all day. Monsters. Buildings that aren't there. Dead people."

"Not dead, most likely," Lulu said. "There's a whole lot more range between dead and alive than they taught us when we were kids, Spyder."

"What are you talking about?"

"There's a lot no one taught us. Deep, dark secrets. Other worlds. Other kinds of people. Hidden, but right in front of us."

"This is a mistake."

"I wish. There's monsters in the world. Some of 'em were born and some were made. I was made."

"This isn't happening. I'm still in the alley. I'm knocked out and I'm dreaming."

"I'm so sorry, darlin'. You're not ready for this. You were never supposed to see or know about it."

"Know about what?" Spyder shouted. "What are you?"

"I'm Lulu, baby. Just Lulu." She sat down next to him again, a horrible, broken toy. "You're just seeing another part of me. And I'm so sorry for that." Tears fell from her empty eye sockets, staining the paper drawings taped there.

Spyder walked across the room and sat on the floor with his back against the counter. "I refuse to accept any of this," he said.

Lulu got up and locked the door to the studio, then sat back in the chair in front of Spyder. "Darlin', we've known each other since we were six years old. You're the first person I came out to," she said. "I guess I'm coming out again."

"As what?"

Lulu leaned forward and laid her hand on his knee. "Please don't touch me," Spyder said. She withdrew the hand.

"I'm not really a monster," said Lulu. "I'm a damned fool, but I'm not a monster. I just got into something a little over my head."

"That part's obvious."

"I just had my eyes opened, so to speak," she said, pulling her exposed muscles into a smile. "Just like you." She slid down next to him on the floor, careful not to let her body touch his. Spyder shifted away from her a few inches.

"Remember four, five years back when I was all messed up on Oxy? I couldn't work. Couldn't do much of anything but steal and score."

"You still owe me a CD player," Spyder said.

Lulu let out an airy laugh, like wind through a keyhole. "Cheapass county rehab didn't work. Then, I met some people through this dealer. They said they could get me clean. Make my hands steady, so I could work again. Of course, I said *Yes.*"

"When was this? I remember you getting better in rehab," said Spyder.

"Jesus, Spyder. I didn't last ten days in there," Lulu said. "I wouldn't let you visit, remember? I always called you? I checked out and was on the street scoring until I met these people."

"Who were they?"

"Monsters. Real ones," she said. "'Course I didn't know that back then. They offered me the deal of a lifetime. I'd get clean, get my brain and get my hands back. Can you imagine what that meant to me back then?"

"How'd you end up like this?"

"You know how is it with dealers. First one's always free. Then the price just keeps going up. You got a cigarette?"

Spyder pulled a pack of cigarettes from his jacket pocket, took one, gave one to Lulu and lit them both. They smoked in silence for a few moments.

Lulu blew a series of small smoke rings through the center of bigger rings, something Spyder had been watching her do since junior high. "The price for giving me back my life was my eyes," she said. "They said that sight's mostly in the brain and they could make it so I'd see better without them." Lulu took a long drag off the American Spirit. Spyder wanted her to stop talking. "They were right, only they didn't tell me it wouldn't last. Every year or so, my sight would start to go and they'd show up, ready to deal. They'd already taken my eyes, so they took something else each time. Stomach. Liver. Skin. I don't know what all anymore. But not my heart. You'd be surprised what you can live without, but not your heart." Another long drag. A cloud of blue smoke. "Each time, they'd do their little voodoo so my body'd keep going, till the next visit. No one ever noticed the difference. When they took my eyes I saw a whole new world. The world, I guess, you're seeing now. Shit, Spyder, no one knows anything. All the teachers and cops and priests and shrinks they sent us to, they don't know what's really going on. When I saw the real world, knowing how long I'd been blind scared me a lot more than the monsters."

"You think this is some kind of goddam gift?" asked Spyder.

"For you it is. You got it for free. It cost me a little more."

"Fuck this world and fuck this gift."

"I'd rather fuck your sister."

"I'll trade you for your mom."

"Deal," said Lulu.

"Goddam," said Spyder. "It is you, isn't it?"

"'Fraid so."

Spyder slid his arm around Lulu's shoulders and pulled her to him. She relaxed and lay her head on his shoulder. They sat on the floor until the sun went down and the studio was dark. People knocked on the door, but they didn't answer.

SEVEN

SHADOWS

Many years ago, Ishtama was the mother of birds, Setuum was the mother of fishes, and in a golden city in the south, Coatlique, the Lady of the Skirt of Snakes—her body decorated with skulls, serpents and lacerated hands—gave birth to the first man, Mixcoatl.

Mixcoatl's sisters were the stars in the sky and he brought one to Earth to be his wife. Their children were the human race.

As much as Mixcoatl's wife loved him, she missed her sisters and longed to visit them in the sky. Mixcoatl went to Apsu, the lord of the birds, to ask him to fly his wife back to Heaven. When Mixcoatl arrived, however, Apsu wasn't there. Apsu's wife, Tiamut, told Mixcoatl that his Shadow Brother, Marduk, had murdered Apsu. Apsu was a friend and Mixcoatl grew very angry at this news. He climbed to the top of the tallest mountain in the world and cut out Marduk's heart with an obsidian knife, throwing the Shadow Brother's body into a deep gorge that led to the center of the world.

When Mixcoatl went home, he told his wife what he had done. She was afraid. "Our mother, Coatlique, the Lady of the Skirt of Snakes, is dead. Your Shadow Brother, Huitzilopochtli, burst from her breast in battle armor and a bone sword."

Mixcoatl told his wife, "I have no brother, shadow or otherwise."

His wife said, "Before she died, our mother warned that at some moment in our life, all men and women create their shadow form, born from their desire and rage. These shadow forms do not manifest themselves in flesh unless called into being by an act of violence or madness, a blow at creation itself. When you rashly killed Marduk, you brought forth your Shadow Brother and released pure chaos into the world. Huitzilopochtli is you reborn as a soulless void. If you do not destroy him, he will kill you and take your place."

Mixcoatl put on his armor, called his sons to his side and took them to war. For years they roamed the earth looking for Huitzilopochtli, but they didn't find him. At night Mixcoatl had terrible dreams and awoke in the morning pale and weak. Finally, Mixcoatl grew sick and his army rested by the banks of the frozen sea at the bottom of the world.

One night, Mixcoatl awoke from fevered dreams to find Huitzilopochtli sitting on his chest. Mixcoatl was too weak to resist and Huitzilopochtli cut out his heart saying, "I've eaten you piece by piece in your dreams, Brother, but don't hate me. I'm not your enemy. I have no choice in killing you and if I smile as I do it, remember it's only the joy a humble servant feels when he restores order to a disordered house, because, of course, there can't be two of us walking the earth."

Huitzilopochtli took his brother's place on the throne of the world. His flightiness and endless cruelties inspired many beings to unwittingly turn their shadows into flesh through acts of treachery or revenge. The different Shadow Brothers—kings and farmers, birds, fish and horses—ruled the Earth. This was the era of blood and massacres that caused the world to be divided into Spheres, because no matter how the Shadow Brothers tried to reason together, they couldn't. They were soulless voids, and even the most cordial exchanges usually ended in murder.

Thousands of years passed before the living things of the earth rose up and killed all the Shadow Brothers in power. To make sure that shadow forms never ruled again, each realm of life appointed auditors to keep the world in balance. These celestial officers had the power of life and death and could roam all the Spheres at will. They had different names among the different animal tribes—such as Soul Weavers, Holy Clerks, Black Scribes, and others. These beings didn't destroy the Shadow Brothers, but they kept their influence in check, even when they sometimes had to collaborate with individual Shadow Brothers to set the world right. The loyalties of these auditors weren't to animal, plant or man, but to the universe. And like the gods themselves, their plans were their own, subtle and unknowable.

They were thought to be beyond the influence of any god or beast in the universe, and this was true. What no one considered were things outside the universe.

EIGHT
SLOW CHILDREN

"Did you ever feel like you were a million miles from where you'd thought you'd be when you grew up? Like you thought you were heading for a weekend in Vegas, but ended up in Mongolia instead?"

Lulu was lying across the three wooden garage-sale chairs they kept up front for customers. Her arm hung down and a lit American Spirit between her fingers pointed at the floor, illuminating the scars on her arm with a faint red light.

"Sometimes," said Spyder. "But then I remember the scariest truth about being a grown up: that no one really knows anything. Maybe where most people want to be is as wrong as where they end up."

"We've been taking our happy pills, I see," said Lulu. "Know what we never, ever talked about: What did you really want to be when we were kids?"

Spyder stood up and stretched, saying, "That's easy. A private detective. You know, a Sam Spade thing. The whole world'd be in black and white and the streets would be slick with rain and lit like a film noir set."

"Sam Spade was always lonely and miserable, least in the movies."

"But at least he knew something. That makes him the exception."

"When I was a girl, I wanted to be Mary Magdalene," said Lulu. "The most hated woman in the world, but Jesus saw her true heart and loved her for it. I wanted that so much. To be hated by the riffraff, but loved by that one perfect, bright-eyed soul who knew me from the inside out. I used to jerk off to the picture of Jesus over my bed. He looked just like Jim Morrison before the alcohol bloat." Lulu took a drag off her cigarette. Spyder still wasn't sure how she was able to smoke with no lips. "When I realized I liked girls more, I jerked off imagining Jesus fucking Mary Magdalene. I was Jesus, of course. I wonder, does that make me narcissistic?"

"No, you're more like Mother Teresa."

"I'd have fucked Mother Teresa."

"You'd have fucked Nancy Reagan if she'd of held still."

"If she was in that pink Jackie O outfit she wore to Ronnie's second inauguration, hell yes. I'd've bent her over the big desk in the Oval Office and slipped her the high hard one next to the Bible Ronnie had Oliver North give the Iranians. Hell, I'd have bent Ollie over, too. Gotta love a man in a uniform."

"You're a damned pervert, Lulu."

"What's Dennis Hopper say in *Blue Velvet?* 'Don't toast to my health, toast to my fuck.'"

"I wouldn't be Dennis Hopper," said Spyder. "I'd be Orson Welles. He can act, write, direct, he married Rita Hayworth and you know, deep in his heart, he's a stone killer."

"That arty fuck never has happy endings. He's always dead or betrayed."

"Yeah, but we all end up there if we live long enough. I love the guy's certainty. He was willing to ruin himself for whatever he was doing. That's the definition of balls." Spyder checked the door again to make sure it was locked, then turned on the light in the studio.

Lulu shielded her paper eyes and softly said, "Shit."

"So, what happens now?" asked Spyder. "Do we open up tomorrow like nothing's different?"

"Things are only different if you act like they're different."

"Bullshit. Everything's different."

"I've been exactly what I am for years and it didn't affect things. Why should that change now?"

"That was before," Spyder said, groping for words. "I was going to say the world has changed, but it hasn't. I'm changed. And I fucking hate it. I take back what I said about Sam Spade and knowing things. I enjoyed my ignorance. Give me three wishes and that's what I'd ask for first."

"Reality sucks," said Lulu sitting up on the chairs. "But, if you wait long enough, everything becomes normal. You'll see."

Looking out the studio window onto Haight Street, Spyder watched the people outside going through their happy, blind lives. Couples were going to dinner, ducking into bars. On the corner, a girl with blue hair was kissing a boy in a cop shirt and vinyl shorts. Softly Spyder sang, "When I'm lyin' in my bed at night, I don't wanna grow up, Nothin' ever seems to turn out right, I don't wanna grow up." He looked at Lulu. "Know that song?"

"Tom Waits. Jenny gave me the CD for my birthday."

"When I see the price that you pay, I don't wanna grown up, I don't ever wanna be that way, I don't wanna grow up…" For the first time, Spyder was glad that Jenny had left him. He couldn't imagine trying to explain all this to her. Where was she right that second? Was she happy? He hoped so.

NINE

HARD THANKS

Spyder straightened up when he realized that he and Lulu were no longer alone.

Three smiling men, dressed like bankers in an old movie, were standing in the studio. One of the men carried a large snakeskin ledger. All three men were very pale and carried long, curved knives in their belts. The banker in the middle was wearing the face of the businessman Spyder had spoken to in the street that morning. The face was held in place on the banker's head by shiny brass clasps that stretched the skin like taffy.

"You are not alone?" said the banker in the middle, the one with the book.

"Who the fuck are you?" asked Spyder.

Lulu stood up and pushed him against the wall. "Shut up, Spyder." She looked at the bankers. "I wasn't expecting you. It's not time yet. I can still see fine."

All three men were wearing skin masks. From under the stolen meat, their flesh seemed to give off a cold chemical glow, like fungus on the walls of a cavern. There was nothing at all human about the men's presence, Spyder thought.

"This visit is not for you," said the banker in the middle.

"It is for us," said the one on the left.

"For accounts balance?" said the one on the right.

"I don't owe you nothing. My account is balanced," said Lulu.

"For now," said the banker in the middle, who appeared to be the leader. "Our concern lies with the future?"

"I saw what you did to that guy. Get the fuck out of here!" said Spyder, grabbing one of the chairs and starting at the men.

The banker with the ledger calmly pulled his knife and pointed the blade at Spyder. "This is not for you, young man. Please do not interfere."

"Look at her. She doesn't have anything left to give you."

The three pale men nodded and laughed. "She lives and breathes? Yes. There is always something. Her heart?"

Spyder looked at Lulu. "You said they didn't take hearts."

"We take hearts, when life is not honored or appreciated. But the oblation can not live without one, so we take them last."

Spyder weighed the chair in his hands, knowing the moment to hit someone had passed. When he set the chair down, the middle banker put the knife back in his belt.

"You can't have her," said Spyder. "But from what she told me, you don't care about that. You just want a payment, right?"

"Accounts must be balanced. This is our burden," said the one on the right.

"Any will do, if given freely?" said the one on the left.

Spyder nodded, still trying to parse their odd, singsong speech. "Then take something from me."

"Shut up, Spyder!" shouted Lulu.

The middle banker said, "You owe us nothing. If we took from you, we would be in your debt?"

"No. You'd leave Lulu alone, so we'd be even."

"This is possible."

"And you said this was for the future, so you wouldn't need anything from me right now…?" Spyder asked.

"Correct."

"Okay then. It's a deal. I'll see you down the fucking road. The door is that way. Use it."

"There is no deal yet," said the middle banker. He stepped forward and grabbed Spyder's arm with shocking speed and strength. With his knife the banker cut a symbol into the underside of Spyder's left wrist. "Now we have a deal." He smiled at Spyder. The flesh the banker wore didn't quite synch with his muscles, so the smile came in stages. First the facial muscles worked, then the teeth appeared, and then the outside flesh stretched into something a schizophrenic might call a smile. "So that you will not forget? And no one else can claim you."

Spyder had been tattooed, pierced and had a ritual scar on his chest, but nothing he'd ever done prepared him for the pain of the banker's knife. It managed to be freezing and branding-iron hot at the same time. And it didn't feel as if the blade was cutting, but raking away large sections of skin and muscle. However, when Spyder looked there was a small, neat incision that was already cauterized.

"Pardon us?" said the banker, and all three men started toward the back of the shop.

"Hey, Barry White, tell me something," said Spyder. "You knew she wasn't alone, didn't you? This whole scene was just a vaudeville act. You weren't here to collect from her, but to rope in someone new."

The middle banker nodded to his companions, then to Spyder. "You. The girl. This does not matter. The debt matters. The restoration of balance? This is our burden." One by one, the three men entered the little bathroom at the back of the studio. When Spyder opened the door a moment later, they were gone.

"What was that word he called you just now?" Spyder asked Lulu.

"Oblation," she said. "It's a kind of sacrifice. The kind you're supposed to give with thanks."

"It's not enough they zombify you. You're supposed to send them a thank you card, too?"

"Pretty much. You wouldn't think it to look at them, but the Black Clerks are all about having a good time." Lulu put her hand lightly on Spyder's shoulder. "You have no idea what you just got yourself into."

Spyder kissed the top of her head. "It's all right. I think I know someone who can help."

TEN
DOA

After dropping Lulu at home, Spyder took at cab to the Bardo Lounge. He'd always preferred the night, but now he was falling in love with it.

Spyder couldn't really deny the angels in the sky or the anacondas with the faces of crying children hiding in the palm trees along Dolores Street, but in the dark the smaller curiosities were swallowed by shadows, mostly invisible. Besides, night had always seemed a time of madness and possibility. The visions just felt more natural at night.

The neighborhood around the Bardo Lounge had taken on a heavy, wet jungle feel, as if the cab had stumbled into the abandoned set of some expensive dinosaur movie. There were always a lot of film crews in town and, for a moment, Spyder thought that they might have genuinely rolled onto a set. But sacrifice poles dotted the corners, animal heads and flowers dripping in the thick, humid air.

The Bardo Lounge was packed. Rubi was serving drinks. She gave Spyder a kiss on the cheek and brought him a tequila. He was relieved to see that she was entirely normal, with none of Lulu's mutilations.

The bar was alive with a happy, drunken weekend crowd. Leather-clad boys and girls with hair in cotton-candy colors and lips shining brighter than their vinyl skirts. Spyder wanted to wade out and dive into their beauty, and be baptized by their sweat and saliva. But for the first time since he was an awkward teenager, he couldn't think of anything to say to them. He felt as removed from the crowd as the monsters he'd been seeing in the streets all day. Spyder turned away and drank his tequila.

There was a demon sitting on the stool next to Spyder. It was a huge bare-chested olive-skinned man, his features lost beneath cascading rolls of glistening fat. White geometric designs covered his arms and chest, some kind of tribal markings. Considering everything, he didn't look too bad, Spyder thought. Pretty human, in fact. Not at all like the monsters in Jenny's mythology textbooks. The demon stole the beer of the girl sitting next to him and poured the whole thing into a wide, toothless mouth that split open in the middle of his chest.

Spyder sighed and the demon caught him looking. The demon leaned in close and said, "How do you get twelve humans to wear one hat?"

"How?" asked Spyder.

"You bite the heads off eleven."

Spyder turned back to his drink. "Sorry for not laughing, but I'm going to be over here ignoring you."

"I'm Bilal," said the demon, " You're the little prince, aren't you? The one Shrike killed for. What's your story?"

"There is no story. I'm just an inker who had to take a leak."

"That's beautiful. Maybe they'll carve that on your tombstone? You'll be an inspiration to future generations." A stoned couple stumbled by and Bilal delicately plucked the cigarette from the mouth of a cadaverous, lavender-lipped boy. The demon sniffed the cigarette once and dropped it into his chest-mouth. "Though I was really hoping you could justify your existence. Like maybe you were some minor deity on pilgrimage. Or a diplomat off to a secret rendezvous to stop a war."

Bilal blew out a long puff of smoke out through his regular mouth.

"What's it like being a demon here in a place like this?" asked Spyder.

"I don't know. What's it like being a human?"

Spyder looked in the mirror behind the bar, taking in the crowd. There were other demons, mostly talking to each other. A couple of guys playing pool were cut up in a way that looked like the work of the Black Clerks. "Weird and getting weirder," Spyder said. "Like Salvador Dali weird, all melting clocks and checkerboard deserts."

"Welcome to the world, boy. As for my personal complaints, you can add having to deal with idiot talking meat like you." Bilal pocketed a two-dollar tip someone had left for Rubi. "See, that demon who died last night was Nebiros. He was a friend of mine. In fact, my best friend in this sorry Sphere." Bilal put his hand on Spyder's arm. Each of the demon's fingers was tipped with a scaly lizard mouth lined with tiny needle teeth. The lizards bit into Spyder as Bilal squeezed his arm. "You owe Nebiros a life, and me, well, I miss my friend and that makes me mad. You know what I mean?"

The enormous mouth opened wetly in the demon's chest and he pulled Spyder closer. A leathery, black tongue darted out, licking Spyder's face. "Shit!" yelled Bilal, slurping the enormous tongue back into his chest. He turned Spyder's arm over, revealing the Black Clerk's mark.

"You must shit candy and piss champagne, son. Everyone wants a piece of you," said Bilal.

"You mean you can't hurt me because of this mark?"

"I didn't say that."

"It sure as hell looked like it."

"Smile while you still have lips. The Clerks have you penciled in. What they'll do to you is a hundred times worse than anything I'd do."

"I'm looking for Shrike," said Spyder.

"Just because I'm not eating you doesn't mean I'm your pal."

"Yeah, but if I find her and get her to help me, maybe she'll get in trouble with the Clerks, too. You'd like that, wouldn't you?"

"Shrike's not that stupid," Bilal said. He took the last of Spyder's tequila and swallowed it, glass and all. "Still, she likes them pretty and dumb. You might drag her down to your level." Bilal spat broken glass onto the ground at Spyder's feet. "She's got a room at the Coma Gardens. It's a flophouse down by Pier 31."

"I've never heard of it."

"It's not for your kind."

"Right. Thanks."

"Go to Hell."

Rubi asked Spyder if he wanted another drink. He shook his head. "You okay?" she asked. "You've been here muttering to yourself all night."

"Just replaying that last fight with Jenny. I keep trying it different ways hoping it comes out right."

"You poor thing," said Rubi.

"I've seen you in here a hundred times before. I've stolen your drinks and I've spit in them. But you've never seen me," Bilal said to Spyder. "How does it feel to suddenly have to live in the real world?"

"It's the worst thing that ever happened to me."

"Good." All of the demon's mouths smiled. "I've been around and I can tell the ones who are going to make it once they get the Sight and you're not one of them. You'll be dead by Christmas. A bullet. Maybe you'll cut your wrists. I don't see you as the hanging type."

"I'm going to kill myself just because I see uglies like you? Not likely, princess."

"No, you're going to kill yourself because you can't stand the real world. Reality is a two-ton weight strapped to your balls. And they just keep getting heavier."

"I'm going back to ignoring you now."

"I've seen it a hundred times. You're changed and there's no going back.

And everyone knows it. Look around. All those pretty girls who used to flirt with you, your friend behind the bar, they're all watching you having a nice chat with an empty barstool. They're already starting to wonder about you. Tomorrow they'll tell their friends. Maybe I can't hurt you, but I have friends who can influence mortal minds. Reinforce the doubt that's already there. By Monday, you're going to be Charles Manson to these people," said Bilal. "Yeah, you're going to kill yourself."

"Tell me something, when you jerk off, do those little lizards on your hands bite? I bet you like that."

"And then there are the Clerks. They've claimed you and you know what that means. They're going to pick you apart like a maggot-covered carcass. Could you feel them slicing you up with their eyes, deciding what piece they'll take first?"

Nick Cave's "Red Right Hand" came on the jukebox. A girl whooped drunkenly and Rubi turned the song up loud.

"I take it back. You won't make it till Christmas," said Bilal. "You won't even make it to Halloween."

"Get a costume and come on over. I'll put razor blades in some apples for you. Enough for all your mouths."

Bilal leaned over the bar and used the lizard mouths on his fingertips to spear some cherries from Rubi's drink set-ups. The demon popped the cherries into his face-mouth one at a time. "Give Shrike a big kiss from me. She'll be so happy to see you, little prince."

Spyder got up from his stool and started for the door. He couldn't help noticing that people were pointedly getting out of his way. At the door Spyder heard Bilal yell, "An OD! You're going to OD! How could I have missed that?"

ELEVEN

THE VOICE OF THE SPHINX

Spyder wondered what time it was. He was in another cab and doing his best to ignore the chatty driver. It pained Spyder that he hadn't ridden his bike that morning. Without the bike, he always felt tied up and weighed down.

Ever since he could ride, Spyder had always had a motorcycle of some kind. "You never know when you're going to need to get the hell out of Dodge," he told friends. "And you can only run so far in a cab." He told the driver to pull over.

"This ain't even near the piers," said the cabbie.

"I feel like walking." Spyder paid the man and got out. He checked out the landscape as the cab made a U turn and headed back the way they'd come. Spyder had lived in San Francisco for ten years and during a brief breaking-and-entering period in his early twenties, had prided himself on knowing every backstreet, alley and bypass in the city. Right now, however, he didn't know where the hell he was.

Ahead of him, where he was certain the waterfront warehouses should lead to the Fisherman's Wharf tourist traps, were well-trodden sand dunes sloped down to San Francisco Bay. A lot of the city had been built on reclaimed beach. This, he was certain, was what the waterfront probably looked like a couple of hundred years ago. Spyder's reflexes told him that ahead, past the dunes, was where the piers lay. But his eyes told him that there was nothing but shifting beach and black water. Then he saw a flicker—an orange light from the far side of the shifting sands. In that moment of illumination, Spyder could see a line of silhouettes moving along the edge of the dunes, heading over them. Some of the silhouettes carried burdens on their backs. Others were merely misshapen. It was enough. Spyder's started walking.

At the top of the last big dune Spyder looked down onto a maze of market stalls that sprawled down to the water's edge. As he got closer, sounds and smells hit him: the screams of hawkers, a dozen different musics pouring from out-of-tune instruments and cracked speakers, the heavy smell of roasting meat, spices and creosote. There were toys and piles of mismatched shoes, fresh vegetables, dried chameleons and flowers that sighed when you smelled them. There were orreries and telescopes, cracked eyeglasses and black eggs that hatched kittens who (according to their seller) spoke perfect ecclesiastical Latin. Sellers tugged at Spyder's arm and waved squirming things, glittering things and mechanical things at him.

By a stall selling decomposing medical books and sex toys made of black lacquer and amber (some with ominous-looking beetles sealed inside) Spyder bumped shoulders with a tall, handsome man.

"Sorry," said Spyder. "My fault."

"You should watch your step, little brother," said the big man. "Not everyone in the market is as reasonable as I. Some are downright belligerent." The man's voice sounded the way black velvet looked and felt. Spyder wondered if it might be some kind of magic trick. Not that he actually believed in magic, but he was beyond ruling out that much anymore.

Though they were physically the opposite, the tall man reminded Spyder of Shrike. He held himself with the kind of grace that Spyder had seen in the swordswoman. But the man was huge, more than a head taller than Spyder. His face, while classically handsome, was marked with deep scars that, at first, Spyder thought might be ritual, but then decided were some terrible accident. Chainmail covered the man's upper body and he wore pants that seemed to Spyder like modified motorcycle leathers. Metal plates and studs had been affixed along the legs, which were tucked into heavy steel-toed boots. At his side, the man wore a wide-bladed Kan Dao sword like ones Spyder had seen in maybe a thousand kung fu movies.

"Do I know you, little brother?" asked the big man.

"I don't think so," said Spyder. "I'm new here."

"Still, you seem familiar."

"I've got one of those faces."

"Perhaps that's it."

The tall man picked up a particularly elaborate sex toy from the stall and shook it. Six little legs sprang from the bottom and some kind of spring-wound plunger popped from the top and began pumping the air vigorously. The little legs kicked as if looking for something to grab on to. When the tall man laughed at the thing, Spyder noticed that color on his face was unnaturally intense. He realized that the man was wearing makeup, trying to cover his scars. The sudden insight made Spyder feel oddly more at home. Even here, down the rabbit hole or wherever the hell he'd ended up, people still had egos and still worried about how they looked.

"I'm looking for a place called the Coma Gardens. Do you know it?" Spyder asked the man.

"Very well," he replied. "Go down this aisle and turn toward the water at the Sphinx. Be sure not to speak to her. She will never let you go. Keep walking and when you see the Volt Eater, the Coma Gardens lie just beyond. You can't miss it."

"Thanks," said Spyder, desperately wanting to ask what the hell a Sphinx and a Volt Eater were, but thinking the better of it. He knew he'd find out soon enough.

He wasn't disappointed. Following the crowd in the direction the tall man had pointed, Spyder saw a Sphinx. A living, breathing Sphinx, like the sculptures in Golden Gate Park. The Sphinx sat up on its haunches, its lion body acorn brown, muscled and sleek as a cruise missile. Gathered around the Sphinx was a rapt crowd. They were clearly in awe, maybe hypnotized, thought Spyder. The Sphinx's face—the face of a human woman—was easily the most beautiful he had ever seen. Spyder looked away when he caught himself staring, but the Sphinx had already noticed him.

"Don't be shy, my friend. Come closer. I can answer all your questions and tell you your destiny."

Spyder half-turned in her direction. "Nope. Sorry. No thanks," he said.

The Sphinx's eyes narrowed with sudden interest and the crowd turned to see who she was looking at. "Yes, you should keep moving," she said to Spyder. "Don't let anything or anyone stop you from getting where you're going." Lowering her voice, the Sphinx spoke to her adoring crowd. Spyder slowed his gait, listening to her words. "See what passes, my children. A blind fool. A golden champion. What could he be seeking under Heaven's rough gaze? We have a mystery in our midst." When Spyder turned to sneak a last look at the Sphinx, she was staring him right in the eye. The beautiful beast gave him a smile and a wink. "It looks as if heroes are coming smaller this year."

Spyder's head spun. He turned away and hurried down the aisle. At the end, he found what he figured must be the Volt Eater. An exotic bare-breasted beauty, her skin oiled and gleaming, she was inhaling in long draughts from a wrist-thick cable attached to a gas-powered generator. After each breath, she spat lighting bolts, snaking and crackling, over the heads of the happily screaming crowd. People threw money at the Volt Eater's feet after each demonstration of her electric skills. It made Spyder a little sad to see her. On any other night, she would have been the hands-down highlight. He would have been in temporary love and dreamed about her as he went home with whomever he was with that night. Tonight, however, the Volt Eater was just a pretty girl spitting watts, no more or less miraculous than Bible-quoting kittens or the lion-woman who'd just pronounced him both a fool and a hero.

Just when Spyder thought he would never be surprised again, he came to the edge of the market and saw the Coma Gardens. Bathed in light the color of blood and pumpkins, the whole building was engulfed in a spectacular fire. Part of the roof collapsed and flames shot fifty feet into the night sky. The only thing more shocking than the fire was the fact that no one in the market was paying the slightest attention to it. They went on with their selling and haggling even as the whole structure cracked and caved in on itself.

TWELVE

CYANIDE RECALL

The Coma Gardens kept on burning. The beams glowed as if they'd been injected with magma, shedding hot jets of flame and debris over the sales stalls. Spyder walked along the cement broadway between the market and burning hotel, unsure what to do.

If Jenny hadn't taken the cell phone, Spyder thought, he could call 911. Of course, he wasn't sure exactly where he was. Still, all he'd have to tell them is that there was a burning building on the pier. The fire trucks would be able to see it from all the way down at Fisherman's Wharf. In fact, someone had probably already called the fire in, which was both good and bad. It was good in that the fire department would put it out. It was bad in that it brought Spyder back to the fact that he had no idea what he would do if Shrike was inside the burning building. He didn't want to think about it. Spyder turned around one more time to see if anyone in the market was forming a bucket brigade. The market went on as it had all evening—oblivious, a world unto itself.

Then Spyder saw someone at the edge of the crowd. She was talking to a man wearing an enormous, jeweled bird mask, one that covered his entire head (or actually was his head, Spyder later thought). The woman wore her shades, and moved her white cane from one hand to the other so she could shake the birdman's feathered mitt. Spyder ran to her through the smoke of the smoldering Coma Gardens.

"Shrike!" he yelled. The woman turned her head toward him as the birdman walked away. Spyder ran up and grabbed her happily by the shoulders. "It's me, Spyder. You saved my life the other night."

The blind woman gave him a crooked smile. "Oh yes. The pretty pony boy. How are you?"

"I'm…" He started to answer, but realized he had no idea what to say. He felt giddy at having found her, but there was the accumulating wreckage of the rest of his life. "I'm fine," he said. "I can see things now.

The real world. That's how I found the market. And you."

"Good for you," she said. "Maybe you're more clever than I thought. A trick pony. Me, I'm off to find new lodgings."

"I can see why," said Spyder.

"What do you mean?"

"What do I mean? Look! Your hotel is an in-fucking-ferno."

"No, it's not. I would be able to feel the heat."

"Of course it is. I can see it burning from here."

"Really? Because the Coma Gardens isn't going to be built for another fifty years," she said. "And it's not going to burn for another twenty after that."

"Then how were you staying in there?"

Shrike breathed deeply and nodded. "You can see things now. And it's all brand new and you don't know what to think of it, do you? Take a walk with me." Shrike reached out and took one of his hands and led him through the crowded market, swinging her white cane gently in front of her feet. The effect of that cane was less that of a blind person feeling her way along than her warning people that she was coming, Spyder thought. Everyone and everything got out of her way.

"People are afraid of you," said Spyder when they reached a less crowded part of the market.

"They're afraid of rumors and tall tales. And I let them be afraid. It makes my job easier."

"What is your job?"

Shrike sniffed the air as they passed a perfumer's stall. "Smell that? Raw ambergris. There's nothing else that smells like that. It's one of those magical substances that makes everyone—humans, demons, angels, ghosts and your little dog Toto—all swoon. There are merchants whose entire trade is delivering ambergris to the markets in Purgatory."

"A couple of days ago, I would have considered that a very odd thing to say."

Shrike nodded. "Yes. Your little vision problem," she said. "First of all, that burning hotel you saw... I'm sure by now you've noticed that the world is a much more flexible place than you're used to. Time isn't the same everywhere you go. And space can change depending on what time it is. Understand?"

"Hello. My name is Spyder and I'm five years old. Have you seen my mommy?"

Shrike smiled and looped her arm around his. Spyder liked how she felt. "Listen," she said, "the waterfront is one of the places where the edges of all the Spheres, the planes of existence in which we live, meet. It's why the market's here. I was able to stay at a hotel that hasn't been built yet in this Sphere of existence because it's already been built in another Sphere. Unfortunately, time being a slippery and relative thing here, the hotel has already burned down in another Sphere. That's what you saw. For me, though, it hadn't burned down. I was booted for an exorcism trade show."

"You went into the future, but you went into the wrong future?"

"Close enough. I was already in the future and the future I didn't want, the one with exorcists in party hats, drifted close enough to make my room reservation disappear. I have to find another place to sleep."

"You can crash at my place," Spyder said.

"No, thanks."

"I'm not coming on to you. My girlfriend's moved out. There's plenty of room."

Shrike removed her arm from his and leaned over to retie one of her boots. "I'm sorry about your girlfriend, but my client isn't expecting to find me in some cozy Victorian flat. Don't take it personally. This is a work-related rejection."

"What the hell is that?" said Spyder. They were at the back of the market, walking back in the direction Spyder had come earlier that night. San Francisco was white and chilly with fog. Looming out of the mist exactly where it shouldn't be was a gigantic stone archway sporting Roman columns. On top was a tarnished copper chariot being pulled by four enormous horses. Shrike sniffed the air, turning her head this way and that.

"It smells like Berlin," she said. "Near the Brandenburg Gate."

"Berlin? Like, the real Berlin?" asked Spyder. "I always wanted to go there."

"Here's another secret for your scrapbook. There is no difference between San Francisco and Berlin. In all the world, there is only one city. Because of how mortals perceive things, the one city appears as different cities, broken up and scattered all over the globe. But if you know the right doors to open, the right turns to make, the right tunnels and rocks to look behind, even mortals can find their way from one city to every other city. There are maps and trackers, ancient, hidden smuggling routes that only a few in the thieving guilds know."

"That's supposed to make me feel better? I almost had enough frequent flyer miles to take Jenny to Prague. Now, she's gone and we could have walked there all along." Spyder stood in the quiet beyond the market, looking up at the gate. When he looked down again, mist was beading on his jacket and he was growing cold. "I can't do this," he said. "I need help. Can you put me back the way I was?"

"I'm sorry. I can't."

"Can anyone?"

"Maybe."

It might have been better if that thing had gutted me at the club, Spyder thought. He said, "Why did you help me the other night?"

"I don't know. I just had to. You were so clueless."

"Why can't you help me now?"

"I'm on my way to meet a client."

"You didn't answer me when I asked you earlier. What exactly do you do?"

"You've seen what I do. I kill things," Shrike said. "People. Beasts. Demons. Whatever a client wants dead."

"The Black Clerks?"

"No one kills the Black Clerks. They're elemental forces. Killing them is like trying to kill wind or light. Why do you want to know?"

Spyder pushed up his jacket sleeve and put her hand on the scar on his arm.

"Damn," she said. "By the pike, you're a fool."

"There's nothing to be done about this?"

"Not by me. When they come for you, offer the Clerks a better deal."

"I could offer them you."

Shrike moved close to Spyder. She smelled of musk and jasmine. She whispered in his ear. "If I didn't know you were such a fool that remark could cost you your head."

"I'm sorry," said Spyder backing away from her. "I'm falling apart. I would never do something like that."

"I know that. I have a pretty good nose for treachery and dangerous folk."

"Where do I fit on the danger scale? Say that one is a pretty little butterfly and ten is the thing that beat me like a two-dollar drum the other night."

Shrike thought for a moment, then reached into the pocket of her coat. "I don't know exactly what you call one of these. It was a present from my niece." She held out a blue plastic rabbit that fit snuggly in the palm of her hand. Shrike wound the rabbit up with a silver key in its side and the toy started to vibrate while a little bell jangled inside. "I suppose this could get stuck in an enemy's throat and choke him, so it's a one. You're a bit bigger and a little smarter, though. I rate around a two." The toy wound down and Shrike dropped it back into her pocket.

"You're Death Valley. You know that? Beautiful, but harsh," said Spyder. He sat down on a sand dune and Shrike sat beside him. "I never got to ask, if you're blind how did you kill that demon?"

"I've trained for this all my life. My father taught me. Then a friend, before he turned out to be exactly the bastard I'd been told he was. Besides," she said, "there's blind and there's blind."

"What does that mean?"

"Just what I said."

"My head is spinning. I have this magic juju sight and've seen such demented shit in the last twenty-four hours. I wouldn't mind being blind for a while."

"It's not really magic sight, you know," Shrike said.

"Then what is it?"

"Memory," she replied. "When that demon had you, some part of it—saliva, a fragment of tooth, a fingernail—infected your blood. Everything you're seeing now you've seen all your life only you've chosen to forget it an instant later. If you remembered anything of this part of the world, it was in your dreams and nightmares." Shrike pulled up Spyder and started walking. "Don't feel bad. Forgetting is the way it is with almost every living thing in this Sphere. But now you can't look away and you can't forget."

"Poisoned with memory. And you can't help me."

"That's right."

"Can you at least point the way back to civilization?"

Shrike pointed back at the market with her cane. "Follow the stalls to the right until you come to a café in an old railroad car. You'll see streetcar tracks just beyond. Follow them along the waterfront and they'll take you all the way to more familiar territory."

"Thanks," said Spyder. "Good luck with your client."

"Take care. You know, I forgot to ask you. Are you Spider Clan?"

"I have no idea what you're talking about. Which is probably the perfect way for us to say goodbye."

"Take care, pony boy."

Spyder walked slowly back to the market, following the route Shrike had described to him. He passed horse traders and what looked like a kind of sidewalk surgery, with a hand-lettered cardboard sign describing procedures, from amputations to nose jobs, along with prices. Spyder found the train car café a few minutes later. He was colder now. His body ached from his injuries and his shoulders were knotted with tension. Somewhere in the dim back of his brain he knew he should be worried about the Clerks and what he was going to do with Lulu and how he was going to open up the shop tomorrow, but none of it got through the fog of exhaustion that was narrowing the universe to thoughts of walking and sleep.

At the edge of the market, by the last big dune, some teenagers were juggling fire without moving their hands. They stared silently and the balls of flame moved through the air all by themselves. Spyder started walking up the dune, when he heard someone call his name.

"Spyder, are you there? It's me!"

He turned and saw Shrike running after him through the sand.

"I'm here," he said quietly, and she hurried toward his voice, to the base of the dune.

"I've been thinking about it and I have a proposition for you," Shrike said, a little out of breath. "This client I'm meeting, she's expecting me to have a partner. But my partner isn't here. Stand in for him and I'll pay you."

"My rent's covered. I want my life back."

"I can't give you that. But some of the people I work with have power. If this client is who I think it is, she might be able to help you."

"Might?"

"It's the best I can do."

"What would I be? Your bodyguard? Your windup rabbit?"

"Your job will be to stand next to me and say absolutely nothing," said Shrike. "I'll do all the talking."

"I'm a mute?"

"People interpret silence as strength. In your case, the less you say, the better you get. I need you to look more dangerous than you really are."

"And maybe she can help me."

"No guarantees."

Spyder walked down the dune to where Shrike was waiting. He stood a little above her in the sand. "I'll help you get your bags from the hotel," he said.

"That's not necessary," Shrike said. She removed a battered leather book from an inside pocket of her coat. "Everything I need is right here." She opened it and little paper shapes stood up from the pages. Horses. Swords. Things that might have been exotic fruits or vegetables. To Spyder, it looked like a kid's pop-up book.

Shrike put the book away and led Spyder over the dune in the opposite direction. "Jean-Philippe, the bird-man, told me about a lovely deserted warehouse where we can spend the night."

"Feel that fog? We'll be ice pops by morning," said Spyder.

"Don't worry. I'll read to you," said Shrike. "A good book will always keep you warm."

THIRTEEN
JOURNEY INTO FEAR

Shrike led Spyder over the dunes toward North Beach, the old Barbary Coast, for two hundred years the traditional haunt of pirates, thieves and the kind of regular citizens who want to vanish into oblivion or into newly invented lives.

Behind an abandoned furniture warehouse under the Bay Bridge, they ducked through a hole in the hurricane fence and stomped through weeds and smashed glass to the back of the building.

Spyder, who had broken into more than his share of warehouses, spotted a smashed window near a rusting fire escape on the second floor. "Looks like we can get in through an upstairs window," he said to Shrike.

Shrike was feeling her way along the back wall of the warehouse. When she came to a door, she jiggled the knob, but the door was locked.

"Hey, there's an open window," said Spyder.

Shrike kicked in the door with her big boots. Her cane had already flicked up and transformed into a sword. She held it in striking position as she strode into the warehouse. Spyder was impressed, but kept quiet.

"Stay behind me," she whispered.

"Hear anything?"

"Rats. People. Shh."

The interior of the warehouse was a black hole decorated with a few grimed windows inlaid with chicken wire and decorated with graffiti. Shrike moved cautiously, but quickly, seemingly sensing where the trash and broken furniture lay and avoiding it. Spyder stumbled along behind her trying to keep up.

"Is it all open down here or are there any rooms?" Shrike asked him.

Spyder tried to see as deeply as possible into the dark. "I can't see much, but it looks all open down here. I think I can see some offices upstairs."

"Show me."

Spyder led Shrike upstairs and she checked all the rooms until she found one that was still locked.

"Move back," she told Spyder.

Faster than his eye could register, Shrike brought her sword arcing down and sliced the padlock off the door. The lock clattered to the floor noisily. Half of it skipped way and rattled down the stairs. Spyder heard low voices as doors leading to some of the other rooms opened.

Shrike turned toward the darkness, holding her sword at waist-level. "You're all welcome to stay here, but anyone stupid enough to come through this door will end up like that lock."

The interior of the office was dusty and littered with paper and rat turds. It looked as if it might have been a records office. Old filing cabinets stood against one wall along with a tilting, three-legged desk. Spyder had stayed in worse places, but not recently. He described the scene to Shrike, who walked from wall to wall, pacing off the room.

"Would you push the old furniture into a corner?" she asked.

When he'd dragged the rusting junk out of the way, Spyder said, "There were some old sofa cushions and maybe a futon out there. I'll go get them."

"If you want to sleep on mildewed trash, feel free. I prefer something clean."

Shrike had her pop-up book open to a page that, in the dark, looked like a scene from *The Thief of Bagdad*. She whispered a few words and the storage room was flooded in light and warmth.

The light came from burning braziers set at each corner of the room. The floors were covered with Persian carpets and bright pillows. There was an enormous bed against one wall and storage vessels and cabinets against the opposite. The place smelled instantly of incense and spices.

"Welcome to my home away from home," Shrike said.

"When I was five, I had a metal folding cup that I thought was the coolest thing in the world," said Spyder. "But I was wrong."

"I'm glad you like it. You're my guest. Please sit down. Are you hungry?"

"Now that you ask, yes."

Shrike dropped her coat and sword onto the big bed and went to the cabinets without hesitation. Spyder sat down on the edge of the bed watching her sure movements. Even though it was occupying an alien space, he thought, this was clearly her room.

"I've been on the road for a while, so I'm not really Suzy Homemaker these days," said Shrike, opening and closing the cabinets. She came back to the bed with a couple of bundles. "All I have is some wine and focaccia."

"The breakfast of champions," Spyder said.

"My glasses are all broken, so we're going to have to share the bottle," Shrike said.

"That's okay. It'll give me a chance to look butch for once tonight."

Shrike smiled and sliced the wax and cork from the top of the bottle with the edge of her sword, then handed the wine to Spyder. It tasted like wind felt at the top of a hill on a summer night. He handed the bottle back to Shrike. "Wow," he said.

Shrike took a long drink. "Don't forget to eat, too. Give it a chance, and this wine will leave you half-naked, shoeless and wearing a dog collar, with only a vague memory of how you got that way."

"Does the wine have a sister?"

"You wish."

Between bites of spicy focaccia Spyder said, "You're not at the Coma Gardens. How is your client going to find you?"

"Magic."

"You're not much like most girls."

"I'm going to take that as a compliment."

"That's how it's meant."

"Slow down on the wine, pony boy. You don't want your mouth getting too far ahead of your brain."

"How long have you been living like this? Out of your little magic book?"

"A long time. Since… Almost half my life."

"You and your business partner, the one I'm standing in for."

"He'd be the one."

"What happened to him?"

Shrike chewed with great deliberation for some time. "He was killed by assassins. Hellspawn."

"You don't ever do anything halfway, do you? It's not enough that your friend got iced. He was done in by hell's hit men."

"I didn't ask for an exciting life, believe me. I crave boredom."

"I know the feeling."

"I don't remember what seeing is like," Shrike said.

"You used to be able to see?"

"Yes. After I went blind, I could still remember things. Colors. Moonlight. My father's face. It's all gone now, though."

"When you cut that lock, I thought you were playing me. A pretty girl just pretending to be blind to look less dangerous."

"You're not the first person to think that," she said, and took off her shades. "But I really am blind."

Spyder looked at her for a long time. He wanted to be sure that what he was seeing wasn't a trick of the firelight. Shrike's eyes were fractured, like cracked glass. The misshapen pupils were ants trapped in amber. Shrike's eyes were bright, but dead.

"That can't be natural," he said.

"I was cursed."

"The bastard lover you talked about?"

She nodded. "It's a story I don't feel like telling right now." Shrike drank more wine and lay back on the bed. "I've answered enough questions for now. Tell me about you, Spyder Lee."

"I'm a Leo. I like wine and focaccia, Seventies Kraut-rock, and I dig chicks with their own swords." Spyder lay down next to Shrike and kissed her hand. She let him, he noted, but a moment later she put her hand on his chest to keep him from going any further.

"Slow down, pony boy."

"Sorry," he said. "To answer something you asked earlier, I'm not Spider Clan. Or, hell, maybe I am. My father loved cars and he loved James Dean. I'm named for the model of Porsche Dean raced. It's also the car that killed him."

Shrike laughed. "You're named for a dead man's car?"

"I think the saddest day of my father's life was when I saw my first James Dean movie and only thought it was okay."

"What did he do?"

"Nothing. We already had some problems, then he just sort of lost interest in me. He wasn't mean or anything. We just didn't ever talk much after that. I think I broke some kind of sacred bond I didn't even know was supposed to be there. It was his own fault. He took me to see *Journey into Fear*. The old man had James Dean, but on my planet, Orson Welles was the man."

"I've heard of him. Tell me more."

"*Citizen Kane*'s still the greatest movie ever. People don't even know that it's a pure special effects flick. It all looks so real, so natural. But there's also *Journey into Fear*. Most people haven't even heard of that one. Welles directed it, but the studio fucked him and he didn't get credit. He plays a Turkish cop. He looked ten feet tall. I wanted him to be my father and I wanted to be him at the same time." Spyder sat up and fumbled in his pockets for a cigarette. The wine had left him lightheaded, but happily so. He found half a pack of American Spirits and lit one. Shrike held out two fingers in a V shape. Spyder placed the cigarette there. She took a drag and handed it back to him.

"He was just a little older than me and had already made the greatest movie ever, and was instantly washed up," Spyder said. "I always wanted to do something like Welles."

"Be washed up at an early age?"

"No, dummy. Do something great. Something permanent. Even if it was just a new tattoo style. Something that would tag some little part of the universe so that I could say, 'I did that.' That's mine."

"And here you are, huddled in a warehouse with a blind stranger surrounded by snoring winos."

Spyder brushed stray hairs from Shrike's face. "I'm not complaining."

"What's it been, two minutes?"

"Thank you for pointing that out, princess. Okay, I told you my shameful film-geek secret. Tell me yours."

"You already guessed it. I'm a princess."

"Like with a crown or did your daddy just dote on you?"

"Both. I even had my own castle. Well, a wing of my father's. Before it all came down around us."

"Let me guess: the bastard lover?"

She nodded. "He was a general in my father's army. Unfortunately, we were in a period of prolonged peace. Without anything to conquer, some generals can grow restless. When he wasn't screwing the king's daughter, he was studying magic with the most powerful wizards he could bribe or blackmail. He studied hard enough that he became a powerful wizard himself. Powerful enough to depose my father, throw my lands into chaos and make himself king."

"Damn. He's still running things?"

"No. He went completely mad. Some of his senior officers were still sane enough to see this. They banded together and killed him, burning his body and scattering his ashes in three different oceans."

"Why didn't you go home?"

Shrike frowned. "He still has potent allies in power. And I don't even have a business partner, much less an army." Shrike held out her hand and Spyder again placed the cigarette in her fingers. She smoked quietly. "I didn't intend to tell you because I thought you'd laugh at a princess caught up in a nasty little fairy tale."

"How does the fairy tale come out?"

"The princess dies," said Shrike, handing the cigarette back to Spyder. "If the story goes on long enough, that's how they all end. It's what happens in between that matters."

"I never kissed a princess before."

"You think you're going to kiss one now?"

"Pretend I'm a ten-foot-tall Turkish cop. That's your type, right?"

Shrike laughed and when Spyder leaned down to her, she didn't pull away. Spyder felt her hand in his hair and she kissed him back hard, as if she hadn't kissed anyone in a long time and had missed it. She rolled on top of him, grinding her crotch into his as they tasted each other's mouths. Spyder slipped his hands under her shirt, sliding over smooth skin and hard muscle, to cup her small breasts. Whatever cord or clasp was holding Shrike's hair back came undone. Her hair fell in fat dreads and braids halfway down her back and brushed Spyder's cheeks. Mostly black, her hair was streaked purple, crimson, yellow and grasshopper green. Spyder rolled Shrike onto her back and pinned her hands above her head. He kissed her and ran his tongue down the side of her throat. When he bit her shoulder, her legs wrapped around him and squeezed. Spyder felt her shudder.

Shrike broke her hands free and took Spyder by the shoulders, telling him gravely, "I am a princess and I order you to take off every stitch of clothing at once."

Happy to play the diplomat, Spyder did exactly what he was told.

Later, covered in sweat, focaccia crumbs and spilled wine, Spyder kissed Shrike on the neck and said, "Tell me more about the princess biz." Shrike was curled against his side, her head tucked into his neck. "Is your kingdom somewhere I would have heard of?"

"No. It's not even in this Sphere. Where I'm from, magic runs the world. Your Sphere built the internal combustion engine. In mine, we transmuted gold into lead."

"Do you miss it?"

"I miss my home. And my father."

"Did he escape?"

"He's dead. I don't even know where he's buried."

"What about your mother?"

"My mother died when I was born. I never knew her."

"Sorry. What's the best and worst part about princessing?"

Shrike thought for a moment, running a hand idly around Spyder's nipple. "The best part was the shoes and learning to fight. The worst part was state dinners where you had to be charming with a full mouth."

"Did the princess have a horse named Princess?"

She pinched his nipple. "I didn't call my horse Princess because he wouldn't have liked it. He was a hundred shades of gray and terribly sick when he was a colt. I nursed him and when he grew strong, I named him Thunder."

"Thunder is just the boy version of Princess."

Shrike bit his ear.

"Why was your partner murdered?" asked Spyder.

"I don't know."

"Was it for someone you two killed?"

"Maybe."

"Does it have something to do with this new client?"

"I honestly don't know. But, yes, it could."

"Peachy," said Spyder. "By the way, when this is all over, can I tattoo my name on your ass, princess?"

"Kiss me and I'll think about it."

FOURTEEN
WHAT ARE LITTLE BOYS MADE OF?

In Spyder's dreams, a man was flicking lit matches at him. The little flames arced out of the dark and hit him in the face, the arms and the chest. All around him was machinery.

Age-grimed engines the size of skyscrapers blasted flames and blue-black smoke into a dingy green sky. A forest of enormous furnaces lay ahead of him and wretched workers (twisted limbs and curved spines, as if their backs had all been broken and not allowed to heal properly) shoveled pale things into the flames. When his eyes adjusted to the light, Spyder saw that the slaves (there was no other word to describe their condition) were shoveling whole corpses into the fire pits. Where there were no corpses, there were piles of desiccated limbs or putrid mountains of human fat. The crippled workers shoveled each of these into the furnaces as diligently as the corpse stokers.

The man was flicking matches again. "You're a fool," he said to Spyder. "A lost puppy. A sparrow with a broken wing, trapped on an anthill. A little boy who's fallen down a well. It's enough to make a good man cry."

"Who are you?" asked Spyder.

"What's the opposite of a good man?" asked the stranger. Spyder could see him better now. He looked like one of the Black Clerks, but his movements were more fluid. "We have three brains, you know. A reptile brain wrapped in a mammal brain wrapped in a human brain. We're all three people in one body. Which do you want to answer your question?"

"Where am I?"

"The dark side of the moon. Over the rainbow. Under the hill." The next match struck Spyder in the eye and he flinched. "But it's never too late to go back home."

"I want to. I want to go home."

"Liar," said the man. "You want to play." He rushed at Spyder, his broken black teeth bared in fury. He was one of the Black Clerks. Or what Spyder would look like if he were a Black Clerk. The man's skin was held loosely in place by hooks, leather straps and brass clasps. He pulled off his face to reveal some pitiful thing beneath, a blackened stick figure that smelled of roses and shit, leaking an oily yellow dew from every orifice.

"Let's see what's under your mask, little boy," said the Clerk Spyder and he dug his spiky, broken nails into Spyder's face, ripping away chunks of flesh and muscle. "What are little boys made of? Meat and tears and bones and fear, that's what little boys are made of!"

Spyder awoke with a stifled scream.

Sitting on a small, child-size chair that looked like it was intended more as a decoration than a functional piece of furniture was a pale, small man in a brown suit at least two sizes too small for him.

"Who are you?" asked Spyder, hoping he wasn't about to start the whole dream over again.

The man stood up and made a small, stiff bow. "I am Primo Kosinski. I have been sent to fetch the Butcher Bird to Madame Cinders' home."

Spyder shook Shrike, then realized she was already awake and playing possum. "I heard him come in," she said. "I just wanted a little more sleep."

"I am to bring you to Madame Cinders at your earliest convenience." The words rushed out of the little man's mouth in a high, breathy voice.

"We heard you the first time," Shrike said. She snuggled closer to Spyder. "I'm not a morning person."

"It's afternoon, ma'am."

"Damn," she said. "All right."

The little man remained standing as Spyder crawled out of bed and began to look for his clothes. Primo's attention was anxious and unnerving. Like what a herd dog must make a sheep feel like, Spyder thought. "Would you sit the hell down and relax?" asked Spyder.

"Certainly." Primo sat, but it didn't help much. He perched on the edge of the little chair, his attention as keen as ever. "And close your eyes while she dresses," Spyder added. The little man closed his eyes and covered them with his hands.

"I don't care," said Shrike. "It's not like there's anything here worth lusting after right now." Spyder knew how she felt. Whatever kind of wine they'd been drinking, it left him lightheaded, clumsy and oddly forgetful. Even when he found his clothes, it took him a few minutes to decide that they were his. It was some small consolation that Shrike, too, was moving slowly and painfully. The wine had kicked her ass, too. Good, he thought. At least we're starting out the day even.

"How far is it to Madame's?" Shrike asked.

"From here, perhaps three hours," said Primo, his voice muffled by his hands. "There is a boat and then the Blegeld Passage."

"You've arranged transport through the passage?"

"Yes, ma'am. A very agreeable tuk-tuk. Very luxurious."

"There's no such thing as a luxurious tuk-tuk," said Shrike, pulling on her boots.

"Yes, ma'am."

The day was starting slow, but all right, thought Spyder. He remembered that Shrike had not wanted him to speak much. That request was working out fine since, once again, he didn't know what she and Primo were talking about other than they were all going somewhere and, happily, using a boat for part of the journey. At least he'd recognize something.

When they'd dressed, Shrike ordered both Primo and Spyder out of the room. She stood in the doorway with the little book open flat on her hands and said a few words. As Shrike slapped the book closed, the bed and carpets were gone and the room was back to its original dingy state. Even the dust hadn't been disturbed. Shrike tucked her cane under her elbow and took Spyder's arm. "Lead us to the boat, Primo."

"This way, please, ma'am." He hurried down the steps ahead of them as Spyder walked down with Shrike. Spyder couldn't tell if she was walking slowly because of the hangover or because she wanted to appear relaxed and indifferent to their journey. In any case, it was pleasant to have her on his arm again. Though all through the walk, Spyder felt as if he were floating beside his body watching himself. He was so out of it, in fact, that Primo was handing them the boat tickets before he realized they were back at the ocean, on the edge of Fisherman's Wharf.

"These are tickets for the tour boat to Alcatraz," said Spyder.

"Yes, sir. You're very observant," said Primo brightly.

Spyder let it go since another thought had popped into his mind. "We're going to get in line for the boat. Please give us a moment alone, Primo."

"What the hell are you doing?" asked Shrike as Spyder pulled her away from the little man and toward their gate on the dock. "It's dangerous for us to be alone like this. He might think we're plotting against Madame Cinders."

"That wine we had last night. What was in it?" asked Spyder.

"Grapes. Spices. I don't know all the ingredients."

"Was it some kind of magic wine?"

"No. Not magic."

"Then chemical. My mind keeps floating and my memory feels like it's been pissed all over. And don't tell me this is normal for a hangover because I've had about a million, none like this."

"It's a special wine," said Shrike. "I didn't know you well last night. If it had gone badly I would have let you drink a little more. I would have had more, too. Then we would have both forgotten. That's all. It's just something I keep around for passing situations that might turn sour. No one needs that kind of thing cluttering up their head. You understand, don't you, pony boy?"

"Passing and sour, you know how to make morning-after sweet talk, don't you?"

"I didn't let you forget it all. I didn't forget, either. And it turned out to be better than passing. Kind of nice. If you could remember, you'd know that I stopped you from drinking too much."

"If I could remember," said Spyder.

"Don't worry," said Shrike. "When we do it again, I'll make sure it's memorable."

"When we do it again? You've got it all figured out."

"I'm a girl with her own sword. That's your type." Then she added quickly. "Don't kiss me now. Primo will be watching. Wave him over. Be careful from here on. No smiles and no talking. You're the quiet, deadly type."

"Easy for you to say. You don't have a hard-on."

"Shh!"

FIFTEEN
I LUV LA

They crossed San Francisco Bay to Alcatraz Island with a hundred other tourists and their children. Spyder hadn't been to the island in a couple of years. He'd always regarded the place as a bore and used the foggy crossing and general gloom that surrounded Alcatraz's abandoned maximum-security prison as compelling seduction tools. It usually worked.

Jenny had been the last woman he'd taken there and it felt odd to be going back again. He looked at Shrike. She was at the bow of the boat, looking fierce in the bay wind, and clearly enjoying the feel of it on her face. Primo stood a few steps behind her and from where Spyder stood on the opposite side of the deck, the little man looked even more ragged than he'd first thought. Not only was Primo's suit too small, but the seams and the fabric itself looked frayed and was clearly torn in places. Spyder wondered, if this Madame Cinders is such a big deal, can't she dress her help in something that doesn't look like it was copped from a dumpster behind the Salvation Army?

When they moored at Alcatraz, Spyder and his companions waited until most of the families had gone ashore before exiting the boat. A park ranger was giving the group a canned orientation lecture, explaining that they shouldn't damage the facilities and that donations were always welcome. From earlier visits, Spyder remembered that the place had originally been a military prison during the Civil War. He'd hated being there, even for a few hours. He couldn't imagine what being locked up for years in that frigid, wind-beaten rock would be like. Alcatraz made him think of a nasty monster-movie castle looming over a doomed village. He wondered what Shrike's castle had been like. Nothing like this, he hoped. If, of course, she were telling the truth and there was a castle. It occurred to Spyder that she might have been telling him a tall tale. She'd slipped him a Mickey Finn because he didn't matter. Why should she bother telling him the truth about herself? She was beautiful, but he resolved to be more careful around her, then smiled to himself knowing how unlikely that was. He was into something whose depths he couldn't begin to guess. This was pretty much a hang-on-and-hope-you-get-to-wear-your-skin-home situation and that didn't leave much room for being aloof.

The ranger finished her spiel and the tourists split into smaller groups to explore the island. Spyder and Shrike followed Primo up the hill toward the prison cellblocks. As they climbed the steep grade, Spyder became aware that many of the tourists, especially the fathers in family groups, lumbered under the weight of demonic parasites that were attached to their bodies. Some of the parents bore scars from the Black Clerks. Spyder met one man's gaze—he still had his eyes—and the look the man gave Spyder was filled with such resigned despair that Spyder had to turn away. Out of the corner of his eye, Spyder watched the man herding his wife and children into the prison gift shop.

Past the cellblocks, on the edge of the island looking back toward San Francisco, were rusted steel double doors. They were chained loosely together and, with a little effort, Primo was able to push himself through the opening. Shrike, smaller, slid easily through the gap. Spyder had to take his leather jacket off to get through and even then there was a lot of grunting and dragging himself inside by inches. But he finally made it.

"I probably could have picked that lock," he said once he was inside the tunnel.

"Don't worry. I have a key," said Primo, and walked away into the darkness.

"Then why…?" Shrike elbowed Spyder to remind him not to speak. He followed them, giving up trying to understand his companions' logic.

"This is one of the old animal pens," Primo told them eagerly. "The soldiers kept their horses here during the winter rains. You can still hear them whinnying if you put your ear to the wall during storms."

In the near, but never total, darkness, they climbed down ladders and through storm grates. They walked passages with floors of mud, passages lined with planks, cobblestone passages and some whose floors seemed to be some kind of soft, spongy metal that made Spyder want to run like a little kid. He was sure that there was no way all these passages were part of the prison complex. This was confirmed for Spyder as they moved through a rocky tunnel whose walls were lined with clay water pipes marked with inscriptions in Latin and Greek. Were they moving in time as well as space? Spyder wondered.

They went through underground vaults and what looked like old sewer sluiceways. Occasionally, they would meet another group moving in the opposite direction. Some were dressed in rags, some looked like ordinary city dwellers, while others looked like escapees from some particularly mean and decrepit Renaissance Faire. The groups never acknowledged each other. Spyder got the impression that the passages weren't the safest place to be.

Up ahead, he noticed that Primo had slowed down and was nervously wringing his hands. At a watery intersection that reminded Spyder of the high gothic sewers where Orson Welles met his bloody fate at the end of *The Third Man*, Primo stopped. The little man turned in slow circles, peering into the distance. He stared hard at the walls, as if looking for a message.

"What's wrong?" asked Shrike.

"Our transport isn't here. A tuk-tuk was supposed to be waiting."

"Did Madame Cinders pay them in advance?"

"Naturally."

"That was your mistake."

"No. She knows this family well. They are reliable. That's why she employs only them to transport her guests."

"Maybe they broke down," said Shrike. "If they were anywhere nearby, we could hear the damned racket from the tuk-tuk's engine."

"We shouldn't remain still too long. It's dangerous. I suppose we should start walking."

"That would be my suggestion," said Shrike. Spyder didn't like the idea of being in the passages any longer than they had to. He looked back the way they had come and saw things moving in the darkness. Golden eyes glinted and slid along the floor. Spyder caught up to Shrike and made sure not to fall behind again.

After what seemed like hours, they were moving through a passage lined with old red brick and dry rot timbers. A cool breeze touched Spyder's face. Sand had piled in miniature dunes where the timbers met the floor.

"Oh dear," said Primo leaning over a broken machine in the tunnel ahead. Twisted wheels lay on the bricks. Spyder could already smell the stink coming from the wreck. Melted rubber, gasoline and burned flesh.

"I'm guessing this is the tuk-tuk we were waiting for?" said Shrike.

"It would seem so," replied Primo. "Hmm. I don't believe this was a motor accident. There appears to be an arrow in the driver's eye. I wonder who could have put that there?"

"That would be us," came a croaking voice from the roof of the passage.

Four men (and the gender of the intruders was just a guess on Spyder's part) dropped to the floor. The men weren't holding anything, so Spyder wasn't sure how they'd been holding on to the ceiling. But what seemed more important to him now was the men's elongated faces and crocodilian skin. Each was dressed differently—one in a firefighter's rubber overcoat, another in priestly vestments, the third wore shorts and an I LUV LA T-shirt and the fourth was wearing a high school letter jacket. Spyder didn't want to think about where the lizard-men might have acquired their clothes, but the rust-colored stains on the LA T-shirt gave him some idea.

"Excuse me, gentlemen," said Primo, and he gave the lizards a bow. "I am Primo Kosinski and I am conducting these guests to the abode of Madame Cinders. The Madame has negotiated safe passage through the Blegeld Passage for herself and all her guests."

"She didn't negotiate with us," said the lizard-priest in a gravelly, hissing voice.

"That's because the compact is universal. No one may ignore or prevent—" Primo began. Shrike cut him off.

"What will it cost us to get through?" she asked.

"The pretty green. Piles of it. Do you have that?"

"You know we don't," Shrike said.

"Good," hissed the lizard in the letter jacket. He took a step toward Shrike. Just as she was bringing her sword up, Spyder saw Primo ram his shoulder into the lizard's midsection, smashing him against the wall in an explosion of bone, blood and dry skin. Next, Primo rounded on the priest and back-fisted him, ripping off a good portion of the beast's face. Spyder was pulling Shrike back from the carnage. As awful as it was, he couldn't turn away. The first thing he noticed, aside from the fact that Primo had the last two lizards by the throat and was slowly choking the life from them, was that the little man's clothes were no longer loose on him. In fact, they seemed a little tight. His skin had turned a bright crimson and long, thorned hooks protruded from every part of his body, ripping through the fabric of his suit. Primo growled with animal fury as he crushed the throats of the lizards until their heads hung at odd angles on limp flesh. Dropping the attackers' bodies, Primo turned to Spyder and Shrike asking, "Are you both all right?"

"We're fine," Shrike said. "Thank you."

The little man, for he was already shrinking back to his original size, approached them, cleaning his hands on the T-shirt he ripped from the body of one dead lizard. "Forgive me, please," he said. "You were under my protection and should never have had to even raise your weapon. You may ask Madame for my life, if you like."

"Don't be silly," said Shrike. "You protected us and we're grateful."

"I'm happy to be of service."

"You're of the Gytrash race, aren't you?"

"Yes, ma'am. Members of my family have been guides for Madame Cinders and her friends for over a thousand years."

"Your family should be very proud of you, Primo."

"Thank you. I believe they are. At least, they sit well with me."

Spyder felt Shrike's hand on his arm, quieting him until Primo had moved away to inspect the lizard-men's bodies. When he was out of ear-shot, Shrike whispered quickly. "The Gytrash are nomads and escorts for travelers. They are a very practical race. They eat their dead for nourishment, but also as ritual. It's their highest act of love and praise."

"We're almost there," said Primo. "Shall we continue?"

"Let's," said Shrike. Spyder walked beside her trying to decide which member of his family, in a pinch, he could eat.

SIXTEEN
THE BIRTH OF MONSTERS

When the world began, there were no such things as monsters. Demons were just fallen angels who, booted out of Heaven and bored with Hell, wandered the Earth sticking little girls' pigtails in inkwells and sinking the occasional continent.

The word monster didn't really exist until the Spheres separated and the humans and beasts in the First Sphere forgot about their brethren in the other Earth realms.

In fact, most of what people call monsters are at least partly human. Many are the offspring of Romeo and Juliet encounters between mortals and races from the other Spheres. The first monster was the offspring of a man, Chrysaor, and Nyx, the snake queen. Their daughter, Lilith, was the first of the Lamia race. When she fell in love with another human, Umashi, and created the long-nosed Tengus. It wasn't just humans coupling with the older races. Earth was a romantic free-fire zone before the Spheres split. Old races mated with the new ones, which created still newer races, new cultures, new myths and new possibilities. Later, when mortals only saw the other races of the Earth in their dreams, they called these long-forgotten siblings monsters.

Of course, mortals weren't always tops on the invitation list for parties, either. A number of animal races, especially the ones in the oceans and air, didn't regard humans as truly sentient beings and considered mating with them to be the grossest kind of bestiality. This generally low opinion of humanity was widespread in the outer Spheres and didn't change for thousands of years, until certain mortal stories trickled out to the hinterlands. Gilgamesh, for instance, was quite a hit with the swamp kings and lords of the air. Other stories of reluctant heroes and reborn champions, characters such as Prometheus and the trickster Painted Man, elevated humanity in the eyes of the other races because in all those stories the heroes die or give up some core part of their being for their people. That humans could grasp the idea of self-sacrifice was big news in the outer Spheres. Humanity was cut some sorely needed slack from races that previously regarded them as a kind of chatty land krill.

Of course, while the creatures of the outer Spheres no longer thought of humans as vermin, they didn't really want to live next door to one, either.

SEVENTEEN
CANNIBAL ORCHIDS

They emerged from the tunnel into what looked and felt like noon light. After the darkness and relative quiet of the subterranean passages, the city was overwhelming.

The first thing that hit Spyder was the heat, then the din of car horns and the heavy reek of exhaust fumes. They had emerged from a storage room in the back of a small open-air café where bearded men in long white garments sipped mint tea and smoked unfiltered Winstons.

Spyder had a hard time focusing on individual objects in the dazzling light. Shrike looped her arm through his and they followed Primo through narrow, unfamiliar back streets that smelled equally of raw sewage and cumin. Shielding his eyes with his free hand, Spyder was able to focus better and realized that the reason he couldn't read the signs on the shops was that they weren't in English, or even Roman letters.

"Where are we?" he asked, knowing it violated his promise not to speak, but not caring.

"Alexandria," said Primo. "The Medina. The old city."

"How far are we from Madame Cinders'?" asked Shrike.

"Very close. Just a few blocks, ma'am."

Spyder had always wanted to go to Egypt, though he'd always imagined going there by a more conventional means. Still, he told himself, he was there with a cute girl on his arm and a guide who knew his way around. For being utterly lost and nearly crazy from confusion and fear, it could have been worse.

They turned a corner and were surrounded by the ruins of a burial and temple complex that looked as if it were left over from the time of the Pharaohs. Sandstone blocks the size of SUVs lay at odd angles amidst a litter of columns and statues of animal-headed gods. Silent children watched them from the tops of the shattered temples. Whole families were living in the necropolis, Spyder realized, though he couldn't say if they were from his time, some antediluvian past or some weird future. The temple inhabitants wore stiff, bulky robes the colors of the stones they walked on. In their odd garments, they looked almost like living stones themselves. The men were butchering the carcass of some large buffalo-like animal and dragging bloody slabs of it off to their families.

Just past the necropolis was an old walled fortress. Over the outer wall, Spyder could just see the top of a golden onion dome and a tall minaret. Primo picked up his pace, breaking into a stiff-legged trot that made him look like an oversize windup toy. Even though it hadn't been more than an hour or so since the fight in the tunnel, Spyder was having a hard time picturing Primo as a killer. Which might have been the little man's greatest strength, he thought. He looked at Shrike. She was lean and exuded confidence, but if he hadn't seen her in action with her sword he wouldn't have imagined her strength, either.

As Primo worked the stiff lock on the gates of the fortress, Spyder shielded his eyes from the sun. Frowning to himself, he remembered his first tattoo: barbed wire around his neck. It was a traditional prison tat. Spyder had told people that the tat was a memorial to his friend Gus who had died in the San Luis Obispo county jail in a fight with a member of a rival bike gang. And that was half true. It had genuinely broken Spyder up when Gus died during what should have been nothing more than a weekend in the drunk tank. But Spyder knew enough about tattoos to know how people would back off when they saw what they thought was a symbol of his having survived serious jail time. Thinking about it now, in the company of two genuine killers who looked anything but dangerous, Spyder saw much of his early ink less as a tribute to the art and more to his own neuroses. He wore his fear on his skin for everyone to see.

Spyder had avoided thoughts like these his whole life and, as Primo wrestled the gates of the fortress open, they came down on him hard. Fear and covering up fear had probably been his primary motivator since childhood. Oddly, now that he had real monsters to deal with and not just the neurotic shadows that he'd dragged with him from childhood, none of it was as bad as he'd imagined it would be. Maybe because he wasn't alone. Shrike's arm was solid against him. If he wasn't really brave, maybe he could watch her and learn to act bravely. A line he used more than once to sell tattoos to uncertain customers popped into his head: "Sometimes changing the outside is the first step to changing the inside."

Beyond the wall, the fortress was another world. Olive and orange trees lined the inside of the courtyard, providing shade and cooling the air to bearable levels. A fountain filled the air with the pleasant sound of running water and a tile walkway pointed the way into the main domed building. Primo ushered Shrike and Spyder inside to an opulent room of cushions and low, inlaid tables on a polished teakwood floor. Primo gestured for them to make themselves comfortable by a table piled high with fresh fruit and bottled water. When they were seated, Spyder put Shrike's hand on the fruit and she eagerly took a fig from the pile. Spyder peeled an orange and said, "I could get used to this."

"It's very nice," replied Shrike. "It's also for our benefit. Letting us know that she can take care of us."

"I like the sound of that."

"It's very nice when you're on good terms. It's also a way of letting us know that her wealth and power can hurt us if things go badly."

"You're getting a lot more from that fig than I'm getting from this orange."

"Keep quiet. There are people listening."

"Where?"

Shrike inclined her head to a grating set into the wall. Spyder looked and saw numerous pairs of eyes staring at him through the wooden latticework. As soon as he focused on them, the eyes were gone. He crawled over the cushions and looked through. Beyond the wall was a large, formal room. Serving girls and white-clad boys were cleaning the place and taking great pains not to look in Spyder's direction.

"She'll see you now." It was Primo, down at the far end of the chamber. Spyder gave Shrike his arm and they followed the little man down a long, cool passageway past dozens of rooms, out the back and into a sprawling Victorian greenhouse. The glass walls and roof were white with steam. Inside, it was like a sauna. Spyder was immediately drenched in sweat. Primo led them deep into a thick internal jungle filled with tropical plants whose thorns and poison sap tugged at their clothes.

They entered a wet crystal-walled room filled with orchids of every imaginable size and color. Servants were gently tending the flowers with potions and fertilizers. Using a silver scoop, a young boy tossed ground meat into the soil. The orchids bent gracefully and used their fleshy blossoms to gather up the bloody scraps. Those that couldn't reach the meat ripped the petals from nearby flowers. The place smelled like a cross between a department store perfume counter and a slaughterhouse.

Spyder felt Shrike stiffen and when he looked, Madame Cinders was being rolled into the greenhouse in a gilded wheelchair, as elaborately decorated as any Louis XIV throne. Attached to the wheelchair was an intricate pump system tied to an intravenous tube that slid under the rich folds of Madame Cinders' sky blue hijab. The woman's face was entirely hidden by the headdress. There was only an oval-shaped grid across her eyes, and through it, Spyder could see nothing but darkness.

Primo walked into the center of the room and stood straight, striking an awkwardly formal pose. "This is the mistress of this house, the Last Daughter of the Moon, the protector and destroyer of Ail-Brasil, Madame Cinders. She will ask you a series of questions. You will answer these to the best of your ability. You are not permitted to question Madame Cinders at this time. If Madame decides to avail herself of your services, then questions may be asked in a less formal setting. Do you understand all these points?"

Shrike stepped toward Primo's voice. Spyder let her and stood where he was, nervous, but careful not to show any emotion. He simply frowned.

"We understand," said Shrike.

Primo rubbed his hands nervously and looked at Shrike and Spyder. "There is, um, one more stipulation," he said, and reached behind an enormous elephant ear plant to pull a hidden lever set into the floor. Gears ground beneath their feet. Pistons hissed and pulleys clanked into action. From the ceiling, a gigantic metal flower lowered itself and opened slowly, like a blossom in the morning sun, to reveal dozens of serrated blades, each longer than Spyder was tall.

"Because of the delicate nature of this commission, if your services are not needed you will not, um, be permitted to leave. Madame Cinders regrets any inconvenience this may cause you."

Spyder shifted his gaze to Shrike. She hadn't moved, so he mimicked her indifference.

"We're ready," Shrike said.

Primo went and stood beside Madame Cinders' wheelchair. The old woman hadn't budged since her entrance. When her voice came, it filled the room, surprisingly strong, deep and clear.

"What is your name, child?" She was addressing Shrike. Spyder looked at her.

"I am Alizarin Katya Ryu." She gave the old woman the slightest of bows.

"Is that your only name?"

"I'm sometimes called Blind Shrike," she said. "Sometimes Butcher Bird."

"Why do you carry the name of a harmless little hatchling?"

"The shrike is a hunter, Madame, though a diminutive one. So am I.

The shrike skewers its prey on thorns and continues to hunt. Like the shrike, I hunt until the hunt is over. The name was given to me by those who've seen my skill."

"You're an assassin, child?"

"Yes, Madame."

"But you are also a thief."

"No, ma'am."

"Did you not eat my figs without asking? That's thievery."

"We were led to food and drink by your servant. We assumed the fruit was for your guests," said Shrike flatly.

"Is it your habit to conduct your life and work based on assumptions?"

"I use common sense. When food and drink are offered by someone asking for my service, I feel free to eat and drink. If I was wrong in this case, if I have offended you, I apologize. But do not forget, Madame Cinders, that it was you who sought out my help. If it is not wanted, then we'll be on our way."

"You have a temper, child."

"Not temper. I simply dislike wasting time, yours or mine."

The old woman paused. Her head moved, ever so slightly. Spyder stared deeply into the blackness where he knew her eyes to be. "Your companion, does he speak?"

"Only when he has something to say."

"Tell me, are you a traveler?"

"If you are asking if I am willing to go where a patron needs me, the answer is yes."

"What if the destination is beyond this Sphere? Beyond every Sphere you know?"

"I go where I'm paid to go."

"Will you go to Hell for me, Blind Shrike?"

"I'm confused, Madame. I'm an assassin. What use would I be to you in a place of the dead?"

"What indeed?" The little pump attached to Madame Cinders' wheelchair chuffed into life. An inverted bottle of some thick purplish fluid bubbled on her IV stand. She sighed a little as the fluid drained into her. "As a traveler, what can you tell me of Hell?" Madame Cinders asked.

"It's very far. It is a city underground, or so surrounded by mountains that it appears to be underground. There are many entrances and exits, if one knows the way. Mostly, I know that you want to avoid the place, if possible."

"Is that all?"

"As I said, Madame, my concern has largely been with living, breathing adversaries."

"You are not doing well, child. Not well at all. Do you wish to be fed to my little flowers?"

"The question is insulting," said Shrike.

The old woman was silent for a moment. Then asked, "If you were to go to Hell on my behalf and you met the great beast called Asmodai, what would you say to him?"

"Who, Madame?"

"No questions, please," said Primo.

"What would you say upon meeting the beast Asmodai?" asked Madame Cinders.

"Good day to you, sir beast?"

Madame Cinders shook her head wearily and turned to Primo. The little man looked at the lever that controlled the metal flower hanging over their heads.

"I would say his name," said Spyder. He took a step forward so that he was standing next to Shrike. Her head snapped in his direction. "If I were wearing something on my head, I would remove it and I'd say Asmodai's name three times, once to each of his heads. Once I've done this, he'll kneel down and answer all my questions truthfully."

"And if you met Paimon?"

"I would only speak to him facing the northwest and never, ever look into his eyes."

"Better," said Madame Cinders. "Between the two of you, I see one good hunter and one good hunter is all I need."

The woman made a slight, almost invisible gesture. Primo jerked the lever that controlled the metal flower. Gears ground again and the blades began to retract. Spyder, his stomach knotted with tension, relaxed. Until he heard a click. The flower stopped retracting and the blades sprang open. The metal blossom shot down at them as if fired by a cannon. Spyder couldn't move. There was nowhere to go and he was mesmerized by the gorgeous meat grinder falling toward their heads.

Something blurred past his eye.

Shrike's blade was up and out. She hadn't struck the flower, but had wedged her sword into the central shaft around which the blades spun, jamming the mechanism. When he realized it had stopped, Spyder grabbed on to Shrike's sword, reinforcing her hold on the flower.

Madame Cinders' deep rasping laugh filled the room. "Better and better," she said. "You've earned the commission." Primo pushed the lever again and the flower retracted completely, disappearing into the ceiling. By then, the old woman had gone.

EIGHTEEN
A WEAPON FOR OTHERS

Primo took Spyder and Shrike from the greenhouse to Madame Cinders' private quarters, which was located at the top of the minaret they'd seen from outside the compound.

They climbed a stone spiral staircase that had been worn smooth over centuries of use. Spyder had no idea how Madame Cinders got up and down the tower since it didn't seem big enough to house anything resembling an elevator. Shrike tugged on Spyder's arm, holding him back and letting Primo get ahead of them on the stairs.

"Since when are you an expert on demonology?" she asked. "You didn't even believe in demons until two days ago."

"My daddy used to say, 'Just because T-bones are better eating, doesn't mean you shouldn't know the zip code of the brisket.'"

"What the hell does that mean?"

"It means, that even a useless tattooist can pick up a few facts that aren't about girls or ink," he said. "Jenny was an anthropology major. Studying medieval Christianity. I used to read her textbooks when she was finished. You'd be surprised how hot and bothered a little demon and saint talk gets Catholic girls. I still know Hell's floor plan, all seven Heavens and which angels rule each one."

"You saved us back there."

"That sword trick helped. Someday you're going to have to show me how that thing goes from a cane to a blade so fast."

"Stay useful and I will."

They entered Madame Cinders' private quarters. The room was dark, as the shutters, which were carved in traditional Muslim geometrics, were closed to keep out the heat. Enough light came through the skylights that the opulence of the room was unmistakable. The walls were hung with tapestries and dark purple velvets. The furniture, a mixture of low Middle Eastern-style pillows and benches, was mixed with elegant European pieces and upholstered in rich brocades. Delicate lamps of brass and milky glass dotted the room. Above an Empire-style desk was an oil portrait of a young woman. Her skin was creamy and pale, like liquid pearls, and her hair long and dark. She wore a high-necked turquoise gown of a simple cut, but even in the painting it was obvious that it was of exquisite material and expertly made. In her hands, the girl held a book whose tattered cover and cracked spine indicated its great age and constant use. Spyder wondered if the girl in the picture was Madame Cinders in earlier, happier times. It was hard picturing the wheezing wreck in the wheelchair as a girl, much less a pretty one getting her portrait painted on her birthday.

"Yes, young man," said Madame Cinders. "A book. That is what I've brought you here for."

"You want us to steal a book, Madame?" asked Shrike.

"The one in this painting?" Spyder asked.

Madame Cinders shook her head, moving the fabric of her hijab slightly. Spyder realized that the awful stench back at the greenhouse wasn't the exotic plants, but Madame Cinders herself. The heavy incense in the tower couldn't disguise the stink of her flesh.

"You're right, I am rotting."

Spyder looked at the woman. He realized that she could read his thoughts. Or was she just picking it up from body language? He resolved to stand completely still and look directly at her.

"Do that, if it comforts you." Madame Cinders nodded toward Shrike. "She has no such worries, you see. Her world is black and full of secrets buried in darkness and deeper darkness. That's why she's so valuable to me. What's an affliction to some, is a weapon for others." Madame Cinders paused as her pump started up again. "I know you both have questions, but let me tell you how the girl in that portrait became the creature you see before you.

"Since the time of the Great Divide, when all the Spheres of the world broke each away from the other, my family has guarded a book. The first book. It contains the true names of all things. Someone with the understanding to use the book could blot out the sun. Turn the oceans to blood. Or close forever the doors of existence.

"The book was stolen from this very room and spirited to Hell by a demon. The same Asmodai I asked you about earlier. Asmodai is known to possess vast and arcane knowledge, so I assumed he had stolen the book for himself. After years of trying, I managed to pursue him into Hell to retrieve the book that was my responsibility to guard.

"In Hell, I learned that Asmodai was now in the employ of a powerful wizard who now makes his home in that dank and depraved realm. It was he who transfigured me from the young girl in the painting to the half-alive thing you see now. All of my strength and knowledge goes into keeping myself alive. I haven't the power to fight for the book anymore."

The pump stopped and Madame Cinders seemed to sag for a moment, then sat up straight in her chair, renewed by whatever potion or tincture had entered her dying blood stream.

"I was arrogant," she said. "Full of pride in my magic and fury at losing the book. I forgot a fundamental law of the universe: that no mortal may look upon Heaven or Hell and walk again among the living. What power the enemy wizard didn't bleed from me, I used up weaving a spell to escape that horrid place."

"That's why you sent for me," said Shrike. "Not because I'm the best assassin, but because I'm blind."

"Because you are both, Butcher Bird."

"I'm not blind. What about me?" asked Spyder.

"You keep her on course, it's easy to see. She's a burning fuse. You keep her from burning out. And you can be made blind temporarily, with a simple spell."

"No way."

"Then blindfold yourself and hope for gentle winds in the underworld."

"Excuse me, Madame Cinders," said Shrike, "I don't want to be crass, but what will be our payment for performing this service for you?"

"Why, child, I'll give you back your eyes."

"Can you fix mine? Make me the way I was before, able to forget all this?"

"It is an odd request and I will not be so rude as to ask why, but, yes, with the book I could do that for you."

"It's not enough," said Shrike. Spyder looked at her. "You're asking us to go to the most awful place imaginable and face both the legions of Hell and the wizard who almost killed you, a sorceress with more magic than I could ever hope to summon. And our payment is to be nothing more than becoming who we used to be? Madame, there must be something more you can offer us or, despite whatever threats you might care to make, we will have to refuse your offer." Spyder was surprised by Shrike's tone, but could tell that she was in full-on haggling mode. The traders in Tangiers had been the same way. It wasn't the easy-going bargaining of Nepal or Mexico, but a verbal fistfight. Spyder looked at Madame Cinders, waiting for her counter.

"What would be enough, Butcher Bird? Your kingdom back? Revenge on your enemies? Your father?"

"I barely recall my kingdom and my enemies will be damned in time. But to taunt me with my father's death, I didn't expect such low behavior from a lady of your standing, Madame."

Madame Cinders laughed and it sounded like bubbling sludge. "But your father isn't dead, Butcher Bird. He's merely mad. Would you like to see him? He's here, not two rooms away from us."

NINETEEN
WHAT MEN NEVER UNDERSTAND

Whirring ahead in her wheelchair, Madame Cinders led Spyder and Shrike to a padlocked room where the walls were padded with thick, stained silk.

Primo unlocked the door. In the darkest corner of the room, away from the light cast by the lone window, a man lay in a fetal position. His gray hair was greasy and wild. With dirty, bandaged fingers he mindlessly picked at the white padding that spilled out from a rip in the wall. The man's eyes were unfocussed, wide and wild.

From the door, Shrike said, "Father?" She stepped into the padded room, but Madame Cinders put up an arm to bar her. Shrike grabbed Spyder's shoulder. "What does he look like?" she asked.

"He's a mess," said Spyder. "Like those homeless guys you see eating out of dumpsters. I'm sorry."

"He is not in his right mind, child. He is quiet now, but can be quite dangerous."

Shrike pushed past Madame Cinders and felt along the wall until she found the huddled man. Spyder moved into the doorway, but hung back. He heard Madame Cinders muttering, "Brave girl. Stupid girl. She has to see everything for herself."

Shrike knelt by the old man and put her hand on his bony chest. "Father? It's Alizarin…"

The old man screamed and his hands flailed out, knocking Shrike back. Spyder darted across the room and pulled her back to the door. The old man kept on screaming, batting at invisible attackers, kicking at the empty air. Deep scars lined his cheeks where he'd clawed his skin away. He was reaching for something and if he hadn't been chained to the wall, he looked like he would be clawing past Spyder and Shrike and anything else he could get hold of. What is he trying to grab? wondered Spyder. He described all this to Shrike.

"What's wrong with him?" Shrike asked Madame Cinders.

"We found him in an asylum in Persia," she said. "He's been made mad by a curse, just as you were blinded by one. Only what your father is suffering is much, much worse."

"What is he fighting? What does he see?"

"He is seeing Hell, child, dwelling in two Spheres at once. His body is here, but his mind is chained below in some abyssal dungeon. What he is fighting off are the demons that torment him."

Shrike stood facing her father, though Spyder knew she couldn't see him. Still, he could feel her body shaking almost imperceptibly. She was trying to see him, trying to will his face into her mind.

"There is only one way to restore your father. And that is to free him from the diabolical shackles that keep him bound below. Otherwise, this is his fate until his heart or his mind finally crack forever."

"I understand," said Shrike, cutting off the other woman. "But I have to ask you again—and I don't ask this arrogantly, but out of fear that I can't truly help my father—how do I assassinate spirits? I fight the living."

"You kill the dead with the weapons of the dead," said Madame Cinders. "Give it to her," she told Primo. The little man came forward and pulled a long-bladed knife from an inner pocket of his jacket. He pressed the knife into Shrike's hand and stepped courteously back. Spyder could see by the way Shrike held the weapon that it was heavier than it looked. The hilt was some kind of black horn inlaid with fine silverwork and a blood-red ruby on each side. Shrike slowly pulled the blade from its scabbard, getting the feel of the thing.

"A hellspawn stole from me, so before I left that cursed place I returned the favor," Madame Cinders wheezed before lapsing into a coughing fit. "That is the knife of Apollyon, also called Abbadon. Do you know of him?"

"His name means 'The Destroyer,'" said Spyder.

"The Destroyer," repeated Madame Cinders. "The blade will kill anything in this world or the next."

"Why would a powerful demon need such a weapon?" asked Shrike. "What aren't you telling us?"

"Clever girl," said Madame Cinders. "You see far beyond your blindness."

"Answer the question, please."

"Apollyon is a general in Lucifer's army. He is part of a loyal faction that opposes Asmodai and the ambitious wizard. You see, Hell is in turmoil, Butcher Bird. The devil's throne is no longer secure. The wizard and his followers are sewing discontent among the other fallen angels. This mutiny has thrown the entire underworld into confusion. While it makes Hell a more dangerous place to dwell, it also makes it an easier place to enter and from which to escape. I'm asking you to be my thief in the land of the dead, but there should still be killing enough to satisfy even a Butcher Bird."

"Where is the book now?"

"Lucifer captured it and it now rests in his palace, Pandemonium."

Shrike slid the demon knife back into its scabbard. "If that book can save my father, I'll go," she said. "I accept your commission."

"Bring me back the book," said Madame Cinders. "The killing, I leave to your discretion. Slaughter armies or creep in and out like a church mouse. It doesn't matter to me. But remember this, Lucifer's ambitions are simple: He rules in Hell and wants vengeance on Heaven. There are revolutionaries in Hell whose ambitions are more like a man's, rooted in hunger and animal desire. Given the chance, they will use the book to overthrow Hell and then bring Hell to Earth. Fail to rescue the book, child, and we may all end up like your father."

"I won't fail," said Shrike. "I'll get your book and free my father. And keep Hell in its place."

"You leave tomorrow at dawn," said Madame Cinders, reversing in her wheelchair and leading them back to her quarters. "Primo will go with you. He knows your route to the Kasla Mountains, through whose highest peak Hell is accessible."

"There are things I need from the city," said Shrike.

"Go back, by all means. I've arranged a tuk-tuk for you. A more secure one, this time."

"Do you know who arranged the attack on our first ride?" asked Spyder.

"Wizards in league with the madman in Hell. Rebel angels, perhaps, knowing that I am coming for the book. I have a key forged by Lascaux imps, the greatest thieves on the mortal plane. It will open any lock, even in Hell. Come closer, child, so that I may give it to you."

Shrike went to the old woman, but instead of putting the key into her hand, Madam Cinders slid both her hand and the key into Shrike's chest. Shrike gasped and pulled away. Spyder held Shrike as she fell back. Madame Cinders' hand was empty.

"What have you done to me?" screamed Shrike, her sword up and at the old woman's throat.

"It's all right, girl. I've put the key somewhere no one can steal it. It will travel through you, with your blood. When you reach the cage where the book is housed, you will find the key again in your hand. Until then, it is safe."

"And unrecoverable, right?" spat Shrike. "This way, I can't betray you."

"Unless you fancy evisceration. And you can't live forever with that thing in your body. You must complete the task you have agreed to."

"Or she'll die," said Spyder.

"It's what we mortals do best," said Madame Cinders. "Don't fool yourself, boy. I haven't betrayed the girl. I'm merely holding her to our bargain. She's a woman and knows the difference between bargaining and treachery, something men never seem to understand."

"Fuck you, you twisted old bitch," said Spyder. Shrike laid a hand on his arm and stood up.

"She's right," Shrike said. "It's just part of bargaining and as fellow women we can, of course, trust each other." She gave Cinders a thin smile.

"You see?" said Madame Cinders. Though he couldn't see her face, Spyder knew she was smiling, showing black rotten teeth under her veil.

"And here is my last bargain," said Shrike, holding up Apollyon's knife. "When we've returned your book, if you don't deliver everything you've promised, I'll make sure this gets back to it's original owner with the name of the person who took it and where, precisely, to find her." Shrike bowed to Madame Cinders. "I promise this to you. As a woman."

Shrike turned and walked out, with Spyder following her. Primo trailed along behind, keeping his distance, clearly nervous.

Madame Cinders had been right about their transportation. A tuk-tuk, a loud, three-wheeled motorcycle that spewed black exhaust and rattled like a glorified lawnmower, was waiting for them in the tunnel. Spyder, Shrike and Primo rode in silence until they came to the wet crossroads where they'd paused earlier. Primo led them back on foot through the passages to Alcatraz. Shrike didn't say a word on the way back, but on the windy deck of the tourist boat back to San Francisco, she turned to Spyder and leaned against him. He put his arms around her and held her there. She sighed and relaxed into him.

"This is nice," Spyder said. He felt her nod. "You warm enough?"

"Yes," she said.

"I'm not going with you," Spyder blurted. "I thought I could, but I can't. I drank tequila with a demon. I talked to a sphinx. I almost got hacked into fertilizer and fed to man-eating daisies. And now I'm supposed to go to Hell. Only I'm not going. Somewhere between the alligator men and the demon knives, I hopped off this train."

"It's all right to be afraid," Shrike said. She pulled away from him. "I'm afraid, too."

"You're a killer. You've trained for this. A couple days ago, my greatest fear was leaving a message for one girl on another girl's answering machine."

"This is funny. I'd planned on ditching you after Madame Cinders offered us the job. I didn't want you to get hurt. But I don't know anything about Hell and I need your help."

"Why? So demons can use your skin to shine their boots? This isn't sneaking into the drive-in with your fuck buddies. This is putting one over on the Prince of Darkness and an army of fallen pissed-at-God-and-the-universe angels."

"You know I have to go."

"You're a cute girl, Shrike. I can say that because your intestines are still on the inside."

"I have to save my father."

"I don't save fathers. I couldn't save mine from drinking himself to death and yours looked pretty far fucking gone, too."

"You don't have to enter Hell itself. It'll take days getting to the Kasla Mountains. Tutor me. Bring your friend's books and teach me so I won't get lost in the underworld."

"That thing in a wheelchair said that if I see Hell, I'll be stranded there forever."

"You won't see it, I promise. I know this isn't your problem. I know you fell into this. But I need you now."

Spyder leaned against the rail and closed his eyes, feeling the rocking of the ship as they docked at Fisherman's Wharf.

"If you're coming, meet me at dawn. Primo will be here with our transportation. You hear me, pony boy?"

Spyder kissed Shrike on the cheek. "Good luck, Alizarin. Come back safe. And thanks for trying to help me out." He turned and walked away.

TWENTY

BADLANDS

Spyder grabbed a cab at Fisherman's Wharf and took it back to his warehouse.

When the driver tried to engage him in tourist chitchat, Spyder ignored him and stared out the window. It was dusk. The sky was midnight blue and shot through with glowing stripes of salmon. Lights were coming on as they drove through North Beach. Strip clubs, punk clubs, sports bars and Italian restaurants hissed by. On the corners were groups of tourists shivering as fog came down upon them in their Alcatraz Swim Team T-shirts. Fidgety clusters of students, street kids and sailors in dress whites ran through the traffic, eager to get on to the next good time.

And there were the mutilated, sipping cappuccinos at sidewalk cafés. The beautiful Volt Eater from the night market was being ferried down Broadway on a glittering sedan chair. Outside a twenty-four-hour sex shop at Broadway and Columbus, a blue-robed angel sat atop a sacrifice pole holding a pale, bloody angel in its arms and weeping.

Spyder dug the crumpled pack of cigarettes from his pocket and lit one. He thought of something Lulu had said when he first discovered her awful secret: "After a while, no matter how messed up it is, everything becomes normal." There's a lot of truth in that, he thought, watching the animal-shaped airships drift through the evening sky. Nothing was bothering him at that moment. With a little practice and the right drugs, he was certain that nothing would ever bother him again.

At his place, Spyder handed the driver a wad of bills and got out of the cab without waiting for change. Inside, the warehouse was cold and not all that comforting. As much as Spyder loved to travel, he was always thrilled and relieved to be back in his own comfortable, messy rooms. As he flicked on the light, however, the familiar piles of books and DVDs, the scattered clothes, felt odd and alien. He grabbed a fresh pack of cigarettes from the kitchen counter and hit the button that rolled up the big garage door that took up most of the west wall of the warehouse. Dropping onto the seat of the Dead Man's Ducati was the first thing that felt right to Spyder since leaving the boat at Fisherman's Wharf. He hit the button to lower the door and popped the clutch. Ducking at the last possible moment, Spyder cleared the weather stripping on the bottom of the door by an inch. He roared onto the 101 Freeway.

Shooting off at the first exit, Spyder headed up to Haight Street with the throttle wide open, blowing red lights and double-parked trucks the whole way. He didn't let up on the gas until he was a block from the tattoo parlor. Fog was drifting in when he rolled the bike between an SUV and a battered El Camino with NUESTRA RAZA stenciled high on the windshield.

Spyder was standing in the street before he realized that Route 666 Tattoos was gone. The area where the parlor once stood was a charred ruin cordoned off with yellow caution tape.

Spyder's mind was a complete blank as he ducked under the tape and stood where his customers had scanned the walls, looking over the flash designs. What he felt eventually was surprise. He'd only been gone a day, yet the place had burned and all the debris had been hauled away. Street people had already started a little colony of shopping carts where the back of the shop had stood. A couple of them (Men? Women? He couldn't tell in their layers of bulky coats.) stared at him while passing a bottle of Four Roses back and forth. Spyder kicked at the garbage that had begun to accumulate on the site. In the trash, he found the fried remains of one of his tattoo guns. He picked it up and weighed the thing in his hand. Dead metal. Worthless. Spyder stood up and let the tattoo gun fall back into the debris.

Jogging back to the Ducati, he gunned it to life and tore across Haight Street, up onto the sidewalk and through the caution tape into the shop, scattering trash and splinters of blackened wood. Revving the throttle, Spyder turned donuts in the debris, smoking his rear tire and scaring the winos enough to huddle together in the back. As a foot patrol cop came running into the burned shop, Spyder slammed back onto the street and away.

The light was on in Lulu's Mission District apartment. Spyder rang her bell and, when there was no answer, yelled up at her window. When that didn't work, he climbed the fence into her backyard and went across a neighbor's roof until, with a jump, he could reach the bottom of the fire escape. Spyder hauled himself up to the bottom landing and climbed the stairs to Lulu's apartment on the fourth floor.

Through the half-open window, he could see Lulu in her old orange robe, passed out on the couch. Pushing open the window the rest of the way, Spyder stepped inside. There were little packets of foil on the coffee table, along with burnt spoons, medical tubing and a syringe with a white, crusted tip. Spyder shouted angrily at Lulu.

"Wake up, asshole. Move. Look at me."

Lulu was limp, but she made a feeble attempt to push him away. Spyder knew that was a good sign. "Look at me, girl. It's Spyder. Open your eyes." He stopped shaking her for a moment when he remembered that she didn't have eyes to open. It didn't matter, she was rousing herself by then, holding on to his sleeve and pulling herself up.

"Spyder? That you?"

"Yeah, it's me. What the hell've you been doing?"

Lulu was sitting up shakily, staring in his direction with the little pieces of paper over her hollow eyes. She began to cry quietly and punched him hard in the chest. "Where you been? I thought you'd gone. Run off 'cause I'm a monster."

"You're no monster, Lulu. And I was only gone a day."

"A week!" yelled Lulu. "You've been gone a goddam week and no word at all!"

"Oh, baby." Lulu grabbed him and cried against him, holding onto his jacket like a child. "I went away to get help for us," Spyder said. "It didn't seem like a week, but we went some funny places where the clocks run different."

"They burned down the shop, Spyder."

"Who did?"

"A bunch of people. Friends!" Lulu wiped her nose on the sleeve of her robe. Spyder handed her a bloody Kleenex from the table where her works were scattered. "They were crazy. Neighbors from Haight Street. People from the Bardo Lounge. They came in saying all kinds of insane shit. You're a murderer or some shit. And, like, we kidnap kids and do things to 'em in the back. They started tearing the place up and someone had a gas can. I thought they were going to burn me, too." She was crying again. When Lulu blew her nose, Spyder saw fresh scars on her wrists. Deep and running along the inner length of her arm, the scars were dry, like ruts dug into hard-packed sand. Spyder touched the scars and Lulu laughed.

"Funny, huh? I can't even off myself. There ain't enough of me left to suicide."

While he'd been gone, Lulu had done other things to herself. She'd inserted slivers of glass and rusty nails through her skin, like parodies of her piercing jewelry. Spyder opened her robe and Lulu didn't resist. Her bare body was decorated with stingray quills and surgical needles. She'd pulled the rubber insulation off wire and laced the bare copper through her skin, ringing the shark's teeth she'd set above her bare pussy. It was mad. But Spyder had seen it before. It was anger mixed with ritual—Lulu's fury at her body and an attempt to reclaim her desiccated flesh through pain and action. Spyder closed Lulu's robe and said, "You're coming with me."

"Get away from her!" Spyder hit the deck as someone slammed into him from behind. He managed to get his boots flat on the floor and roll on top of his attacker, pinning their arms down. It was Rubi. She was screaming at him.

"Get out of here, you freak! Killer! You child-molesting fuck!"

"Rubi, calm down," said Spyder, not daring to let go. When it was clear he wasn't going to release her, Rubi stopped struggling.

"You going to rape me, too, asshole? Everyone's on to you. Such a big man. What you do to children, you sick fuck…"

"Rubi, whatever you think you know about me, it's not true."

"Don't you hurt my Lulu!"

From the couch Lulu said, "This is what everyone's like when they talk about you. What did you do? You're like Charlie Manson all of a sudden."

"I killed a demon's best friend," Spyder said. "Lulu, put some stuff in a bag. You're coming with me."

"No, she's not!" screamed Rubi. "I won't let him hurt you, baby."

"I don't want to go anywhere, Spyder. I'm scared."

"And you're stoned, too. Listen, it's not safe for you. If this curse or spell or whatever made people think I'm a killer, it means sooner or later, some of that's going to land on you. If they can't get to me, you're next on the menu."

"No! Don't listen to him, Lulu. He's sick. He's a murderer!"

"I'm so sorry, Rubi. I like you. I really do." Spyder held the bartender down and punched her as hard as he could across the jaw. Rubi was unconscious immediately.

"Rubi? Oh shit, Spyder."

"Lulu, don't fade on me now. We have to get you out of here." He held up the dirty syringe. "If these deluded assholes don't kill you, you're going to do it yourself."

He pulled her from the sofa and walked Lulu to the bedroom closet. "Get dressed," he told her, and grabbed the small leather backpack that Rubi always carried. Spyder dumped the contents on the bed and pulled shirts, underwear and socks from Lulu's dresser, shoving them in the pack until it was full.

When he was done, Lulu was sitting quietly, dressed in a scuffed pair of Doc Martens, black jeans with ripped knees and a pink Hello Kitty T-shirt. Spyder put Lulu's favorite '50s gas station attendant jacket on her and led her back to the living room. Rubi hadn't moved. Spyder knelt and listened to make sure she was breathing all right. She was. He got some ice from the freezer, wrapped it in a washcloth and laid it on Rubi's jaw. He dialed 911. When the operator came on, Spyder said, "There's been an accident. A woman's hurt," and gave the address.

"Bye, Rubi," whispered Lulu as Spyder hustled her out of the building.

"Hold on to me," he told her as they got on the bike. Lulu wrapper her arms around his waist and leaned heavily on his back. Spyder kicked the Dead Man's Ducati into gear and took back streets across town to a twenty-four-hour diner he knew down by the waterfront.

For all her scars and drugged despair, Lulu seemed better after a second cup of coffee. She took a long breath and even smiled the now familiar raw flesh smile.

"Aren't we a pair? A couple of real desperadoes. Like those kids in *Badlands*. Kit and…who was his girlfriend?"

"Holly."

"Yeah, that chick from *Carrie*. She was really something." After a moment, Lulu said, "I never saw you punch anybody like that before."

"Sure you have."

"Not a girl."

"Yeah," said Spyder. "That was new."

"I love her."

"I know you do. She going to be all right."

"You sure?"

"I promise."

Lulu looked out the window, apparently satisfied for the moment. They drank coffee, ate pie and french fries, and Spyder watched the clock over the counter creep ever so slowly toward dawn.

"So, what happens next to a couple of outlaws like us, hopped up on caffeine and sugar, and on the lam?"

"I figure it's a lot like *Badlands*," said Spyder. "We leave here, get a ride and go straight to Hell."

TWENTY-ONE
JUBILEE

At the far end of Fisherman's Wharf, past the eager early morning tourists and their blear-eyed children, a jeweled airship hung in the air.

The balloon portion resembled an enormous, ruby-colored seahorse. Below this was a comfortable-looking gondola of a dark, lacquered wood with gold filigree. Spyder saw the seahorse blocks away, but wasn't worried. By now he knew that no one else could see the thing or would remember it for more than a few seconds if they did.

Spyder parked the Dead Man's Ducati by a clam-chowder stand in front of Fisherman's Wharf and left the keys in the ignition. Taking Lulu by the hand, he led her down the long wooden walkway connected to the piers. Long before Fisherman's Wharf had been transformed into a video game and fried fish tourist trap, the place had been a working pier for fishing boats coming in from beyond the Golden Gate. Even weekend sailors avoided the place now, however. It wasn't just the tourists. The few places left to tie up boats had been staked out by hundreds of growling and extremely territorial sea lions. Mostly, the animals used the piers to sun themselves, so in the cool morning air there weren't more than a dozen or so sacked out on the deck. Spyder walked Lulu carefully around the sea lions to the airship.

Primo waved to them from the end of the pier. Shrike was sitting on one of the pilings, her face to the sun. Her pale skin was outlined in the orange and pinks of dawn light. Spyder stood behind her. She got to her feet, put a hand on his chest and smiled at him. "I never doubted you for a moment, even if you doubted yourself," Shrike said, and pecked him on the cheek. She went to the balloon and Primo helped her into the gondola, then Lulu. Spyder followed them inside as Primo cast off the rope that tethered them to the wharf. For a second, it seemed as if nothing was happening. Then, they rose straight into the chill morning sky. Spyder's stomach dropped with the nauseous sensation of riding in a freight elevator.

Shrike was passing around cups and a thermos full of hot coffee.

"Hey, I'm Lulu," Lulu said to Shrike. "A friend of Spyder's. I was at the bar with him the night you two met."

Shrike nodded. "Have some coffee," she said, then turned and went below deck.

Spyder poured coffee for Lulu and himself and watched Primo at the front of the gondola operating a spider web of lines and pulleys, positioning the airship to catch the bay winds. Spyder took his cup and approached the little man.

"Want some coffee?" Spyder asked.

"I don't drink stimulants, sir."

"Need any help with the ropes?"

Primo grinned. "Oh, no thank you. I'm fine." He pulled enthusiastically on one line and let another slide through his hand as they turned away from the coast and drifted toward the Golden Gate Bridge, steadily gaining altitude as they went.

"You look like the cat who ate the canary, after fucking it," said Spyder.

The little man nodded. "I'm doing what I love," he said. "I serve Madame Cinders because that is my duty. She gave my clan sanctuary centuries ago and we always honor our debts. But living sedentary in her palace isn't the happiest life for me."

"A ramblin', gamblin' man."

Primo laughed. "We Gytrash are travelers both by profession and by disposition. I grew up on horseback, in trading ships clad in gold and on endless overland treks through all three Spheres.

"This airship reminds me of one I was on many years ago. My clan landed on the island of Montes Lunae to make repairs and take on supplies. Montes Lunae is a rich, green island in the Second Sphere which, back then, was ruled by Chashash, the Raven King. It was the hundred and fiftieth year of Chashash's rein and in keeping with Lunae tradition, he'd declared Jubilee."

"That some kind of party?" asked Spyder.

"It's much, much more than that, sir. During Jubilee, all laws are suspended, all slaves freed, all the lands won in battle are returned to their original owners. Jubilee is a time of renewal and madness. A time to burn the fields—both physical and metaphysical. Prisons became art galleries. Art galleries became bordellos. Bordellos became courthouses. Then it all changes again over night.

"As time goes on, the laws of physics begin to fall apart. Mortals can fly…badly, in my experience. On Montes Lunae, many aeronauts cracked their skulls before they got the hang of it. And when they did learn the basics of flying, they'd still get airsick. It was a bad idea to enter some neighborhoods without an umbrella.

"There was a method to all this madness. Everyone who lived on the island, including visitors like us, were given tattoos with colored shapes—circles, triangles or squares, along with alchemical symbols. This complex combination of colors and symbols told you who you were in relation to everyone else on any given day. On my chest, I received an inverted red triangle with the symbol for quicksilver.

"The night my clan received its tattoos (each of us received a different combination of symbols), we had no idea of our place among the islanders or to each other anymore. We were saved when I saw a captain from the Raven King's army. I had met the man earlier, but that night he prostrated himself before me. He was a slave, he told me, the lowest of the low in relation to those who carried my symbol. I had him explain the pecking order to my whole clan, so that we might fit in with the celebrations. When I saw the captain again a few days later, he was the lord and I was the slave. This is how it was during Jubilee. Anyone could be anyone else on any given night. Even the Raven King himself was, on occasion, both a prisoner and a slave. I know this because I, Primo Kosinski, of the Black Iron Gytrash, for three full days became king of the Second Sphere.

"I was in prison when it happened. Everyone ends up in prison during Jubilee. What I didn't know was that the Jubilee kings and queens were chosen in prison by a lottery. My lottery card bore the outline of a wolf's paw. This meant nothing to me since a number of other prisoners had similar symbols on their lots. But through a combination of the wolf, the configuration of the stars in the sky and my tattoos, I was declared king and taken to the royal palace high atop the World Poplar.

"I loved being king. Pretty girls—exotic dancers who were now the legislature—would bring me fruit and legal documents. I often signed the documents without reading them, assuming I would learn what they were eventually.

"We passed new Jubilee laws constantly, then would make it illegal to enforce them. The laws were often deliberately ludicrous. It became illegal to carry a small dog while smoking a pipe. It was further illegal to attempt sexual relations with an animal while either party was on fire. No one could smile while wearing white, or frown while in the presence of a man in stripes. Those found guilty of these charges might find themselves banished to the sewers with nothing but a candle and a baseball bat. Or they might be made archbishop.

"The only law that remained constant and coldly rational throughout Jubilee was simple: Everyone on Montes Lunae, resident or guest, must participate in Jubilee wholeheartedly while he or she was there. This was a hard thing for some people. It was a hard thing for my family.

"Eventually, my mother found herself subordinate to a man she didn't like, a marriage broker who was also a card cheat and a libertine—two things my mother couldn't abide. She refused to serve the man when it was her time. When the broker insisted, my father and brothers beat him. My family was arrested and brought before me. I was king. I had no choice. They had broken the most basic law of Jubilee.

"I executed them."

Spyder looked at Primo hard as the little man made subtle adjustments on the lines that controlled the airship's progress.

"But this isn't a sad story," Primo continued. "To honor my family's death, I prepared their bodies as a great feast on my last night as king. I invited all the citizens of the island to dine with me. Everyone ate and through the citizens' digestive tracts, my family became a part of every person on Montes Lunae. When those citizens had children, a tiny piece of my family was passed on to them. To this day, I am welcome in any home on the island, from the highest to the lowest, because, in a sense, every person on Montes Lunae is a blood relation."

TWENTY-TWO
BEWITCHED

"It occurs to me that I have no idea where we're headed."

"To the desert. The Kasla Mountains," said Shrike. "They're our entrance to Hell."

Spyder and Shrike were in the galley below deck and she was mixing a strong tea fortified with red wine and spices. Spyder liked the smell and he enjoyed watching Shrike work, feeling with her small, sure hands for each utensil and ingredient as she prepared the brew.

"I've never heard of the Kaslas."

"They're on the island of Kher-aba in the Sunkosh Sea."

"This is going to be one of those places that regular people can't see, right? And I'm going to recognize fuck all."

"Chances are."

"Tell me how nice I am for coming along."

Shrike smiled. "You're an angel. A lifesaver. My prize pony."

The living quarters in the airship were like a flying palace, an equal, in miniature, of Madame Cinders' ornate quarters. The place smelled of cedar, mahogany and Shrike's herbal brew. Nearby, Lulu slept on a heavy Chinese fainting couch, delicately carved in the shape of an emperor dragon. Though smaller than his warehouse, the airship was easily the best place Spyder had ever lived.

"I'm the teacher here, school girl. You're not allowed to sexually harass me."

"You're missing your chance, Humbert. I was going to do my best Lolita for you."

"How is it that a princess who knows about Lolita has never heard of stuff like James Dean or a Porsche?"

"Sorry if I skipped Pop Culture 101 before we met. I've lived in this Sphere on and off and I've picked up a few things. TV I learned about from my old partner. He would describe the shows to me."

"You never told me much about him."

She shrugged. "He was a boy I met in the Third Sphere, Ozymand Riyahd, a thief and the son of a sword maker. He helped me train and perfect my skills. But it was dangerous for us. Soldiers from my kingdom were still looking for me. We bribed a wizard for the magic to get to the First Sphere. Neither swordsmanship nor magic helped, in the end. Ozymand was murdered. Is that what you wanted to know?"

"Sorry. I didn't mean to go all Jimmy Olsen, but I needed to know what it was between you two."

"Why?"

Spyder shrugged. "Because you have my interest. Because you're not like anyone I ever met before which, I know, is an understatement. I like you, but I don't want to go shaking my tail feathers where they're not wanted."

"Ozymand was my friend and will always own a piece of my heart. But he's gone now. We murderers are a practical bunch. Just like on TV. When the first Darrin left *Bewitched*, they got another."

"You know about *Bewitched*?"

"Uncle Arthur makes me laugh. But TV witches aren't much like the real ones."

Shrike finished preparing the tea and handed a cup to Spyder. It was warm and revived him after his sleepless night.

"Maybe you can get a job as a demon consultant in Hollywood."

"I'll be a stunt person for all the famous blind female action stars," said Shrike. She laughed. "I liked Jean Harlow. Is she still in movies?"

"Not for about sixty years."

"Oh. The way her voice sounded made her sound so beautiful."

"She was. Good guess."

"I told you: there's blind and there's blind."

"Which means what?"

"I'll explain later. Tell me about your friend. Is she an expert on Hell?"

"Lulu? Not hardly. She's a friend. Sort of my little sister. I couldn't leave her behind."

"Can she fight? Can she find water in the desert? Navigate by the stars?"

"She can give you nipple rings and a nice labret."

"Then why did you bring her? You know where we're going. Every step of this journey is going to be over razor blades and landmines."

"Things back home are steel-wool panties—somewhat uncomfortable and crawling up your ass. A demon's pissed at me, and now everyone thinks I'm Ted Bundy's cabana boy. If I'd a left Lulu behind, she would have offed herself or been offed by some solid citizen. You should understand about wanting to protect a friend."

"She's not one of your little harem girls?"

"Lulu's my oldest friend in the world. And if she was going to do the Dance of the Seven Veils it would be for you, not me."

"Ah. A girl's girl."

"She'd likely prefer 'Soft Butch,' but yeah. You're not jealous or anything are you?"

"You're the one whose penis has its own answering machine. I heard and smelled a woman coming on board..."

"And thought I was bringing a snack? Thanks for letting me know you still think I'm an idiot."

"I don't think that. We just don't know each other that well, yet. In my kind of work, trust is important. And I don't give it easily."

"Neither do I, and I'm not even a killer."

"Then, you should understand that I'm enjoying your company, but I'm not entirely at ease with it yet."

"I'm right with you there, Calamity Jane."

"We'll know more by the end of the trip."

"Not me. Aside from you, I want to forget every bit of what I've seen," said Spyder. He lit a cigarette.

"These things are never that simple," Shrike said. "I'm from another Sphere. When you lose the sight, I'll be gone, too. If you saw me at all, it would only be as a ghost."

"Balls. Madame Cinders said her book has the power to create and uncreate things. She should be able to bend a few rules about what can and can't be seen. I want to see you. I don't want to see anything that's going to eat me; I don't want to see demons or talking snakes; and I don't ever want to see anyone with horns or wings."

"Some of my best friends have horns and wings."

"I'll be your hillbilly boyfriend. Purty, but slow."

"No problem there."

"See? We're halfway home."

"And if Madame Cinders can't bend the rules? What if, to regain your precious ignorance, we never see each other again?"

"We'll deal with that when it happens. Besides, I don't know what the hell I'm doing out here. I'm probably going to get eaten by a demon dachshund or shanked by a fire-breathing tea cozy. That'd solve everything."

"Stick with me, pony boy. The talking dogs will have to get through me to get to you."

Shrike laid her hand on Spyder's chest. He didn't move, but became aware of his heart beating and the movement of blood through his body.

"I think you're sexually harassing me again, but I'll let it go for now," he said.

"Did you bring your books?"

"Jenny took most of 'em. But I know the important stuff, the grand schemes. The first, most important thing you need to understand about Hell is what Hermes Trismegistus, a famous alchemist, said: 'Hell is like anywhere else. Only worse.' Course, that sounds better in Latin."

Spyder talked into the night, telling Shrike about the pits and traps of Hell—the cunning lies demons tell, the slowly spinning trees full of knives in the abattoir forests. Lulu slept nearby in the hold. Spyder checked on her from time to time and made her drink water. They sailed west all day and all night. Like bright toys, airships drifted in the distance.

TWENTY-THREE
DEATH IS NOT THE END

A mong the greatest lies ever told, probably the greatest is that death only comes in one flavor.

Depending on the time, the place, the species of the deceased and its general standing in the universe, the nouveau-dead can find themselves experiencing any number of different types of death.

Most often, the classes of death experienced by humans fall into three categories:

Total Death. This is the typical human death. Sleeping the big sleep. Taking a dirt nap. The spirit has moved on and the body is empty meat in the cold ground. Nothing, short of some expensive special effects or an act of God, is going make a Total Death anything but a common separation of spirit and a feast for worms.

Hungry Death. This is a loathsome kind of half-death. Typically, the hungry dead end up as zombies—slow-witted, gluttons for human flesh and smelling like an abandoned pig farm. This is the category where you never want to find yourself. Too deranged for Heaven and too unstable to accept damnation in Hell, there's no love lost in any Sphere for the hungry dead.

Petit Mort. The little death. This is the most elusive, but perhaps the most sublime human death. It's reserved for those enlightened souls to whom death and life aren't separate states, but the continuation of a single thought. Once they've made that initial transition between life and death, your typical Petit Mort spirit slips continually been the Land of the Dead and the Living Earth, wherever the action happens to be at the time.

Each state of death has a very different cast. Not all bad ones are punished. Not all good souls are rewarded. Luck or the lack of it, timing and intelligence are as important in death as they are in life.

A few of the humans who've experienced Total Death are musicians Buddy Holly and Bob Wills (plus most of his Texas Playboys); comedian Andy Kaufman; aviatrix Amelia Earhart; Picasso; cosmonaut Valentina

Tereshkova; Marilyn Monroe; and Hitler.

The hungry dead also include a number of musicians, most notably Jim Morrison; also actress Jayne Mansfield; serial killer (and the real Jack the Ripper) Frederick Bailey Deeming; author Ayn Rand; big-eyed child painters Margaret and Walter Keane.

The small Petit Mort roster includes most of the major prophets, plus a few artists, such as the painter Marcel Duchamp; singer Robert Johnson; inventor Nikola Tesla, and Lilith, the first wild wife of Eden. Also in this category is a peculiar class of being, not quite human and not quite divine. These are the Tricksters. They slip between life and death for the simple reason that they refuse to take either state seriously. The Tricksters—Loki, Legba, the Painted Man, Coyote, Kubera and others—are pure chaos. Some cultures are certain that the Tricksters created the universe as a colossal practical joke, while others believe that as a joke is how they will end it.

TWENTY-FOUR

AMAZING GRACE

Spyder awoke sometime around dawn. Lulu was curled up next to him under a blanket on a big love seat. Spyder looked around for Shrike, but she wasn't anywhere in sight. Water was boiling on the little stove.

He got up carefully, trying not to wake Lulu, and went outside. The steady wind was wet and frigid. Spyder wrapped his arms around himself and went to the bow where Primo and Shrike, in her heavy coat, were talking. As he rounded the corner of the cabin, Spyder saw what the two were talking about. Another airship was hanging twenty or so yards off the port bow. It was shaped like an immense black scorpion. A metal cable was slowly extending from the scorpion ship's gondola, which hung from the end of the stinger.

"What's going on?" asked Spyder.

"According to Primo, they've been shadowing us all morning," said Shrike.

"What's that line they're sending over here?"

"A communication device," said Primo. "I believe."

"You don't know?"

"It's similar to devices I've seen, but I can't be sure."

"In any case, they'll be tethered to us. I don't like that," said Shrike.

"What's up, Spyder?" came a voice. He turned to see Lulu coming from the cabin.

"The neighbors want to borrow a cup of sugar."

"Holy shit," Lulu said, coming up behind him. "Are we happy about this?"

"I don't think we have any choice," said Shrike. "Spyder, not that I want you doing anything crazy, but would you go into the cabin and get that demon blade that Madame Cinders gave us?"

"Apollyon's knife?"

Shrike nodded. "It's wrapped in a silk scarf. If anything comes off that

94

ship, I want to know we can kill it."

"We going Texas Chainsaw on the other blimp, too?" asked Lulu. She pointed off to starboard.

"Spyder…?" said Shrike.

"Another ship's coming out of the clouds," he said. "A burning heart wrapped in thorns. It looks like a Christian sacred heart."

"It's the Seraphic Brotherhood," said Primo, "pledged to the archangel Michael. They're warrior priests."

"Are they approaching us?" asked Shrike.

"No," said Spyder. "They're just hanging parallel a mile or two away."

"There's others out there, too," said Lulu.

"She's right. I can see a half-dozen other ships, but they're mostly just dots."

"Get the blade, Spyder," Shrike said.

He ducked below deck and Lulu followed him.

"Lulu, I want you to stay in here," said Spyder. He stalked around the cabin looking for the silken bundle.

"I'm no cotillion queen, Spyder. I can take care of myself."

"Not when you're coming off junk."

"I wasn't that deep in this time."

On the kitchen counter, he spotted the bundle. "In any case, I'll feel better knowing you're safe." Spyder found a butcher knife on the stove and tossed it to her. "But if anything with more than one head comes through the door, feel free to stick it."

"That's pretty much always my policy."

"That's my girl." Spyder grabbed his leather jacket and headed back onto the deck.

"Hey, Spyder!"

"Yeah, Lulu?"

"Your kamikaze girl outside? She's a sweet slice of honeydew."

"That she is."

When Spyder got back to the bow of the ship, the cable that had been spooling from the scorpion had settled onto the port railing, clamping itself in place with a single golden claw. A rotating disc had flipped open at the top of the claw and there was a grainy image of a young man flickering on a small screen before the wheel. The young man's face was cut through with snowy scan lines. He wore a dark uniform of a severe cut (and marked with numerous medals and campaign ribbons) and a kind of silver ring around his head. To Spyder's relief, he was clearly human. The young man and Primo were speaking rapidly in a language Spyder didn't understand.

"Did I miss anything good?" Spyder asked Shrike.

"We're being offered a bribe," Shrike whispered. "The young pup doing all the talking is Bel, the crown prince of the Erragal Clan. One of the powerful houses of the Third Sphere."

"What exactly are we being bribed for?"

"They know where we're going and what we're bringing back. They want the book."

"I'm guessing these aren't the kind of people Madame Cinders would have over to tell her troubles to."

"It's unlikely," said Shrike. "Did you bring the knife?"

"I've got it under my coat."

"Don't do anything until I tell you. For now, we're just playing a diplomacy game. Primo is politely telling the prince thanks, but no thanks."

"What if he gets mad? Last time I looked there was fuck-all but water under us."

"Those other airships should keep him in line. The Erragals are powerful, but they wouldn't want to be seen shooting an unarmed ship from the sky."

"Pardon me," said Primo, "but the young prince is becoming very agitated. I don't think that anyone has every refused an Erragal royal bribe before."

"Tell him we're on Hajj. Religious pilgrims can't accept bribes."

"Yes, ma'am."

Off to the starboard side of the ship, the sky opened like a sunbeam slicing through a cloudbank. A pale, sexless, beatific face appeared between the ship and the Seraphic Brotherhood's floating heart. The face was glowing, like a child's dream of angels, and when it spoke, its voice was like thunder.

"Fuck me," whispered Spyder.

"I know that sound," said Shrike. "God's Army to the rescue."

"What are you talking about?"

"Listen."

All Spyder could hear was the echo and rumble of the transparent head hanging in the cold ocean air. The voice and the size of the thing weren't what was most awful about it; it was the utter blissfulness of its expression. Spyder had seen faces like that before—especially the eyes—when being analyzed by court-appointed psychiatrists and being sentenced by compassionate judges who sent him off to juvenile work camps for his own good. They were the understanding eyes of kindly folk who burned witches alive to save their souls. But when Spyder glanced back to the prince, he saw that Primo had dropped out of the conversation completely.

Lulu emerged from the cabin, clutching the butcher knife to her chest. "Are we dead yet?" she asked.

"Getting there," said Spyder. He nodded toward Bel's image. The young prince's flickering face was creased with anger. He was clearly no longer addressing Primo, but the Seraphic Brotherhood's ghost representative. The wraith head nodded and calmly answered the young prince's furious chatter. "The bribers are bitch-slapping each other," Spyder said.

"Or arguing over who gets to suck our bones," said Lulu.

"We'll know soon," said Shrike.

"Hey, Spyder?"

"What, Lulu?"

"When we were kids, did you ever picture yourself freezing to death while God and a big scorpion tried to decide who was going to eat you?"

"It's not god, Lulu. It's just some magic trick," said Spyder.

Lulu hunched her shoulders and went over to the railing. She gave the angels the finger and began to sing at the top of her lungs, "Onward, Christian soldiers, marching as to war, with the cross of Jesus going on before…"

"Quiet!" Shrike yelled. "Primo, before I push these fools overboard, what's happening?"

"I believe it's over, ma'am."

Spyder looked toward the beatific ghost head. It was fading from the sky. On the bow railing, the prince's spinning disc was folding itself up and retracting into the cable still hooked to the port railing.

"He's right," said Spyder. "Everyone's packing up and backing off."

"We were lucky," said Shrike. "Primo, set the course and come into the cabin with the rest of us."

"Yes, ma'am."

"Come on, Lulu," said Spyder.

"I don't think I like that Christian soldiers song anymore," Lulu said. "I never thought about the words till now. Doesn't seem very Christian singing about how fun war is."

"It's someone's idea of Christian."

"Not mine," said Lulu. "When I die, make 'em play 'Amazing Grace' at my funeral, okay?"

"I don't know that they're going to have 'Amazing Grace' on the jukebox at the strip club."

"What strip club?"

"The one we're going to have your funeral at."

"Cool. Can I come?"

TWENTY-FIVE
ANGEL FIRE

It was warm below deck, but Spyder shivered. He tucked Apollyon's knife into his belt and pulled his jacket around himself.

Primo was pouring whiskey for everyone from a crystal decanter that looked like it was worth more than everything Spyder had ever owned put together.

"I thought we were on some kind of secret mission," said Lulu. "Not much of a secret if every balloon jockey in Never Never Land shows up for the run."

"Someone's been ratting us out since day one. We got ambushed on the way to set up this job," Spyder said, downing his whiskey in a gulp.

"Thanks for inviting me along, bro. This is tons better than being at home under the covers with Rubi." Lulu, too, swallowed her whiskey and gave an exaggerated shake of her shoulders.

"Primo, did Madame Cinders tell anyone about trying to retrieve her book?" asked Shrike.

"Not that I know of."

"How many people knew she had the book in the first place?"

"A great many. Every truly powerful practitioner of magic in all the Spheres knows about the book of true names."

"Did Bel say why he wanted the book?"

"No, ma'am. In fact, I don't think he knows what it was. He just kept offering more and more gold. I got the distinct impression that he was acting on behalf of someone else. Perhaps behind his family's back."

"Did he say that?" asked Spyder, pouring himself and Lulu more whiskey. Shrike and Primo weren't drinking theirs, but, Spyder noted, seemed to take some comfort in simply holding the glasses.

"No. He was very evasive."

"So, you're just guessing."

"I'm observing. I'm a traveler. We learn to read people or we don't survive."

"No offense, man," said Spyder.

"None taken, sir."

"What do we do now?" Spyder asked Shrike.

She finally drank her whiskey, in two long gulps. "Sail on," she said. "Quickly. The sooner we reach the Kasla Mountains, the better."

"The young prince is still attached to the bow," said Primo.

"Get him off and get us out of here," Shrike said.

"Right away."

"So, the plan is we run real fast and hope they don't pounce on us like a cat on a baby chick?" asked Lulu.

"There's not much else we can do, bobbing along like a damned cork."

"This balloon idea was bullshit."

"A ship, a caravan or a magic pumpkin pulled by mice. It doesn't matter. Someone was going to try and stop us from getting to the gates of Hell. I was just hoping we'd get more of a head start."

Spyder was no longer gulping the whiskey, but sipping it. Still, its warmth wasn't particularly comforting. Just when he felt like he was getting used to the high weirdness that had swallowed his life, that lost-at-sea feeling was coming on him again.

When Jenny was packing to leave and the warehouse had iced over into glacial silence, Spyder had rewatched what, in his opinion, was Orson Welles's most peculiar movie, *Mr. Arkadin*. The flick was a puzzling mishmash of *Citizen Kane* crossed with a baroque postwar crime melodrama sort of spot-welded onto the side. *Mr. Arkadin* was about an ambitious young smuggler who's researching how the mysterious financier, Gregory Arkadin, made his first fortune. Arkadin himself ends up hiring the smuggler to finish the project. Apparently, he had amnesia and didn't know his own early history. The story dragged the young ne'er-do-well through the junk and small-time gangster debris of postwar Europe, taking him from a flea circus to fleabag motels to mansions where drunks hinted at escapades in white slavery. As the bad guys who were murdering the people the ne'er-do-well had interviewed got closer and closer to him, Spyder didn't understand why the guy didn't just take his pocket full of expenses money, hop a train and head for the hills.

One thing about the movie had always stuck with Spyder, however: Arkadin's amnesia story. Spyder wondered what that was like, waking up in some stranger's clothes, afraid to touch anything because it might be a mirage, or a papier-mâché prop on a movie set or a museum artifact wired to an alarm. The cops would come running in and beat you, maybe kill you, before ever you had the chance to explain that you were simply lost. Drinking his whiskey, Spyder felt definitely lost, trapped in someone else's life, imprisoned in some other loser's skin.

The airship shook. Then shook again, knocking the whiskey decanter and teakettle onto the floor. Outside, the booming voice of the Christians' talking head was back.

Spyder ran out onto the deck, followed by the others. The sacred heart airship had come much closer. At this distance, its size was shocking. The other ships, which had been keeping a discreet distance, were also closing in. When Spyder described the scene to Shrike, she yelled, "Primo, get us moving!"

"I can't! The prince's ship is still attached," Primo yelled, struggling with the claw that still gripped the railing.

"Get that thing off us," Shrike told Spyder. "Primo, get back to the navigation. When Spyder shakes us loose, take us low and away from here."

Spyder kicked at the golden claw and managed to put a few cracks in the surface of the rail, but whatever the rail and line were made of, they were very tough. Lulu ran over and kicked along with Spyder, but both the claw and railing remained where they were. Then Lulu stopped what she was doing.

"Shrike, get away from the railing," Lulu said.

Spyder turned to see what had caught Lulu's attention. The Seraphic Brotherhood's great burning heart was slowly opening, like the doors of a hangar. A burst of light and angels (or angel-shaped things) poured from the opening, flaming swords out before them. They scattered across the sky, some coming toward their ship, some toward the scorpion, while others headed for the more distant ships. The sound of cannon fire erupted across the sky as several of the more distant airships began to shoot at the angels and the Brotherhood's heart.

Something scraped against Spyder's side, and he remembered Apollyon's knife. Pulling it from its scabbard, Spyder swung it down. The blade split the claw and sliced through the railing so easily that, at first, Spyder thought he'd missed. A thick black fluid pumped from the claw's wrist as it and its tether fell away. The scorpion ship shuddered, perhaps in pain or perhaps in response to the angels slashing it with their burning blades.

Lulu was crouched with her back to the wall of the cabin, yelling, "Shit, shit, shit…" over and over. Shrike was at the far railing, slashing any angel that dared fly too low. Finally free of the claw, Primo had more control of the ship, but the angels overhead slashed at the steering lines. The deck swayed as the little man had less and less influence over the vessel. Spyder held onto the railing to keep from being thrown overboard. In the distance, a ship like a crystal skull was burning and a jeweled Garuda was sliced nearly in half before exploding.

The prince's scorpion ship wasn't faring much better. One of its enormous claws was falling away, on fire. At least they're shooting back, Spyder thought, as something streaked across the sky between their ship and the scorpion. Angels fled from the flying thing. The ones that didn't see it coming were sliced to pieces in its wake. Then the thing dived and was gone, only to emerge from under the far side of the deck, near Shrike. It flew right at and through the sacred heart, before circling back through the angel swarms, killing and maiming dozens as it swung back toward their ship.

Their seahorse was losing altitude fast. Spyder went forward to where Primo was struggling with the ship. Control lines and splintered sections of rigging lay at the little man's feet. As Spyder reached him, he was wrestling with the few lines that still worked.

"Please take this," Primo said. Spyder grabbed the line and was almost lifted off his feet by the weight. Primo had been holding it with one arm.

"Can you get us out of here?" Spyder asked.

"It's doubtful. I'm just trying to make our crash as easy as possible."

"What can I do?"

"Don't let go of that line." But it went slack in Spyder's hand as more angels swooped down and slashed at the ropes. Shrike jumped to the base of the rigging and slashed the heads from two angels. Too late. The deck trembled and the whole vessel dropped thirty feet in a second, then seemed to catch itself. Primo strained against the remaining lines.

"It's dead! Leave it," someone shouted.

Hovering off the starboard bow was a small, flat black flier. Its tapered body was curved like a wasp's, and its veined, quadruple wings were streaked with angel blood. The pilot had pushed back the canopy and was gesturing to them. "Get on board! You can't stay aloft much longer!"

"Don't have to tell me twice," said Spyder.

"I'll keep us steady and join you in a moment," Primo said.

Angels, debris and flames were thick overhead. Spyder kept his head down as he ran. He grabbed Lulu by the arm and yelled, "Shrike, we're leaving," then pulled her to the flier at the bow of the ship. The tall pilot leaned from the cabin as Spyder helped Shrike over the rail. Taking her hand, the pilot pulled her inside. Lulu followed.

"Primo!" Spyder yelled. "Come on!" An angelic sword slashed at Spyder. He fell back, his arm scorched, his vision blurred by the flaming sword. When he could see straight again, Spyder saw Primo, swollen to his fighting size, spikes slick with blood. He was burned and bleeding; dead angels lay all around him. An angel in Primo's grip fought weakly as he strangled it. Another angel dropped down from the overhead lines, slicing off Primo's right arm. The little man screamed. Spyder, Apollyon's knife out, felt the blade nick a rib as he buried it in the chest of the angel who'd cut Primo. The little man picked up his severed arm, then with Spyder's help, they stumbled to the black flier, grabbing on as the seahorse groaned and slid toward the ocean in flames.

Spyder pushed into the flier's cramped cabin, but Primo, in his exaggerated fighting form, was too big to fit through the opening. He crouched on the wing and held onto the canopy with his good arm as the flier dropped below the battle. And kept dropping.

"We're too heavy," said the pilot.

"There's land ahead," Primo yelled.

Through the breaking clouds, an island was spread out in the cold sea. The pilot struggled with the controls, circling toward a stretch of open beach. Spyder held onto Primo as best he could, while Lulu huddled against Shrike. The pilot yelled something, but all Spyder could hear was the white-noise hiss of the wind as it shrieked into the cabin. The beach came up fast. The pilot pulled back on the wheel. They bounced once and there was a snapping sound as the wings came off, taking Primo with them. The flier nosed down and dug into the sand and that was the last thing Spyder remembered for what felt like a very long time.

TWENTY-SIX

MY ENEMY'S ENEMY

"Shit," said Spyder.

"Aw, baby's first word," Lulu said. "Guess you're all right, cowboy."

Spyder opened his eyes. He couldn't sit up or quite focus on any one object. He recognized Lulu's blur because he'd seen that before in plenty of bars. A blur that might have been Shrike, left what was probably a campfire and came to where Spyder lay.

"How are you feeling?" asked Shrike.

"Alive. Gangbanged by gorillas."

"It was a hard landing."

"A soft crash is more like it," said Lulu.

"But everyone made it," Shrike said.

"It's hard to breathe," said Spyder.

"You may have broken some ribs," said Shrike. "Count Non did a healing spell on you, but it's still going to hurt for a few days."

"Count who?"

"Count Non," said Lulu. "The flyboy who saved us. He's the coolest. Steve McQueen fucked Superman and they had a baby. I already almost cut off some fingers playing with all his weirdass weapons."

"How about Primo? He fell off the wing."

"See for yourself," said Shrike. "Can you sit up?"

With Shrike and Lulu's help, Spyder managed to sit upright in the sand. Every breath was an adventure in pain. He gasped and took shallow breaths. That helped. Over by the fire, Primo sat, his injured shoulder wrapped in a clean bandage. He was drinking with a tall man dressed in leather and chainmail. The stranger had a scarred but darkly handsome face and eyes that glowed like a cat's in the firelight. He nodded at Spyder. Primo turned and smiled when he saw Spyder awake.

"Good to see you up, sir! Thank you for your help off the ship!"

Spyder tried to shout back, but his ribs spasmed and he couldn't get his breath. He gave Primo a pained smile and a little wave. The stranger, Count Non, raised his glass at Spyder.

"I've seen that guy before," said Spyder.

"Yes, he said he knew you, too," said Shrike.

"He doesn't know me. We just saw each other at the weird market with the Sphinx. How did he end up near our ship?"

"He was coming to knock us out of the sky."

"He said that?"

"Yes."

"A good dresser and honest as a preacher," said Lulu. "Why can't I find a girl like that?"

"Why is he still here if he came to bury us?" asked Spyder.

"Because I changed my mind," said Count Non.

Spyder's senses clearly weren't hitting on all cylinders yet. He hadn't seen the Count coming over.

"You need to move around or those muscles will stiffen up. Let me help you," Count Non said, reaching down and effortlessly lifting Spyder to his feet. It hurt like hell to be upright, but Spyder swallowed the pain. He didn't dare let go of the Count's shoulder as the man walked him slowly to the fire.

"How's the arm, Primo?" asked Spyder. "Or, well, you know what I mean."

The little man smiled and turned to let Spyder see his empty sleeve. "Like you, I'm a bit sore, but the Count has an extensive knowledge of healing magic. And it's hard to kill us Gytrash."

"Lucky for us," said the Count. Spyder watched the little man smile broadly. It was weird, but the Count had that kind of air about him. Spyder wasn't sure what it was, but the man's title fit him. There was a weight to his presence that was oddly—Spyder couldn't think of another word for it except "regal." He turned back to the Count.

"You look better without the makeup," he said.

Count Non chuckled. "Do you think so? If I'd known I wasn't flying right back to civilization, I would have packed it. My scars bother some people."

"I think they're cool," said Lulu.

"Thank you."

"What do you do, Count. When you aren't trying to kill us?" asked Spyder.

"Don't be rude," whispered Shrike.

"It's all right," said Count Non. "He's right to feel uneasy, being saved by his executioner. I was all set to kill you, especially when I saw you dealing with that pig prince of the Erragal Clan. Then I saw the Brotherhood attack your ship and knew that we were on the same side."

"What side is that?" asked Spyder. "I didn't even know there were sides."

"The Brotherhood is scared enough of your expedition to try and stop you, and that's good enough for me," said Count Non. "'O mine enemy: when I fall, I shall arise.'"

"I'll drink to that," said Lulu, picking up a glass.

"The Count is coming with us," said Shrike. "We can use the help, getting where we need to go."

"He's on our side now? Okay, asshole, who paid you to get us?"

"I was hired by the Wizard's Guild. I wasn't told why, but I understood that you were about to acquire something that would upset the balance of ethereal power in all the Spheres."

"So, you're some kind of magician union buster?"

"The Brotherhood doesn't believe in magic, but is more than willing to use it to its own ends. As we all recently witnessed. I knew then that whatever you were up to could only weaken them. The wizards will just have to sort out their business themselves."

"Just like that?" asked Spyder. "You're not afraid of a whole army of pissed-off magicians?"

"I have my own sources of protection," said Count Non.

"Like me, the Count is royalty without a country."

"Not quite," he said. "We're far from conquered. I'm traveling all the Spheres looking for help."

"How? By working as a merc?" said Spyder.

"What better ways to meet other warriors and adventurers such as yourselves?"

"Spyder, listen to me," said Shrike. She sat beside him in the sand and put her hand on his shoulder. "You've been unconscious for a full day. And the Count and I have been talking. I believe him. Please trust my judgment on this. I want him to come with us."

Spyder reached out to where Lulu was pouring drinks from a leather sack with a bone spout. She poured a glass of amber liquid and handed it to him. Spyder took a pull and felt the liquor burn where sand had scoured the back of his throat.

"Fuck every single little bit of this," said Spyder. He rubbed his temples. "So, where the hell are we?"

"We made it to Kher-aba, the right island to get to the Kasla Mountains," said Shrike. "But we're on the wrong side."

"How big is Kher-aba?"

"Big enough," said Lulu. "Walking is not plan one." Sometime during the night she'd lost the pieces of paper she'd kept taped over her eyes. The empty sockets were black and deep. Spyder tried not to stare.

"Before we landed, we spotted a city a day or so through the desert to the north," said the Count. "There's a fres- water river nearby. We'll follow that to the city."

"What city is it?"

"We don't know," said Shrike.

"It's not one I know," Primo said.

"That doesn't sound like a good thing," said Spyder.

"It doesn't mean anything, necessarily," said Shrike. "How long has it been since Madame Cinders went looking for the way into Hell? The city could be a recent vintage."

"In any case, we have no choice. We need transportation," said the Count.

The liquor was making Spyder lightheaded. He remembered that Shrike said he'd been unconscious for a day, which meant that he hadn't eaten in all that time. The liquor buzz made the ache around his middle seem far away.

"Thanks for fixing my ribs," Spyder said.

"Glad to help a fellow fugitive."

Spyder finished his drink and held out his glass for another. "So, Count, Lulu tells me you have some wicked bad weapons?"

Count Non's face widened into a smile, showing perfect white teeth. It embarrassed Spyder that he suddenly felt like a little kid who'd just been given a compliment from his favorite teacher.

TWENTY-SEVEN
THE HALL OF MIRRORS

The sun was up and the air was warm when Spyder awoke. It was the kind of early morning heat that he knew meant that the afternoon would be an inferno. Hope the river water's cool, he thought.

Spyder rolled over and groaned. His side hurt less, but now his right arm was sore. He'd spent a good part of the previous evening drunkenly playing with one of Count Non's odd weapons. What had he called it? Spyder tried to remember through the haze. It was something unpronounceable, with a lot of back-of-the-throat "ch" sounds. Spyder had just ended up calling it a Hornet, he recalled. His high school football team had been the Hornets and the weapon buzzed like a stinging insect when it was spun properly.

Spyder held his side and let out a groan when he stood up.

"The more you move around, the better you'll feel," said Count Non. The big man was packing his gear into a pair of leather saddlebags, like the ones Spyder had installed on the Dead Man's Ducati. The Count's bags looked hand-tooled, with squids or some weird animals stitched all over them. Spyder envied the bags.

"That'll fix my side, but what'll fix this arm?" he asked, rotating his shoulder painfully.

"You just need more practice. At least you didn't cut off your own head with it. I saw someone do that once."

"Thanks. I'll be playing that little movie over and over in my head tonight."

"Here, drink some water," said Shrike. "We're all going to have to be careful not to dehydrate out here."

Spyder sat down next her and took the canteen she offered. The water was cool and delicious.

"That's about perfect," he said. "Did this come from the river?"

"Yes, the Count and I brought it back this morning."

108

"You were out there all night?"

"A good part of it. We wanted to know if anyone or anything was coming down that river."

"Was there?"

"Not a soul. Just night animals having a drink."

"Must have been boring."

"We talked."

"About anything in particular?"

"Different things."

"Different things are good. I like different things."

Shrike took her coat from the ground and, after testing with her hand to see if the ashes were cool, scooped the charred remains of the fire into the lining. She then tied the whole thing in a bundle.

"What are you doing?" asked Spyder.

"I don't want to leave a big arrow pointing to where we've been or where we're headed. We brought some reeds from the river and can drag those over the sand to dampen out footprints. The wind will do the rest."

"Any ETA on that city?"

"A day or two, depending on our pace," said Primo. He was already smoothing the sand on the far side of the fire with another bundle of reeds.

"I don't suppose we have any food?"

"No, but we have a fresh water source and that's more important," said Shrike.

"And lord knows we've got weapons," Lulu said, using the bottom of her Hello Kitty shirt to polish the blade of a long, thin knife with a yellowed bone grip.

"When do we move out?"

"Right now," Shrike said. "Ready?"

"As I'll ever be."

"If the wind will not serve, take to the oars," said Count Non, hoisting his saddlebags onto his shoulders.

"What?"

"From the Romans. Not as poetic as Marcus Aurelius, but not bad. In this case, it means that we should start walking." He tossed Spyder the weapon he'd been playing with the night before. "Here. Work with that some more. You really weren't doing too badly. And it can't hurt to have as many competent fighters as possible on this journey."

"Thanks," Spyder said, not sure if he'd just been insulted or not.

The river was a few yards beyond the nearby dune wall. The water looked clean and clear. Animal tracks by small stands of reeds and algae-covered rocks lined the banks. Spyder leaned down painfully and scooped some of the water onto his face. It was icy, runoff from the mountains in the distance, he figured. They headed inland, straight toward the unknown city. The Count and Lulu were talking up front, with Primo trailing behind. Shrike dumped the remnants of their campfire in the water and used her cane to navigate the sand and rocks. Spyder walked with her. He had his leather jacket tied around his waist, holding Apollyon's knife in place.

"So, straight up, how do we stand right now?" he asked.

"We were blown out of the air. We're moving too slowly. And we're too many people."

"Why do I think that last one includes me?"

"I didn't say that, but I still don't want to see you get hurt."

"I appreciate that and double-down on that particular wish. But we're alive and moving. Besides, we've got the Count with us now. The way I see it, Lulu and I are the only dead weight."

"I don't believe in dead weight when it comes to people. People are too complicated. Too capable of surprises."

"For an ex-princess stuck in the desert with a bunch of semi-cripples, you're awfully Up with People."

"I like the heat. It reminds me of home."

"What's your reading on the Count? Sounds like you spent a nice day and night getting to know each other."

"That's an odd way to put it."

"He's sure your type. Tall, armed to the eyeballs, a hunk of burnin' love. He even has better saddlebags than me. I don't have any illusions about you and me, you know."

"Now who's jealous?"

"This isn't jealousy. This is the voice of pure reason. I just know that slumming for a few nights with a drunk ink monkey doesn't mean anything. Hell, he's even royalty. You can compare scepters."

"I'm not picking out bridesmaids dresses yet."

"Red is in this year. It goes with everything."

"I asked you silly questions when you brought Lulu, remember? We're still working on this trust thing."

"That remains the sad truth."

"Tell me a story," said Shrike.

"What kind of story?"

"Something about your life before. Something illuminating and revealing.

Not tattooing or sexual conquests. An adventure."

"You don't think sex is an adventure? Tough room," Spyder said.

He played idly with the Hornet. The weapon had a long cylindrical grip wrapped in a light, tough leather. At the top hung several whip-like strands of a stiff, saw-tooth metal. From the weight and feel of the weapon, the metal strands seemed to slide around the edge of the cylindrical grip on some kind of internal runner. With a little practice, Spyder discovered that he could spin the metal strands until they hummed like a swarm of locusts. When he had the rhythm right, the whirling strands formed a kind of shield that pulverized anything they made contact with. It was like holding off an enemy with a wood chipper. Spyder remembered Lulu and Primo taking turns chucking rocks and burning wood from the fire at him. The only times anyone hit him was when he lost the rhythm that kept the strands moving at top speed. He wondered what those saw-tooth blades would do to flesh.

"Okay, I have a story," Spyder said. "This was on, probably, my second trip to Paris. You been to Paris?"

"I passed through."

"I went there with this girl, Trina, one Christmas. She came from money and knew a lot more about the high end of the world than me. I was used to staying in squats and youth hostels. When I was with her, we stayed in an actual French hotel. The Hôtel Esmeralda, across from Notre Dame. It was cold and wet that time of year. We were under-dressed and freezing, but we did all the usual tourist stuff. The Louvre. The Eiffel Tower. Café Deux Maggots.

"There was this older Spanish guy, worked the front desk at night. Really nice. Later, he told us he was Peruvian. We asked him what bar we should go to and he offered to drive us around, give us an insider's tour of the city.

"It's a little after midnight when the guy, Pablo, gets off. He pulls around the front of the hotel in the smallest car I've ever seen. This car'd give a fetus claustrophobia. I'm polite, so I squeeze into the back. Pablo and Trina are up front.

"He starts driving and we don't know where the hell he's taking us. I'm suspicious, because that's my nature. But Pablo is cool. He takes us by some old buildings where Jean-Paul Marat and other French Revolution psychos used to live. He takes us into a dark, wet park where it's just starting to snow. This is the park where the best hookers hang out. Sure enough, there's a woman in a fur coat standing at an intersection, looking like she's waiting to cross. As we pull near her, she opens the fur coat. She's naked underneath, a Victoria's Secret wet dream. Pablo asks if we've ever seen Versailles. We hadn't, so he drives us out."

Spyder spun the Hornet's metal strands, and thumbed a stud on the grip. Spring-loaded spikes popped from both ends of the weapon. The Count had explained that when a fighter destroyed an enemy's sword, the spikes could be driven into the opponent's midsection as a finishing blow.

"Now, this is after midnight on Christmas Eve. In Paris. Everything is closed. Does this stop Pablo? Hell, no. He drives us all the way around Versailles until, in the back, we spot a guard gate that's open. This is too good to pass up. We sneak inside.

"There's a guard house maybe ten feet away, and we can hear the guards inside getting juiced on Christmas cheer. They don't care that three idiots are sneaking into a national monument. Did I mention that we'd been drinking?"

"I took that for granted."

"By now, the snow's stopped and there's mist everywhere. We're not drunk enough to try and bust into the palace itself, but there's acres of gardens out back. We wander back there for an hour, whispering, hoping not to set off any alarms. At times, the fog is so thick, we can't see anything, even standing next to each other. Leafless trees appear out of nowhere and then vanish again into the gloom. We sit on benches and smoke and try to peek inside the palace to see the Hall of Mirrors or where the Sun King might have shagged a mistress in secret.

"We couldn't see anything and the cold was starting to sober us up. Now we're getting nervous, so we decided to get out of there. Of course, when we went back, the guard door was locked. There's nothing to do but climb one of the stone walls to get out, and the only wall low enough to climb was right by the guard shack. We started up and hoped to god that the guards stayed put. We had to walk along the top of one wall and drop over the side of a second to get out of the place. The whole time we were going, I was praying, Please, Lord, don't let them find us sneaking out of there with a Peruvian. They'll think we're Shining Path guerillas and never believe we didn't plant a bomb or something."

What was weird about the Count's weapon was that, as polished and well-balanced as it was, its surface felt uneven and rough. Like maybe it hadn't been built—and even here, in this insane new world he inhabited, it struck Spyder as an odd idea—but as if it had been grown, like a flower.

"Is that it?" asked Shrike.

"I didn't get to the good part. The guards came outside with their stinky cheese and we had to shoot our way out."

"You did not."

"No, we didn't. We drove back to the hotel, ran upstairs and hid, waiting for the gendarmes to come and take us to jail on Christmas Day. But they didn't come and we got away with it. I suppose, it's not much of an adventure, as far as adventures go. There's no sex or imminent death or flying monkeys, but for some reason it sticks in my mind as a kind of perfect night."

"And the cynical tattooist is revealed to be a romantic."

"All losers are romantics. It's what keeps us from blowing our brains out."

TWENTY-EIGHT
SUSPICIOUS MINDS

"We'll reach the city by midday tomorrow, if we get moving by dawn," said Count Non.

"Good news," said Primo. "We need to reach the Kasla Mountains by the full moon. A shadow cast through a certain rocky promontory is the only way to find the entrance to Hell. If we miss the moon, we'll have to wait a month until the next one." He made a face and rubbed the shoulder where his arm was missing. Spyder felt for the guy. His side was hurting after the all-day hike.

"Fuck that," said Lulu. "Fuck that with Michael Jackson's pet monkey."

"Full moon's just a few days off. Think we can make it?" Spyder asked Shrike.

Shrike was smoking Spyder's last cigarette, puffing, then passing the butt to him. Spyder took a drag, then passed the precious smoke to Lulu, who opened her mouth to accept it like a communion Host. She smoked and passed the butt to Shrike, who leaned on her cane, lost in thought.

"We have to make it," Shrike said. "We can't hide out here like bugs in the sand for a month. We're lucky to have made it this far."

They sat in the entrance of a shallow cave, which served as cover for the small fire they had going to ward off the cold desert night. Earlier in the evening, they'd stacked brush at the cave entrance to diminish the glow of the fire, hoping not to be spotted by any scouts from the Seraphic Brotherhood, the Erragal prince or any of the other far too interested parties who might be looking for them. Spyder wasn't sure if "lucky" was the word he'd have used to describe their situation, but they were alive, and he had to admit that that counted big time in the luck department. But his gratitude lessened with every stab of hunger and throb of his injured ribs.

"I wonder what Rubi's doing right now," said Lulu.

"Missing you," Spyder said. "Cursing me."

"Blue moon, you saw me standing alone, without a dream in my heart, without a love of my own…" Lulu sang softly. "Elvis should have stopped right there, you know? He never did fuck all after he left Sun Records."

"If he'd stopped there, he wouldn't ever have done 'Suspicious Minds.'"

"Was it worth dying on the shitter for?"

"For 'Suspicious Minds'? Most definitely."

"I'm going to have to give you the benefit of the doubt on that one."

Spyder was sorry that Lulu had brought up Rubi. It made him think of Jenny, whom he no longer really missed, but who remained a kind of sick ache in his stomach. He couldn't even describe the sensation, but it was compounded of regret and the sense that he'd failed as a human in some fundamental way and that her desertion was the starkest proof of that. On the simplest level, though, it just made him gloomy to think that someone he'd been so connected to was walking around hating him. He gave Shrike the last of the cigarette, went to the cave entrance and sat down, letting the night breeze blow over him. The cold made him stop thinking.

He heard someone coming up behind him and saw Shrike settling down.

"You're quiet tonight," she said.

"It's a quiet night."

"You're thinking about home."

"I'm not thinking about anything right now."

"I liked your France story."

"Did you?"

"Would you like to hear one of mine?"

"Not right now. I mean, I want to, but I'm hurting and tired and won't be able to listen right."

"All right," she said. She held up her face to the wind as it blew into the cave. Spyder thought she looked like a young wolf when she stretched her head up like that. She was beautiful.

"Tell me about being blind," Spyder said. "About how there's 'blind and then there's blind.'"

Shrike poked at the sand with her cane. "You probably sensed that I have moments where I appear to see things."

"From the first night we met."

"It's not really sight. It's simple magic, the only kind I know. I never had any formal magic training and just picked up things along on the road. Traded for spells. Bought them. Stole them. There has always been a little magic in my family, but my mother had that knowledge and she was dead. I studied weapons because it made my father happy.

"When our kingdom was scattered and I was on the road, I only had the possessions I could grab from my bedside. A few family heirlooms. One of these was a kind of bracelet with a casting of a bird on top. A shrike. That's my family's totem animal.

"We also had family gods which we prayed and made offerings to. All the royal families have household gods. You need a deity or two on your side to keep other Houses from taking what's yours. Those who knew how could petition the gods for favors. I didn't have that knowledge. But I got it.

"I'd run off some bandits from the property of an odd little man, Cosimo Heisenberg, a kind of mechanical wizard. He made machines that were like people. 'Karakuri,' he called them. Little windup men and women who could sing an aria or write a sonnet or sew a wedding gown.

"He wanted to pay me with a new set of eyes, but I didn't like the notion of depending on mechanical, windup sight. So, he helped me use the gifts I already had better. He made this cane for me, which, as you've seen, is more than a cane. He also examined my heirlooms to see if there was anything of value. He was the first person I'd trusted since leaving home.

"He checked out the bracelet with the bird and figured out what it was for. You see, it made no sense as jewelry. The maker had cast the bird's claws from razor-sharp steel and fitted them to the underside of the piece, so that they were in contact with the skin of the person wearing the bracelet. There was also a spring mechanism to rake the claws down the wearer's arm. What use could there be for something like that?"

"Cutting. Blood," said Spyder, who'd seen his share of bloodletting and scarring rituals among the *überhipster* modern primitive crowd in San Francisco.

"Exactly. The bracelet was an instrument of sacrifice, a device for making a blood offering to my family gods. Say the right incantation and release the spring on the silver shrike. The blades would take your blood and help you get what you want. On a small scale. It's not much of a sacrifice. Only good for small favors. Like a second or two of sight."

"What do you see? Is it like normal vision?"

"Nothing at all. It's like I'm floating above the scene, looking down on everything happening. I can see myself and my opponent, plus the nearby landscape. The visions never last for long. Just long enough for me to get my bearings and a sense of an opponent. I can't do it too often. The gods get tired of these dime-store sacrifices. I have to be careful not to ask for their help too often."

Spyder frowned. "I wondered why you kept that coat on, even in the heat. You're hiding the bracelet."

"And my arm," said Shrike. "It's not something to see."

"How many times have you used the bracelet?"

"I don't know. Sometimes you make a blood offering without asking for anything in return. Sometimes, when you're boxed in, say, you use it more than once. More blood sometimes means more sight. Sometimes not. I've been using it for ten years."

Spyder reached over and pushed up the sleeve of Shrike's coat. The bracelet was on her right forearm. It was a beautiful object. Like something that belonged in a museum, he thought. He turned Shrike's arm over and worked the bracelet's clasp, sliding the thing off her arm. Shrike's skin was streaked with years of ragged scar tissue. The back of her arm was red with new scars, still in the healing process. She'd used it on the airship, Spyder thought.

He set the bracelet over his own arm. It was too small to go all the way around, so he held it in place and pushed the metal shrike back until he felt it catch. Feeling around the bird's wings, he found the release button and pushed it. The bird raked down his arm, sending an electric pain all the way up to his shoulder. When Shrike heard the bracelet snap, she started a little and reached for him.

"What did you do?" she asked.

"I wanted to know what it was like," Spyder said. He leaned down and kissed her scars before putting the bracelet back on Shrike's arm. She leaned into him and he put his bloody arm around her.

"Where I come from, this isn't your standard dating scenario," Spyder said. Shrike laughed at little. "But I guess it's one way to get to know each other."

"Excuse me."

Spyder looked up. Primo was standing over them.

"I hate to intrude, but I need to speak to madame Butcher Bird."

"Meaning you want me to take off?" asked Spyder.

Primo was silent.

"It's all right, Primo. Spyder is part of this and can hear anything you have to say."

"Yes, ma'am," Primo said. He groaned as he sat down. "There's something Madame Cinders didn't tell you, afraid that you might not agree to perform the service she requires."

"She wanted you to tell me when we were on the road and in too deep to turn back."

"Yes, ma'am. I'm sorry. I would have preferred not to do things this way."

"It's all right. I understand that it wasn't your choice. What is it that was too awful for me to know?"

"The mutinous spirits in Hell, the confusion that is to be our cover?"

"Tell me."

"Some say that it is led by the Golden Bull, Xero Abrasax."

Shrike was silent. She stabbed the ground with her cane.

"Shrike?" said Spyder. "You know this guy?"

"Yes."

"He's the…"

"Yes, he's the bastard traitor who fucked me, took my father, my sight and my kingdom."

"There's more, I'm afraid," said Primo.

"Fuck that sick bitch," Spyder said.

"Be quiet," said Shrike. "Tell me the rest, Primo."

"The key that Madame put into your body. You know that it was forged in Hell. It is not an object that is compatible with life. If you fail to reach the cage in which the book rests, the key will move through your body, as it is doing even now, and pierce your heart. You will die."

"We should turn around right now," said Spyder. "We've got the Count with us. She'd never expect an ambush. We'll kick her chair over, pull out her tubes and stand on her fucking throat until she takes that thing out of you."

"I can't do that. Loyalty is all people in my profession have."

"Excuse me, ma'am, but Mr. Spyder has a point. Whatever you decide, this I'm telling you as a friend and a Gytrash: Madame Cinders does not always honor her bargains gracefully. When this is over, you must be wary."

"Swell," said Spyder. "If we fail we're screwed and if we succeed we're fucked."

"Thank you for telling me. You're a true friend," said Shrike. She reached out and squeezed the little man's hand.

"What are you going to do?" he asked.

"We have to go forward. Without the book, we have nothing to bargain with. With it, we have a chance."

"We can cut and run," said Spyder. "Disappear into that city ahead. Or trade for a ship and go somewhere."

"There are too many people looking for us," said Shrike. "There's no ship that can sail us away from this mess. And I need to get this key out of my body. The only way to do that is to get to Hell and succeed."

"I'm going with you," said Spyder.

"You can't. One glimpse of the underworld and you'll be trapped there forever."

"I'm not going to sit by the door reading the funnies, wondering what time you're getting home from work."

"This is just stupid and dangerous. Why are you doing this?"

Spyder kissed Shrike's cheek. "Didn't you get the memo? Heroes are coming smaller this year."

They went and sat back down at the fire with Count Non and Lulu. The Count had his long legs propped against the far wall of the cave. Spyder watched as a tarantula worked its way down from the ceiling, stepped onto Count's boot and crept up his leg. When it reached his hip, Non grabbed the tarantula and tossed it into the fire, where it writhed and sizzled. Spyder looked at the man.

"When you cut out the poison sac, tarantula tastes a lot like crab," the Count said.

"There must be some seriously fucked up Boy Scouts where you come from," said Spyder.

Lulu was making shadow animals on the wall. She wiggled her fingers to create a giant spider.

"The Count and me were having a chat, and we agree on the whole Elvis thing. 'Suspicious Minds' is a fine song, but Tom-fucking-Jones could've sung it as well. Probably did, too. I don't have any Tom Jones CDs."

"I have a bootleg of Elvis doing 'Suspicious Minds' live that I'll play for you when we get back," said Spyder. "You'll see it's worth suffering any number of white-leather Vegas jumpsuits. For a song like that, you've got to take the good with the bad."

TWENTY-NINE

BERENICE

"It's Berenice," said Shrike. "We're lucky we followed the river."

"Now we know what town it is," said Spyder. "We could have just walked here through some sewer pipe and skipped the whole Hindenburg drama."

"No. Berenice isn't like other cities. It isn't really here. Only the memory of the city."

"A city like the Coma Gardens?"

"Berenice is where memories live when we're done with them. It's where they're born and it's where they eventually die."

"What good does it do us? We can't ride the memory of horses to the mountains."

"There are humans in Berenice," said Count Non. "Someone has to be there to bear witness. Otherwise, the memories fade away. To make money, the human inhabitants trade with travelers."

"Trade what?" asked Lulu.

"Lost keys, lost pets, lost dreams, lost hope," said Shrike. "I passed through there once before. It can be dangerous. Psychically. You don't want to turn a corner and run into your own lost virginity."

"Speak for yourself. I'd do me at fourteen," said Lulu. "Let's follow the goddam yellow brick road."

"No road, Lulu. Just the river," said Spyder.

"Shit."

"We'll swim," said Shrike. "We just have to get past the city walls. Inside, there are walkways along all the canals."

"You cool with swimming, Lulu?" Spyder asked.

"Excuse me, son. You were the civilian. I was a lifeguard at YMCA summer camp, remember?"

"Yeah, but that was a while back before your troubles."

"You think my empty eyes and guts are going to fill up with water and drown me? That ain't going to happen. But thanks a fuckload for bringing it up."

"I'm just worried is all."

"Don't be," Lulu said, and waded into the river. When she was knee deep, she turned back. "There aren't any sharks or things with stingers out here, are there?"

"Nothing that can hurt you," said Shrike.

"Count, you get on one side and I'll get on the other. We'll put Shrike and Primo between us. Make sure no one wanders off course," said Spyder.

The Count smiled. "A fine idea."

"Primo, are you all right swimming with one arm?" asked Shrike.

"I'll be a little slow, I think," he said.

"Slow's fine. No one's in a rush to find their lost socks," said Spyder.

Shrike took Spyder's arm as they waded into the river. When she swam, she did so with ease and confidence. Spyder realized quickly that she didn't need much looking after. He kept an eye on Primo, who was doing a kind of modified dog paddle with his one good arm. The swimmer Spyder kept wondering about was the Count. How he managed to stay afloat while still wearing his chainmail amazed Spyder. Lulu was ahead of them, a strong, steady swimmer. She'd tied her jacket around her waist and on certain strokes, her Hello Kitty shirt slid up her body, letting the morning sun glint off the glass and metal she'd inserted into her wounded flesh.

Something brushed along Spyder's legs. Fingers touched his chest, tugged at his arms as they entered the water on each stroke. "What the fuck is happening?"

"They can't hurt you," Shrike said. "They're just memories. Drowned sailors, corsairs, anyone who died in water."

Spyder suddenly wanted very much to be out of the river and done with Berenice. The towering city walls, through which they soon passed, also seemed to be made of water. Not ice, but liquid water, pulled upward and carved into imposing barriers. If all that water ever came down, Spyder thought, it would wash the city away.

Lulu was already out of the water when the rest made it to the walkway. She helped Spyder out and he grabbed Shrike. The Count leaned down and practically lifted Primo from the water. The little man bowed in thanks.

"Where to?" Spyder asked.

"*Uptown Saturday Night*," said Shrike.

"You know some weird shit, girl."

"That's an old movie, right? It just popped into my head. That happens here."

As they walked along the marble concourse beside the canal, Spyder asked, "Earlier, why did you say that we're lucky we followed the river?"

"There are four entrances to Berenice. Water, air, fire and earth. Fire is the memory of violence and war. Air is the perpetual hurricane of anger and lost souls. Earth is a freezing mountain of despair and fear."

"The memories of the drowned are like the welcoming arms of your family compared to what lives in those other places," said Count Non.

"Wonder what would've happened if I'd tossed in a handful of Alka-Seltzer back there?" asked Lulu. "Would it piss those dead guys off or make 'em feel better?"

THIRTY
A UNIVERSAL JOKE

Their clothes dried quickly in the bright sun, and by the time they reached one of the great boulevards that divided Berenice into its local parishes, no one would have guessed that they'd had to swim into the city.

From the interior, Berenice was much more impressive than it had seemed on the approach. At each corner of the boulevard was a white-washed ziggurat topped with a gilt sun, angled to catch the light at different times of the day. Crystal globes hung from polished streetlamps. Spyder counted a dozen large bronze statues to different gods on the one street. Who knew how many there were on the others? Handsome residents came and went from temples and tailor shops, butchers and herbalists, paying no attention to the travelers. The street on which they stood was paved with pale pink flagstones, but green, yellow and sky-blue streets intersected it.

"Okay, we're here, somewhere. What do we do now?" asked Lulu.

"Let us not sleep, as do others; but let us watch and be sober, putting on the breastplate of faith and love; and for a helmet, the hope of salvation," Count Non said.

Spyder looked hard at the Count.

"St. Paul's First Epistle to the Thessalonians," he said.

"Yeah, I was just about to say that."

"We need to find stables or a market," said Shrike. "Some place big, with professional traders. And remember, you can't tell the wandering memories of people from real humans simply by looking at them."

"Then how do we know who we're talking to?" asked Spyder. "How do we trade for anything?"

"It's a question of attitude," Shrike said. "If you're talking to the memory of a trader, his responses will be mechanical and rote. A memory isn't active. It can't really do or say anything new or original. A human trader will be more eager and unpredictable."

"Makes sense."

"I'm going to go alone," said Shrike. "A poor blind girl can sometimes count on a pity discount."

"You'll be able to find your way back here?" asked Spyder. "Maybe you should take Primo as backup."

"I'll be happy to accompany you, Butcher Bird. And a one-armed man with a blind woman might evoke even more pity from an anxious trader."

"All right," said Shrike. "We'll meet back here in two hours. Can I trust you three to find your way back?"

"Don't worry, I'll look after Lulu and the little brother," said the Count.

Spyder felt a pang of awkwardness as he and Shrike went off in different directions. He felt, somehow, that he should give her a goodbye kiss or something, but simultaneously wondered if he was supposed to acknowledge anything between them at all. In the end, they both went their own way.

They walked three abreast through the strange town, Spyder near the street and Lulu near the buildings. Count Non walked between them. "The first time I ever went to Tijuana on my own, I got lost," said Spyder. "Ended up in this shantytown somewhere up in the hills. This place went on and on. Plus, it was one of those days where you don't wake up hungover, you wake up still drunk. So, I'm wandering around, trying to figure out a way back to town, and this kid, a student, starts chatting me up. He wants to practice his English. Only whenever I ask him how to get back downtown, he suddenly can't understand me. I tell him to fuck off and keep walking. But these Tijuana shantytowns are like a goddam anthill. Houses made of broken cinder blocks, cardboard and big cans of vegetable oil pounded flat.

"Fast forward a few hours and I'm somewhere, but nowhere I've ever seen before. And now the sun is going down. Out of nowhere comes the kid who wanted English lessons. At first I think that I've just walked in a big circle. Then, I realize that the little fucker's probably been shadowing me all day. My eyes are red and my head's full of broken glass and dust bunnies. I was wearing a brand new shiny pair of two-hundred-dollar New Rock boots. I had to trade 'em to the kid to get out of there, and walked back to my hotel barefoot."

Spyder couldn't quite figure out a pattern to the city. A street would be laid out like an ordinary one in any town, but then a building would be gone and in its place would be a pile of junk. Lost things, Spyder guessed. Not objects, but the memory of them. There were mounds of keys, piles of every kind of money, great meals laid out on endless banquet tables, the wan clowns and listless trapeze acts from forgotten circuses, lost limbs (fingers still trying to grasp some long lost something, feet flexing with somewhere to go). There were packs of dogs, flocks of birds, colonies of house cats and stacks of dirty aquariums holding every kind of fish imaginable, lost pets all.

They stopped to look at the trinkets laid out on tables in a small street market on a yellow boulevard that intersected theirs. A trader with leathery skin and blue, chapped lips clasped his hands and greeted them eagerly. He stared at Lulu. "I see you've been doing some renovations, my dear." He took a bite of a juicy, green-skinned fruit. "What will you take for her?"

Spyder didn't bother looking up at the man, but kept studying the charms on the table. "She's not for sale."

The merchant leaned in close, speaking in intimate tones. "You think I won't keep her well because she lacks eyes. Don't worry. Those are not the organs that interest me."

Spyder tucked his hands in the waist of his jeans, pushing back his jacket to make sure the man saw Apollyon's knife. "I missed that. Say it again," Spyder told the man.

The merchant's gaze flickered from the knife to Spyder's eyes. "You misunderstood me, friend. There is no business here," said the merchant, licking his thin lips. "Thank you. Have a good day." He walked quickly away.

Spyder turned to Count Non, who loomed close behind him. "I was doing all right, you know. I don't need you doing Hulk Hogan over my shoulder."

"Perhaps neither of us frightened him," said the Count. "Perhaps for once he heard his own words and was appalled."

Lulu said nothing, but swept her arm across the merchant's table, knocking his wares to the pavement.

"Yeah, he seemed like the real reflective type," said Spyder.

"'God hath chosen the foolish things of the world to confound the wise; and God hath chosen the weak things of the world to confound the things which are mighty.'" The Count laughed. "I like you, little brother. You disguise your nobler qualities to play the fool."

"Uh, thanks."

"Would you take some advice from someone with a bit more experience of the world?"

"You don't look that much older than me."

"Trust me. I am."

"Are we talking Paul McCartney old or Bob Hope old?"

"More like those mountains in the distance."

"Damn. You must get all the senior discounts."

"Be quiet," said the Count. "It's not necessary to fill every moment with your own voice. Silence terrifies you. You see your own existence as so tenuous that you're afraid you'll pop like a bubble if, at every opportunity, you don't remind the world that you're alive. But wisdom begins in silence. In learning to listen. To words and to the world. Trust me. You won't disappear. And, in time, you might find that you've grown into something unexpected."

"What?"

"A man," said the Count. He started out of the market and back to the main boulevard. Spyder and Lulu followed.

"Don't feel badly. This is just a chat between friends, not a reprimand. If you feel lost and foolish sometimes, don't worry about that, either. All great men begin as fools. It's one of life's little jokes."

"Spyder, he just called you a joke of the universe. Kick his ass," said Lulu. She put an arm around Spyder's shoulders. Count Non smiled at her.

"Food for thought," said Spyder. "We'll cover more ground if we split up for a while. I'll meet you back at the corner where we started."

"I was just fucking with you, man," said Lulu, but Spyder was already rounding the corner in the other direction.

THIRTY-ONE
THE FUTURE

In a street of nightmares, Spyder saw the Black Clerks.
The street had been roofed over, like the souks of Morocco. The sound attracted Spyder to the spot, a strange and deliberate animal wail—screams extracted with mechanical precision.

Inside the dark, cramped street was a gallery of horrors. Men turned over bonfires on huge metal spits. Women crushed under rolling boulders studded with surgical blades. Children screamed as spiders and oversized ants tore at their young flesh. Terrified people were tormented up and down the length of the street, shrieking and tearing at the arms of pass-ersby as they were chased by snarling animals or angry mobs. Spyder took a breath and reminded himself that none of this was real. It was just the collective memories of bad dreams, the night terrors these poor saps could never forget. It reminded him of paintings by Bruegel and Goya, and, while he tried to work his way around the thought and not let it invade his consciousness, the memories of the paintings made him think of the underworld. If this is what Hell was going to be like, Spyder wasn't sure he could take it. Of course, he was going to be blindfolded so, unlike here, he wouldn't have to actually look at Hell. It was a small comfort, but Spyder was ready for any comfort he could get.

At the far end of the street, Spyder spotted the Black Clerks. At first, he took them to be part of another nightmare and stopped to watch them pulling the guts out of a cop who had been crucified across a writhing pile of drug-starved junkies, their withered limbs (oozing pus and blood from running sores) strained against the barbed wire that held them to-gether. The head Clerk, the one who always held the reptile-skin ledger, looked at Spyder and beckoned him over.

"You are quite a long way from home?" said the Clerk, in his peculiar singsong cadence.

"You see me. I thought you were someone's bad dream."

"We're as real as you?"

"How about him? Is he real, too?" asked Spyder, inclining his head toward the tormented cop.

"He thought he could escape us," said the Clerk. "Sometimes it is not enough to take what is ours from the body, but to insinuate ourselves in the mind and memory. A warning and object lesson for others? This is our burden."

Spyder started to walk away.

"I hope you aren't running away, trying to cheat providence?"

"No way, José. I'm true blue," said Spyder.

"You don't wish to stay and watch us work?"

One of the Clerks had placed an elaborate metal brace into the policeman's open mouth and was studiously sawing off his lower jaw.

"Why would I want to see that?"

"Because you're lying. And most people want to know their future."

Spyder backed away and quickly left the street of nightmares.

THIRTY-TWO
DOMINIONS

Before this world, there were other worlds. Before this universe, there were other universes. Before the gods you know now, there were plenty of other gods.

Gods like to think of themselves as eternal. It's what gets them through the eons, but there are only two true eternals: birth and death. Everything else is junk washed up on the beach. The tide goes out and the pretty pink shells, the gum wrappers and the dead jellyfish are all washed away. Gods and universes come and go this way, too, but a living god knows some tricks. A god can mold energy and matter into anything it wants, or nothing at all. Gods can appear in an instant. Gods can disappear faster than the half-life of Thulium-145.

To save themselves, gods can scheme and they can hide. Some gods learned to hold their breath and float like kelp in the elemental chaos that rules the roost when one universe ends and the next hasn't quite kicked in.

Each of these trickster gods thought she or he alone had outwitted Creation by crouching in shadows of the universal attic. Then a young God called Jehovah took a band of rebel angels and tossed them, like week-old fish, from his kingdom into the dark between the worlds. As the burning angels fell, the old gods laughed and heard each other. For the first in a long time, they knew they weren't alone.

Worlds collapsed as the old gods, called the Dominions, got to know each other and learn one another's favorite games. Galaxies flickered and went out like cheap motel light bulbs. Whole Spheres of existence burned like phosphorous. Though this took a few million years in human terms, it was just something to do over lunch for the Dominions.

But the universe had its own agenda. When the Dominions tried to slip back into our universe from their refuge in chaos, they took a header out of the starry firmament, every bit as violent and humiliating as Lucifer's fall from Heaven. Not coincidentally, the Dominions fell along the same path as the exiled angels, straight into Hell. But unlike Lucifer's hordes, they didn't stop there. The mass of these beings was so great, that they fell through Hell out the other side, into a dead universe, one whose last echo hadn't yet faded away.

There was no life in this other universe except the Dominions themselves. Nothing to destroy but empty worlds. No one to torment, but each other. And no new games to play. The Dominions loved games. That's why they devoured stars. The best games, to them, were the ones played in the dark where only the sounds of screams and the taste and smell of evanescing lives let you know when you were winning. Their plan was to go from world to world, playing different games until there was no one left to play with. Then, they'd hide in the dark between universes until a new universe came into being, and they'd start all over again. Now, however, there was no one to play with and no way out. They'd fallen out of the living universe and didn't know the way back in.

In some stories, the Dominions have grown even madder in their isolation. They slash their empty worlds. They burn each other. But nothing makes them happy. When the Dominions sleep, they dream about us and how sad they are that we're so far away and not able to play. Sometimes they gnash their planet-size teeth in the dark. They're always looking, scratching at the edges of time and space for a way back into our universe. Sometimes they find a crack and peek through at us. When your skin goes cold and you feel like you're being watched, but no one is there, it's them. We're their drive-in double feature, with a Cherry Coke and free refills on popcorn.

THIRTY-THREE
THE KILLER INSIDE ME

The plaza was full of papers, kicked up by sluggish crosswinds. The papers were pages from old books and yellowed newspapers. Spyder stood at the bottom of a mountain of books taller than the highest ziggurat in Berenice.

He picked up a leather-bound volume embossed in gold Cyrillic on the cover. Inside the book were equations, a swamp of calculus problems and diagrams. He tossed the book back on the pile and picked up a paperback copy of *The Killer Inside Me* by Jim Thompson. It had the same cover as the edition he'd read as a teenager. Spyder hadn't seen a copy in years. He read a page at random and felt the same tingle at the base of his spine that he'd felt when he'd first run across Thompson's spare, hardened-steel prose at fifteen. Spyder wondered what would happen if he put the book in his pocket and just walked away.

"An interesting choice," said a man around the far side of the pile. "Considering the choices available."

Spyder craned his neck to see a short, round man in a kind of leather kaftan. Over the kaftan yards of barbed wire had been looped, encasing the man in spiny metal. On his face, the man wore a wooden mask depicting some grinning Japanese demon. Spyder remembered that Shrike had said something about masks. Some of the humans in Berenice wore masks, she'd said, to keep lost memories from attaching themselves to them and becoming false memories of a life they'd never led.

"I had this book when I was younger," said Spyder, tossing the Thompson back on the pile.

"I knew there was a reason and the reason was emotional, rather than an intellectual attachment. You picked up the book which moved your heart, not some great work of literature meant to impress others."

"I was a junior varsity criminal and had a few run-ins with the cops, so the book was a big deal to me back then."

"Of course it was!" said the round man. "If you enjoyed that, may I show you some other, rarer volumes at my stall nearby?"

"I'm just passing through. I'm not buying."

"No, no. No buying. Just looking. Come. It's a pleasure to meet a man of similar interests. I guarantee you will enjoy my wares. Books never written. Paintings never painted. Films never committed to celluloid. All only ever existed in the minds and hearts of the artists who dreamed them." The man turned and said to Spyder, "I am Bulgarkov."

"Spyder."

"Are you Spider Clan?"

"Whatever." Spyder followed Bulgarkov. "Nice zoot suit. You expecting a stampede?"

"Are you referring to my garments? The streets are full of dreams and men, two equally dangerous organisms. The mask keeps the hungry memories of men at bay and the wire keeps away the men themselves."

"I don't think I'm going to have time to look at anything," said Spyder, intending to leave the man at his stall. Spyder picked up a copy of *Poodle Springs* by Raymond Chandler. He vaguely remembered the book. Chandler had died before finishing it, but left notes and a partial manuscript. His publisher had hired some other hack to finish the novel years later. There was no second name on this *Poodle Springs* title page. Spyder flipped to the ending. It wasn't what he remembered in the patched-together version he'd read.

The stall was piled high with books. Paintings were stacked against the back wall and 35mm movie film cans were piled on wooden shelves and floor. The title on one caught Spyder's eye.

"This movie doesn't exist," he said.

"Of course it doesn't. If it did, I wouldn't have the thing in my shop."

"This says *Heart of Darkness*, directed by Orson Welles. Welles never directed *Heart of Darkness*. The budget was too big and the studio wouldn't pony up the money. That's why he made *Citizen Kane*."

"And yet you hold that very film in your hands. Do you know why?"

"No."

"Because Mr. Welles made the film in his mind. He saw it in his dreams, and the memories of those dreams have manifested themselves in the ethereal celluloid you see before you. Would you like to buy it?"

"I told you, I'm not here to buy. And I can't play a film like this. You need a movie theater projector. My VCR doesn't even work."

"Would you like to see the film?"

"Of course."

"There is a small cinema nearby. It is for people such as ourselves, the humans who inhabit our quaint little city. I allow all my films to be shown there. It's very good publicity."

"I can't," said Spyder. "I have to meet some friends."

"You'll just go for a little while. Not for the whole thing. When will you have this chance again?"

"You aren't trying to hustle me, are you? Because I'm going through kind of a weird period right now and it's left me cranky. Someone trying to hustle me would definitely go home limping."

"Why would I need to hustle you or anyone? I have the rarest merchandise in all of Berenice—the dreams of great artists. What will you give me to see Mr. Welles' wonderful film?"

"I have a little cash, but that's probably not worth anything here."

"No, no. Money is trash to me." He looked Spyder up and down like Spyder had once seen his uncle size up a neighbor's '57 T-Bird. The uncle came back that night to steal the car, but the neighbor was waiting and shot him in the head with a thirty-ought six.

"That ring," Bulgarkov said. "I'll take that."

"My ex gave me that."

"Even better. The memory of the gesture will still live in the metal."

Spyder looked at the ring on his left hand. It was a half skull that wrapped around the back of his finger. Jenny had given him the ring on their six-month anniversary. It was a cheap thing, but he'd always loved it.

"I don't know," he said.

"Mr. Welles is waiting. I am waiting. You are waiting, too. The girl, obviously, is gone. Let the ring go and get on with your life."

Spyder thought about it. Things hadn't always been bad with Jenny, and the ring was a reminder of a time when things had been close to great. These days, every memory of her felt like five hundred pounds of nails. That wasn't what made the decision for him. In the end, he gave the ring to the merchant for the same reason he'd done so many things in his life: "Why the hell not?" he said, and slid the ring off.

Bulgarkov dropped the ring into a pocket beneath his loops of barbed wire and said, "The cinema is this way." He pointed back toward the plaza and came from his stall to show Spyder, but tripped over the frame of an unknown Francis Bacon self-portrait. The merchant started to fall and Spyder instinctively reached out to grab him. Bulgarkov's barbed wire ripped through the palm of Spyder's right hand.

"Shit!" yelled Spyder.

"Take this," said Bulgarkov, going to the back of his stall and return-ing with a silk scarf. He wrapped the material tightly around Spyder's wounded hand and stanched the flow, but blood had already splashed on the pavement and the floor of the stall.

"You're a goddam menace in that suit, man," Spyder said.

"I'm so sorry." Bulgarkov grabbed a book from the stall and handed it to Spyder. "Here, the book you were admiring, please take it, with my apologies."

"I'm okay. It just startled me, is all," said Spyder, but his hand was throb-bing. "Don't go square dancing in that get-up. Adiós." He took the book and headed off, following the directions Bulgarkov had given him.

As Bulgarkov said, the cinema was indeed small, a converted café, full of silent patrons, with a wrinkled sheet for a screen at one end and a clattering film projector at the other. Through the front entrance, Spyder could see a sliver of the face of a young, handsome Orson Welles. He was sweating and his eyes were wide. Welles' voice came through the open door: "Did he live his life again in every detail of desire, temptation and surrender during that supreme moment of complete knowledge? He cried in a whisper at some image, at some vision—he cried out twice, a cry that was no more than a breath…

"The horror! The horror!"

A shadow moved across Spyder. "When they told me you were in Ber-enice, I knew you'd show up here."

Spyder looked at the man. He dropped Bulgarkov's book, seeing his own face, ten years younger.

THIRTY-FOUR

THE GHOST OF CHRISTMAS PAST

"Boo," said Spyder's younger self. "I am the ghost of Christmas past."

"How long you been rehearsing that one, you little shit?"

"I had it for a while, but I was saving it for a special occasion, grandpa."

"At least I know what you are."

"What?" asked the younger Spyder.

"What's the line? 'An undigested bit of beef, a blot of mustard, a crumb of cheese, a fragment of an underdone potato.'"

"'There's more of gravy than of grave about you!' Of course, we never read the book, did we?"

"It's just a story. Not really a book. And, actually, I have read it since then. But I still prefer the movie."

"*A Christmas Carol*, nineteen thirty-eight, directed by Edwin L. Marin," said young Spyder.

"With Reginald Owen as Scrooge."

"The only real movies are in black and white. We're secret snobs."

"I'm a snob. You're just the memory of a lot of bad speed. Who told you I was here?"

"Mutual friends."

"The Black Clerks? They send you to spy or just to fuck with me?"

"I do what I want, old man. When I heard you were around, I came by. I wanted to see how I turn out."

"What's the verdict, son?"

"Nice ink. But the rest of you is old and soft."

"That's what you always said to everyone over twenty-five," said Spyder, flashing back on using variations of the line on uncles, cousins, cops and counselors throughout his teens. "It's true, then. You little Casper the Ghosts really can't say anything original. You just remix what I said

135

an ice age ago."

"I hear tell you're a tamed little bitch these days. You really getting led around by an eyeless flatback?"

"She's an assassin, not a prostitute."

"Maybe now but I heard that in her lean and hungry youth she had another line of work."

"Didn't we all?"

"Yeah, and it was fun!" said the younger Spyder. "You gave it up, didn't you? You have that housebroken look. Way too upstanding to steal for your supper these days."

"What can I say? Unlike you, Peter Pan, I grew up."

"That's your excuse for what you've become? That's stone pitiful."

"I'm not going to justify myself to someone who doesn't even exist. However, on the off chance that it means something, I'll tell you this. Remember Santos Raye?"

"Fat, white-haired fucker at the chop shop. Everyone called him Santos Claus."

"That's him. You're too young to know this, but Santos got murdered. Iggy Atkinson did it."

"So what? Santos was a snake-mean, drunk fuck who got what he deserved."

"Yeah, but I talked to him that morning. And Santos was Iggy's partner. Then Santos disappeared. No body, no nothing. But everyone knew what happened. I was a happy car thief, but I never pictured myself as a murderer. And I knew if I stuck around, sooner or later that's what I'd be. That or dead."

"You pussyed out. On both of us."

"We were always playing walking a fine line, painting and drawing in the day, stealing cars for Iggy and Santos at night. It was cool and fun. We were artists and above it all. Then Santos was dead and I knew who did it and I wasn't above shit. I made a choice. Art or crime. I chose art."

"You made the pussy choice."

"It's my life, and you're just the ghost of something I don't want to be, I don't even want to know about."

"Hey, remember this?" Young Spyder pulled a punch knife from behind his back.

"I'm you. You can't hurt me."

"I saw that *Star Trek*, too. But it's not how things work here. That bloody hand hurt?" His youthful reflexes were still streetfight quick. He slashed Spyder's already bloody fist.

"Fuck!" Spyder yelled, grabbing his cut hand.

Spyder went down on one knee. He'd liked kicking people in the head in his youth. When his younger self approached, Spyder doubled over as if in pain, reached into his own waist band and slashed the kid's right knee with Apollyon's knife. Young Spyder went down hard, clutching his leg.

"Fuck you, fucker! You're gonna die, you sell-out motherfucker. When the Clerks gut that dyke cunt and your girlfriend, I'm gonna hold you down and make you watch!"

Spyder felt an overpowering desire to run away. Seeing his young reckless self lying bloody on the ground and cursing him, another powerful desire took over, however. Spyder kicked the kid in the temple. Then in the ribs. Then the groin. Then he just kicked to feel the thrill of his boot making contact with a body. When he stopped, the boy wasn't moving. Spyder wrapped the silk scarf tighter around his wounded hand and ran into the side streets of Berenice, hoping he could find his way back to the rendezvous point. He didn't want to get lost and have to trade away another pair of good boots.

THIRTY-FIVE
UNSTRUNG

When Spyder finally found his way back to the corner on the pink flagstone street, the others were already there.

Lulu waved to him and Shrike cocked her head in his direction as he approached. Spyder wondered if she recognized his footsteps. He'd heard that blind people could sometimes do that sort of thing. His hand felt as if it were on fire.

"Hey, we got us horses. We're real cowboys now!" said Lulu happily. "Damn, what's up with your hand?"

"Are you all right, Spyder?" asked Shrike.

"Let me see the wound," said Count Non.

"Later. Let's get the fuck out of here."

"You know how to ride?" Shrike asked.

"The end with the face goes forward, right?"

They walked to the stables where Shrike and Primo had traded the last of her jewelry for horses, saddles and feed. Riding down the long boulevard, they left the city using a smuggler's route they'd bribed the stable owner to reveal: a refuse tunnel that swept away the waste and trash produced by the city's human population. The place was dark, stinking and, at times, the ancient masonry ceiling was so low that even lying flat on their mounts, the riders' backs slid along the slimy tunnel roof. But, it was better than trying to swim with the horses, or braving the sandstorm, fire or freezing waste at Berenice's other gates, Shrike reminded them, before vomiting into the filth. That set Spyder and Lulu off. Eventually, the tunnel ended at a sluggish stream in the open desert, just beyond the city walls. The fresh air and light was as thrilling as anything Spyder remembered in his life. They turned north, with Primo, the traveler and natural geomancer, in the lead. Lulu and the Count followed, and Spyder and Shrike rode at the rear.

"What went on back there?" asked Shrike. "Did you have words with

Count Non?"

"Nah. He had words with me. Listen, can you hurt those things back there? Those memory ghosts?"

"Tell me what happened."

"I had a run-in. With myself. It got out of hand. I might have killed him."

"I don't think you can kill those spirits. Do you still have the memory of the part of yourself that you fought with?"

"Yeah, I think so."

"Then it's still alive back there. The only one you hurt is yourself. There's so much pain in your voice."

"He was just a kid. I was just a kid. I wanted to kill him. I wanted to wipe him out."

"That's not how you're going to get rid of him, you know."

"What is?"

"Learn to forgive him."

"Did you forgive the guy who betrayed you?"

Neither of them said anything for a while. His hand had stopped bleeding, so he wiggled his fingers to see if they worked properly. They did, but moving them was agony. "Don't tell the others about this, okay?"

Shrike leaned to him in the saddle. "Kiss me," she said. Spyder was happy to oblige.

"Are you cured?" Shrike asked. "Back home, at the Autumn Encomium—it's a lot like Christmas—members of the royal family must kiss any ill or injured person who asks. The kiss was supposed to cure all maladies."

"Did it work?"

"Tradition says yes. As far as I'm aware, no, not even once."

They stopped to water the horses at a spring a few hours later. Berenice was long out of sight and before them was nothing but open desert and the Kasla Mountains in the distance. As the horses drank, the group ate some bread and meat Count Non had traded for in one of the street markets. The meat was stringy, but spicy and rich tasting. Spyder started to ask what kind of meat it was, but decided to leave well enough alone.

"How's your hand?" asked Lulu, between mouthfuls of bread.

"It's all right. The Count put on some ranch-dressing-smelling goo. It doesn't even hardly hurt," said Spyder, flexing his fingers.

"You see the fight barkers back in Berenice?"

"Think I must've missed them."

"Damn. You'd've loved it. After you took off, the Count and me were kind of looking for you. We went down this one street and there's all these sideshow freaks and retards in a big metal pen with all these locals staring 'em down. Pinheads. Guys with arms where their legs should be. Or their bodies stop just south of their nipples. Monster-headed hydrocephalic she-males. It's totally Tod Browning. And the real twisted part? These freaks fight each other while the barkers take bets!"

"And I thought I was having a twisted time."

"It gets worse," said Lulu. "I asked some old guy what the deal was. He said they were the broken memories. Like the memories of schizos or dying people. They're like the deranged homeless of Berenice, roaming the streets, attacking each other and normal memories. I guess some humans figured how to make some money off 'em. You'd never guess those shiny, happy people would be into that, would you? I mean, all those clean, straight streets, and here's the guy who made your shoes betting that the blind geek in the corner can bite the fingers off the legless tranny."

"They made money tossing Christians to the lions, why not memories?"

"Everything's show biz, in the end."

"Truer words were never."

"Couple of those clowns thought I was with the geeks on account of my unique look. The Count straightened 'em out."

Spyder wondered if he should tell Lulu about running into the Black Clerks, but he decided that the news wouldn't do her any good. He handed her the canteen of water Shrike had given him. Lulu took a long drink. A red and black snake burrowed up out of the sand, tasted the air with its tongue and dove back underground.

"And you say I never take you anywhere nice," Spyder said to Lulu.

That evening, they camped in a small dune valley, out of the night wind. They hadn't seen any airships all day, so the others started a fire while Primo showed Spyder how to hobble the horses. He didn't feel it while riding, but once on his feet, Spyder's ass and back were sore. It took him a while to pour grain into the horses' feed bags, as he couldn't grip either bag properly with his injured hand. The Count found him and helped him slip the bags onto the horses' heads.

"Back in Berenice, I upset you. That wasn't my intention," said Count Non.

"No harm, no foul, man," said Spyder, slipping the feed bag on the last horse. "I'm just a little on edge. You and Shrike, you're used to this Conan the Barbarian stuff. I'm just passing through and it's getting to me."

"It is a situation. I can see how ending up here unwillingly could leave one unstrung."

"That's it. I am un-fucking-strung," Spyder said. "What's your story? You don't sweat anything. That some stiff upper lip blue blood thing?"

"My father certainly wouldn't say so. Unlike Shrike, I can't claim a tragic seduction or a kingdom stolen. I'm nothing more than a bad son who can't go home."

"What did you do?"

"What does any son do? I didn't love my father enough. And he didn't have the patience to let me find that love on my own terms."

"We've got something in common, then. The last thing my father ever said to me, before he disappeared into a sea of Jack Daniel's, was, 'You are my greatest mistake.' I was twelve."

The Count nodded and stroked the neck of one of the horses. "Making our own way toughens us. Look at you. Not everyone could take the shock of being snatched unwillingly from one world and dropped into a new one."

"Halfway to Hell, man. I thought I'd cleaned up a little, and was going the other way. Or, at least, holding steady."

"It's not a kind universe. I've lived many places since leaving home, many much worse than this. Compared to where we could be, this isn't so bad at all."

"The idea that we could die out here doesn't bother you?"

"There are worse things than death. Would you rather change places with Shrike's father?"

"No thanks."

"For now, we have this sky and the moon, warm air in our lungs and good companions. I can tell you one thing for certain, little brother: In this life, no matter what anyone promises you, what allegiances of love or fealty they swear or what gods they pray to, you will never have more than what you have at this moment."

"Goddam, Count, you cheered me all the hell up. I might just dance."

Count Non looked up at the sky. "'Every night and every morn, some to misery are born; every morn and every night, some are born to sweet delight; some are born to sweet delight, some are born to endless night.'" He motioned for Spyder to follow him away from the horses. "Show me how well you can use—what are you calling it?—the Hornet."

Spyder held up his injured hand. "The wing's clipped."

"As it may well be in battle. Come on, I'll show you some tricks that will impress the girls."

"You make a convincing argument."

THIRTY-SIX

HIGHWAY TO HELL

"**M**y left ring finger," said Spyder.

"My little toe. Either one," replied Lulu.

"I suppose I could lose an ear."

"A nostril."

"Nope. It's the whole nose or nothing."

"Picky fucker. I'll keep my nose. How about my pancreas? I could lose that. What the hell does a pancreas do anyway?" Lulu asked.

"That's where your Islets of Langerhans are."

"What the hell are they?"

"I have no idea. I just remember the name from high school biology."

"I wonder if I even have a pancreas anymore."

The group was riding north, into a waste of dust and heat. It was early in the day and the air was still crisp. The lemon sun had bleached the sky to a pearly blue.

"If they took it, they must know what it's for, so someone's getting some use out of it."

"As long as someone's happy."

"Smell," said Spyder.

"Smell? That's a sense. Smell's not a part of your body you can lose."

"Excuse me, Nurse Ratched, but smell is a neurological response in the olfactory cortex in the temporal lobe of your brain. Ipso goddam facto, 'smell' is a part of your body."

"Fuck you and the Discovery Channel," said Lulu. "It's still a stupid answer. Without smell, you'd never get laid again. Sex is all about smell. Pheromones and all that invisible shit that let's you know who wants to ride you like a rocking horse and who just wants to steal your smokes." Lulu turned around in her saddle. "Am I right, Shrike? Guys are such idiots."

"She's right, Spyder. Sex is smell. Smell is sex."

"You're all against me," Spyder said. "Primo, you lost something the other day. You should be playing, too. What part of your body would you lose first if you had to lose something?"

"I don't think I'd like to lose anything more, thank you," said Primo.

Shrike said, "You don't want to play game this with Primo. He'll win."

"Why's that?" Spyder asked.

"Primo, what did you do with your severed arm?" Shrike asked.

"I ate it, ma'am."

From the desert floor rose the detritus of long-dead cities. Spyder slowed as they rode among the ruins. He ran his fingers over broken pillars that curved up from the sand like the ribs of a fossilized giant. Spiral stairways curled into the empty sky. Faceless, wind-scarred statues stood watch over the wreckage of enigmatic machines of corroded brass gears and cracked mirrors, stained ivory, springs, sprockets and shattered quartz lenses.

"I've never seen anything like this before," he said. "It's beautiful."

"I have seen all the works that are done under the sun; and, behold, all is vanity and vexation of spirit," Count Non said.

"It's shit like that that most weeks made me cut Sunday school," said Spyder. "I got a beating for it, but I'll take that over brainwashing. Everything we do or try is corrupt? What are we supposed to do with our lives?"

"According to a number of prophets," said Non, "our true calling is a lifetime of worship and nothing more."

"Praise the lord and pass the ammunition," said Spyder. "Thanks, but no thanks."

"I agree."

"You've got quite a stack of biblical pickup lines, Count. You in the seminary or something?"

"I am the victim of a classical education. I learned at a young age that a good quote allows you to appear smarter than you really are."

"'In Italy for thirty years under the Borgias they had warfare, terror, murder and bloodshed, but they produced Michelangelo, Leonardo da Vinci and the Renaissance. In Switzerland they had five hundred years of democracy and peace, and what did that produce? The cuckoo clock,'" recited Spyder. "Welles says that in *The Third Man*. I remember it whenever life goes all abstract expressionist."

"That's every other weekend for you, right?" said Lulu.

"Fuck you, Martha Stewart."

Along a high ridge to the east, desert nomads were salvaging junk from the sand. They had sheets of sand-scoured metal, ornate urns and statues piled on long sleds that they hauled, by hand, across the dunes.

"Should we stop and say hi?" asked Lulu.

"Why?" asked Shrike.

"I don't know. So we don't seem like assholes."

"This is their desert," said Count Non. "They're more likely to think we're thieves after their salvage than their new best friends."

"What about food and water? Maybe we could trade with them," Spyder said.

"We have enough food. And there's plenty of water in the desert," said Shrike. "Primo's taking us along a route with springs and wells, aren't you?"

"Give me a single leaf and I will tell you the shadows of the birds that have crossed it. Give me a stone and I will tell you what army has marched past and where the freshest water can be found," Primo said. "That's the earliest bit of wisdom the Gytrash learn in childhood."

The day was heating up quickly. The tracks of the nomads' sleds paralleled their trail for several miles, then cut to the east and disappeared. Spyder pulled off his leather jacket (causing shooting pains throughout his injured hand) and draped it over the saddle horn.

Shrike rode up beside him and offered him some of her water. Spyder drank and kissed her hand as he gave her back the canteen.

"Tell me more about Lucifer's kingdom," she said.

A few yards ahead of them, Spyder could hear Lulu singing quietly, "I'm on the Highway to Hell..."

"Some cultures see Hell as a pit of torment. Others as a workhouse as big as the universe," Spyder said.

THIRTY-SEVEN
A BAD GOOD NIGHT

"You sure you never see anything when you're not doing your blood magic? I swear, sometimes your eyes lock on me and they're wild and wide. There's fireworks going off inside and bolts of lightning, like from a tesla coil."

Spyder and Shrike had just finished making love on a Persian carpet Shrike had manifested with her magic book behind a dune near their camp.

Shrike smiled. "It's funny to hear you say that. No one ever talks to me about my eyes. Even Ozymand didn't. Everyone thinks I'm sensitive about it or something."

"Maybe they're afraid to piss off a hard girl with a really big sword."

"You're not. That's why I like you, pony boy."

Spyder took a handful of sand and slowly dribbled it between Shrike's breasts.

"You shit," she said, brushing herself off.

"If you ever get bored and decide to off me, my preference is being fucked to death."

"Duly noted. And I won't let Primo eat you. Not all of you." Shrike's hand slid down Spyder's body and wrapped around his cock. "I wish I could see your face. I wish I could see you hard. You feel good inside me."

Spyder kissed her and started to become hard again.

"What was that?" he asked, pulling away from her.

"What?"

"Listen."

They both lay quiet for a moment.

"It's the ruins," said Shrike. "Underground machines. Some of them have been humming on their own timetable for a thousand of years."

"Shit. I was afraid it was one of those balloons."

"Relax. Non's watching for them. Do you have any cigarettes left?"

145

"No. I wanted to trade for some in Berenice, but I decided to get mugged instead. We going to live through this, you think?"

"That's the plan. At least if we die in Hell, we'll be close to where we're going to end up."

"You can always find a little rainbow for me," said Spyder. "Does killing mean anything to you? I know its your job, but does it ever get to you?"

"It's not my dream job, but it's better than the alternatives. I'm not ready to be a beggar or a prostitute. When I was thrown out into the world all I had was a little magic and my skill with a sword. One day, I'll use it to win back my kingdom," said Shrike. She turned on her side facing Spyder. "I'm glad I don't see the faces of the people I've killed. But I'd rather die a fighter than a victim."

Spyder smoothed her dreads back from her face. "You are a fighter. A life-taker and a heartbreaker, and you don't need anyone. Certainly not someone like me. I can barely get my pants on to go to work in the morning. But when I look at you, I have this ridiculous desire to watch out for you."

Shrike nuzzled into Spyder's chest. "Sweet boy," she said.

From the other side of the dune someone cleared their throat.

"Who's that?" called Shrike, sitting up and grabbing her cane.

"Quiet," came Primo's low voice. It was the first time Spyder had heard him give anything like an order. "Something is about. Count Non would like you both to come back to camp."

"Tell him we'll be right there."

Spyder pulled on his pants and helped Shrike find her clothes. They left the carpet and ran back to camp.

"What's up?" Spyder asked. The others sat around a small fire, drinking the mint tea Lulu had bought in Berenice.

"Sit down and have some tea," said Count Non. "Don't look around. There's something out in the dunes."

"We heard machines earlier. From the ruins," said Spyder.

"This isn't machines or horses or even wolves looking for a quick meal."

"Men," said Shrike. "How many?"

"Eight, at least."

"Shit," said Spyder.

"Can you reach the Hornet?" asked the Count.

"It's right by my saddle, on the other side of the fire."

"Don't reach for it now. You'll fight with that and not the knife. The

Hornet will give you some distance from your opponent. Smile. You and the Butcher Bird are relaxed and happy and in love."

"How can you be sure they're going to attack?" Spyder asked.

Lulu handed them cups of hot tea. Shrike blew on hers to cool it. "You send one or two men to spy," she said. "When you send eight or more, it's a raiding party."

"Is it those desert rats we saw earlier today? They didn't look like much," said Spyder.

"Anyone who can live in this open desert is going to be hard as stone and fierce as a demon," said Non.

"I'm boosting morale with cheap bravado," said Spyder. "On my planet, we refrain from telling people how fucked they are."

"My mistake."

"How are you doing, Lulu?" asked Spyder.

"I could use a fix. Or a drink."

"We need you bright-eyed and quick like a bunny right now."

"No problem," Lulu said. She moved her leg to reveal the smooth butt of a sawed-off shotgun. "A four-ten. Small enough to love. Big enough to kill."

"You have any more guns in that bag?" Spyder asked Count Non.

"Sorry, no."

"Damn. I'd feel a lot better with a gun."

"You'll do fine."

"Shh," said Shrike. "They're close."

"How can you be sure?" Spyder asked.

Out in the dark, one of the horses whinnied and a small throwing knife thunked into the sand by Shrike's leg. She was up instantly, her cane blurring to a sword as the first attacker came charging out of the night. Spyder didn't even look. He knew she could handle what was coming, and dove for the Hornet.

Spyder came up off-balance and couldn't get the metal flails at the Hornet's head to spin properly. He heard Lulu blasting away with the four-ten and turned in her direction, just in time to see the tribesman that was rushing him. The attacker had a length of sharpened pipe raised above his head and was too close and coming too fast for Spyder to get out of the way. Already off-balance, Spyder let himself fall backwards, pushing the stud on the side of the Hornet to release the spikes from the ends. The tribesman impaled himself on the shaft of the weapon and landed on top of Spyder.

He struggled from under the man's body and finally got the Hornet spinning properly. It hummed like an angry swarm of insects. As throwing knives shot toward him from the dark, they were shredded in midair. Out of the corner of his eye, Spyder saw Shrike hold off three attackers simultaneously, spinning to slice the legs off one, before gutting and decapitating the others. Lulu picked off attackers and whooped out rebel yells while Primo crushed tribesmen with his fist, the Hulk in a cheap suit. Count Non fought almost as impressively as Shrike. He charged with his broad Kan Dao sword in one hand and a Morningstar in the other, alternately slashing and crushing the skulls of his opponents.

Another attacker was on Spyder, one who understood what the Hornet was. He didn't rush into the saw-tooth flails, but feinted and moved around, trying to find a way past the spinning shield. Spyder's injured hand was a white-hot ball of pain. He could feel blood running down his arm. That was the side on which the tribesman made his attack. He drove his sword to the opposite side and when Spyder turned to parry him, the attacker spun smoothly, slipping around the flails. In his haste to avoid being sliced to giblets, the man came around a touch wide and barely managed to drag the tip of his sword through the top Spyder's right arm. Before the man could come back with a killing blow, his midsection exploded. He fell and Spyder saw Lulu standing there with her shotgun smoking. Spyder returned the favor by slicing off the arm of another attacker who lunged at Lulu's back.

And then it was over. No more men came over the dunes. Spyder and Lulu turned in slow circles, waiting for someone else to rush them from the dark, but no one came.

"Spyder, stop spinning that thing," said Shrike. He dropped the flails into the sand to stop them. Shrike turned once, her head up, listening. "If there are any left, they've run off to lick their wounds."

Spyder put his arms around Shrike and she held on to him. "A fighter, not a victim. Understand now?" she asked.

"Yeah," he said. But he thought, I killed a man tonight. More than one. Spyder pushed Shrike away and puked into the sand.

"Pussy," said Lulu.

THIRTY-EIGHT
DEAD EYES TALK

"The horses are gone," said Lulu.

"All of them?" asked Shrike.

"The ones that aren't dead."

"Goddam," said Spyder as Count Non wrapped his injured shoulder in gauze he pulled from the saddlebags. He pressed a poultice to Spyder's wound and wrapped that, too.

"What's that?"

"Herbs with Saint Cosmas' dust," said the Count. "The shoulder and your hand should be healed by morning."

"You didn't even get scratched."

"Unlike some people, I try to avoid being stabbed."

"You got something against bleeding?"

"Blood belongs on the inside, little brother."

"Duck and cover. Got it."

"This one's eyes are gone," said Primo. "And this one."

"This one, too," said Lulu. "Shit they're all cut up. Oh god…"

Spyder looked at Lulu. She was kneeling by the body of a dead tribesman, her hands over her mouth. The dead man's robe lay open, revealing his chest and belly. They were scarred and stitched in the same haphazard manner that was becoming very familiar.

"Are they cut, Spyder?" asked Shrike.

"Sliced and diced, just the way the Black Clerks do it."

Lulu touched the face of the dead man in the sand. "Is that how I look?" She spoke in a child's voice, like she was in shock. She pulled her jacket closed and crossed her arms, tucking her hands underneath. "They all that way?"

"Yes," said Primo. He was walking from body to body, moving their clothing with his foot, checking them for scars. Spyder could tell that he didn't want to touch them. Going to where Lulu knelt, Spyder got her to her feet.

"Come away from there," Spyder said, and sat her by the fire.

"Why would they come after us like that?" Lulu asked.

"In our clans, there's a saying about the Black Clerks," said Primo. "'They watch the world through silent eyes.'"

"What does that mean?"

"It means that taking a part of someone's body gives the Clerks some power over the remaining body," said Shrike.

"It's still just static to me."

"I believe it means that the Black Clerks might not take eyes simply because they are foul and need to replenish their organs," said Count Non. "Perhaps they are able to see where those eyes should be, watching through the empty sockets they once inhabited."

"The Clerks are in my head? They're looking through my fucking eyes?" Lulu shouted. There was hysteria in her voice.

"Is that right, Shrike?" asked Spyder.

"It's possible," she said.

"I saw the Clerks in Berenice. I thought it was just a coincidence," Spyder said. "They must want the book, too. Or to spook us from it."

"I led those slugs right to us," Lulu said. "The Black Clerks have seen everything we're doing and know right where we are." She stood and snatched up the shotgun. "Fuck that."

"What are you doing, Lulu?" Spyder said. He started over, but Lulu pointed the four-ten at him.

"Stay put, Spyder. I'm ending this right now." Lulu was walking backwards into the dark, keeping the gun pointed at the group. "Those bloodless motherfuckers think they can watch TV out of my head? I'm going off the air, like I should have done a long time ago."

"Don't do anything stupid," said Spyder.

"Look at me!" Lulu yelled. "Look at what's left of me! I've pretty much used up all my stupid for this lifetime. I'm done." She ran into the dark.

Spyder ran after her, pausing at the dune line in case she was waiting. He didn't think that Lulu would want to shoot him, but she still might out of fear or surprise. He moved slowly down the base of the dunes, letting his eyes adjust to the dark. Finally, he saw a woman running. Spyder lit out after her.

"Lulu!" Spyder yelled. "Lulu!"

When he reached her, Lulu was on her knees in the sand, the four-ten wedged under her chin.

"Stay the hell back, Spyder."

"Give me the gun."

"I didn't want you to get hurt. And I didn't mean for you to get involved in my shit. The Clerks are coming for you now, too. For all of us."

"They're not coming for anyone. We're going to get that magic book and get clean."

"Look at us, Spyder. Those people back there have a clue. We get loaded and hunt for girls. We can't help them."

"Not dead, we can't."

"We'll mess everything up."

"That's a possibility."

Lulu looked at Spyder. "I really love you, you know. You're the best person I know. But I can't have those things crawling around inside my skull." Spyder heard Lulu pull back the hammer on the four-ten.

"Before you do anything, I want you to listen to me, Lulu," Spyder said in a calm and even voice. "You listening?"

"I'm not putting the gun down."

"Fair enough. You hold on to it, if it makes you feel better."

"Okay."

"The Clerks took your eyes. We know that and are agreed on it, right?"

"Yeah."

"Did they take your ears?"

"No. I've still got them."

"Right. So all they can do is watch TV with the sound off. You following me?"

"Not really."

"If the Clerks are spying on us through your eyes it's because that's all they can do. They can't listen to us. They don't have your ears. That means, all we have to do is keep you from seeing where we are and they're blind as a bat."

"You think that'd work?" Lulu asked. She moved the gun from under her chin and scratched the side of her head with the barrel.

"We just cover up your little eyeholes and the Clerks get to play Three Blind Mice till we're home, drinking tequila and winking at college girls."

"Maybe," she said.

"If you're nice, I'll get Shrike to slip the blindfold on for you. You like a little bondage with your morning coffee, right?"

Lulu seemed to think about it for a moment. "I'm not giving back the gun," she said. "I've been useless and naked up till now. But I know how to use this."

"I'm sure the Count won't mind. Come on over here."

Lulu got up and went to Spyder. He kissed her cheek and hugged her tight. "Don't scare me like that again."

"I won't," she said, and hugged Spyder back. "So, can Shrike really put my blindfold on? That sounds kind of hot."

Spyder slid his arm around her shoulders and led Lulu back to camp.

"Christ, you got a cigarette?" Lulu asked.

"Nope. Don't worry. We're almost to Hell. Bet they have plenty of smokes down there."

THIRTY-NINE
ANTHROPOLOGY

"We're moving too slowly without the horses," said Primo. "I'm afraid we won't make it to the mountains in time."

"When will the moon reveal the entrance to Hell?" asked Shrike.

"Tonight, I think. Perhaps tomorrow, too. After that, it will be invisible for a month."

"Where are we exactly?"

Primo looked up at the stars, then at the mountains ahead and behind them. "Perhaps halfway between Mount Cholula and Mount Culhuacan, near the Tajin burial mounds."

Shrike nodded. "If we push through, we can make the base of the mountains late tonight," she said. "But we'll have to rest at midday."

"I'd rather not, ma'am."

"I know, but we all have injuries and no one's had any sleep. I don't want us limping and yawning into the underworld."

"You're right, of course."

They'd been walking most of the night, since an hour or so after the attack. Food and water was weighing heavier on their backs with each step. Spyder had a length of the Count's rope tied around his waist and this was tied to Lulu's left wrist. She was blindfolded with a yellow scarf, like a Tibetan prayer flag, Shrike had taken from a boudoir conjured by her magic book. Lulu didn't have much to say as they trudged through the sand. She never let the four-ten drop from resting on her shoulder, Spyder noted.

"How you doing, Lulu?" Spyder asked.

"Feel like I'm your Rottweiler bitch you're taking out for a whiz. Find me a fire hydrant so I can mark my territory."

"You're lots sweeter than a Rottweiler. Hell, you might be a Shih Tzu. Maybe one of those little teacup poodles old ladies like."

"It's not wise to taunt a woman with that much firepower," said Count

Non. "That gun is enchanted and will never run out of shells."

"I have this demon-made knife Madame Cinders gave us. Is that some kind of demon blunderbuss?" asked Spyder.

The Count sighed. "The way you people use words, it's a wonder you understand each other at all. Every vaguely inhuman creature you find unpleasant or frightening or just strange is a 'demon' to you. And everything conjured or made by these creatures is 'demonic.'"

"Back in San Francisco, there was a fat fucker with a monster mouth right in the middle of his chest. He wanted to eat me. You telling me that wasn't a demon?"

"He was no more a demon than Primo. Primo is Gytrash. Simply another humanoid race. A different kind of human animal. A more interesting and durable species than you ordinary humans, and probably a bit scary to you First Sphere bumpkins."

"So, what was Mister Mouth?"

"He sounds like a Bendith," said Primo. "They're a particularly ugly sort of troll and aren't averse to human flesh."

"A Bendith or possibly a Nagumwasuck," said Count Non. "You boring one-headed, two-eyed humans are scattered through all the Spheres. Take our Butcher Bird. Like you, she's an ordinary human, but clearly she didn't grow up in some First Sphere backwater. She's lived with other intelligent races and understands the infinite varieties of life, the magical possibilities, that spring from the conjunction of different living species."

"I was right there with you, Count. Up until the bestiality stuff right at the end," said Lulu.

"Humans and animal entities have been mating and producing offspring since the world began, little sister. It's still quite common in regions of the Second and Third Sphere."

"Okay, Shrike, Lulu and me are white trash, Primo is a Second Sphere *Übermensch* and you're some incredibly old rich kid slumming from Upper Coolsville," Spyder said. "What the hell is a demon?"

"A fallen angel," said Count Non. "Demons are from Hell. They serve Lucifer, command his armies, run his cities and, when called upon, torment the souls that have been consigned to the underworld. True demons travel throughout all the Spheres and while they can seduce and despoil almost any creature that catches their fancy, they can't produce offspring. The demons that exist now are the same ones expelled from Heaven long, long ago. Give or take a few."

"What happened to the demons that aren't around anymore?"

"The prophets tell us that a few managed to beg and cajole their way back into Heaven. Others are dead. Demons can be moody company and while a human exorcist can, for instance, expel them from a possessed body, they can't kill them. Only God or another angel can kill an angel, fallen or otherwise."

"Or an angel's weapon," said Spyder, pulling Apollyon's knife from his belt. "This was made by a demon to kill demons."

"The weapon is ready, but are you? You will have to get very close to use that. You've never even seen a true demon. Will you be able to walk up to your worst nightmare and stick that toothpick in its gut, little brother?"

"The babe to my left is the killer. I'm just here to hump gear and look pretty."

"You're doing a fine job," said Shrike.

"Thank you. Where'd you get all this Trivial Pursuit data, Count?"

"I study life. It's what my people do. We are infinitely curious about the forms that life takes, from insects to angels. We know them and treasure them all."

"You're like an anthropologist or something?"

"Both really. That's the best way of putting it."

"An anthropologist with a big goddammed sword," said Lulu.

"'God will put his angels in charge of you to protect you wherever you go. You will trample down lions and snakes, fierce lions and poisonous snakes,'" recited the Count. "Self-preservation is no vice. If a black widow spider tried to bite Charles Darwin, I doubt he would have had much guilt about crushing it under his boot. Loving life doesn't mean being soft."

"Amen to that," said Shrike.

When the sun was almost directly overhead and the sky was unbearably bright, they rested in the belly of a ruined metal storage tank in a scattering of industrial ruins. The night and first part of the day had been rough. Now, they drank water and ate dried meat and what little bread hadn't been lost in the fight the night before. Things buzzed gently in the ground beneath them. If he weren't so tired, Spyder imagined that he might have found this alarming.

Later, Shrike lay down beside Spyder. "Thousand fingers massage," he said.

"What?"

"The buzzing downstairs. It doesn't feel so bad."

"Mmm," Shrike said, and was asleep against him. Spyder closed his eyes and in a few moments, he, too, was asleep.

Spyder was in a scrap yard like the lot behind Santos Raye and Iggy

Atkinson's chop shop, only this scrap yard stretched to the horizon in all directions. Piles of dead cars burned in the distance, sending up gushers of flame and black smoke that boiled together like entwined snakes in the sky. Spyder looked down at the ground. It was wet and bones protruded from the red soil. The burning cars threw his shadow, long and distorted, behind him. When he looked again, Spyder saw his younger self there. He wasn't surprised. The kid had always been just a step or two behind him. He looked worse than ever. His clothes hung from him in rags as if he'd been in a terrible accident. His eyes were gone and his body looked like something dragged off an autopsy table. Spyder's shadow-self smiled. He was still holding the punch dagger he'd had in Berenice. The blade was still slick with Spyder's blood.

Spyder knew what was coming. He dragged a heavy femur out of the wet ground so that he could hit the kid when he made his move.

Something came clattering toward Spyder across the scrap yard. A filthy old man with a bit in his teeth was pulling a flaming chariot. The chariot's rider wore a golden war helmet with a mesh face-shield. He pulled that off and Spyder saw that the chariot driver had the same face as the old man with the bit in his mouth. The rider then pulled that face off to reveal a lean, foxlike face that Spyder didn't recognize. "How many masks are we wearing today?" shouted the rider, and he pulled at the face of the old man dragging the chariot. The old man's skin came off his skull, a limp rag, exposing muscle, bone and mucous. Spyder was still considering this vision when a white-hot blow to the back staggered him. The punch dagger, ruby-red with blood and glittering like Christmas lights, was sticking out of his chest. It had been pushed clean through him, back to front. He felt weak, but the shock to his body was so great that the wound didn't even hurt.

Shrike screamed and startled Spyder awake. Before he could move, Shrike was up and out of the tank, charging across the desert with her sword drawn. Spyder ran after her, and finally caught her by a collapsed brass tower thirty yards away. Shrike shook and cried, but her body was tense, ready to spring, ready to kill something.

"Were you dreaming?" Spyder asked

"Yes. My father was in Hell being tortured by the bastard, Xero Abrasax."

"Was he pulling a chariot?"

"Yes," said Shrike. "How did you know?"

"I think I might have had part of your dream."

Shrike breathed deeply. "We're close to Hell. It can creep into your dreams. That's good. It means it was just a nightmare and not an omen."

"Yeah. We just dreamed what scares us the most."

"But why did you dream about my father?"

"I don't know. I know I'm not going to sleep again, that's for sure."

"Me neither."

"Listen, let's just go till we reach the mountains. No more bullshit. No more pit stops. We wait for it to cool off and we walk till we drop."

"You're right."

Shrike nodded and they walked back to the tank. The others were all up, looking pale and agitated, as if they, too, had been awakened by disturbing dreams. There wouldn't be any arguments about pushing straight on through to the Kaslas.

FORTY

THE POSSIBILITY OF FLOATING

"Have you thought about what you're going to do, little brother?"

"When?"

"When we reach the gates of Hell."

"Not much, no."

"Maybe you should. I've listened to you talk about the place and, while I admire your scholarship, I wonder if it's enough."

It was just after sundown and the sky along the horizon was the color of rust and bruises. Spyder was spinning the flails of the Hornet over his head, speeding and slowing the serrated metal as they walked. Count Non was beside him. Lulu and Shrike walked ahead, led by Primo. Lulu said something that made Shrike laugh.

"What's ever enough? In for a dime, in for a dollar," said Spyder.

"Does that attitude make you a hero or a fool, I wonder."

"They're the same thing. Fools get themselves cornered. Heroes are just the fools who get out of it."

Count Non nodded. "Being a fool might just be your greatest strength. A fool can do what a wise man won't," he said, and shifted his pack from one shoulder to the other. "In the Tarot deck, the Fool is depicted as a young man about to step off a cliff into empty air. Most people assume that the Fool will fall. But we don't see it happen, and a Fool doesn't know that he's subject to the laws of gravity. Against all odds, he just might float."

"If fucking up is power, I should be the Hulk by now," said Spyder. He took a breath. "Goddam. I'm going in. I told myself I wasn't. I've been sort of turning it over in my mind this whole time."

"Thinking goes against the Fool's strengths. Just do what you have to do."

"Truth is, I kind of always knew I was going, from the first time Cinders brought it up. But I couldn't admit it," Spyder said, spinning the Hornet from side to side. "There's an old Buddhist saying that whenever you ask a question, you already know the answer."

"I'm glad to hear you bring up the Buddha," Count Non said. "All that medieval Christianity that informs your descriptions of Hell had me worried. We can learn a lot from the Buddha. In Hell, you'll be all right if you remember his most basic advice: follow the Middle Way."

"All the books say that Hell's a naked roller derby on broken glass. It's nothing but extremes. Think there's a Middle Way down there?"

"If you're on fire, do you jump into the pool of water or the pool of gasoline? Even in the most extreme circumstances there's a choice."

"I wish I could see the place. Being blindfolded the whole time sounds like balls."

"That's the first choice you have to make. Is seeing Hell's décor worth being trapped for eternity?"

"I'd have to give that a big No," said Spyder. "How about you? How do you feel about playing blind man's bluff?"

"It's all the same to me. This won't be the first prison I've visited. I've been locked away in dark places. After a while, the darkness becomes a comfort and light is the stranger."

"You've been there, haven't you? Hell, I mean. You're dancing around the subject, but I have this feeling."

"My people have done business there."

"What kind of business?"

"It varied. I'm not proud of much of it."

"Why didn't you say anything when I was wanking on about it? If you know the place better than me, why didn't you speak up?"

"You were doing a fine job. I didn't see any reason to interrupt."

"Is there something you can tell me that I should know? Anything that can help us?"

"That's not permitted," Count Non said.

"What does that mean?"

"Hell is a place of extremes, yes, but extremes are relative. What's extreme for Spyder isn't extreme for me. Shrike's extreme isn't Primo's or Lulu's. The details of Hell are different for everyone. Telling you about my dealings wouldn't do you any good and might just confuse you. I wouldn't want to be the cause of you getting hurt. Or worse."

"You're killing me with tender mercies. There's nothing you have that can help us?"

The Count sighed. "I've been talking about it this whole trip, trying to prepare you. You're as ready as you're going to be. Remember the Buddha's advice. And don't ever lose heart. Hell is designed to drain lost souls of hope. Don't let that happen. We've already agreed that you're a fool and so far, despite a few bruises, you've been lucky. That's halfway to a hero. No matter what happens, what you see or hear or experience, be the fool that lives. That's my best advice."

"I was hoping for a magic helmet or something."

"Don't be afraid, little brother. The stars are on our side. When the moon points to the hellmouth, the underworld's defenses are down and all the gates are open. 'In that day the Lord with his sore and great and strong sword shall punish Leviathan; and he shall slay the dragon that is in the sea.'"

"You can talk some shit, Count."

Count Non tossed a stone straight into the air. As it arced down, Spyder tilted up the Hornet and ripped the stone to powder.

"There's airships over us," said Spyder.

"Angels, too," the Count said. "To the west."

"If your people did business with Hell, did they work for Heaven, too?"

"Of course."

"You aren't on the flying monkeys' side, are you?"

"You mean the Brotherhood and their angelic lapdogs? They can all kiss my ruby-red arse," said Count Non. "Would you prefer it if I was on the other side?"

"Both sides can blow me right about now," said Spyder. "I'm just jumpy is all. That Bible talk of yours had me wondering."

"It's a family habit and hard to break."

"You aren't a preacher or something?"

"My father is."

"I knew it."

"When the urge hits, perhaps I should switch to Greek."

"It couldn't hurt."

FORTY-ONE
VANILLA ROSES

"**I**s this the place?" asked Shrike.

"I believe so," Primo replied.

"Believe?" Spyder asked.

"A figure of speech. This is the place."

"What happens now?" asked Lulu.

"We wait," said Primo, "for the moon to move across the sky and reveal the location of the entrance to Hell."

Shrike crouched on the ground leaning on her cane. Spyder knelt down beside her. The desert night wind came in dry, frigid gusts. He shivered.

"Does this feel right to you?" Spyder asked.

"As far as I can tell, we're where we should be," she said. "We're in Primo's hands now. Is the moon up?"

"Been up for a while. That's what worries me. We might have missed it."

"We still have tomorrow night."

"We lost all our food and most of our water back at the OK Corral."

"Then, let's hope we still have a chance tonight."

"Can we start a fire or something?" Lulu asked. "The wind comin' off these hills is giving me some serious raisins."

Count Non shook his head. "That's not a good idea. Not with enemies overhead. They would spot even a small fire."

Lulu shivered in her light cotton jacket. "I'm seriously dying over here." Spyder took off his leather jacket and draped it across her shoulders.

"What about one of those caves?" asked Spyder. "We can do like the other night, start a small fire and stack some of this scrub over the entrance. Maybe cover it with our coats."

"It's still dangerous," said the Count. "What do you say, Shrike?"

"If nothing else, moving around and gathering brush will warm us.

Do you see anything yet, Primo?"

"No, ma'am. Whatever your decision about a fire, I'm going to stay here and watch the moon."

While Primo and the Count kept track of the sky, the others began pulling the dry, shallow-rooted brush from the loose desert soil and piling it in a nearby cave. While Lulu and Shrike broke up some of the brush into kindling, Spyder spread their coats over a pile of brush at the cave opening. Count Non volunteered a heavy wool cloak that he pulled from his weapons bag.

When he'd covered the entrance, Spyder slipped inside, trying not to disturb any of the brush that kept in the light. Kneeling next to Shrike and Lulu, he struck a match and lit the kindling they'd laid out. The sticks caught quickly and the little cave filled with light. The heat came up more slowly, but in the frigid night, they felt their skin begin to warm and it felt good. Spyder leaned into Shrike as Lulu huddled up on the other side.

Lulu pulled off her blindfold. "All they can see is the fire, right?"

"Yeah. They won't know where the fire is," said Spyder. "We having a good time yet?" Spyder asked.

"Shit, this is better than dinner and a spanking," said Lulu.

From outside the cave came Count Non's voice. "Sorry to disturb you, but you should come and look at this."

"Who should?" called Lulu.

"All of you."

"Dammit."

They crawled out of the cave slowly, gloomily, leaving the warmth behind. It felt even colder and more miserable now that they'd had a few minutes of comfort. The three of them remained huddled together as they went to where Primo and the Count were waiting.

Spyder followed the men's gaze upward to the night sky. "It's the moon," he said. "Been there. Done that."

"Look beyond that peak," said Primo.

"Oh man," Spyder said.

"What is it?" asked Shrike.

Spyder felt Lulu shiver.

"Two moons," Spyder said. "There are two moons in the sky."

Shrike lowered her head, but didn't say anything.

"Who has the juice for this?" Spyder asked.

"The Brotherhood, perhaps," said Count Non. "Perhaps the Black Clerks, though I've never heard of them doing anything remotely this mad before."

"It could be a confederacy. Two or three of the groups wanting to stop us could have combined their powers," Shrike said. "This is bad."

"There's something worse," said Lulu, looking back at the cave.

Spyder turned and saw that the fire had ignited some of the brush by the entrance. The whole cave was burning like a merry beach bonfire on the Fourth of July.

"If someone's looking for us, I think we just sent 'em a flare," said Lulu.

"There's something in the flames," Primo said.

Black, moiling smoke slid from the cave, up the mountainside. But a slower, heavier smoke hung white in the air, turning in slow motion tornadoes. Things coalesced inside the spinning whirlpools, shape-angled, skeletal. A glimpse of bared teeth. A sharp arc of metal. Heavy, restless boots.

"Soldiers," said Spyder. "Primo, that cave we want is above us, right?"

"Yes, sir. Up the mountain."

"Maybe we should go now."

Spyder took Shrike's hand and they ran up a narrow switchback that cut back and forth across the face of the Kasla Mountains. Coming from far behind them, Spyder heard the clattering of metal and leather. He hoped the smoke soldiers were slow, or still smoky, so the mountain wind might blow them away. As the group ran, however, the sound of the soldiers' weapons came closer. Shrike pulled away from Spyder and ran back down the mountain, her sword up and ready to strike. Spyder was frozen in place, his mind a blank. What was she going to do against a soldier made of smoke? But when Shrike made her first slash, Spyder saw the blood and heard a scream. He realized that while the soldiers might have come from smoke, they were now just flesh and blood. He, Primo and Count Non charged down the hill while Lulu opened up behind them with the four-ten.

Spyder sent a couple of the soldiers off the edge of the trail as they tried to avoid the spinning Hornet, while the Count gutted one, then another of the smoke soldiers. Spyder saw other soldiers forming at the foot of the mountain. While the others attacked the remaining few pursuers, Spyder grabbed Shrike.

"Do you know any magic to make the wind blow harder?" he asked.

"One spell."

"Use it."

Shrike got down on one knee and rolled up her sleeve. Whispering a low incantation, she pulled back the metal bird on the lancet, locking it into place. A moment later, the bird snapped down and Spyder saw blood run down Shrike's hand. The wind kicked up at their backs, pushing them toward the edge of the cliff. Spyder grabbed Shrike and pulled her back against the mountain.

Below them, the hurricane that now blasted down from the mountain scattered the burning scrub from which the soldiers were coalescing. Half-formed soldiers splattered onto the sand, a wet corruption of skin, bone and exposed organs.

Overhead, immense, dark things blacked out parts of the sky. Search lights played across the desert floor, illuminating the underbellies of the airships. The lights pooled around the bodies of the dead soldiers near the cave.

Count Non and the others trudged up the hill into the wind, finally reaching Spyder and Shrike.

"We should keep moving." The Count had to shout to be heard above the wind.

"Can you turn the wind off now, pretty please?" Spyder asked.

Shrike raised her hands and uttered a few words. Nothing happened. She indicated that they should start up the hill. "Sometimes it takes a few minutes," She said. "This isn't like turning off the TV."

They started up and within a few minutes, the wind began to slack off. The airships kept up their search, lighting up the bodies of the slaughtered soldiers on the trail below. Looking for us among the dead, thought Spyder. He felt a surge of excitement, having come through another fight. Primo came up from the rear, still scanning the sky, trying to find some clue in the mad light and crisscrossing shadows cast by the twin moons.

"That archway in the rock above us," he said. "I think it's pointing to an opening in the rock face."

"Lead the way, man," said Spyder, and slapped him on the back. Primo flinched from the blow. Spyder saw that he was holding his side. Blood stained the front of his white shirt, and oozed from between his fingers.

"You're hurt."

"It's nothing," Primo said. "We'll be away from them soon."

Primo went quickly up the trail, but Spyder could tell that he was more badly hurt than he was letting on. The little man constantly looked northward at a stone archway in the rocks above. In the crazy mix of shadows, Spyder couldn't really see what had Primo so excited.

Thunder rumbled behind them, then lightning. The ground shook. Heat and a wave of static bristled over their skin. Spyder could tell that it wasn't thunder in the sky, but more of the light weapons he'd seen back in the airship battle. Rocks tumbled down at them as searing white bolts blasted into the mountain. They pressed themselves as close as possible to the rock face and kept moving. Looking up, Spyder thought he saw angels circling the mountaintop, high above.

"There!" yelled Primo, between thunderclaps. The mountain rumbled up through their legs. "I need to climb. Please give me a leg up."

Spyder still couldn't see where Primo wanted to go, but he crouched by the little man's leg to give him a boost. Primo took a breath. His remaining hand was bloody and his balance was a little shaky. Holding on to Primo's shoulder, Count Non steadied him enough to step onto Spyder's hands and begin the climb.

He must have cat eyes, thought Spyder. Using his one arm, the little man climbed steadily up the rocks, reaching a deep, recessed shadow just a few yards above their heads. "We would have walked right past it," Spyder said to himself. The ground shook and rocks came down, almost knocking Primo off his perch at the lip of the cave.

"This is it!" Primo called. "Climb!" The mountain trembled and Primo used his one arm to brace himself in the cave entrance. Where his bloody hand touched the mountain, the rock turned black. The blackness spread outward and around the cave like paper crisping in an invisible fire. "Hurry!" Primo shouted to them.

"Look out!" Spyder screamed.

Primo frowned, cocking his ear, trying to hear Spyder above the thunder. The little man was now standing in a circle of curdling black set against the mountain. Spyder tried to wave him away from the entrance.

"Do you smell something?" asked Shrike.

Above them, Primo screamed as crooked black spikes spun out of the rock, drilling through Primo's body, pinning him to the rock. As Primo struggled, Count Non started climbing toward him. Too late. Double-edge blades, as long as Primo's arm, sprang from the sides of the mountain and closed on Primo like the jaws of a colossal mechanical beast. The blades sliced cleanly through the little man and he was silent. Then the spikes rotated out of Primo's mangled body, allowing the pieces to fall quietly over the rock face. If there was any sound, Spyder couldn't hear it above the thunder and his own screaming. As the spikes disappeared into black rock, the side of the mountain turned back to a dull gray.

Count Non dropped down beside Spyder.

"They're gone. Primo and the cave," said Spyder. "I can't see anything." Rocks tumbled down the mountain at them.

"We can't stay here!" shouted Lulu.

"Help me up," said Shrike. "I'm climbing."

"It's gone!" shouted Spyder. "We can't see anything."

"I don't need to see it," she said. "Can't you smell it?"

"What?"

"Flowers."

"The smell of the Inferno is like vanilla roses," said Count Non. "If you can follow that scent, we'll follow right behind you." Shrike nodded and the Count lifted her onto the rock face. Shrike climbed slowly, carefully, feeling her way up the wall, groping with her hands and feet for each purchase on the cliff.

Below, the desert floor was turning red and liquid as the sand super-heated to glass where the airships' light weapons hit. Spyder pressed his forehead into the mountain. For the first time in what seemed like a long time, he stepped outside himself and looked at where his sorry ass had landed him: clinging to a murderous mountain on some imaginary island, with warrior angels above and demons below. "If you could see me now, Jenny," he whispered. "If you could see me now."

Count Non put his hand on Spyder's shoulder. Spyder looked up and saw Shrike kneeling on a ledge, gesturing for them to come up.

"You're next, little brother. Don't leave the lady waiting," Non said, giving Spyder a leg up the rock. As he climbed, Spyder heard Lulu huffing and cursing behind him. When he reached the ledge where Shrike waited, she grabbed him and pulled him inside. Spyder turned and pulled in Lulu, as Count Non came up behind her. Outside, the killing light from the airships was hitting all around the cave entrance. Dust and stones rained down on them from the ceiling. The smell of roses was sickening, cloying and overripe. Spyder was suddenly afraid. A light bolt hit just below the lip of the entrance and threw them deep inside the cave.

"We're not safe here," said Count Non. "We have to get down below."

"Back here." Shrike's voice came from deeper in the cave. "Stone doors. They're warm. And they smell like an abandoned florist."

Spyder and the others scrambled to her through the dark. At the rear of the cave, stood two massive doors, forty feet high, carved from the mountain itself.

"How do we open them?" Spyder asked.

"They feel light," said Shrike. "I think I can just pull them."

"Wait," said Count Non. "Shrike and Lulu are safe, but Spyder mustn't forget his blindfold." Non slid Lulu's blindfold from where it hung around her neck, unknotted it and stepped behind Spyder to tie it on.

"Shouldn't we put that back on Lulu?"

"Don't worry. Even the Clerks can't see through dead eyes into Hell."

"You sure?"

"My father knew the place well."

"I hope you're right. I didn't like the idea of stumbling around down there with all of us blind."

Quietly, Non said to Spyder, "We made it, little brother. The entrance to the Inferno. 'I will give thee the treasures of darkness, and hidden riches of secret places.'" As the cool cloth of the blindfold slid over Spyder's eyes, something nicked his left ear. Then his arm. He heard something shoot by and strike the wall.

"Get down!" screamed Lulu.

Spyder didn't have a choice. Count Non had collapsed against his back, knocking them both to the ground. The Count was dead weight on top of Spyder. He slowly crawled out from under the Count's body. Things flew by over his head, but he made it behind a bend in the rocks. From there Spyder looked back and saw Count Non's body bristling with at least a dozen golden arrows. Bright angels were pressed shoulder-to-shoulder at the cave entrance, arrows and quivers raised.

"Get ready to open the gates," Spyder shouted to Shrike. "Now!"

He brought the Hornet up and spun the business end as fast and hard as he could. The angels' arrows flew at them, but were vaporized by the Hornet's flails. Spyder kept the weapon between the angels and them. The angels advanced steadily into the cave. Some stood over Count Non's body, and that made Spyder angry. He spun the Hornet faster as a blast of heat and the stink of rotting flowers washed over his back.

A strange light filled the cave when Shrike pulled open the gates of Hell. The walls turned a deep russet, and the light seemed to bubble, as if it were boiling to the surface of the world in sluggish waves, weighed down by the malevolent gravity of Hell below and the miles of earth it had to pass through.

The forward-most angels' skin and wings turned dark and shriveled in the Hell light. The ones that didn't cook and collapse immediately, backed quickly out of the cave. When they were gone, Spyder went to Count Non and checked his pulse. He was dead. Spyder pulled the blindfold from the Count's hand and set the Hornet gently down beside him.

"I can't use this blind. Maybe it'll do you some good wherever you are," Spyder said.

There was a spiral wrought-iron stairway beyond the open gates, and sounds came from deep below. Some were rhythmic, others random. The rhythmic sounds were like the banging of vast and relentless machines. The arrhythmic sounds were screams. The walls of the cave flickered as if someone were quickly clicking a light switch on and off.

Before they entered the gates, Shrike knelt on the floor, took a handful of dust and sprinkled it over her head. "Count Non and Primo Kosinski. Strength to your spirits, my comrades, my friends."

"Vaya con Dios," said Spyder quietly.

"Sweet dreams, guys," Lulu said.

She slipped the blindfold over Spyder's eyes and made sure it was tight. Shrike took Spyder's left hand and he took Lulu's left. They walked through the gates of Hell and started down the long spiral staircase into the abyss.

FORTY-TWO
IZANAMI AND RED DRAGON

The first great war on Earth took place millions of years ago when the warrior princess, Izanami, fought Red Dragon, the rapacious prince of the west.

With her army following behind, Izanami ran all the way across the land of Jodo to fight Red Dragon. Izanami finally cornered and defeated Red Dragon in a battle that lasted for years and destroyed a third of their kingdom.

Izanami had a secret known only to a few of her most trusted officers. Izanami didn't defeat Red Dragon because she was a cleverer tactician or a stronger warrior. Izanami won because she was insane.

She came to the battlefield in a heavy cloak, under which she was wrapped in chains. As she entered the battlefield, she looked small and lost. It was only when she was released from all her heavy restraints that the full power of her madness was brought down up on Red Dragon. Izanami won the battle by exploding a volcano in the Khumbu Mountains. The lava and ash almost destroyed the world, but killed Red Dragon and his army first.

Izanami was the first hero on Earth, though few have ever heard of her historic combat. Her story remains popular with her people, but even among scholars across the three Spheres, Izanami's story is obscure.

The Nio, Izanami's people, were smoke wraiths. The entire epic war between Izanami and Red Dragon lasted no longer than the span of a human breath—but for the Nio, that breath was a lifetime. And that was Izanami's other secret. She knew how insignificant her people and their victory were in the universe. Its insignificance made the victory seem all the sweeter to Izanami, proving once again that the logic of Tricksters and the enlightened are hard to tell apart.

FORTY-THREE
EATEN ALIVE

They seemed to walk forever, but they never grew tired or hungry or thirsty.

"What a lousy day to stop smoking crack," said Spyder, stumbling on the staircase for maybe the fiftieth time. He had a deathgrip on the metal railing. It had never occurred to him that something as simple as walking down a flight of stairs could be such a pain in the ass when blind. His balance was off, his whole sense of where he ended and other objects began was gone and every new scream and sound from below startled him.

"I knew this reporter down in LA. He was doing a series of stories on local subcultures for one of the alternative weeklies. You know, the kind of scene-hopping bullshit that desk monkeys and teenyboppers read to feel edgy. Eventually, his editor wants him to write about the Hell's Angels. He gets a hookup to their clubhouse and he's surprised by how smart and cool most of the Angels seem. At the end of his formal interview, they tell him they're having a party and he should come, so he can get a better idea of what's what. Sure, he says, expecting a phone call or a flyer or something." Spyder stumbled again. Shrike caught him by the shoulder. "Thanks. About three in the morning, he's in bed. When he opens his eyes, he finds about a half-dozen Angels in his bedroom. 'Get dressed,' they tell him. He's no dummy. He does what he's told. Outside are about a dozen more Angels. They rev their bikes loud enough to peel paint off the neighbors' houses and roar out into the canyons over the Hollywood Hills, with my reporter friend riding bitch on the back of some guy's bike.

"The thing about those canyons is, there's a lot of bodies buried out there. A million years from now, archeologists are going to understand us from all the bones of the dead TV producers, junkie musicians, porn stars and coke dealers scattered through those canyons. And my friend doesn't know if he's going to get laid or stomped or shot in the head and buried in a shallow grave. Then they round a corner and he sees the lights and hears the music. The Angels promised him a party and, sure enough, there's a party going on.

"But an Angel party isn't a regular kind of party. There's a lot of guys on massive doses of acid, playing William Tell with fifty caliber handguns. There's knives flying by and gangbangs and more beer than in all of Milwaukee. And here's my little artsy-fartsy weekly newsrag lit major buddy trying to be Cool Hand Luke with it all. The thing he said, though, and I believe this, was that after a while he really was cool with the savage craziness. The party went on all night and into the next day, and the way he put it, 'You can only be terrified for so long.'"

"I guess you're still looking for your happy place on this trip," said Lulu.

"Working on it. I figure Hell can't be any worse than Houston."

"Are we close to the bottom, Lulu?" asked Shrike.

"Damned if I know. It just keeps going down."

"It's getting hot," said Shrike.

"Yeah, but it's a dry heat," said Spyder. No one laughed.

"Why can't the Prince of Darkness have an elevator? Ozzy would," Lulu said.

"Don't disrespect the demons in their own house, dear."

"Yes, daddy."

"Maybe this should be a quiet time, while we try to get our bearings," said Shrike.

Spyder stumbled again, cursed. He leaned over the railing and felt a warm wind rising from somewhere below. It still smelled of roses, but there was an undercurrent of something musky and subterranean, darkly fungal. Spyder had to admit that he was a little surprised and kind of annoyed with himself. After all the reading and study he'd done concerning the underworld, now that he was actually here, he kind of wanted the place to be a furnace full of guys in red suits, pointy beards and pitchforks. Those childhood images and fears never go away and never really get updated, he thought. You can add on new ones, but you never completely bury the old nightmares.

"How many angels are there?" asked Lulu.

"Depends on who you ask. Some claim a hundred and forty-four thousand. Other guys a million, a hundred million, or even a billion, but those are probably just bad translations. Anyway, a third of Heaven went down with Lucifer when he got the door."

"You're saying, there's between a hundred forty thousand and a few million crackhead angels down there?"

"Give or take."

"How fucked are we?"

"It could be worse," said Shrike. "We're sneaking into to a mad place at a chaotic time. War is a perfect cover for crime."

"What's going to be down at the bottom of this staircase?" asked Lulu.

"I wish I knew," Spyder said. "Hell's pretty flexible. Different to different people at different times. It's got a geography, all these little fiefdoms controlled by Lucifer's lodge buddies. There's the big boy's palace in the biggest city, Pandemonium. Some prophets say Hell's just a big, pointless machine, that all the damned souls are cogs and gears and that the machine's only purpose is to grow with no purpose at all. Others say that life in Hell's just like life on earth, only more hopeless and boring. Some traditional types still go with the fire and brimstone story, and why not? Someone's got to have that old school stick up their ass." Spyder shrugged. "I've talked to Shrike about the demons and laws and traps I've read about, but, we're not going to know what's down there until we're on the ground."

Lulu laughed.

"What?" asked Spyder.

"I'm just rememberin' something. After I came out to my folks, all the times they told me this is where I'd end up. And here I am."

The air grew hotter and more fragile, brittle almost. Not like the desert. It felt artificial, as if someone had left on a giant dehumidifier and it was sucking the moisture from everything. The rising air from below was full of an itchy grit that settled on everyone's skin and instantly itched. Hell already sucked and we're barely through the door, Spyder thought.

Spyder felt Shrike's hand close around his. "When we get down there you stick close to me, pony boy."

"Why didn't you tell me that being blind was such a drag?"

"You get used to it.

"This probably wasn't the time to start."

"Damn. We're here. The bottom," said Lulu. "Be careful stepping down."

"Where do we go now?" Spyder asked.

"I was going to ask you, Mr. Wizard. What is this?"

"Describe it. I'm Stevie Wonder over here."

"Right. Sorry," she said. "Okay. We're in a big cavern at the bottom of the stairs. There's light, but hell if I can tell where it's coming from. In front, there's three really big doors. There's no signs or nothing, but all of the doors have the pug ugliest demon faces carved on them. Looks like we're marching down some monster's gullet, whatever we do. But which one do we open?"

"This wasn't in any of the books," Spyder said. "What do the demons look like?"

"Like demons. Big scary teeth and huge goddam claws."

"Do the demons have snouts? Like dogs or wolves?"

"Yeah. Kind of. What are they?"

"I think I got it," said Spyder. "It's not 'they.' It's 'it.' This is Cerberus. The three-headed hellhound. Some stories say Cerberus guards the entrance to Hell. Some say he *is* the entrance. To get inside, Cerberus swallows you. Only you have to pick the right mouth, otherwise, he shits you out into chaos. Not Heaven or Hell, just stone-cold nothing."

"So, which head gets the bone?"

Spyder hesitated. He heard someone moving around by the doors. Shrike. She was muttering a spell that wasn't working. The situation was so frustrating. Spyder wanted to rip the idiot blindfold off his eyes and not have to stand around like a crippled child.

"The one on the right feels light on its hinges. It's been used the most. Maybe it's the way," said Shrike.

"Or it's a trick to get us down the beast's belly," said Lulu.

"We go in through the center," Spyder said.

"How do you know?" asked Shrike.

"Count Non knew things about Hell. He told me to be like the Buddha. Buddha always took the Middle Way."

"Are you sure?"

"Open it."

He listened to Lulu going to the door. Hesitation. A footfall. Silence. The sound of dry hinges grinding and a door scraping over a dirty floor.

"Lulu?" asked Shrike.

"There's a tunnel. Something's moving at the end. People. And like a river, I think." She pushed the door open wider. "Hey man, thanks for not dooming us right off."

Spyder smiled. "All part of the service. I guess we're supposed to go in there now."

Someone fell. The sound was dry and hollow in the warm, thick air of Hell. Spyder moved toward the sound.

"Shrike, are you all right?"

"I'm fine. Let me catch my breath."

"Lulu?"

"I've got her. Follow my voice over here."

Spyder found them sitting on the floor. Shrike was leaning on the cavern wall. Her hands were wet and cold.

"Something in my chest," she said. "I think it's the key Madame Cinders put inside me. I can feel it moving. It must know we're getting near the book."

"When you're ready, we'll go," said Spyder.

"I'm ready," she said, and got up slowly.

The middle tunnel through Cerberus' gullet was warm and wet. When Spyder touched the wall, the stone was fleshy and yielding. They all hurried through as quickly as they could.

FORTY-FOUR
DADDY LONGLEGS

"Hello?" Lulu called. "Anyone back there?"

"What's wrong?" asked Spyder.

"I thought I heard something behind us in the tunnel. Who'd a thought there'd be weird sounds in Hell?"

"Is there a river ahead?" asked Shrike. "We have to cross it to get to Pandemonium."

"Yeah, there's a river, and no problem crossing it."

"Lay it out for us, Lulu," said Spyder. He had his back to a stone outcropping just beyond the tunnel. Around them were dozens of voices, people screaming and talking, people on crying jags. From above came a metallic humming punctuated by momentary squeals, the wail of rusted wheels and rotten gears. Spyder didn't like the idea of machines that he couldn't see hanging over his head.

"I don't know where to start. We're in a what's his name? Bosch. We're in a Bosch painting," Lulu said. "Hear all those people? They're standing around waiting to get across the river. I bet you don't smell roses anymore, do you? There's pipes all around dumping what looks a lot like shit, blood, carcasses and lord knows what other puke into the river. Jesus fuck!"

"What is it?" Shrike asked, her sword half-raised.

"Something, like a big, white worm just popped out of the water, latched on to one of those people and dragged 'em under."

"They aren't people, Lulu. They're souls. Don't worry, they can't drown," said Spyder

"No, but I bet that thing can chew on 'em for a good long time."

"What else do you see? Can you tell how we get to the other side?" asked Shrike.

"Yeah. There's these metal cars, like the sky cars at an old amusement park, slung on wires over the water. Shit. I don't know if I want to ride on one of those with those hungry worms waiting for us to drop."

"We have to," said Spyder. "Listen, the thing that grabbed that guy, it wasn't random. Souls are sorted all over Hell, starting right here. This is the Bone Sea. The ones who end up in it are so foul that even Hell doesn't want them. The ones wandering around this shore and on the other side, they're maybe worse off. Completely lost. They can't get into Heaven and they won't go into Hell. They'll spend eternity right here by this river of shit. We don't have that option. If we don't move, Shrike's going to die."

The voices of the wandering souls grew quiet, then came back louder than ever. Lulu said, "Remember how I used say it was all ironic with you named Spyder, that you're so afraid of spiders?"

"We worked that over once or twice."

"Be glad you're blind right now. I shit you not, there's a twelve-foot-tall spider strolling down the shoreline kicking people out of his way like he's Donald fucking Trump."

Spyder reflexively pressed his back into the outcropping and went very cold inside. He wanted desperately to find the tunnel and go back up the way they had come, but Shrike grabbed him and held on.

"We have to go on," said Shrike. "Trust me. I'll take care of you."

"Weird," said Lulu. "That spider looks sort of mechanical. Like someone took about ten junked cars, some old TVs and prosthetic limbs, wired them together and taught them to walk. And it gets better. The thing's got a human head."

Feedback knifed through Spyder's head, bringing back memories of a hundred sweaty clubs on a thousand drunken nights. A voice crackled and boomed, broken, imperious and mad.

"Move along, you desperate scum, you noxious void of the earth's bowels, move along! Your fate lies across the Bone Sea, not on my shore! Across the river is the eternity you courted your whole corrupt and sorrowful lives. No one remains on my shore. Move along, you lost lambs, you food for the wolf. Lollygag and your suffering will begin all the sooner!"

"Shrike, get your sword up," said Lulu. "Daddy longlegs is headed this way, twelve o'clock high."

A rhythmic clanking filled the air, along with the smell of burning oil, decaying flesh and overheated circuit boards. Spyder sensed some enormous presence looming over them.

"My god. You're alive," came the voice. It was low and human. The madness was gone. "Forgive me for that scene a moment ago. They make me say and do those terrible things. The beasts that run the machines. I'm attached, you see."

"Who are you?" asked Shrike.

"Cornelius…something, I think," said the spider machine. "I was once one of these poor souls. Lost and terrified. I don't belong here. I don't deserve Hell. I refused to cross the Bone Sea. Demons came with nets and rounded us up like wild animals. When I awoke I was the foul thing you see before you."

"You must've gotten on someone's bad side, then super-sized it," said Lulu.

"I can't remember," Cornelius said. "Kind souls, will you kill me and free me from this endless torment?"

"I don't think we can kill you, Cornelius," said Shrike. "You're already dead."

"Am I? It's been such a long time. I don't remember."

"Cornelius, we need to get to Pandemonium. Can you help us?"

"I would if I could, dear lady. I've never been there or even seen the place, but I hear it's glorious. I've never been anywhere but this shore." Madness was edging back into his voice.

"That's not true. You were a man," said Spyder. "Don't ever forget that."

"A man. Was I? How nice. Yes, I remember. I was a boy and we lived by the sea. In Brighton. There were trains and gulls. It was lovely…" Circuits fried. The spider machine lurched and Spyder felt the ground shake.

The demented, amplified voice was back. "Move along, you wandering excrement, God's pitiful blunders. Move along and despair!" Cornelius moved back in the direction of the shore, hunting wandering souls. His voice faded as he went, but its echo filled whatever space enclosed them.

"I think it's time to go," said Lulu. She led Spyder and Shrike to the edge of the stinking, clotted water and helped them into one of the elevated cars. Souls fell back as they went. Spyder felt their hands caress him, as if looking for warmth. The car lurched into the air and carried them over the Bone Sea.

"I seriously wonder if we're gonna make it out of here," said Lulu. No one replied.

FORTY-FIVE
PINK BOY

It seemed to Spyder that it was taking a long damned time for the little cart to clatter and squeal its way over the Bone Sea.

"Talk to me, Lulu," said Spyder. "Where are we?"

"'Bout halfway across," she said.

"How's that possible? We've been crossing for hours."

"Daddy, are we there yet? Daddy, are we there yet?"

"We're not in the world anymore," said Shrike. "We can't expect time to run here the way it does at home."

"This is an E-ticket freak show, I wanna tell you," said Lulu. "You sight-impaired types are missing some severe shit, which you don't need to know about. Not if you ever want to eat again."

"Tell us," said Spyder.

"I'm just babbling 'cause I'm a little scared. You don't need this stuff in your heads. My guess is there'll be plenty of monsters before this is over."

Spyder shifted in his seat, trying to find a comfortable position. The sheath for Apollyon's knife kept jabbing him in the leg. When he tried to stand, Lulu pulled him back down.

"There's things on the wires. Like baboons with porcupine quills all down their backs. The quills are matted together, like knives. They're eating this green fungus growing on the wires. The bored ones are grabbing souls from the other carts and dropping 'em into the sea. Oh Christ!"

Spyder nudged Lulu with his boot. "Hey, forget the stuff. Sing something."

"Like what?"

Very quietly and not entirely in key, Spyder started to sing, "We're caught in a trap, I can't walk out, because I love you too much, baby." In a moment, Lulu picked it up, "We can't go on together with suspicious minds…"

Lulu said, "Praise Elvis. We made it." A moment later, the bottom of the cart dragged across a beach that crunched underfoot, like crushed shells. They jumped out and landed safely on the ground, as the cart continued its endless roundabout journey.

Lulu grabbed Spyder and pulled him and Shrike to their feet. "Let's move. We're attracting a crowd. More of those hangin' around dead folks."

Spyder didn't need her to tell him. He could hear them coming, crunching lightly across the beach toward them. Their voices were like whispers drifting through a long ventilation duct—flat, distant and insistent. Spyder stumbled and went down on one knee, cutting his hands on the sharp shells. Lulu and Shrike started to help him up, but other hands were there, pulling him away, purring and cooing and desperate.

"Blood. He's alive!"

"Please wizard, do me a service in Hell and I'll tell you where to find a great treasure back on earth…"

"Take my place in the Inferno and your heirs will rule a vast and wealthy kingdom!"

"So pretty. The red. Life."

"Save me, my lord. I am a virtuous woman…"

There were so many lost souls on this side of the Bone Sea, and they were much more aggressive than the souls who'd refused to make the crossing. None had much individual strength, but their combined desperation had Spyder pinned within their massed presence. It was like being slowly crushed under a ton of feathers. Spyder felt his leather jacket rip and his shirt come apart. The souls gasped and fell back.

"His skin marks…"

"L'homme peint…"

"A warrior…"

Their hands were on Spyder's back, and running over his arms and face. So many of them, he couldn't breathe. They pulled his hair and clawed at his cheeks. He tried to push them away, but it was like pushing at air. Fingers slipped under his blindfold and into his eyes. The souls' fingertips glowed inside his eyeballs like eerie deep-sea creatures.

"Get back!" Spyder yelled.

The weight of the souls instantly left his body—but a second later a hand swept across his face. Among the faint gasps and wails, Spyder heard the distinct sound of laughter. He turned toward it and was shoved down hard onto his back. The fall knocked the wind out of him and Spyder slowly opened his eyes. It took his mind a few seconds to register that the streaks of gray and white he saw weren't ghostly fingers in his eyes but the bone beach. When his eyes focused, the first thing he saw was the dim, colorless souls crowded around him, then Hell's rough, black cavern walls. They seemed to go up forever.

"Back off!" Spyder screamed as he scrambled to his feet. He heard the sound of laughter again and spun toward the sound, pulling Apollyon's blade from his belt. When the sound came again, Spyder swung the blade at the nearest specter, a big man dressed in the leather and iron of an ancient Roman soldier. The knife passed through the soul as if through smoke, but the knife tore him as it went. The soul clutched at the bloodless wound, trying to hold himself together. Too late. He split apart completely, like fraying cloth, and vanished with a breathy sigh. The remaining souls scattered down the beach.

Off to his left, Spyder saw Lulu, laid out on her back, her mouth open in a kind of silent scream. A crowd of souls had her pinned to the ground and seemed to be examining her wounded body. Dead fingers probed her eye sockets and surgical scars. Spyder slashed through the crowd, scattering terrified souls, and pulled Lulu up. She buried her face in his chest, but didn't make a sound. She just clung to him and shook.

Further down the beach, Shrike was holding another group of souls at bay with her sword. She'd used her magic to cover the blade in fire, but the gesture wasn't really stopping the souls, just distracting them. Spyder got Lulu to her feet and pulled her over to Shrike. Some of the group must have seen him dispatch the other souls, because they ran away as he got close.

"Shrike, it's me," Spyder called, and she lowered her blade.

"Lulu?" she asked.

"She's here with me. She's pretty shaken up."

"How did you find me?" Shrike's hands were up searching for him. "You can see me?"

"Yeah."

Shrike found Spyder's face with her hands and felt for where the blindfold should be. When she didn't find it, Shrike sagged against Spyder and kissed him lightly on the lips.

"Damn," she said.

"That pretty much covers it."

"Ooo, a little group action. I like that," came a hissing voice. "Or is this some platonic expression of relief? What a bore. Lust is all that's amusing about talking meat. The faces you make and the all squishing sounds."

Spyder lunged with the Hell blade, jamming it under the chin of the demon staring at them from atop a black obsidian boulder.

"Don't hurt me with that thing!" it cried.

The creature was small, pink, bloated and naked. It had an oversized semi-human head with tiny eyes and a slit that seemed to serve for both a nose and mouth. Its hands and feet were so tiny that they appeared useless, yet its nails were black, twisted and razor-sharp. The thing's cock was thicker than its arm and dragged along the ground like a third leg. Into holes in its skull were set thirteen white candles, which never seemed to blow out. Wax flowed down the thing's head and face like slow-motion tears.

"You know what this is?" asked Spyder.

"I'm not blind," said the creature. "It's the black blade, hungry for death, even among the dead."

Spyder pressed the knife harder into the thing's throat. "Are you the little prick who snatched my blindfold?"

"Why would I do that? You talking meat are vile enough as spirits. Who wants you alive down here, eating and defecating and breathing your foul stenches into the air?"

Spyder withdrew the knife, but kept it by his side. The creature clumsily crawled onto its tiny feet.

"Who are you?" asked Shrike.

The creature proudly drew itself up to its full height of about four feet. "I am Ashbliss, servant and valet to his Divine Abhorrence, the Lord of Flies, Beelzebub."

"Why were you spying on us?"

"This is my day off. I often come here to play about with lost souls. They make funny noises."

"Fuck off, pink boy," said Spyder, "before I carve my initials in your ass just to see what kind of funny noises you make."

"You don't want to do that. I'm here to help you," said Ashbliss. "You're the Painted Man."

"Who?"

"Modesty is such a bore. But I know about you, and you need my help. You're here for the book, aren't you?"

"How do you know that?"

"The same way I know who you are. You're here because you have to be. It's all been foretold. You're not the first champion to come this way. You're not the first talking meat to come for the book. This beach and the roads of Hell are paved with the bones of the champions who came before you."

"How can you help us?" asked Shrike.

"I can take you to where you want to go. To the book."

"Why would you do that?"

"Because I want a small favor in return," Ashbliss said. "You're brave and you have the black knife, the blade that empties all vessels of life. I want to be free of my master. True, his cruelty is boundless and his depravity is deeper and darker than the chaotic void that lies between Heaven and Hell." Ashbliss looked at his feet over his round belly and shrugged his tiny shoulders. "My problem is that I know all his terrors and his tirades. He's a bore."

"So, you're a demon, huh? How's that working out for you?" asked Lulu.

"I enjoy my work. I don't enjoy my master. He's—"

"A bore. We picked up on that," said Spyder. "Everything bores you, doesn't it?"

"I'm hopelessly corrupt," Ashbliss said, smiling. "It's my nature."

"Thanks for the offer, but we know the way," said Shrike.

"So did they." Ashbliss spread his little hands indicating the expanse of bones at their feet. "And anyway, you're lying. I, on the other hand, know shortcuts. Secret paths. Passages that only a being such as myself can navigate."

"Truth is, I'd rather wander aimlessly than take the word of you and your horse dick," said Spyder.

"I understand. You're proud and strong. You're the Painted Man."

"What the fuck does that mean?"

The demon giggled. "I know your voices now," Ashbliss said. "When you need me—and you will need me—just call my name. I'll hear you anywhere in the underworld."

"Don't wait by the phone."

"To show good faith, I'll give you something for free." He pointed at two low hills in the distance. "That path between the hills, were you going to take it to enter the Plains of Dis beyond?"

"That was the plan," Shrike lied.

"Yes, lots of lazybones try that route," said Ashbliss gravely. "Do not, under any circumstances, follow that impulse. Sulfur fumes rise from old mine shafts and mix with the damp fog that drifts down from the cliffs above. The air itself turns to acid. Even my kind shun the place. Go to the southwest, near the old library in the Forest of Lies."

"The Forest of Lies?" said Spyder.

Ashbliss sighed, mumbling, "Fools," under his breath. With a small gesture, he pulled a pen and sheet of vellum out of the air. The demon scratched away at the vellum for a few minutes and tossed it to Spyder.

"A map," said the demon. "That information is free. The next will cost you." He bowed, dribbling wax onto the bone shards at his feet. "Feel free to go back to your lust. I promise not to look. And enjoy your journey." With a jaunty wave, Ashbliss waddled away down the beach.

FORTY-SIX

THE DAMNED AND THE GENTRIFIED

Spyder slipped on the remains of his jacket and followed the others. They went along the route indicated on Ashbliss' map. Every step of the way, they crunched over the bones of other adventurers who had come for the book, but none of them talked about this. Spyder and Lulu led Shrike through tricky fields of loose rock. Looking after each other gave them all something to do, and the contact was reassuring.

"It wasn't supposed to be like this," said Shrike. "It wasn't supposed to go this way. You're trapped down here, Spyder, and I don't know how to help you."

"Then it's best not to dwell on it," he said. Shrike reached out for him, but he walked on ahead, describing the scene to her.

"We're going through a slit canyon. The light is grasshopper green. There are strata of some pale orange and turquoise rock that glows like glass lit from the inside. Along the top of the canyon are the ruins of buildings. They're pretty crude rock and clay shells. They may be some of the first things the angels built when they landed here. No one's used them in a long, long time. The canyon walls are covered in sigils, the magical symbol for each angel's name. I recognize a few. Baal. Pillardoc. Azazel. Salmiel. Beelzebub. Lucifer's sigil is just ahead. It's huge. The size of a whole cliffside. That hellhound took a great big whizz to mark his territory."

When they reached the spot on the map indicating that they should circumvent the Plains of Dis, Shrike stopped. It was on the wind: the faint, but unmistakable rotten egg stench of sulfur. Spyder checked the map and turned them to the southwest, as Ashbliss had advised. "This way," he said. They turned off the road and headed overland, through thick, thorny bushes, following the demon's map.

Soon, they came to the Forest of Lies, where things were seldom as they first appeared. Paths turned to dust underfoot. A bare tree sprouted vicious thorns when Lulu leaned on it to remove a stone from her shoe. The sickly, brooding birds that nested in the twisted branches murmured to them trying to break their spirits.

"She cares nothing for you. She wants the book. The power. When she has that, she'll leave you like all the others."

"You killed your father. With your treachery and lust, you took the snake into your bed and set him loose in your home."

"They still suspect you. They will abandon you here and return to the world and laugh about your torment while they fuck."

The deserted library in the Forest of Lies was an ancient wreck. Its doors and windows were long gone and the pages of its books blew through the woods like the ghosts of dead leaves. Spyder picked up the some of the papers that wrapped around his legs and snagged overhead in the trees. There were love notes, suicide notes, tax returns, forged money, old treaties embossed with government seals, lottery tickets, doctored photos, newspaper articles and religious texts.

They passed from the Forest of Lies into the Valley of Lost Desire. The place was eternally shrouded in a thick fog and lovers wandered through the gray desolation hearing each other's calls, but never finding one another. Ash from a nearby volcano drifted down into the valley, making the fog worse. It looked as if the volcano had erupted sometime in the recent past. Hard-baked bodies lay strewn across the valley floor, like a museum exhibit about the destruction of Pompeii. It wasn't until Spyder tripped over one of the heavily ashed corpses and heard a steady scraping from inside that he realized that the crusted forms each contained a trapped soul. Spyder tried cracking open a few, but the rocks he used always shattered without making so much as a crack in the stony prisons.

They passed from the Valley of Lost Desire into an overheated swamp that on the map was marked only as Rage. Faceless souls chased and savagely beat other souls in waist-high bogs of boiling blood. Once each attack had been accomplished and the victim beaten senseless or drowned, the victim and attacker would exchange roles and the whole process would begin again. The souls didn't seem to notice Spyder and the others as they inched by on a narrow ledge. They were grateful to make it out of Rage without incident.

They passed from Rage into the frozen Plains of Misery. The sullen, suicidal and malicious, who took nothing from existence but pain and who made others' lives as empty and excruciating as their own, lay half in ice, cursing and trying not to look at each other. As they went, Spyder looked down and saw other souls completely submerged in ice, swallowed up by the diamond-blue glacier that inched back and forth across the scarred open land.

They passed from the frozen Plains of Misery into the overgrown Fields of Greed. Souls dug enormous golden thorn bushes from the rocky soil with their bare, bleeding hands and tried to carry them away, only to have the bushes stolen by other souls, driven mad by avarice.

When they tried to carry too many at once, souls ended up buried beneath piles of golden thorns. Others ripped their ghostly bodies to shreds as they fought frantically for the bushes with other souls. A bleeding woman fell at Lulu's feet and when she tried to help the wounded soul, the woman tried to bite Lulu. She clutched a small collection of golden thorns to her breasts, cutting herself to the bone. "You keep away," the woman told Lulu. "These are mine."

When they were finally through the Fields of Greed, the skyline of an enormous city glistened in the distance. "Pandemonium," said Spyder who, despite himself, felt a little shuddering thrill inside as he spotted the place. The city possessed a brutal but elegant beauty, as if the Manhattan skyline had been dropped into the city of the biggest oil refinery in the world.

What puzzled Spyder, however, was the city that lay just beyond Pandemonium. Though the other city was farther away, it towered over Hell's greatest metropolis, dwarfing its tallest towers. The graceful mother-of-pearl domes and minarets of this other city shimmered in the light from an artificial sun that was suspended by some magical force high over the place. In the false but dazzling light, the buildings appeared to be trimmed in gold and silver and inlaid with precious stones. Construction cranes huddled silently at the edges of the bright city.

"That looks brand new," said Spyder.

"Shit," said Lulu. "Demon condos. Yuppies'll even gentrify Hell."

FORTY-SEVEN
MISS FUCKIN' MANNERS

According to the map, they were at a place called the Razor Pits of Merry Vengeance.

Only there were no pits and no razors. Just a cracked alkali plain whose surface had been scraped flat sometime in the not too distant past. Mounds of crystallized mineral salts and dry soil dotted the plain where they'd been left and never removed.

"Are you sure?" asked Spyder. "We've been off the path for a long time. Maybe we're lost."

"I know exactly where we are," said Shrike. "Things are just different."

"So what?" said Lulu. "Shit changes. Those carts over the Bone Sea weren't always there, right? The devil's building Barbie's Dream Hell House. Big deal. Pandemonium's right over there and so's the book. What are we going to do about that?"

"Go and get it, I suppose," said Spyder.

"Just walk in?" Lulu asked.

"We hadn't really worked out a plan yet." He sat down by one of the alkali piles.

"No shit, Dr. No. And under a cloak of darkness isn't going to cover our asses 'cause this place is nothin' but a cloak of darkness."

"Shrike, what do you think?"

"We need to know what's ahead of us. And I only trust that demon so much. He could be leading us into a trap or a dead end just for his own amusement."

"Well, I don't see a Chamber of Commerce to get a new map."

"One of us is going to have to go into Pandemonium, take a look at Lucifer's palace and see if the book is really there."

"I hate this plan."

"If he has the book, it should be easy to find. Lucifer will probably have it on display, a war trophy. Do you think there will be many guards?"

"How should I know?"

"You're our Hell expert."

"Let me tell you, this place isn't exactly like the books said. But, I guess, the psychology's the same."

"How does that help us?" asked Lulu.

"There's this old story about Vlad the Impaler, this kill-crazy Romanian prince. He's the guy *Dracula* is based on," Spyder said. "More than anything, this guy loved killing Turks, and he loved killing them by impaling them on long wooden poles. He'd stake whole fields with thousands of dead and dying Turkish POWs. Everyone was afraid of ole Vlad. A story goes, that he left a golden goblet by a waterfall on the road to his city, a place where travelers could get a cool drink on the long road. This goblet was worth a lifetime's wages for anyone in his kingdom. But people were so afraid of this psycho that no one ever stole the goblet. They didn't want to end up like one of those Turks."

"Thanks for taking us there, bro. But what the fuck does that mean?"

"Vlad left the goblet so people could get a drink. He also wanted to prove what a badass he was."

"There won't be any guards at all," said Shrike.

"That's my guess," said Spyder. "Lucifer knows no one has the balls to steal from him. I bet the place is going to be wide open."

"Who's going to find out?" Lulu asked.

Before any of them could respond, there was a sound. Deep, ponderous and rhythmic, like diesel engines the size of mountains driving wheels the size of skyscrapers. Spyder climbed to the top of the alkali mound and peered carefully over the top.

"What is it?" asked Shrike.

It was an army. At least, that was Spyder's best guess. There were demons and damned souls marching onto the plain to Spyder's right. They were clad in armor. Or maybe not armor, he decided. Machinery? Parts of the souls were definitely machine-like. In fact, some were variations on the spider machine they'd seen back at the Bone Sea. Others were Frankenstein patch jobs, trailing long umbilicals attached to still larger machines driven by demons.

"Lulu, tell me you've still got your shotgun," said Spyder.

"An armed society is a polite society and I'm Miss-fuckin'-Manners."

"I take it we've been found out," Shrike said.

"Found out, sold down the river and the river frozen over."

"You've got the magic knife. Think what Shrike and I have'll stop these demons?" asked Lulu.

"I doubt it. But if they're going to snuff us, I want to send a few home with bad dreams."

"Wait a minute," said Spyder. He shifted position on the mound. "Fuck."

"What is it?" asked Lulu.

"Déjà-fucking-vu."

"What?" asked Shrike.

"Remember that nightmare you had in the desert? The one we both had? With the chariot?"

"Of course."

"We've got the director's cut about to go down right in front of us," Spyder said. He slid down the mound. "That Hell army isn't for us. It's for your friend, Xero."

"Did you see him?"

"I saw a gold chariot, leading a shitload of souls and demons from the opposite side of the field. They were too far away to see any details."

"My father," said Shrike. "What was pulling the chariot?"

"Same as his army. Souls and demons."

"One of those souls is my father."

From across the plain, came a thundering war cry. Spyder and Lulu crawled around the side of the mound.

"What's happening?" asked Shrike.

Another mad shout.

"They're just yelling and tossing shit at each other. Getting the troops worked up."

"The man in the chariot, what does he look like?"

"He's wearing a helmet. I can't see his face. But he's tall and ballsy. He's shouting something at the Hell army and his boys look ready to chew bullets."

"Xero was a fine general. He fought beside his men. Even when he sent them off to slaughter, they loved him."

"I knew a pimp like that back in Houston," said Lulu.

"Something's happening," Spyder said.

At some unseen signal, both armies surged forward. They slammed together with the sound of a crashing jumbo jet. Xero drove his chariot into the middle of the massacre, spearing demons and souls with an enormous longbow that never seemed to lack for arrows. When shafts hit his enemies, they didn't just skewer them, but went clear through, gutting one opponent, then taking out the one behind, as well.

Shrike charged around the mound, past Spyder. "Father!" she screamed. "I'm here! It's Alizarin!"

Spyder grabbed Shrike's shoulder and pulled her back, as much to shut her up as to comfort her.

"I can't stay here. I have to fight," said Shrike.

"No problem," Spyder said. "As of now, we got both sides coming at us."

"Good," said Shrike. She stood, brought up her sword and climbed to the top of the mound.

"Xero Abrasax, the men you betrayed took your head," she shouted, "And I, Alizarin Katya Ryu, the woman you betrayed, is here to take it again!"

"Tell 'im, girl," shouted Lulu. She and Spyder both ran from the mound as the few first few soldiers from Xero's army reached them. Shrike was already in the air, doing a perfect somersault and slashing the throats of three demons as she landed. As Spyder slashed away with the black knife, he saw that Shrike's left arm was streaked with blood. She'd called up some kind of magic before leaping into the fray. It must have been heavy because her own blood splattered on the ground with the demons' as she split them open with her sword.

Spyder slashed his way through the battle, picking up a fallen demon's shield to defend himself as he went. Souls came apart when cut by Apollyon's blade, but demons seemed to be burned by it, their eyes popping and their skin crisping as if heated from the inside. Lulu was pumping her shotgun to Spyder's right. It didn't seem to kill the demons, but it exploded heads, arms and torsos, leaving them nicely crippled.

Things suddenly went very quiet. Spyder lunged at a hyena-headed demon, but slashed empty air when the thing backed away and knelt down. Shrike and Lulu's opponents mimicked the move. Spyder looked around and saw a slave-drawn chariot rolling slowly toward them. Behind it, Xero's men were mopping up the remnants of the Hell army, most of whom were sprawled on the ground, slaughtered or twitching like broken toys.

The chariot stopped a few yards from Shrike. "My eyes and ears did not deceive me. It is you, Alizarin," said the man in the golden helmet. "What a charming surprise. Say hello to your father. He makes a fine mule." He reached down to a blank-eyed old man and petted his head the way you might pet a dog.

"I'll kill you, Xero," Shrike said.

"You can't, child. I'm already dead." Xero pulled his helmet off. Spyder was surprised by what he saw. After all of Shrike's vitriol and the terrible dream they'd shared in the desert, he was expecting a brute. What he saw was a refined and strangely handsome face. It was long, with a wide forehead, bright eyes and the kind of nose his grandma would have called "noble." Xero's smile was wide and toothy, giving him an elegantly feral look. It was no mystery why a younger, more naïve Shrike would have fallen hard for the man.

"I'll burn your soul from existence," she said.

"Lucifer said the same thing and he hasn't managed it. What makes you think you can?"

"I hate you more than the devil does."

Xero laughed. "That, I believe," he said. "I'll make you a proposal. Stay here with me in Hell and I'll release your father from his curse. I'm going to win this war soon. I already control the outlands and am slowly strangling Lucifer. When I take his throne, I'll have more use for a bride than a broken-back nag," he said, pulling Shrike's father's matted hair.

"I trusted you once and it destroyed my world. I won't trust you again."

"Please reconsider. For both your sakes. It's a reasonable offer. When I have to make the offer again, the terms will diminish and they'll diminish each time I ask you, until you agree."

"I'll cut my own throat first," said Shrike.

"Perfect. Then you'll end up right back here with me."

Spyder saw it just before it happened. In Xero's presence, Shrike was still that furious, irrational, deeply wronged teenage girl. And she was losing her shit completely, he thought. She shrieked and went right for Xero, her sword up in killing position. Xero brought his bow up and fired off a volley of arrows at her, but he didn't really seem to be trying to kill her. He was laughing the whole time. Shrike spun and parried, splitting the arrows in the air. Spyder was already hacking his way through Xero's army when one of the arrows slashed Shrike's right arm. But she kept coming, even while Xero took aim right at her heart.

Spyder reached the chariot and lunged blindly, not knowing or caring where he hit. He jammed the black blade into Xero's right thigh. The general groaned and backhanded Spyder off the chariot, harder than any human had ever hit him before. Spyder blacked out for a moment, but shook himself awake enough to see Xero pull out the knife as his leg was cooked black. Apollyon's blade even burned his hand. He tossed it away, and his demon troops scattered from the knife as it fell. Spyder scrambled to retrieve it and was almost run down by Xero as he shifted his chariot to slip Shrike's sword blow. Kicking his chariot forward, he took off fast across the blood- and machine-oil-splattered plain. His surviving troops followed behind on foot.

Spyder, still winded from Xero's blow, staggered to where Shrike was on her knees. When he touched her, she was softly crying, and pushed Spyder away.

"I lost him," she said between sobs. "My father was right here. I lost him and it's my fault."

"Xero played you," said Spyder. "You weren't ready for him. You will be next time."

"I will," she said. "Are you all right? I didn't mean to push you."

"It's all right."

Lulu dropped down on the ground nearby, breathing hard. Seeing her, Spyder had to laugh.

"I guess we can forget the element of surprise," he said.

They were filthy, covered in sweat, demon blood and fluids Spyder didn't want to think about.

"It takes a big man to get down on his knees and beg," said Lulu.

"It's why us sissies carry knee pads. Ashbliss, can you hear me?"

The little demon was suddenly standing on a nearby alkali mound, wringing his pudgy hands.

"You're all so damp and exhausted. Am I too late for the rutting?"

FORTY-EIGHT
TREACHEROUS AND BORING

"Okay, little man, let's make a deal," said Spyder.

"Lovely," said Ashbliss. "You know my terms."

"We'll cut you loose from Beelzebub, but first we need the book," said Shrike.

"Nonsense. You have the knife. First my master, then your book."

"We have the knife, but that might not be enough. To use the knife, we have to get close to your master and that might not be possible. If we have the book, we can use its magic to safely free you."

"Or destroy me. I'm not sure I want to help you after all."

"Ashbliss, don't be that way," said Spyder. "We're not demons. We're human. If we make a bargain, we keep it."

"Humans are the most treacherous animals in existence! Everyone knows that!" Ashbliss shouted. "It's not even fun going to Earth and corrupting you because you're all halfway there."

"How can we prove to you that we intend to honor our bargain?" asked Shrike.

"There is nothing you can say or do. I don't trust you. Accept my bargain as stated or I'll be on my way. I'm sure other talking meat will be along shortly, after your bones are used to fill potholes in the road to Gehenna."

"All right, you got me, you clever boots," said Spyder. "We were messing with you, but you foxed us. We'll do it your way. First the boss, then the book."

"Spyder, it's too dangerous," said Shrike.

"I'm open to suggestions. Xero knows we're here. This runt knows we're here. Some of Lucifer's demons high-tailed it out of here during that fight, and they knew we're here. We've got to do something and we've got to do it now."

"He's right, Shrike," said Lulu. "I know you're the smart one and the warrior and all, but we're not gonna tunnel out of here with a spoon and positive thinking. We need the book, however we can get it."

Shrike was silent a moment. "I know," she said. "Give me the knife. I complicated things by losing my temper. I'll kill Beelzebub."

"You sure you're up for this?" Spyder asked

Shrike nodded. "I told you I'd take care of you down here. I haven't done a very good job so far. Let me do this."

Spyder pulled Apollyon's knife from his waist and gave it to Shrike, taking her hand for a moment after he handed her the blade. He looked at Ashbliss. "We're not going to hump. Don't even ask."

"Treacherous and boring," muttered the demon.

A fireball streaked at them from across the plains, turning away from them at the last possible moment. At the edge of the field, it turned and circled back, scorching a circle once around the group, enclosing them in a ring of fire. When the circle was complete, Spyder could see something in the flames. A man stepping down from a chariot.

"I couldn't leave you all without saying goodbye," said Xero. Great waves of heat cascaded off his body. He didn't seem to be covered with fire so much as made of it.

"Do you remember that I was the one who taught you your first magic, Alizarin? But I gave you so little considering how much I got in return. Your bed. Your kingdom. Your father's soul. I even had that boy gutted. Your old partner, Ozymand," said Xero. Shrike held the black blade before her. Xero approached, but carefully stayed beyond her reach. "Your friend there, the pretty fool, injured me when my back was turned. I should be resting, but I needed you to know that even wounded, I'm stronger than you."

"I'm not afraid of you. And I'm no longer shocked," said Shrike calmly. "You don't have any power over me."

"You misunderstand. I'm not here to hurt you, girl. I'm here to give you a gift. Once upon a time, I took your sight. Now I'm giving it back." Xero puckered his lips and blew across his hand, as one might blow a kiss. A roiling fireball enveloped Shrike for a second. When it faded, Xero was gone and Shrike was on the ground. Spyder ran to her and saw, thankfully, that she was unburned by the magic flame. He and Lulu propped Shrike up between them as Ashbliss peered from behind a pile of demon corpses.

"Are you alive?" Ashbliss asked. "The bargain is off if you're dead."

"Shut up!" shouted Lulu.

Spyder was murmuring into Shrike's ear and patting her cheek. "You're all right. You're all right. Wake up, Alizarin. Come back."

She awoke with a start. Spyder felt her go rigid in his hands. She screamed once and went very quiet.

"Can you hear me?" Spyder asked. "Are you all right?"

Shrike's hands went to her face. She pulled off her shades and looked at Spyder. The ruin of her eyes, the cracked-glass irises and spidery pupils were gone. Her eyes were greenish gray, perfect and open wide.

"I can see," she whispered.

"I'm so sorry," said Spyder.

"You're sorry your woman can see?" said Ashbliss. "You mortals really are bastards."

"I'm sorry because now she's stuck here in Hell forever, like me," said Spyder.

"I've already been stuck here for millions of years. Pardon me if I'm not more sympathetic."

"Can you shut it for a minute?" Lulu said.

"Fine," said Ashbliss. "In fact, you seem less and less like the champions I thought you were. I think I'm going to have to nullify our deal."

Spyder snatched the black blade from Shrike's hand and tackled Ashbliss, pinning the demon down with his legs.

"Are you mad?" Ashbliss cried. "My master will destroy you! Gigantic scorpions will suck the marrow from your bones! Beelzebub will fill your still-living carcass with molten lead!"

"No, he won't," said Spyder. "Because I'm going to kill him for you. And then you're going to take me to the book, just like we agreed." With the black blade, Spyder cut off one of the candles on Ashbliss' scalp. The little demon screamed piteously as black blood flowed from the waxy stump. "If you don't stick to our deal, I'm going to use this magic Ginsu to cut off your arms and legs and make you my doormat. And that's just the warmup. I'll devote the next million years to inventing brand new ways of making your existence pure misery."

"No!" cried Ashbliss.

"With the most treacherous animal in existence, you do not fuck. Got me?"

"Yes! Yes!" screamed the demon.

"We've got a deal, right?"

Ashbliss nodded.

Spyder rolled off the demon and helped him to his feet. He held up the candle he'd sliced from Ashbliss' head and when the demon reached for it, Spyder snatched it away.

"You can have this back in a minute," he said.

Shrike was on her feet, but unsteady. She looked around Hell in child-like wonder.

"It's been so long since I've seen anything, I don't even know how to make sense of it all," she told him. She took a step toward Spyder and wobbled. "My balance feels funny. All the cues are wrong."

"Sit down," Spyder said. He and Lulu helped her to the ground, so she wouldn't fall. "Listen to me. I'm going to Pandemonium with Ashbliss. I'm going to put his boss to sleep and then I'm going to go and find the book."

"It's too dangerous," Shrike said.

"You can't do it. You can't even walk," he said. "Lulu can't go. Cut up like she is, she'll attract too much attention. That leaves me."

"I hate this plan," Shrike said, and laid her head against Spyder's chest. He hugged Shrike, then Lulu.

"You come back safe or I'll find your ghost down here and kick your dumb, dead ass," Lulu said.

"Take care of Shrike while I'm gone," Spyder said.

"You got it."

Spyder went back to Ashbliss and held out the demon's candle to him. Sullenly, Ashbliss took it, and with a great deal of groaning and swearing, poured wax on the stump and stuck the candle back in place. The little flame popped back to life.

"I really am going to keep our bargain," Spyder said.

"You had better. Now, get down and roll in the dirt like the pig you are."

"What?"

"You'll need a disguise to get into Pandemonium. You're going as my slave. Get down and dirty yourself, meat."

Reluctantly, Spyder did as he was told. When he'd rolled in as much filth as he thought necessary, Ashbliss took pains to inspect him, slapping more dirt onto Spyder's face and especially his ass, "To give you an authentic sex slave patina," he said.

"We done?" Spyder asked.

"Nearly. Get on your knees."

"Don't get carried away with the sex slave fantasies."

"I need to chain your neck."

"Where're you going to get a chain out here?"

"Right here," said Ashbliss. He squatted down and his face turned a deeper shade of red as he strained. A second later, a shockingly long length of silver chain slid from out of his round, pink ass.

"No goddam way."

Ashbliss smiled. "If you want to call off our deal…"

"Put it on," Spyder said, lowering his head.

As he and the demon started toward the city, Spyder heard Lulu singing Aretha Franklin's "Chain of Fools."

FORTY-NINE

THE GARDEN OF EARTHLY DELIGHTS

"So, are you any particular kind of demon?" asked Spyder.

"Why do you care?"

"Just making conversation. You're a horny little bastard. I thought maybe you were some kind of incubus or succubus or something."

"Lust is just my hobby. I'm simply a demon."

"Before you fell, were you any special kind of angel? Seraphim, cherubim, throne, archangel?"

Spyder and Ashbliss were stepping over the remains of demons and damned souls as they crossed the carnage-strewn alkali plain. The place stank, a combination of rotting flowers and scorched engine oil. Ashbliss was leading Spyder by the chain wrapped around his neck.

"I was simply an angel," said Ashbliss.

Spyder made a wounded sound. "Huh. That's sort of bottom of the barrel, isn't it? What are there, like nine ranks of angels? And you're all the way down in the basement. Janitor of the universe."

"We had to keep watch over the Earth. That's how I learned what beasts you talking meat really are."

"Is that how you ended up like this?"

"What do you mean?"

"Your demon form. Looks like you were dragged behind the ugly truck over rocky roads all the way down from Heaven. They wouldn't have pulled that on one of the heavy angel ranks, a seraphim or a throne, would they?"

"I like my form."

"Course. I mean, you'd have to. Not having any choice and all."

"Hush," said Ashbliss, and yanked the chain hard.

They came to a rough highway that curved gently into the distance toward the city. Along both sides of the road were hundreds of crucifixes, stretching as far as the eye could see in both directions. Men and women, their skins stripped off, were secured to the crosses with nails through their wrists and wire around their chests. Their legs, which were free, high-kicked in unison, like some zombie movie chorus line. As he got closer, Spyder could see umbilicals running into their empty skulls. All their mouths were propped open with pockmarked mesh screens and tinny music flowed out. Polkas. African tribal dances. New Orleans jazz. Techno, and a dozen other styles Spyder couldn't identify.

"You opening a theme park or something?"

"You looking for a job for eternity?"

"Seriously, what's with all the urban renewal? Why'd you fill in the razor pits back there? And what the hell are you building over there?"

Spyder pointed into the distance at what looked like the boarded-up mine shaft in the distance, but it was not like any earthly mine. The entrance went up for miles, and each wooden plank across its face could have represented a whole forest. The metal beams that buttressed the planks could each have been melted down and have provided enough steel for a battleship.

"That was like that when we got here. They didn't even bother finishing Hell before they cast us down here. It's very rude, I think," said Ashbliss. "As for the razor pits, they were fun, but never necessary. We had to clear the land for the project."

"Which project would that be?"

"The only project. The only one Lucifer and the other master demons care about, at least."

"And that is…?"

"Heaven," said Ashbliss. "We're building Heaven."

"Interesting. I kind of thought there already was a Heaven. And they kicked your sorry asses out."

"That's God's Heaven. This one is for us."

"I get it. God looks down and sees your new and improved Heaven and slaps his forehead, realizing you fallen angels were right all along. Then—*bang!*—you win the argument."

"You're not as stupid as most of your kind. But you make up for it by talking to much."

"Is that what that city is, beyond Pandemonium? Part of the new Heaven? Is that what Hell really is, one big hardhat zone?"

"You tell me," Ashbliss said. "Behold."

When he was still a child, Spyder had found a book of his mother's. It was an art history text, left over from her brief attempt at community college. She'd lasted less than a semester and bad-mouthed the curriculum, the teachers and the other students nonstop whenever the subject came up. But even as a child it puzzled Spyder why she'd kept her school books if they brought back such painful memories. It wasn't until years later that he realized that it was probably his father's nagging that had propelled his mother out of school. Spyder's father considered all forms of self-improvement, short of studying innovations in Detroit horsepower and chasing strip-club tail, useless and, in all likelihood, un-Christian. Spyder never understood why his mother had said that he was so much like his father. He knew that they were nothing alike, and he'd hated her for saying that. He hated his father just because.

The picture in his mother's art history text that had captivated him as a child was the Hell panel from Hieronymus Bosch's triptych, *The Garden of Earthly Delights*. It wasn't the clever and artful ways the demons tortured the damned souls that had fascinated Spyder. He'd studied the top, the far background of the painting, where none of the sexy tortures were happening. That section of the painting depicted a ruined, burned-out city, or a city that had been built along very different aesthetic lines from a human city. The buildings and the sky above were black, as if grimed under a permanent layer of soot. Shafts of lemon-colored light shone from the windows of each building and sliced through the smoky darkness, which only added to the feeling that this was ground zero for some unknown holocaust.

All those memories and images came back to Spyder as Ashbliss led him down the chorus-line road and into the enormous construction site for Heaven 2.0.

The scale of the project was so vast, Spyder's mind couldn't take it all in. Looking at the place was like being in a car accident—it came to him as a series of still images flashing into his brain, but the whole of it was beyond his comprehension. In the far distance entire mountain ranges were being blasted away or gobbled up by machines whose steel jaws were almost as large as the tops of the mountains themselves. A white sea of activity surged around the giant machines and Spyder realized that this ebbing and flowing tide was made up of millions of souls moving the ore mined by the machines to the horrible open-pit foundry nearby. Flames, miles high, rose from the foundry and molten steel flowed into molds down dozens of chutes, each as wide and as deep as the biggest river Spyder had ever seen.

There were workshops nearby where demons supervised souls in some of the more delicate work needed for the structures: the polishing and cutting of precious stones, the stripping of huge sheets of mother-of-pearl from enormous shells, the goldleafing of delicate statuary. Outside the workshops fortunes in diamonds, rubies and sapphires were piled, along with amber boulders the size of a man.

Millions of tons of concrete sluiced into giant foundation holes from thousands of storage tanks. At the bottom of the holes, souls were directing the lines that spewed the wet concrete evenly across the floor. Souls too slow to move or too clumsy to escape slipped under the gray, oozing mess like they were drowning in quicksand, and disappeared. The skeletons of a thousand new buildings were being lifted into place by massive claws and welded together by souls linked to other machines through yet more umbilicals. The one constant Spyder could make out in all the chaos was that the demons were the supervisors, while the damned souls were the work-gang slaves. This knowledge was nailed down when Spyder looked to the far side of the site and watched demons feed the bodies of injured and unruly souls into huge presses that squeezed all the fluids from them. The liquid was drained into tanks to be used as lubricant for the construction machines.

Spyder's heart was beating fast. His brain was on overload. This was not the Hell in the books. A demon grabbed a soul sporting a mohawk, kneeless black jeans and a safety-pinned T-shirt, some squirming, hard-luck punk, and tossed him into the fluid press. A stray thought popped into Spyder's mind: Jenny, you would love this.

FIFTY
HOLY SHIT

Spyder and Ashbliss skirted the edge of the construction site and entered Pandemonium by a side street in what appeared to be the butchers' quarter.

Heavy-muscled demons in stiff rubber aprons hacked, gutted and sliced mystery meats in stinking shops on a dim boulevard whose gutters ran black with blood as thick and dark as chocolate syrup. Wriggling tentacles and the snouts and bellies of giant coal-colored hogs hung on rusty meat hooks next to the egg-white entrails of horse-size beetles.

They rounded a corner and entered a wide public plaza. The place was spotlessly clean and a pleasant scent of roses filled the air. Across the boulevard was a great, domed crimson building. Below the large central dome were a cluster of smaller domed outer buildings, with spiraling white minarets at the cardinal points. The place reminded Spyder of Hagia Sophia in Istanbul, though this structure was a dark and dismal parody of the ancient church-turned-mosque.

"Is that the palace?" Spyder asked.

Ashbliss pulled him quickly through the plaza. "Of course. Keep your head down. Don't speak unless you're spoken to, slave."

"Let's walk by the entrance and see if there are guards."

"There aren't. We're going to my master's home."

"I don't trust you. Five minutes isn't going to kill you."

"It will if one of Beelzebub's other attendants sees us and asks questions."

Spyder stopped in his tracks, but Ashbliss didn't notice. When he reached the end of the chain, he was jerked back and almost fell over. The demon yanked Spyder with all his weight.

"Move, slave."

"No."

"We had a deal."

"Let's walk by the palace."

"Someone will see us!"

"They will if you keep arguing with a slave."

"You selfish beast. You want to trick me!"

"No, this one usually keeps his word. Though, some women might argue the point," spoke another more familiar voice.

Spyder looked at a nearby bench, the apparent source of the voice, but no one was there. Then, by his ear he heard, "Bring hither the fatted calf, and let us eat, and be merry. The prodigal son is returned."

"My lord!" cried Ashbliss, dropping onto his belly.

"Count? How did you get down here?"

Count Non smiled and clapped Spyder on the back. "Guess," he said.

"You're on the guest list?"

"I make the guest list, little brother."

Spyder looked at Count Non and in his eyes he saw unfathomable expanses of time. A heart wounded more desperately than Spyder had ever imagined was possible. A pit of reckless and brilliant fury. Desolation and pride—these most of all. They seemed to unfold from Count Non like a pair of dark wings.

"Holy shit," Spyder said.

"That was once my name in a dead Sumerian dialect."

"You're Lucifer."

"That's my name. Don't wear it out."

Lucifer went to Ashbliss and prodded him with his boot. "Up, you rosy turd. I know what you wanted from this mortal, and you can't have it. Normally, I wouldn't care about your second-rate treacheries, but we're at war and I need my loyal generals on their feet, not buried under quicklime in the garden. Understand?"

Ashbliss got to his feet, but stared down at the black and white pavement slabs that formed a checkerboard pattern in the square. "I understand, my lord. Have mercy on me."

"Mercy? You must be thinking of someone else."

"Cut the little creep some slack," said Spyder. "He's supposed to be sneaky. He's a demon for Christ sake. Oh. Is it okay to say that down here?"

"Do you hear that?" Lucifer asked Ashbliss. "This mortal, whom you were about to betray and murder, is pleading for your life. It will be a long time before you see such grace down here again."

"Kill me? We had a deal."

"No, you had a lie," said Lucifer. "This little wretch doesn't work for

Beelzebub. Do you, turd?"

"No, my lord."

"Ashbliss here is a freelance thug. Someone has paid him to dispose of one of my better commanders. Possibly our friend, Xero. Little Ashbliss was going to trick you into doing the dirty work for him and then eliminate you."

"Is that true?" Spyder asked.

Ashbliss wrung his hands.

"Fuck him," said Spyder. "Drag him back to the butchers' quarter and let them hang him up on a hook."

"I can't refuse a guest," Lucifer told the demon.

Ashbliss burst into tears. His candles flickered out, one by one.

"Hell, I'm just blowing off steam. Can't you just lock him up or something?" asked Spyder. Then to Ashbliss. "You'll tell this man everything he wants to know, won't you, asshole?"

Ashbliss looked up with red-rimmed eyes, not sure what to do. He lunged and grabbed Spyder's hand, planting kisses on it with his thin membranous lips. "I will! I will! Thank you!" His candles flickered back to life.

Spyder looked at Lucifer. "Can you make the doggie stop humping me?"

"Come here, wretch."

Ashbliss went and stood before Lucifer.

"You'll begin your rehabilitation by going back to where you left my friend's companions and bringing them to my palace. Go quickly, before you ruin my good mood."

Bowing once, then twice, Ashbliss took off across the plaza as fast as his stumpy legs would carry him.

"Run, Forrest, run!" shouted Spyder.

Lucifer grabbed Spyder in a quick embrace. He was dressed in a striped black-and-gold hakama, the familiar chainmail over this bare chest, and a short jacket of some shiny material—vinyl or rubber. His head was shaved, and from his mid-scalp down the back of his neck, his pale skin was covered with black tattoos, intricate lettering in what Spyder remembered from Jenny's books was a kind of Angelic Script related to the Coptic alphabet. Even in Hell, Lucifer carried deep scars in his handsome face.

"It's good to see you, little brother."

"You know, my father was Baptist and my mother was Lutheran and sometimes I ended up going to both churches on the same Sunday, so I shouldn't be happy to see you," said Spyder. "But I am."

"Being able to embrace contradictions is a sign of intelligence."

"Or insanity."

"That's what the archangel Gabriel once said to me. Just before I cut off his head."

"Damn."

"I didn't have a choice. He would have cut off mine, if I'd given him the chance. I haven't thought about that in a long time. You know, that was the incident that triggered the war."

"In Heaven?"

"None other. You don't really think we're here because of the nice views?" Lucifer put out his right arm and wrapped Spyder's left arm around it. "We can catch up while I show you around my little kingdom."

FIFTY-ONE
OFF THE RADAR

"You son-of-a-bitch. We thought you were dead," said Spyder.

"I was," Lucifer said. "That body was as dead as dead could be. I just ended up back here."

"You wanted us here all along, didn't you? You manipulated this whole thing just to get us here. Why?"

"Xero Abrasax. He came here with some very impressive magic. Enough to rally an army and challenge me. I needed a champion. A mortal to kill a mortal soul. Shrike can kill him. He doesn't show it, but he's afraid of her. There's something in the book she can use against him."

They passed a golden temple, like an Aztec step-pyramid. In front was a kind of sculpture on a tall bronze base. A heavy cloth twisted languorously on top, looping and folding over itself, as if it was spinning slowly in water. The material changed colors as it moved, revealing eye and mouth holes. Spyder realized that it wasn't cloth, but human skins sewn together.

"Even if I believed that, all the shit you put us through, dragging our asses through the desert and across Hell, why do that if you wanted us here all along?"

"The universe has rules for these things. I needed Shrike here. I knew she needed a partner that could help her get here, but would have no personal desire for the book. Besides, do you think you would have come if I'd just popped into your tattoo shop one night around closing and said, 'Hello, I'm the Prince of Darkness. Think you could help me out with a little war next Tuesday, say, sixish?'"

"You had that demon attack me in the alley!"

"I just pointed out to the Bitru that you were carrying its mark."

"I'm suddenly remembering Sunday school. You're the Prince of Lies."

"First, don't try to quote chapter and verse to me, little brother. I know every holy book ever written. I even penned a few of them. Second, the 'Prince of Lies' is Ahriman, the Zoroastrian lord of darkness and brother to Ahura Mazda, the lord of light. Not that I ever met either one, but I'm sure they were lovely chaps. No, before you try telling me how the world is and who I am, remember what Samuel Butler, a mortal, once said: 'It must be remembered that we've only heard one side of the case. God has written all the books.'"

"You're just a victim of bad publicity?"

"Isn't it obvious?" Lucifer asked. "I was the loyal opposition in Heaven. I tested Job and plenty of others, all with Yahweh's blessing. In the early days, mortal faith and free will were new concepts. That's where the conflict began. God gave you free will, but we angels were expected to bow and scrape. I couldn't accept that."

"You were going to steal God's throne."

"I bet you believe everything Republicans say about Democrats. The archangel Michael accused me of wanting to sit in the throne of Heaven, but I didn't want to be God. I didn't want to be God's lap dog, either."

"You've got some serious daddy issues, mister."

The devil smiled. "Pride, too. The books got that right, at least."

"So, you're building Heaven to prove God wrong."

"Something like that. Heaven with free will."

"And not to set yourself up as a new God?"

Lucifer stopped walking and pointed with his free hand. "That's my palace over there. I don't need to remind anyone down here who's in charge. I'm not deluded enough to see myself as God. Over all, the first one did an impressive job creating the universe. It's the details I dispute."

"What's that quote? I've heard it a couple of ways, 'God is in the details…'"

"Also, 'the devil is in the details.' Yes, I'm aware of it. I don't know which version is more insulting."

"Let me get this straight, you're just down here having this family squabble with God for the last few million or few thousand years… I don't get how time works here."

"Don't try. You'll just hurt your brain."

"Cool. And you just want to show God that free will for your kind is hot biscuits and gravy. Then why fuck with us mortals? What's with all the temptation and corruption?"

"Who said that was me? Oh yes, everyone." Lucifer released Spyder's arm and they sat on a stone bench on the edge of the square. "I have to take some responsibility for that. Millions of angels came with me when Father threw me out and changed the locks. I had to give them something to do."

"All those monks and nuns, Jesus in the desert, all the visions of all those righteous types, none of that was you?"

"I'll admit that I've had my hand in a tempting manifestation or two. I was an angry young man, lashing out at all God had created. But like you, little brother, I couldn't help growing up a little."

Demons walked by them through the plaza, glancing furtively at the talking meat chatting with the ruler of Hell. Tall, bile-colored women with snakes for hair and dressed in high-collared latex robes whispered to each other as they passed. Graceful, loping things, like mechanical praying mantises, craned a stalk eye or two at the conversation. A flock of living skeletons, human from the waist up, but birdlike from the waist down, stopped and stared at the men on the bench. The skeletons moved as a group, like pigeons, chittering down one of the side streets.

"What about all those souls remodeling your den? What about the ones being tortured down here?"

"Do you think I invited them here? We've been Heaven's cesspit since time began. I'm just making use of the freeloaders. The tortures are just day-work for my less intelligent brethren. And truthfully, some souls are useless, not even fit for manual labor."

"I'm having a hard time with this poor, poor, pitiful me line, Count. Lucifer. What should I call you?"

"Anything you want, just don't call me late for dinner," Lucifer said. He looked Spyder in the eye. "The truth will set you free. But it might also hurt your feelings: You see, humanity isn't even on my radar. My quarrel is with Heaven, not you."

Spyder looked at Lucifer's palace, thinking over everything he'd seen and heard. "You're my friend. At least Count Non was. I don't really know what to believe right now."

"Admit it. You want me to be a monster. Humanity has to find someone to blame for its crimes. The problem is that you never really believed Copernicus. You still think you're the center of the universe and that all creation revolves around you."

"You've been practicing this speech for a while, haven't you?"

"I'll give you an another example. The snake in the Garden of Eden?"

"Yeah?"

"It was just a snake. Humanity's first real decision was to defy God. So was mine. That's the reason I make you uncomfortable. We're so much alike." Lucifer leaned closer, speaking quietly. "In Heaven, my title was 'The Tester'. I tempted and tormented mortals to test their faith, all with God's blessing. Job, for instance. It's a hard habit to break. But I always worked on the little things. Lust. Jealousy. Greed. Humanity didn't need any help with the big sins. It was you who ate the apple and fell from grace. It was you when Carthage was raped and burned and the earth salted. It was you at Hiroshima and Wounded Knee and Auschwitz and at every lynching of every hapless sharecropper who dared to meet the eyes of a white woman."

"You must really hate us. If we didn't exist, you'd still be in Heaven."

"I don't hate you. You're children, and children don't know any better. If it hadn't been you, something else would have set off my troubles with God." Lucifer shrugged. "Fathers and sons."

"Did you have anything to do with taking my blindfold off?"

"Why would I do that? I don't like many mortals and the few I do care for should be off living their lives, not going mad down here. You were trapped by something else. There's a black cloud around you that I can't see through, which means I can't help you. But you're going to have to deal with it sooner or later."

"Who's the Painted Man?"

Lucifer rolled his eyes. "The boogey man for demons. The Painted Man is the monster in the closet. Dr. Moriarty. Kayser Soze. He's supposedly a creature of pure chaos, neither God nor angel nor demon, who one day will come to destroy us. Why do you ask?"

"No reason. I heard a demon mention him."

"That's all? And you called me the Prince of Lies." Lucifer stretched and stuck out his long legs. "Don't trouble your handsome young head, Spyder Lee, you're not the Painted Man."

"Is Xero?"

"No, but he thinks he is and that makes him dangerous."

"How do you know he's not?"

"If he were I would have smelled him coming. I'd have tasted him. I'd have heard every beat of his heart. If the Painted Man ever sets foot in Hell, I'll know it."

Spyder looked down and saw a half-smoked cigarette lying at his feet. He picked up the butt and smoothed it straight. "Got a light?" he asked. Lucifer handed him a pink fur lighter.

"This is Lulu's," said Spyder.

"She dropped it by the Bone Sea. I was going to return it the next time I saw her."

Spyder lit the butt and dropped the lighter into his jacket pocket. It felt good to pull the smoke into his lungs.

"What's the deal with all the Satanic losers back home? Do you like them? Do they drive you crazy? What about Anton LaVey?"

"I love Anton LaVey. I love all carnies. God can have the meek. I'll take the grifters."

"You've got an answer for everything. I'll give you that, Count."

"We all have to live with ourselves, especially here. I'll tell you something, because I think you'll understand: I know that our Heaven is quite probably a pointless and futile thing, but we'll build it anyway, because it's all the Heaven we're ever likely to have."

Across the plaza, Ashbliss came with Lulu and Shrike. The men rose as they got closer. Both Lulu and Shrike went right to the man they knew as Count Non and hugged him.

Spyder said, "Ladies, let me introduce you to the man in black, his infernal badness, Lucifer."

Shrike and Lulu looked at the fallen angel. Shrike took Spyder's hand. Lulu smiled. "Count Non, you tricky fuck. I knew there was something about you. Not many men can make me question my preferences."

Lucifer looked at Ashbliss. "I'll talk to you later, dung beetle. Vanish." He snapped his fingers and the little demon was gone.

"Here," said Spyder, and handed Lulu back her lighter.

"Where'd you find it?"

"I'll tell you later."

"What happens now?" asked Shrike.

"Under other circumstances I'd probably throw a party. Given the current unpleasantness, I'll just take you to the book."

"Just like that?"

"Unless you'd like to wait around for Xero to attack again." Lucifer nodded to the hills beyond the golden step-pyramid. Men and demons were massing along the ridge.

Lucifer turned to Shrike. "By the way, it's nice to finally see your eyes. They're lovely."

"Thank you. It's good to see you, but a little strange, too."

"I get that a lot."

Lucifer started across the square to his palace as the others followed. Spyder looked over his shoulder and saw Xero's troops starting down the hill for Pandemonium.

FIFTY-TWO

WAITING FOR THE END OF THE WORLD

The entrance to Lucifer's palace was covered in flowers.
Bloody roses snaked on unnaturally long stalks around the main
entrance, a wide portico that let onto an immense reception hall. Inside,
clusters of white lilies and fleshy pink and tiger-striped orchids joined
the roses. The white marble floor was covered with a rich, purple carpet,
trimmed in gold. On one wall were exquisitely detailed anatomy charts
of humans, demons and every kind of animals Spyder had ever seen. On
the opposite wall hung a huge tapestry, a rendering of William Blake's
Great Red Dragon and the Woman Clothed with the Sun. Along the back
wall was what Spyder took to be Lucifer's trophy gallery.

Victorian-style curiosity cabinets were laid out neatly around the gently
curved walls. The first cabinet held a kind of black knotted lump floating
in air behind leaded glass. The little plaque at the bottom of the case read:
John the Baptist's Heart. Next to it was a set of battle armor, blackened,
the metal ripped and melted by some monstrous blast. "That's mine.
From the old days," Lucifer told Spyder. Nearby was a silver trumpet.
"Gabriel's. I nicked it on the way out the door." The next cabinet held a
crown of thorns. "No explanation needed there, I suppose." Rare plants
and animals were lying in bell jars and pinned in display cases. They
were all alive, but trapped. Two cases side-by-side held an assortment
of Fabergé eggs and different kinds of puzzle boxes. Lucifer shrugged
and said, "I just like them." Another glass case contained a kind of black,
swirling nothingness that seemed to suck light into itself. It was labeled,
Chaos. At the end of the row was a cage and in it lay the book. It was
as tall as Spyder and the covers were riveted plates of solid steel, with
runes etched into the surface. When Spyder saw it, he thought, This is
not a human's book.

"I feel sick," said Shrike. She clutched her chest.

"Is it the key?" Spyder asked. "We're near the book. It's probably try-

211

ing to get out."

"I don't know. This doesn't feel right." She took deep, painful breaths.

Behind the cage that housed the book, the flowers began to die. The wave of death spread around the room. The flowers all turned black, shedding their petals before falling to the floor in dry heaps. Spyder's gaze followed the trail of rot around the room. The trail of dying flowers ended at a long staircase where Xero stood, with Shrike's father at his feet. Xero kicked the old man and he rolled down the stone steps, landing in a heap at the bottom.

"Father!" screamed Shrike, and she stumbled to him. Spyder and the others followed, Spyder with the black blade out and Lulu with her shotgun pointed at Xero. As Shrike reached her father, demons dropped down from the ceiling and dragged her up the stairs. Spyder started after them, but Lucifer grabbed his shoulder and held him.

"Don't move," Lucifer said. Spyder turned and watched as Xero's troops quietly streamed in through the front entrance, filling the front of the hall.

"'And I saw, and behold a white horse: and he that sat on him had a bow; and a crown was given unto him: and he went forth conquering, and to conquer,'" Lucifer said to Xero. "You have more gall than brains coming into my capital, and especially my home."

"You have a million idle threats, angel. What you don't seem to have is an army."

"You aren't looking hard enough."

Lucifer closed his eyes. The Blake tapestry on the wall exploded into light and demons poured from it, armed with barbed spears and vicious swords. The opposing troops snarled and growled, showing each other their teeth, beating their weapons against their shields. Neither side attacked, but waited for a signal from their masters.

"Get the key!" shouted Xero. One of the demons holding Shrike pulled a knife from his belt and cut into Shrike's chest. She screamed. Lucifer pulled Spyder back from the stairs before he could do anything.

"Lulu!" Spyder screamed. She opened up at the demons with the four-ten. They fell back as the shots tore up the stairs around them. One demon collapsed with a shot in the chest, and another went down with a head wound. The other demons scrambled up the stairs to cower at Xero's feet.

Lucifer pulled both Spyder and Lulu back across the room to the curiosity cabinets. Spyder shook himself free.

"I thought you were a warrior. What's wrong with you?" he yelled.

Lucifer spoke evenly. "Timing is everything. Never let your temper lead you. Both of you, stay here."

Lucifer went to the center of the room, between the two snarling armies, and looked up at Xero. He looked relaxed. Even happy, thought Spyder.

"You've done very well for yourself," Lucifer said. "You're not the first to ever challenge my position, but you're the first to get this far."

"Save your congratulations. I'm not done yet."

"Why should you be? You've come so far with so little. We're alike in that. When we angels first came to this place, there was nothing. Now look at all we've built. You were just another lost soul when you arrived and look at what you've accomplished. I admire that. I don't like to annihilate talent. How would you like your own principality? You've killed off a few of my less competent generals. Would you like their lands for yourself and your men?"

Xero grinned a wolf's grin. "No thank you. I think I'll take everything."

"You won't," said Lucifer.

Xero kicked the demons cowering at his feet. "Go back and get the key!" Reluctantly, the demons crawled down the stairs to Shrike. She lay quietly, her hand over her bloody wound, watching Lucifer. Spyder tried to catch her eye, but she looked as if she were in shock.

"You won't take my kingdom because you aren't equipped to. Winning a few battles is nothing. Even taking this palace is a pointless gesture."

"Then why don't you just surrender it and leave?" said Xero, and his troops laughed.

"You're a good tactician—for a mortal. And that will be your downfall. Your wars last weeks, months, perhaps a few years. It's easy to plan, to keep your armies together, to believe in yourself. But how long can you do it, mortal? The last war I fought lasted ten thousand years."

"And you lost."

"That was to God. Do you think you're God, little man?" said Lucifer. "I can wait, you see. You can win a thousand victories and I can wait. Time itself can burn out and the universe can collapse in on itself, and I can still wait. And in the last second at the last moment of existence, when even gods and angels must perish, I will find you and slit your throat. And the last thing you'll see before the nothingness takes you will be my face smiling in victory."

Shrike saw the demons coming down the stairs for her. She screamed.

When they tried to grab her, she hacked them with her sword, but she was too badly injured to crawl away.

"What a silver tongue you have. But none of it will happen if I kill you first," said Xero. He raised his arms and waves of black lightning blasted down at Lucifer, along the way vaporizing the demons he'd sent for Shrike, just as one triumphantly held up the key he'd pried from her side. The key went skittering across the floor, leaving a tracery of blood, and came to rest at Lucifer's feet. Lucifer placed his right foot on top of the key. Xero bellowed in anger.

Shrike ducked and pressed herself beneath the bolts. Lucifer didn't move. He appeared to know when something was coming and simply raised his right hand, letting the lightning flow into him and out his left hand, right back at Xero. The stairs exploded around the general, but he kept throwing the bolts, pushing Lucifer back, only to be pushed back himself.

It was too much, Spyder thought. Xero couldn't be bribed. Maybe Lucifer could wait for the end of time, but Shrike couldn't.

Spyder grabbed Lulu and pulled her over to the book. "Help me," he said.

"How?"

"We're going to push the book into that case of chaos. Let it swallow the damned thing. Maybe we'll die, too, but we'll take these demonic fucks with us."

In the center of the room, Lucifer and Xero's battle continued. Shrike slowly, painfully, crawled down the stairs toward her father. The two armies shrieked, growing more agitated by the second. When their taunts and roars reached a mad pitch, someone threw an axe. That's all it took, both armies rushed each other with weapons, claws and teeth.

Lulu came around to Spyder's side of the book cage and pressed her back against it. Spyder grabbed the bars and put his shoulder into them. He felt a funny click and stepped back. The front of the cage fell open.

The battle quieted, then stopped all together. The demons stared at Spyder, as did Xero and Lucifer. Shrike lay by her father and looked at him, dazed.

"He has the key!" screamed Xero.

"No, he doesn't, you idiot," snapped Lucifer. He looked at Spyder. "You haven't been holding out on me, have you, little brother? No secret saint-hood or magic in your past?"

Spyder shrugged, shook his head.

"That cage doesn't pop open for just anyone."

"Get the book!" screamed Xero to his troops.

"It's not yours?" came a quiet voice by the portico. "The book belongs to us."

Spyder turned too look, but he already knew what was there. The Black Clerks, ledger in hand, were walking into the palace straight through the demon armies. The demons fell back, afraid to touch them. Only Lucifer stood in the Clerks' way. For the first time, he seemed truly enraged.

"Out of my kingdom, crawling filth!" he screamed.

The head Clerk stepped forward. He cocked his head to one side. Then he raised a finger. Lucifer was thrown, loose-limbed and helpless, across the room. He landed hard on the stairs above Shrike, stone splintering as he crashed on the marble.

The Clerks turned to Spyder. "Come to us?" the head Clerk told him.

"Fuck you," Spyder said.

The Clerk flicked a finger. The scar Spyder had received earlier from the Clerks began to burn. His vision clouded. He saw things. He saw himself through their eyes. He saw himself looking at himself looking back at himself in infinite regression.

"Not dead yet?" the Clerk said.

"Shit," said Spyder, sorting through the pictures in his head. Dizzy, he grabbed Lulu. "It wasn't you they were looking through," he said. "In the desert. It was me. I helped them follow us the whole way."

"Strong," said one of the other Clerks.

"What do you want with the book?" asked Spyder.

"It's ours," said the head Clerk.

"I don't believe you." Spyder leaned on the book for support.

"No matter," said the head Clerk, and in a fraction of a second, he'd pulled the little knife from his belt and flung it into Spyder's chest.

"Spyder!" screamed Shrike.

He fell back against the cage. The Clerks walked silently toward him. Trying to stand, Spyder grabbed the book with his bloody hands.

"That's not permitted," said the Clerk.

An icy white shock ripped through Spyder's body and he fell to the floor.

FIFTY-THREE
THRENODY 23

The long-extinct scorpion people of Anu sang songs for their dead. Each song was designed to teach a new spirit some skill or valuable lesson for the Afterlife.

Of all the Anu songs set down on tablets and scrolls, only a handful were for those on their way to Heaven. The vast majority of the songs were for those on their way to Hell.

A translated excerpt:

To whom shall I cry to as I go into the depths?

My God who, if she should appear, would destroy me

With her terrible beauty?

God's Enemy, who would consume me in his resplendent terror?

At the bare edge of the abyss, beauty and terror are less than

A burning step apart, each worthy of worship, graced, pure, demanding.

God burns us. The Enemy burns us.

They will light my way through the long dark

And fire me in a sublime pyre, until I am only ash.

Only ash, I enter the abyss to behold

My shadow

My sins

My world laid bare

Surrounded by souls, dust and ash, I go alone.

Dust and ash, I know that we all venture alone, but that we all venture.

And it is only dust and ash that passes through the abyss,

Only dust and ash.

The sublimely consumed. The radiantly destroyed.

Only dust and ash passes through.

FIFTY-FOUR
MORE THAN HEAVEN

He was falling for a very long time. Hours. Years. Eons. He was in the book. He was the book.

Stars twinkled in and out of existence. Dust became planets and cooled into mountains, then became dust again. Life appeared, flourished and died. He felt the immense emptiness of an entire universe devoid of any living, thinking thing. The universe died soon after. He absorbed its passing into every atom of his body.

He saw, felt and tasted nothingness, or as much of nothingness as his mortal mind could fathom. But even in nothingness was life. It passed through him and moved on, immense beyond belief. So large, it didn't notice his microscopic presence. He was at the end of time and the beginning. Some immense wheel was turning somewhere. Existence was done, but not over. Life was too powerful for that. It was beyond time or space or god or death. He couldn't quite get hold of it. The image of life, the idea was too big for his flea-size brain, but he caught a glimpse, as he floated high, so high above the universe (Is this Heaven? Or something more?) that he could look down and see it all laid out below him—clusters of galaxies like strands of pearls. But stars were things. And what he'd glimpsed wasn't a thing, but a force. Something he couldn't quite grasp, like light shining through a prism. He could put his hand into it, touch it, but never really hold it.

It was beautiful and sad where he was. So lonely. He was the oldest living thing in the universe. Or was with it. Or it passed through him, like air moving in and out of his lungs, leaving a little of itself behind—just a few molecules. Each molecule grew into pictures and words. The pictures and words flowed together to form a structure. It had doors and windows and a seemingly endless number of rooms. It was a cathedral. A memory cathedral, the kind monks used to memorize whole sections of the Bible. Spyder had read about them in Jenny's books. But the rooms

217

in this cathedral were filled with something else. Some immensely older knowledge. Each image he touched, each word he mouthed filled him with power and dread. For a long time, he thought he was dead. Then he tripped over an uneven door frame. He caught himself before he fell, but tore the palm of his hand on the frame. His blood dripped onto the floor of the cathedral. This body is alive, he thought. I'm alive.

I'm alive.

And then he was falling again.

FIFTY-FIVE
TABLE SCRAPS

He awoke on the floor of Lucifer's palace. Someone was standing over him. His eyes fluttered fully open and he recognized a woman's face. Tears were flowing from her empty sockets.

A name floated by and he said, "Lulu." She reached down and pulled the knife from his chest. He groaned.

"Alive?" said one of the Clerks.

"He is surprising," said the head Clerk.

Spyder leaned shakily against the cage that housed the book. Lulu spun on her heels and blasted the Black Clerks with round after round from the four-ten.

"Don't," said Spyder, reaching for her.

Each of Lulu's shots hit, but it was like shooting at scarecrows. The rounds went through the Clerks, as if there was nothing but straw to absorb the blasts.

The head Clerk snatched the shotgun from Lulu's hands and tossed it across the hall. "Your debt is past due. We will collect now. Your heart, I think?" he said.

"No," said Spyder. He got to his feet and stretched. "Damn. Sometimes dying is like a week in Vegas."

"Perhaps your head was hurt in your fall?" said the head Clerk. "We move from Earth to Heaven to Hell. Nowhere is closed to us. We swallow life and spit out creation. And you say we will not take this child's tiny life?"

Spyder went and stood close to the head Clerk, close enough to smell the rot in his borrowed flesh. "I know what you are. You aren't gods. You aren't even demons. Come on out of the closet, boys."

"We don't believe you."

"I know, but that doesn't mean dingo's balls. You're hollow. Puppets. I don't even think you're really alive."

"Are you mad? I think so."

"Don't pay attention to the man behind the curtain, that's the best you can come up with? It didn't work on the girl in the ruby slippers and it doesn't mean shit to me."

"Enough," said the Clerk with the ledger. He opened the book and withdrew something that looked like a thick, ragged tree limb. Dropping the ledger, he twisted the limb until a dozen ragged blades sprang from the shaft: killing thorns. The Clerk lunged, but Spyder side-stepped the blow, slipping behind his attacker. Slamming his arm around the Clerk's throat, Spyder held him so that the others could watch, as he whispered a single word into the Clerk's ear. When Spyder released him, the Clerk remained frozen in place, his deformed weapon still in the air.

"A trick? Yes," said the head Clerk.

The frozen Clerk began to shake. His mouth came open and he made a sound that was part wonder and part howl of pain. He shook until he was a blur, and the stitches holding his pale body together began to split. The wan internal light the Clerks always gave off burst through his seams as he flew to pieces. As each broken part of him hit the floor, it vanished.

The two remaining Clerks looked at Spyder.

"I said the true name of time and decay," he told them. "Do you even know what you are? You're the boy-toys of the Old Gods, the Dominions. You need used-up organs because you're trash on two legs. Golems. Animated table scraps. A word made you walk and a word can make you stop. I saw into the book. I learned the words."

"We are the engines of creation and destruction," said the head Clerk. "We balance the Spheres. We prune dead branches, taking life where it is not appreciated, such as in this sorry child?" The Clerk nodded at Lulu. "We pass her breath back into the universe for new souls."

"That was your burden. That's what you used to be. You balanced order and chaos, but something happened. The Dominions got inside of you. Instead of serving the universe, you started serving the Old Gods. You're their delivery boys. You grant wishes to the weak, the wounded and lost, getting your hooks in their souls so the Dominions can feed on them. There's nothing left of your old selves, when you balanced the universe. You're empty shells. This book was made to bring the Dominions back, but I'm not going to let you do that."

"Is someone going to kill someone soon?" Xero called from the stairs. "I was about to win a war."

"You were about to be eviscerated in front of your troops," said Lucifer.

"We know you. You are not a man, but a broken child?" said the head Clerk to Spyder. "You've seen and learned much lately, but you remain a drunken libertine who despises his own foolish weakness above all else. And your mortal body is trapped forever in Hell. But we will take pity and give you the gift of annihilation."

"I'm not afraid of you."

"But it is yourself you hate and yourself you must fight?" The head Clerk raised his hand to the palace entrance, where a figure was waiting.

Spyder saw his reflection. Sort of. A version of himself, but scarred like Lulu, crudely stitched together, like the Clerks themselves.

"He is your Shadow Brother, built from a broken memory you left in Berenice. All the blood you left in the street? A very powerful elixir. We sacrificed a few of the organs we'd collected," said the head Clerk. He turned to Lulu. "Child, do you recognize your eyes in another?"

"You got the jump on me in Berenice, bro," said the lacerated Spyder. "But I'm back and bad and ready for love."

"More golem trash," Spyder said to the Clerks. "You think I won't kill it this time?"

"We're counting on it. He's special. Not you in name and form, but you, literally. A strike against him is against yourself? Show him," the head Clerk told the golem.

Spyder watched his Shadow Brother pull the punch dagger from behind his back and slide it hard across his chest, carving a deep, crimson wound. Spyder felt something like a live wire being dragged over his skin. He looked down and saw that he had a chest wound identical to the golem's.

"You know the true names. Use them. Turn him to dust!" called Shrike.

"I can't. I might dust out, too," Spyder said.

Feinting and teasing, the golem came at him with the knife. Spyder backed up and started to draw Apollyon's blade from his belt, but stopped himself. It would be suicide.

The golem kept making little charges, then stabbed and sliced himself. Spyder twitched in pain and bled, feeling each twist of the blade. The golem circled him, splashing blood onto the marble floor and laughing.

"Why are you running? This is what you always wanted. Life's too hard for people like us. Let me fix it for you," said the golem.

Spyder backed up. Sweat flowed into his wounds, stinging him.

"Remember the Middle Way, little brother!" yelled Lucifer. "Would the

Buddha fight himself?"

Spyder stopped in his tracks, his gaze flicking to Lucifer, then Shrike. He stretched his arms out wide and closed his eyes. The golem rushed him, jamming its knife deep into Spyder's chest. Gritting his teeth at the pain, Spyder wrapped his arms around the golem and held on. They were both bleeding and the floor was slippery with their blood. Spyder lifted the younger, smaller version of himself and spun on his heels, dropping his Shadow Brother onto the book. Gasping, Spyder twisted and threw all of his weight on his doppelgänger, pinning him long enough to pull the black blade from his own belt and swing it once.

Both Spyder's and the golem's heads slid off their shoulders and rolled onto the floor.

FIFTY-SIX

STARS

Spyder rose on wobbly legs and set his head back on his shoulders.

"You know those days when you just can't do anything right? You're having one of them," he said to the head Clerk.

"This is some trick of yours, Lucifer?"

"It's all me," said Spyder. His throat felt full of pins and needles as he spoke.

"No matter? Alive or dead, you are lost, locked in Hell forever. So is the woman."

"Not necessarily. You did us a favor, Brainiac. Shrike makes these little blood sacrifices when she does small magic. All this golem's blood and mine should be good for one big favor, don't you think?"

"What are you doing?" asked Lucifer.

"I'm sorry, man. You're my friend, but Shrike and I can't spend forever down here."

Lucifer looked stricken. "You don't want to do that, little brother."

"No, but I've got to."

The book was already ingesting the blood Spyder and the golem had spilled on the floor. Spyder laid his hands on the metal cover and whispered strange words that seemed to flow into his mind. He was speaking a language he didn't understand, a tongue so guttural and inhuman that it would have been agony even if his throat hadn't been freshly slit.

The runes etched into the book cover glowed and the remaining blood began to boil. Spyder pulled his hands back as the golem's lifeless body, along with the last dregs of blood, were absorbed into the book.

Far across Hell there was a sound like thunder, only it came from beneath the ground, as if the foundation of the underworld itself had cracked.

"Do you know how insane this is?" asked Lucifer.

"I'm the fool, remember? I do shit you sensible guys wouldn't dream of."

Quivering green light, like a fluorescent bulb shining from the bottom of the ocean, blasted through cracks in the ancient, unfinished wall Spyder had seen while walking to Pandemonium with Ashbliss. The colossal iron reinforcing beams began to bend and buckle as some fantastic new weight pressed against the bricks from the other side.

"Glorious! Glorious! They are here!" cried the head Clerk.

"Not for you."

"It is accomplished! We believed the Butcher Bird would free the Dominions, as revenge when you and the slut died. But you have done her job for her. The universe is ours."

"You're talking to a guy who just cut off his own head. You don't get to tell me what's yours and mine," said Spyder. He grabbed the head Clerk and ripped away the stolen skin that covered his face. In shock, both Clerks retreated a pace or two. The head Clerk touched his face, feeling for the stolen flesh that was no longer there.

"Feeling cold? Something missing?" Spyder asked. He then spoke a single word and the Clerks tumbled to their knees. They grew smaller and softer, as if their bones were turning to warm butter, until they were nothing but pale puddles on the stone floor.

Spyder looked back across Hell as the ancient wall began to crumble. Hands clawed at the gigantic bricks from the other side. Strange howls filled the air. Spyder became aware that both Xero and Lucifer's armies had grown considerably smaller since the Dominions had made their presence known. Deserters continued to sprint out the front of the palace.

Lucifer limped to Spyder and stood next to him, watching the ancient wall crumble. "You may have beaten the Clerks so cleverly that you've killed us all," he said.

Xero came slowly down the stairs. "What did he do?"

"He's released the Dominions," said Lucifer.

"Why?" asked Lulu.

Before Spyder could say anything, Xero charged down the stairs to where Shrike was cradling her father in her arms. He grabbed her by the hair and held a knife to her throat. "Come to me, Old Ones! Give me the power to defeat my enemies! I make this blood sacrifice to you."

Lucifer let loose an animal howl and charged, his body morphing as he went. His body went transparent, like living glass, then burst into a blinding silver light. His eyes, however, dimmed to shimmering, pitiless black pits, and he became what Spyder knew had to be a wrathful version of this original angelic form.

Shrike fought Xero's hand from her throat. The man was concentrating on Lucifer. Spyder realized that Xero was reciting a spell.

"Look out!" Spyder screamed.

A blur shot from the great book as Apollyon's knife flew across the room and embedded itself into Lucifer's spine. The Prince of Hell collapsed at Shrike's feet. She swung her sword backwards over her head and buried it in Xero's skull. The general just laughed.

"When I've bled you dry, I'll bring you back here and make you my concubine. I'll rape you in Hell forever."

Lucifer, back in his more familiar Count Non form, staggered to his feet. "Alizarin," he said, and reached out his hand. Shrike grabbed Lucifer and pulled him toward her, hard, throwing herself onto the floor.

Spyder ran to them, covering Shrike's body with his own. Xero screamed. Spyder turned and saw the general pushing madly at Lucifer's body. The tip of Apollyon's blade, which was protruding from Lucifer's belly, had buried itself in Xero's midsection when Shrike had pulled Lucifer down. The general shrieked as the blade burned him. Lucifer grabbed the man and rolled off Shrike, bearhugging him, driving the knife in deeper. Their bodies glowed red. Xero's blackened lips curled back like burning paper.

The general was suddenly very still. Lucifer pushed free and backhanded Xero across the face. The fried mortal soul crumbled, a burned-out husk.

Spyder went to Lucifer and pulled the blade from his back.

"I thought that knife killed demons," he said.

"You're not just any fool and I'm not just any demon," said Lucifer, leaning heavily against the railing.

Spyder snatched the tunic from Xero's corpse and went to Shrike. Holding her upright, Spyder pressed the cloth over the wound in her chest. Lulu, exhausted, collapsed next to Lucifer. Across Hell, the wall finally came down and the Dominions poured through. They were so alien and so massed together, shouldering their way from their exile in chaos, that, later, no one there, mortal or angel, could describe what exactly came into this universe through that ancient breech in time and space. There were shaggy heads and arms that were lined with eyes, reptile wings, tentacles, cocks with teeth, legs like a bird's and legs like machines. Emerald flesh, exposed bones, metal talons, fire, wind and ice.

The Dominions circled the roof of Hell once, twice and on the third pass, shot up together, blasting through and out into the night sky. Gazing up through the glass dome atop Lucifer's palace, Spyder saw familiar constellations. Orion. The Big Dipper. It was Earth. It was home.

FIFTY-SEVEN
JESUS CHRIST AND BRUCE LEE

"So, Spyder, what was the deal with your head back there? Why aren't you completely damn dead?" said Lulu.

"Ask your boyfriend. He's the one who gave me the idea," said Spyder. He turned to Lucifer. The Prince of Hell sat with his elbows on his knees, his fingers steepled, staring out at his ruined kingdom. "How'd you know that my dying would kill the golem, but not me?"

"I guessed," Lucifer said. "You had a fifty-fifty chance."

"Something happened when I went into the book. I was with the Dominions for a second, I think. Some of their life or whatever keeps them going rubbed off on me."

"I think you're right," said Shrike. "Look." She moved the cloth from where Spyder had been holding it on her chest. The wound was closed.

"Come here," Spyder told Lulu.

"Why? You haven't gone all *Dawn of the Dead*, have you?"

"Quiet. Come on down here."

Lulu came down the stairs and sat next to Spyder.

He took both her hands, saying, "I'm not sure what I'm doing, so just close your eyes and relax."

"It's prom night all over again."

The palace was a disaster. The walls were webbed with cracks big enough to put a fist in. Part of the dome had collapsed. Hell proper was in sad shape, too. Millions of tons of rock had come crashing down when the Dominions blasted their way out of the place. Most of Lucifer's new Heaven and much of Pandemonium lay in ruins. The group had all remained on the stairs throughout this harrowing of Hell. Exhausted, bleeding, they were way down the road past both fear and surprise, stalled between numbness and wonder. None of them even blinked when Shrike's father disappeared. They chose to see it as a sign of release, that with Xero's passing the curse that held the old man's spirit in the underworld had been broken.

"That fool's curses were as thin and hollow as his head when I cracked it," Lucifer had said.

"When you're through with my hands let me know, okay?" Lulu asked. "I've got a hellacious nose itch."

"Then it's working," Spyder said. "I think we're about done here."

"Dude, what did you do to me? I feel all hot and strange."

"Go look."

She stepped over the fallen columns and broken glass, navigating her way across the buckled floor to Lucifer's curiosity cabinets. None of them had broken, but they lay at crazy angles against the walls and floor. The *Chaos* cabinet was still standing in its original spot. Lulu went to it and checked herself in the glass. Her reflection stared back with the swirling nothingness behind it.

"It's me," she said. "I look like me again."

"Eyes and skin and everything. Did I get it all right?"

"You tricked me out like an old Chevy. For what? The Clerks still own me. They'll just come and take these eyes, too."

"Lulu, the Clerks are gone. At least the ones who snagged you. If any others ever show up, I'll huff and I'll puff and I'll blow 'em all down."

Lulu leaned her head on the cabinet, holding her belly. "Why do I feel like this?"

"You were empty. They were making you into them. That's what they do. You're alive again. Being alive hurts," said Spyder. "And you haven't had a stomach in how long? That one's probably hungry."

"I remember hungry."

"You okay?"

Lulu nodded. "Yeah."

"I did the right thing, didn't I?"

Spyder couldn't see Lulu's face. Turning, she walked back to the stairs, staring at her hands.

"Yeah, you did good. It's just a lot to get hold of. I didn't realize how much of me was gone."

"For what it's worth, I know how you feel," said Shrike. "I haven't seen colors in so long. I remember them all, but I can't quite recall which is red and which is blue. It's a little overwhelming."

"That's one word for it."

"Sit with me," Shrike said. Lulu came over the wreckage and curled up with her head in Shrike's lap.

"I'd fuck a duck for a cigarette right now," Lulu said.

Lucifer was inspecting his palace. He picked up a couple of fragments of cherry-colored glass that had fallen from the dome. Holding them over his eyes, he peered up through the hole in the roof of Hell.

"Maybe we should put a skylight up there," he said. "I miss the stars sometimes."

"Sorry for busting up the place," said Spyder.

Lucifer dropped the glass. "Sorry for tricking you into the bowels of Hell."

"I was thinking about taking some time off anyway."

Lucifer smiled at some private joke. "This was all one big con job, you know. I manipulated you, but the universe slipped a good one past me."

"By saying 'universe' you're trying not to say 'God'?"

"Perhaps," said Lucifer. "I had to go to talking meat— sorry, mortals— to save my kingdom. Not only did you have the power to save it, but to destroy it, too. Maybe pride really is my sin. The Painted Man was right in front of me this whole time, and I never even saw you coming."

"Hell, you brought him here," said Lulu.

"Thank you for reminding me," he said with mock gratitude. Lucifer picked up a gilded candle sconce, looked around and threw it back into the rubble. Going to his curiosities, he began picking up the cabinets that had fallen over. Spyder went to help him.

"I don't know about the Painted Man thing," Spyder said as they turned the wooden Fabergé egg case upright. The gleaming eggs lay in a thousand pieces on the bottom of the velvet-lined cabinet, bejeweled junk. "I don't exactly feel like Jesus Christ or Bruce Lee."

"Good. That's my job," Lucifer said.

"What happens now?" asked Shrike.

Lucifer pulled the cabinet with John the Baptist's heart from where it was leaning precariously against the wall, setting it flat on the floor. Shifting it inch by inch, he got it aligned exactly where he wanted it. Spyder helped him slide the crown of thorns cabinet until it was just so.

"Deo gratias," Lucifer said. He looked at Shrike. "The Dominions have broken the boundaries of Hell. All bets are off. You can go home any time you like. Me, I begin rebuilding. None of this affects our work here, you know. Yahweh had his little laugh, but we're still building our Heaven." He pulled a scarlet silk kerchief from his pocket and wiped some of the dust off the glass of the cabinet that housed the crown of thorns. "And if he destroys that one, we'll build it again. We have all eternity to get it right."

"We're going to have to take the book with us," said Shrike. "Madame Cinders will want it in return for my father." She brushed some of Lulu's hair out of the girl's eyes.

"Take it. I don't want the damned thing around here."

"Can we really give it to her?" asked Spyder. "I got a glimpse of what it is. I don't know anything about magic and look what it did to me. What could someone with her knowledge do with it?"

"She'll do exactly what Xero was going to do. Make a deal with the Dominions and grab as much power she can," Lucifer said. He opened the case with his puzzle boxes and set them back on their proper display stands.

"We can't let her do that," Spyder said. He went to where Shrike was sitting and knelt down next to her. "We can't give her the key to all that power."

"She'll kill my father. Or worse. Curse him again. He'll be right back in Hell and all of this will have been for nothing."

"I don't know what to say."

"Idiot, you're a hero now. You're going to have to learn to think on a larger scale," said Lucifer. He used his kerchief to slap at the dust that had settled on his clothes. "You just cracked open a hole in the universe, deceived the devil, wrecked Hell and sent the Black Clerks packing. Even I couldn't do all that and I can do a lot. Yet with all that to your credit, you're telling me you can't defeat one dying hag?"

"I wouldn't know where to begin."

"You have a warrior by your side and the Prince of Darkness for a friend. What you don't know is how to ask for help, but that is how we gain knowledge and improve ourselves."

"Okay," said Spyder. He leaned back his head, threw out his arms and shouted as loudly as he could, *"Help!"*

Lucifer shook his head. Shrike covered her ears.

"Damn, I've wanted to do that for days," Spyder said.

Lucifer kicked his way through the rubble until he found what he was looking for. When he picked it up, Spyder recognized the knife the head Clerk had used to stab him.

"You asked for help and here it is," Lucifer said. "When troubled by a diseased sorceress like Madame Cinders, you need a miracle. Look to the saints for a cure."

Lucifer took the knife and went to his curiosity cabinets.

"Come here, so I can give you something," he said. Spyder went to him. Lucifer made one quick slice and wrapped the prize in the scarlet kerchief before handing it to over. "Don't lose that."

"I won't," said Spyder, finding himself suddenly able to be a little shocked again.

Shrike went to where the cage with the book had fallen over. The impact had turned the marble beneath it to powder and driven the book several feet into the floor.

"Any suggestions on how we can move this thing? It's a thousand pounds if it's an ounce," she said.

"Travel for all of you, including the book, is being arranged right now," Lucifer said.

"So, we're probably at the goodbye portion of the evening," said Spyder. "I really suck at this."

Lucifer smiled. "I know. I looked into the minds of some of your exes."

"Find anything good in there?"

"You're not universally despised." Lucifer leaned in to whisper, "That includes Jenny. But you need to learn to let go of things that only exist in the past tense."

Lucifer went to Shrike. She put her arms around him. "You helped me free my father. I'll always be grateful for that," she said.

"You've lived half your life in light and half in darkness. Which do you prefer?" Lucifer asked.

"When I've seen enough of either I'll tell you."

"Fair enough," he said, and leaned in to kiss her cheek. Then reached out for Lulu's perfect, restored hands and gave each a kiss.

"You're a prince, Prince," she said. "You could turn a dyke's head."

"A higher compliment, I'll never receive."

Lucifer went to Spyder and the two of them looked at each other.

"Think we're ever going to meet up again?" Spyder asked.

"Abyssus abyssum invocat," Lucifer said. "'Hell calls Hell.' For better or worse, we are brothers. We'll meet again."

"When you get Heaven finished, invite me to the opening."

Lucifer nodded toward the palace portico. "Your ride is here."

Spyder turned. He knew what was coming from the sound and the word-picture Lulu had painted back at the Bone Sea. Finally seeing the enormous mechanical spider, however, was a much stranger sight than he'd imagined. Still, the contraption wasn't as frightening as what had been in his head back when he'd been blindfolded. The creature moved so delicately on its long legs, Spyder thought that it looked like it was walking on tiptoe.

Lulu walked up to the machine.

"Cornelius, remember me?" she asked.

The head on the enormous mechanism looked puzzled. "I apologize, madam. My memory isn't what it used to be. However, meeting you now is certainly a pleasure," he said. Cornelius turned his attention to Lucifer and bowed deeply.

"You were a gleeful and criminally stupid thug during your life. Do you recall any of that?" Lucifer asked. He approached Cornelius, who continued to hold his deep bow.

"No, my lord."

"We harnessed your brutish tendencies to make use of you while you were in my domain. But I'm prepared to relieve you of this job. Would you like that?" Lucifer made a dismissive gesture with his hand. "Don't bother answering, of course you would. You will take these good people and this book out that hole you might have noticed in the roof. You will take them wherever they want to go and do whatever they ask of you. When they dismiss you, and only then, you will return here to me and we'll discuss finding you some other task that won't wrack your pea-size brain. Do you understand?"

"Yes. Thank you, my lord."

"Pick up the book and wait outside."

Cornelius stood up and moved with delicate, almost mincing steps until he'd positioned his enormous body properly on the uneven floor. Four of his metal legs scrabbled in the wreckage and pulled the book free. When it was secure against his belly, metal jaws clamped down on it, allowing him to lower his legs. He turned and went outside, a bit slower than when he'd entered, weighed down by the book's bulk.

They followed Cornelius out to the plaza and one by one climbed onto his back. Lucifer stood below in the palace portico looking up at them through the cherry-colored dome glass he held before his right eye.

"The good thing about glass is that we can melt it down and use it again. This marble is a total loss, though. Maybe I'll have some bankers dig it out with their teeth." Lucifer bowed deeply to them, waved once, turned on his heels and strode back inside his palace.

Spyder and the others held on tight as Cornelius loped through the wreckage of Pandemonium, out across the plains of Hell to one of the impossibly high walls that were the boundaries of the underworld. Then, they began to climb.

FIFTY-EIGHT
ROLL ME A SMOKE, JOHN WAYNE

"Eight legs good! Two legs bad!" Lulu shouted as they strode across the desert.

They were making good time. Cornelius never needed to rest or slow down, even when walking straight into a sandstorm. Spyder told him to head for Berenice and he started straight across the desert without hesitation. A trip that had taken days on the way out, they now covered in a few hours. Around midmorning, when they caught sight of the city of memories, it was strangely reassuring.

"One step closer to home," said Shrike.

Something was happening around Berenice. Even at a distance, they could see it. A dozen airships were in port on the south side of the city. Spyder wondered if they should turn and head back into the open desert, then flag down a boat when they hit the coast. He didn't like the idea of going up in one of the airships again, and he was reasonably sure no one else did. But there was no telling when anything larger than a local fishing boat would come along. They had to go to Berenice.

"Damn," said Spyder. "I should have asked Lucifer for some of those jewels back on the ground in Hell. We don't have a penny to buy a ride."

"We'll be fine," Shrike said.

"You think?"

Shrike leaned against Spyder, running a hand through the hair on the back of his head. "The Count was right, you need to think bigger."

They caught sight of the first lookout a couple of miles from the city. The boy had been asleep, and his loose dun-colored robes blended into the sand. He awoke suddenly and screamed as Cornelius nearly stepped on him.

The boy ran ahead for a few paces, shouting excitedly to them before stopping, raising a pistol over his head and firing off a flare. Cornelius never broke stride and the boy ran after them.

"You don't think they're a lynch mob, do you?" asked Spyder. "For me doing over that memory?"

"I don't think so," said Shrike. "But if anyone does anything stupid, Cornelius can run us to the coast."

Other lookouts popped out of the sand as they approached the city, gawkers, too. It all made Spyder nervous, and he kept his hand on his knife, but each group smiled and waved at them as they passed. No one seemed upset to see them and better yet, thought Spyder, none of them looked like cops.

A group of twenty or more robed men and women met them at a wadi just outside the city walls. Dignitaries. Local bigwigs, thought Spyder. They had that self-important air about them, like the kind of crowd back home that gave a million dollars to the symphony just so they can get a plaque and their name in a newsletter. What the hell did they want? He slipped Apollyon's blade behind his back and kept his hand on the hilt. Shrike touched his arm.

"Relax," she said. "They're friends. They'll probably give you the key to the city."

"We'll see," he said.

However time and space moved in the underworld, on Earth there had obviously been enough time for word to spread about what had happened below.

"I don't guess it would take Sherlock Holmes to figure it out," Lulu said. "There's a hole the size of Dallas in the middle of the desert."

Just to make sure no one got frisky, Spyder had Cornelius stroll right up to the Berenice officials. The dignitaries looked a bit nervous by the proximity of the giant spider, but they all smiled and applauded as Spyder and the others climbed off. A gray-haired man with fierce Maori-style facial tattoos, clearly the head of the delegation, embraced each of them as they came down. With his hand on Spyder's shoulder, the tattooed man turned to the other dignitaries and began a quick speech in a flowing, melodious language.

Spyder looked at Shrike. "You got a clue what this guy's saying?"

"He's speaking Ubari. It's an old city-state built in the First Sphere. I haven't heard it spoken in a long time," she said. "He's calling us the 'Saviors of Light.' 'Defenders of Light.' Something like that."

"If at any point he says 'prison bitches,' let us know," said Lulu.

The Ubarian ambassador said something while standing next to each of them, gesturing extravagantly, clearly enjoying his moment in the spotlight. The assembled delegates nodded and laughed politely. It looked to Spyder that a lot of the crowd were like him, not understanding the man, but going along with the group out of politeness or ritual. He spotted one man off to the side in the ordinary working robes of a merchant, rolling a cigarette. Spyder held up two fingers in the universal gesture of smoking. The man smiled and handed Spyder the cigarette he'd just finished, and lit it with a small gray stone that emitted a jet of flame when he breathed across it. Spyder took a long puff and bowed a little thanks, and then passed the smoke to Lulu, who took it eagerly.

"It's their great honor to greet us after our battle with the Princes of Despair," said Shrike.

"Who's that? The Clerks, you think?"

"Maybe. All I know is, they're happy to see us and no one is going to be arrested or lynched."

"Good news. He going to shut up soon, you think?"

Lulu came over and handed the cigarette back to Spyder. She dug in the sand with her boot, then half-turned away from the dignitaries.

"That tall blonde guy in the back look familiar?" she asked.

Spyder scanned the crowd discreetly, not letting his gaze linger anywhere too long.

"Should he?"

"Isn't he that prince from the airship? The one Primo was talking to on TV?"

"Bel. His ship got stuck to ours. I guess the prick didn't die in the dogfight, after all."

"Maybe we can get a ride with him. He owes us," Lulu said.

"How d'you figure?"

"We saw him fuck up big time. And we're the Power Rangers of Light or whatever. He'll fart and tap dance for us if we ask."

"I'll settle for a drink and a shower."

"We're invited to a banquet in our honor," Shrike said. "All of Berenice, Ubari and the families of the Second Sphere want to honor us."

Spyder smiled at the man and nodded. "Can we say no?"

"They won't be happy."

"Tell him we need to get your father," Spyder said. "Tell him Dad's sick and in danger. We have to get to him fast."

Shrike stepped forward and smiled at the crowd, with all the dignity she could muster. She spoke slowly, hesitantly, taking long pauses, groping for words. Spyder and Lulu finished the cigarette and Spyder tucked the stub into his pocket. The man in the merchant robes came forward and gave them his bag of tobacco, along with his rolling papers. Spyder accepted, nodding sincere thanks.

"This hero thing doesn't half suck," he said.

"Roll me a smoke, John Wayne," Lulu replied.

When Shrike finished, the Ubari dignitary began chattering and gesturing again. His guests nodded solemnly and looked at Spyder.

"We off the hook?" he asked.

"I think so," said Shrike. "He's saying that we're true champions appointed by god, I think, or some kind of giant bird. That we care so much for humanity that we can't even stop to celebrate a victory…you get the idea."

The Ubarian grew quiet. He turned and embraced Spyder and the others in turn. The dignitaries all rushed forward to shake their hands and kiss their cheeks, as the group made their way back to Cornelius.

When Bel came forward to shake, Spyder held on to his hand. "Tell this asshole we need a lift out of here," he said to Shrike.

She spoke quietly to the prince as the other dignitaries clustered around, praising them in a dozen languages. They're worse than demons, Spyder thought. Demons can't help being creepy.

A moment later Shrike returned. "It's set. We can head out in an hour, when the ship is ready to launch."

"Cool."

When they'd all climbed onto Cornelius' back, Spyder ordered him to rise as quickly as possible. The dignitaries gave a collective "Ooo," as the man-machine whirred and clanked to life and set out around the city walls to where the airships were berthed.

They waited with the prince beneath his new scorpion airship that seemed half again as big as the old one. The prince barked orders to a small group of deck hands waiting on the ground and these were relayed up to the ship in an elaborate series of whistles and arms gestures. A few minutes later, a huge cargo net was lowered down from the ship. Cornelius stepped into the net and curled his legs under his body, settling down like a giant cat. With a jerk, Spyder, Shrike, Lulu and Cornelius were hoisted up and onto the prince's airship.

Half an hour later, the big scorpion banked gently starboard and headed out to sea with a dozen other airships trailing behind. The morning sun turned the edges of the ships to fire, so that Bel's was trailed by a burning swan, a school of fiery fish, a glowing snake skeleton and a perfect silver sphere that reflected the sky, sea and all the other ships nearby.

"You sure this guy knows the way to Alexandria?" Spyder asked Shrike.

"He doesn't, but his navigators know their way through all the Spheres. Relax."

Prince Bel gave them his best rooms. They happily cleaned up and settled in. When they weren't busy sleeping, crew members brought in a constant stream of food and wine. Shrike didn't let on that she could speak the prince's language, and enjoyed reporting what she heard while eavesdropping.

"It's like a game of Telephone," she said. "The rumors circulate, getting bigger and bigger. Spyder is an archangel or maybe the new Lucifer. I get the feeling that a lot of asylums emptied across the Spheres when Hell came down."

Spyder relaxed on a silk-covered fainting couch, with Shrike curled up next to him.

"It's nice to be well thought of for a change," he said.

"Can't argue with that," Lulu said, blowing smoke rings and watching them float away through an open window.

The trip was calm and slow. Exactly what they needed, Spyder thought. He and Shrike disappeared into the unoccupied rooms in their wing of the ship and made love as often as they could. At other times, Shrike went up on deck and practiced with her sword, getting used to having her sight back. However, in the back of his mind, regardless of whatever they were doing, was always the image of Madame Cinders. What the hell was he supposed to do when they confronted her? He shook his head, pushing the thought back into the dark. What had the Count said? "You will never have more than what you have at this moment." If that's true, thought Spyder, it's all right with me.

By the time Bel delivered them to Alexandria, they were getting twitchy and restless. Shrike had spotted angels flying near the ship one night. They couldn't decide if that was a good sign or bad, but decided it was time to get off.

The prince, who'd kept his distance during the flight, appeared in full royal drag when it was time for them to disembark. He and Shrike exchanged a few polite words on deck, but it was obvious that he was as anxious to have them gone, as they were to get away from him. With a wave of his hand, the cargo net lowered Cornelius to the ground in an open area near Alexandria's main port. Spyder, Shrike and Lulu were already on the spider's back.

"It looks like Brighton," Cornelius said. "I think. Maybe not. But it's very beautiful."

What first struck Spyder about being back in an earthly city with cars and humans, pollution and fast-food joints, was how completely unremarkable it felt to be riding on the back of a giant mechanical spider borrowed from a friend in Hell, moving unseen through streets alongside the spirits, angels and fantastic beasts that inhabited the other Spheres. Shrike directed Cornelius to the tangled streets of the Medina, and they retraced the route Primo had taken them just days before. Seems like a century, Spyder thought, as they turned a corner and seemed to leave ordinary Alexandria and entered the ruins of the necropolis complex. As before, thin children stood on enormous stones watching them. This time, though, a few of the older children waved to them and turned to whisper to each other before their parents came and nervously hustled them away.

"That's a bit more honest," said Spyder. "Seems like everyone knows who we are, but someone finally admitted they're not happy to see us."

"Not everyone loves a god-killer," said Shrike quietly.

"You said the Clerks weren't gods."

"They're weren't. But I'm not sure that detail means much to these people."

"Probably know there's a shit storm coming," said Lulu, "If this Cinders bitch is what you say she is."

"She is," replied Shrike. "And more."

At the next bend in the road, the great onion dome and minarets of Madame Cinders' compound swung into view.

FIFTY-NINE
AT THE END OF THE DAY, LUCK ALWAYS FAILS

"You lose my Gytrash and bring me back this useless deviant?" rasped Madame Cinders.

They stood before Madame Cinders in her tower room. The over-sweet scent of mutant orchids and the old woman's rotting flesh almost made Spyder gag.

"One, we didn't lose him. He was our friend and he died trying to get that damned book for you," Spyder said. "Two, we didn't bring Lulu back for you, lady. You don't deserve her used panty shields. And three, if you think deviants are useless, we must not know the same deviants."

"Give me my book."

"What's the magic word all good children say when they want something?"

They'd entered Madame Cinders' fortress without bothering to wait for her servants to open the front gates. Spyder had Cornelius kick his way through. The splintering wood and twisting iron hinges flew to pieces with a very satisfying amount of noise. Ten of Cinders' guards had run into the courtyard, but they scattered when they got a good look at Cornelius. Spyder and the others had strolled straight through Cinders' palace and up her tower with Cornelius guarding their rear. No one challenged them as they went.

"Give me my book," repeated Madame Cinders.

"Pretty please, with sugar on top," said Spyder. "That's what good children say."

It had been a tight squeeze, getting Cornelius up the narrow staircase to the top of Cinders' tower. He had to turn his great mechanical body sideways and crab slowly upward, his head cutting a deep scar into the top of the passage.

Spyder gestured for Cornelius to come forward and drop the book. As it hit the floor, the tower shook as if an earthquake had hit it. Cinders' guards looked around anxiously, as bones, dried herbs and potions tumbled from the shelves, but Madame Cinders showed no outward reaction. Spyder wasn't surprised. She looked even worse, more inhuman than when they'd left her.

"I've heard about your doings in the underworld. You think you have power now that you've defeated a few miscreant angels," she said. "But you know nothing about power."

Madame Cinders was no longer in her wheelchair. She was laid out flat on a kind of mechanical gurney, atop a pile of stained silk pillows. She looked at them reflected in a gold-framed mirror perched at an angle above her head. Spyder was sure she'd shrunk in size. Were her legs missing? The pump system, that injected and drained whatever horrible fluids kept her feeble flesh moving, had doubled in size and complexity, and was nearly as large as the gurney. Still, even trapped in that ruined body, she managed to project both menace and intelligence. Spyder didn't like looking at her. She stank like an old abattoir. Spyder patted his pockets, found the last of the tobacco he'd acquired at Berenice and began rolling a cigarette.

"There's no smoking in the presence of the Madame," said one of her guards. Spyder ignored him. He licked the paper lengthwise and rolled the cigarette closed.

Madame Cinders continued, "Any fool can stumble into luck once, twice, even a hundred times, but at the end of the day, luck always fails. Then, skill and knowledge are required. You have neither. The Butcher Bird has some, but not enough to save you both."

"I have plenty of skill. I'm a pretty good tattoo artist. And I can always pour beer without it getting all foamy," said Spyder.

"The last time you were here, the Butcher Bird was the one who spoke. Now, puffed up and preening, you do all the talking. Or are you the distraction while she carries out some action against me?"

"I'm not speaking, witch, because I have nothing to say to you," said Shrike.

Cinders laughed her awful, gurgling laugh. "But you have your sight, child. And soon you will have your father. I should think you'd be grateful for these things."

"If we're not gushing and grateful it's 'cause you lied to us. The book was never yours. You conned and you lied and you blackmailed us into stealing it for you," said Spyder.

"Did I? How wrong of me." Cinders' pumps kicked into action, hissing and cranking, filling the tower room with noise. A thick green discharge was extracted from Cinders' midsection while separate pink and clear fluids dripped through tubes embedded in her skull.

"Neither your feigned outrage nor your glibness can hide your fear, boy. You forget, your mind is as clear and open to me as the sky in mid-summer. I know you want to keep me from taking the book, but you cannot. You know my vengeance would be fearsome. There's the girl's father. And the other thing."

"What other thing?" Spyder asked.

"How is my father?" demanded Shrike.

"Well. And quite himself. No longer mad," said Madame Cinders. "You've gotten what you wanted, yet you've come here full of malice and with the intention of denying me the book."

"What's the other thing?" asked Spyder.

The old woman laughed. "You have no idea, do you? You really know nothing about power." In the mirror, Madame Cinders' eyes flickered toward her guards. "Kill them."

Shrike was moving before the old woman had finished speaking, slashing one guard across the midsection before his sword was drawn, and then slicing through another's throat. Crouching, she spun and ripped her blade through the knees of two guards who rushed her from behind. As the men fell, she lunged and disemboweled a third. Launching herself into the air, she caught the last guard with a kick to the temple that sent him rolling over a table.

Lulu had the four-ten up at her shoulder and was blowing holes in guards and the walls of Madame Cinders' tower. Spyder ducked as a guard swung his sword at his head. Springing from his knees, he thrust Apollyon's blade up and into the man's heart.

An arrow shot past Shrike's right ear. She whirled around and saw one of the now legless guards reloading a crossbow. Shrike brought her sword down in a sharp arc, slicing off the guard's arm below the elbow. When she advanced on the second legless guard, he held his empty, trembling hands out before him in a gesture of terrified submission. Shrike turned and swung her blade towards Madame Cinders, but the old woman was ready. Later, Spyder realized that Madame Cinders had thrown her guards at Shrike as a sacrifice, knowing that she'd tear them to pieces, but would be distracted enough not to see what was coming.

In the fraction of a second it took for Shrike to turn her blade toward Cinders, the old woman pressed together the withered claws that were her hands. A screeching filled the air, like the metal wheels of a dozen subway trains slamming on their brakes at the same time and Shrike was lifted from the floor in the jaws of one of Madame Cinders' enormous mechanical orchids. The serrated blades of the machine's jaws tightened on Shrike's ribs until she screamed.

"Cornelius!" Spyder shouted.

The spider clattered forward, its metal legs gouging holes in the stone floor as it shot at Madame Cinders. Spyder climbed onto a table and tried to reach Shrike's outstretched hand. Lulu shot at the base of the metal bloom, but her shots bounced off, filing the air with hot shrapnel. Cinders didn't notice them or didn't care. She threw a small glass vial at Cornelius. It broke on the ground before him and where the fluid splashed on him, his metallic body glowed and began to melt. Cornelius screamed in fear and pain as the internal fire spread throughout his body. He turned and ran for the stairs. Blinded by the heat, he missed and smashed into the far wall, exploding into a thousand twitching fragments of bone and metal.

"This, you must have guessed, is the other thing. Taking the thing you love," said Madame Cinders. "You won't attack as long as I can kill the girl. It's in your eyes. See how easy it is to stop you? You know nothing about power." She turned her gaze to the iron orchid and it lifted its head, carrying Shrike almost to the ceiling. She hung limply in its jaws, not fighting anymore. Spyder swore he could hear her ribs crack.

"No one in this world or any other will hold me in this dying body any longer," Madame Cinders said. "The Dominions and I will rule completely. I'm not greedy. Let them have the universe. I'm happy with this one small world."

Cinders reached under the folds of her hijab and pulled, breaking a thin gold chain that held a small vial around her neck. Pushing a button on her gurney, she rolled forward, positioning herself next to the great book.

"I've guarded this vial for a hundred years," she said. "It's the last of my blood. I had it extracted when my body succumbed to the curse, after returning from Hell. I've been a slave to these machines ever since. No more. With this blood sacrifice, I'll be reborn into a new body." Madame Cinders inclined her head toward Shrike. "Perhaps I'll take hers. If I haven't already broken it too badly."

She raised her shriveled hand and upended the vial over the Dominions' book. The thick red fluid spread over the book's face like a living thing. It smoked where it touched the runes. The blood bubbled, and the book began to drink it down. Then it rose slowly and silently until it hovered just above Madame Cinders' head. She pushed open the cover and ran her hand ecstatically over the thick pages. With another small gesture she brought the book closer to her face until it was almost touching her. Then, she bent her head forward and bit into it, chewed and swallowed.

As the old woman ate, Lulu came to where Spyder stood. When he saw her twitch the barrel of the four-ten up a few inches, he reached over and pushed the gun back down. "No," he whispered.

The old woman ripped at the book with her teeth.

"I consume myself. I consume the wisdom of the true gods," she said. It sounded like some spell or prayer. She seemed to have forgotten about Spyder and Lulu, her dying guards, everyone else in the room. "Let their power fill me." Each time she swallowed a piece of the book, her voice grew stronger. When Spyder could see her arms, the flesh was transforming, returning to a more natural color.

When Madame Cinders had eaten all of the book's pages, she sat up on her gurney, looked at Spyder and Lulu and smiled. "You have no idea what this is like. I can see everything. Every Sphere, every creature and blade of grass within. This is what the Dominions see. These are the eyes of god." Her flesh returned quickly, and as she spoke, her face transformed to that of the young woman in the painting above the Empire desk. She was human, almost beautiful. Spyder hated her even more now.

All that was left of the book was the spine, and Madame Cinders devoured it quickly, impatient to finish her meal. With her new, strong hands, Madame Cinders pulled the tubes from her arms and body. She turned and slid slowly from the gurney to the floor, wobbling on her legs like a newborn calf. Spyder looked up at Shrike. She wasn't moving at all. Madame Cinders walked toward Lulu and him. He took a step back, but a fallen table blocked him from moving any further.

She stood in front of Spyder and stretched like a cat, feeling her body coming back to life. Then she leaned toward him and whispered, "Am I not beautiful?" She giggled like a young woman just finding her body for the first time and realizing the power in her flesh. "Do you want me?" she asked him in a purring, seductive voice.

Spyder stared at her. "Fuck you."

"Yes," she said. "Fuck me. No one's done that in a long time. And when I'm satisfied, I'll teach you to use that power you have but are going to squander."

"I don't want anything from you."

"Don't you?" she asked. The metal flower moved and Shrike screamed. Spyder froze where he was.

"All right," he said. "Anything you want. I'll do it." Out of the corner of his eye he could see Lulu, also frozen in place, her face drained of all color.

Madame Cinders put her cheek next to Spyder's. "Will you kill your deviant friend for me? Just for my amusement?" Spyder didn't answer. "No? You care about her that much? Good. I'll keep her with the other to keep you from developing foolish ideas."

"What do you want with me?" asked Spyder. "You're becoming one of the gods now. You can have anyone you want."

She smiled at him brightly. "I want you because you have the power. I can't have that just wandering around in the world," she said. "And because I don't like you, and it will kill you to stay with me, but you will anyway because of these two." She moved her hand toward Shrike and Lulu. "You know nothing about power. But I'll teach you," she said, and leaned in to kiss Spyder on the lips. As their lips came together something sizzled in the air and they were both thrown apart by an electric shock that seemed to burn through every muscle in Spyder's body.

Madame Cinders grabbed onto the gurney and quickly pulled herself from the floor. "Why did you do that?" she screamed, her face a deep and furious crimson.

"I didn't do anything," said Spyder. "It just happened."

"It was very rude. I'll teach you never to be rude to me again." She turned toward Lulu and raised her hand. Spyder jumped in front of her and pulled Lulu behind him. But instead of hurling a spell at them, Madame Cinders doubled over in pain and hit the floor screaming.

"What is this? What have you done?" she yelled.

"It's not my fault," said Spyder. "I didn't expect you to eat it, you silly bitch."

"What?"

"John the Baptist's heart. I hid it in the spine of the book. I thought it would maybe make the magic not work. I sure as hell didn't see this coming…"

Madame Cinders fell on her stomach, her body convulsing, her shoulders twitching. Her head snapped up and lolled to the side. Her eyes were pearl white and flames seemed to dance inside. She drew in a long, harsh breath that began as a hissing in her lungs, rising in intensity until it was the growl of a rabid wolf. Boils, red and livid, grew and burst along her right arm and spread across her body. Her white hijab, now stained with her blood, began to smoke as her skin gave off a black incandescent glow. Her bones were visible beneath the skin, and soon the skin itself was peeling and dropping off in long, dry strips. She seemed to shrink, as if something were draining her from the inside. Runes rose like welts on her blackened skin.

Whatever force she used to control her mechanical flower suddenly broke and Shrike fell to the floor. Spyder ran over and took Shrike's face in his hands. "You all right? Talk to me." He held her until she opened her eyes. "You can't get away from me that easy," he said.

"Look," said Lulu, pointing to Madame Cinders.

The witch was on her feet, her arms out, using every bit of her strength to keep her balance. She seemed paralyzed in place, unable to move. Suddenly, her head snapped toward Spyder. She took one step and the thin blackened skin that still covered her bones, sloughed off and fell to the floor like boiling tar. Her bones sank into the thick mess and disappeared.

Spyder and Lulu tried to pull Shrike to her feet, but she screamed in pain. Spyder lifted her shirt and found the deep bruising and cracked ribs. Her skin was lacerated with the serrated tooth marks of the orchid's blades. Without thinking about it, he lay his hands on her and closed her eyes. Soon, he could hear Shrike's breathing become slow and steady. A few minutes later, she could stand on her own.

They searched every room in the tower until they found Shrike's father—alive, though frail and confused. Wrapping him in a blanket they found in the guards' barracks room, they bundled the old man down from the tower.

Madame Cinders' servants waited anxiously in the courtyard as the four came out.

"We need a coach and horse," Shrike told them. The servants didn't need to be told twice.

They rode back through the Medina and just managed to squeeze the cart into the tunnels that ran to Alcatraz. Shrike held her sleeping father in her arms the whole way, speaking to him quietly as they went. Spyder put his arm around her. She reached up and squeezed his hand. He could see her fighting back tears.

When they reached the old cavalry stables, Lulu asked, "What's it going to be like back home, you think?"

"I don't know," said Spyder. "You're covered, I guess, but I might have to leave town. We'll see."

"Going to be weird to be back. You know with a full set of eyes and insides and skin."

"Weird's not so bad when you get used to it."

"No shit."

They stepped down from the coach, but when Spyder turned to help Shrike and her father, they were gone.

SIXTY
WORSHIPPING CROCODILES

"Oh, you poor things," said Mrs. Porter.

When they got back to San Francisco, Spyder and Lulu, broke and shaky, managed to hitch a ride with the Porters, a family on vacation from Baton Rouge, Louisiana, who'd had their bags stolen off the luggage carousel at SFO.

The Porters were very sympathetic to the nice Texas couple they found stranded at Fisherman's Wharf, after Spyder fed them a story about their brand new Toyota hatchback being stolen. After they'd all piled into the Porters' SUV, with both parents and three kids, Lyle Porter, the husband, launched into a nonstop monologue all the way to Spyder's warehouse.

"These people they got workin' at the airport, they're not stealing to be evil. Where they're from, stealing's a way of life. Everybody does it, from the president to the police chief, from the school teachers to the local witch doctor. Every one of 'em's a goddam thief. Hell, if I was in their shoes, I'd probably steal, too. But this is America. We don't need to do that kind of shit, pardon my French, here. You work hard and you get your reward. But, I suppose, when you're raised worshipping crocodiles or some such nonsense, anything goes. Am I right?"

"Right as rain, Lyle," said Spyder, hoping they got home soon or got hit by a semi.

Lulu crashed with Spyder that first disembodied night back. Realizing he had no idea where his keys were, Spyder had to wheel over a dumpster from the car repair place next door, then climb onto the roof and drop down into the upper loft through a skylight. In the morning, Spyder found his battered old hardback of *Naked Lunch* on the bookshelf and pulled out the hundred dollars in emergency money he kept hidden in the spine. He and Lulu got on his old bike, an oil-leaking Kawasaki Police 1000, and Spyder took her back to her place in the Mission.

For the duration of the ride, Spyder obsessively checked his mirrors and scanned the street, waiting for a siren or a vigilante to point him out as a killer or a child molester. But it didn't happen. As he pulled up in front of Lulu's building, Rubi was coming out. She smiled brightly and kissed both Lulu and Spyder, giving no indication that she recalled Spyder punching her. Lulu gave a shrug and followed Rubi back inside, after blowing Spyder a kiss from the steps.

Spinning a quick one-eighty across the median, Spyder cruised over to the Haight. The tattoo studio was still gone, and the vacant lot still looked like whatever had occupied it had burned. Spyder couldn't decide if that bit of historical consistency was comforting or not.

He left the Kawasaki parked between an art car covered in plush toys having sex with naked Barbies and a Jews for Jesus panel truck. He went into the Long Life Cupboard health food store. Immediately, his stomach was burning and his shoulders were one big knot of tension. Spyder's fight-or-flight instincts were locked on high alert for any funny look, wayward gesture or wandering beat cops. No one even acknowledged him except the cute blonde hippie chick at the register who smiled and asked, "How's it hanging?" as Spyder paid for his orange juice. "Sucks about your shop," she said.

"Thanks."

"You opening another one?"

"We haven't decided yet."

"Let me know if you do. I was thinking about getting a mudra tattooed on my shoulder," she said. "Tell Lulu hi, and don't be a stranger."

"You got it," said Spyder. He smiled awkwardly and fled the place. It was all too much. The city. Too many people. Too much noise. Copper jitters. The angels, demons and strange beasts that had wandered in from other Spheres were there, too, but their presence seemed kind of normal. It was the athletic shoe ads on the buses, the wandering tourists and ultra-hipsters, the panhandling poser kids that were making it hard for him to breathe. Spyder downed his OJ, gunned the bike into traffic and drove home. He'd been social enough for one day. No need to push my luck and find that one guy who still thinks I'm Charlie Manson, he thought.

Back at the warehouse, Spyder sorted through a pile of mail on the floor by the front door. There was an official-looking letter from an insurance company. Inside was a settlement check for the burned studio. The check displayed a prominent *one* followed by many more zeroes than Spyder had ever seen on a document relating to him.

Later that night, he met Lulu for a drink at the Bardo Lounge and showed her the check.

"Rubi, give my future ex-husband a drink on me."

"Just make it a Coke, thanks."

"You feelin' sick?"

"Like I'm wearing borrowed skin."

"Me, too," Lulu said. "Still haven't heard anything from Shrike?"

Spyder shook his head. He pulled out a fresh pack of cigarettes, cracked the pack and removed one. Lulu stole one and lit Spyder's smoke with the pink Zippo she'd almost lost by the Bone Sea.

"Not a word," said Spyder.

"We been sitting around too long. We need to work."

"I'm not ready to even think about opening another shop. Maybe we could get a couple of chairs in a shop on the street. Big Bill's or Colored People."

"There you go."

Rubi came back with their drinks. "Cheers," she said, giving them a big smile. Spyder was almost used to Rubi not hating him.

Lulu raised her glass in a toast.

"The Kaiser's moustache."

"To Lucifer's tail." Then, "To Primo."

"To Primo."

A demon sat on the stool to Spyder's right, nursing a glass of Jäger-meister. Bilal, the demon, fat and shirtless, poured the Jäger into a mouth that opened in his chest. He looked straight ahead, trying not to catch Spyder's eye.

Spyder leaned over to him. "What's the difference between a demon and a glass of beer?" Spyder asked.

Bilal shifted his eyes toward Spyder, but refused to turn his head. "What?"

"Beer's still good without a head." Spyder put his hand on the demon's shoulder. "Remember me?"

The demon turned away.

"Talking meat all looks pretty much the same to me."

"You're Bilal?"

"Maybe."

"Then you should remember me. Or do you curse so many people that we all blur together?"

"You need to go away now," Bilal said. His chest-mouth opened slowly, emitting a growl and hot breath that reeked of wet decay.

"Stop that," said Spyder. He touched the middle finger of his right hand to Bilal's chest. The skin shifted like sand, sealing the extra mouth shut. "What were you saying?"

The demon heaved its enormous bulk from the barstool, feeling for its lost mouth.

"I'll destroy you," it said.

"Yeah, your first one worked out so well. What do you do for an encore? Not swallow my soul?" Spyder took a sip of his Coke and a long drag off his cigarette. It was good to have real smokes again. "I was in the book. I am the book. And your demon noise sounds like cricket farts to me now. I have Apollyon's blade. I'm the devil's brother. I killed the Black Clerks. What are you but some back alley rat-eater who likes to take out his bad moods on people who can't fight back?"

Bilal was breathing hard. He was angry, but Spyder could tell that he was even more scared.

"Leave me alone," said Bilal.

"All I wanted was to be left alone, but you tried to eat me. When that didn't work, you cursed me. Made people think I was Hannibal Lecter."

"That was before."

"Before what?"

"Before I knew who you were."

"And who's that?"

"The Painted Man."

"Don't you forget it. Now, what's the magic word?"

"What word?"

"What do we say when we've fucked up and we want forgiveness?" asked Spyder.

Bilal hesitated, shook his head. He stared at the floor. John Cale's version of "Heartbreak Hotel" came on the jukebox.

"I'm sorry," said Bilal.

Spyder nodded, patted the demon's barstool.

"Climb back up in the saddle, big man. Let me buy you another Jäger."

"You're not going to kill me?"

"Hell no," said Spyder. "I understand about bad moods and being stuck someplace maybe you don't want to be. So, you get to keep your head and I get to not spill demon guts all over this nice, clean shirt."

Bilal gestured to his chest.

"Could you?"

"Sorry." Spyder touched the demon. The skin of Bilal's chest shifted, unsealing his second mouth.

Rubi brought him a shot of Jäger and Spyder passed it to the demon. He clinked his Coke against Bilal's glass in a toast.

"Tell me the truth," said Spyder, leaning in close. "Do we taste more like pork or chicken?"

SIXTY-ONE
THE OTHER SIDE OF THE WIND

A month later, the initial rush of being back home had worn off. Spyder waited for his mind to settle down, his moods to slide into their regular patterns; he waited for the world to become solid under his feet, but it didn't happen.

He ate. He slept. He ordered a new tattoo gun and an autoclave from an online wholesaler. When they arrived, he got as far as opening the box before losing interest. Every day he went out to buy food, but just came home with more cigarettes. When the insurance check covering the fire in the tattoo shop arrived, he finally admitted that he wasn't going to go back to work anytime soon. After a few calls, he got Lulu a table at Luscious Abrasion, just down the street from where their shop had been. He'd visit her there every couple of days.

It had been more than a month, but he was startled every time he saw her. She looked so good, so happy to be back. Soon, it was hard to remember all that the Clerks had done to her.

"You look lost at sea, sailor." Lulu and Spyder were having burgers at an outdoor café near Golden Gate Park. Lulu stole another of Spyder's American Spirits and lit it with the pink lighter he'd taken back from Lucifer while they were still in Hell.

"I'm feeling a little adrift, yeah. No big deal. It'll pass."

"You need to work, dude. Get back to what you know and what you're good at. I bet you could really make the colors dance now that you've got all those Dr. Strange super powers."

He shook his head and took a bite of his burger. The meat was chewy and tasteless in his mouth.

"You'd think so, wouldn't you?" he asked. "But I can't control it. I'm a little scared of my hands. What if my mind wanders—and it's wandering a lot these days—and I turn some baby goth girl into a Black Clerk?"

"If you make any Angelina Jolies, save one for me." She smiled at him and when he didn't smile back, Lulu shook her head. "I don't understand why you can't just do stuff now. You healed me back at Cinders' place. And you fixed Shrike."

"That was all one big rush. Like I was running, and as long as I kept running, I could do anything. But now I stopped and I can't find my feet. The more I think about the magic, the worse I get at it."

"What are you going to do?"

"Don't know. The insurance money came through, so I don't really have to work right now. Besides, I dream about money and there's gold in my sock drawer when I wake up."

"Must be nice," said Lulu, irritation edging into her voice. "What'd be even nicer was if you got over this whiny little bitch thing you're in and you went out and found Shrike."

"You don't think I've tried? I've been back to the night market. Down to the Coma Gardens. I even busted into the tunnel under Alcatraz. Nothing. No one's seen her. She's gone."

"Sorry, bro."

"I should go."

He didn't tell Lulu the whole truth about his home life. The magic or power or whatever it was he'd acquired inside the book was getting more out of control every day. The deeper he sank into his dark mood, the more dangerous the magic became. Each night, he woke up from restless dreams to find his apartment choked with hellfire or locked in glacial ice. His bedroom was invaded by souls wandering in from the edge of the Bone Sea. Galaxies swirled where the ceiling should be, and he could see the Dominions floating between the stars, eating worlds and swimming in swirling clouds of cosmic dust.

Spyder couldn't stand being in the warehouse anymore, so he rented an ancient, rundown metal workshop in the industrial zone on a winding road out by the old Navy yards. The place was just four metal walls and an aluminum roof with a razorwire fence outside. There was nothing inside the shop for him to break or freeze or burn up when he dreamed. All Spyder took with him was his motorcycle, an air mattress, cartons of cigarettes and beer. Everything else he dealt with as he needed. During the day, he kept Apollyon's blade under the mattress. It mostly came in handy on those sleepless nights when he thought he was going crazy. He would take out the knife and feel its weight in his hand, smell a faint echo of Hell when he held the grip close to his face. When sleep refused to come, he thought about hiring an airship and flying deep into the desert to find the hole he'd blown in Hell's roof. Lucifer would be happy to see him and might let him stick around to help rebuild Heaven. Or would he? The fallen angel had told him to go home and live his life, but what did that even mean anymore?

What an amazing place to have gotten yourself to, he thought, when even Hell isn't an option.

In May, on Orson Welles' birthday, an old art house theater in the Mission District had a marathon screening of his films. Spyder had seen the early stuff dozens of times, so he only came for the late-night flicks, *It's All True*, Welles' doomed Brazilian epic, and *The Other Side of the Wind*, a dark, micro-budget film about a bitter director, played by John Huston. He knew there weren't enough guns or tits in either movie to get Lulu to sit through them, so he went alone.

It was almost two in the morning when the movies let out. Spyder went to the corner where he'd parked the Kawasaki and lit a cigarette. It was cold and wet. Heavy fog was blowing through the streets like sparkling ghosts.

"Hey, pony boy."

She was leaning against the front door of a check-cashing shop. Through the open door was a miserable line of restless illegals pretending not to see the down-on-their luck Caucasians who were busy pretending to be somewhere else entirely.

Spyder sat on the bike, took a drag off the American Spirit.

He said, "I have this scar on my arm. Sometimes at night I touch it just to make sure I didn't imagine it. It's where the Clerks marked me. On the floor by my bed, I have this great big knife. I close my eyes and my head is full of the craziest things. Like some kind of acid flashback, only it's not mine. It's someone else's. But when I fall asleep it's all okay because at the end of the craziness, I get the girl. Only I wake up and remember I didn't."

"I'm sorry I ran off. I'm worse at goodbyes than you are," said Shrike.

"How's your father?"

"He died."

"I'm really sorry to hear that."

"Don't be. I took him home, to the Second Sphere. He was happy when he went."

"So, there's a happy ending after all. I'm glad you both got that."

"You don't have to be so magnanimous."

Spyder nodded, took a pull on the cigarette.

"Yeah, I do. Otherwise the walls start doing that closing in thing and I want a drink and I'm trying real hard not to want that."

"You're not drinking? I'm impressed."

"I still drink. Just less." He shrugged. "Leaves more money for cigarettes."

"I'm really sorry I left you like that."

"You said that already."

Shrike walked over to him. Her eyes were clear and bright, though a little dark, as if she hadn't slept in a while.

"My father was dying. I knew it the moment I saw him back in Madame Cinders' tower. I had to take him home," Shrike said. "And I had to get away from you."

"Did I do something wrong?"

"Just the opposite. You saved me."

"Bullshit. You're the one with the sword, the one who knows magic and how to move between worlds. I was just doing card tricks."

"You don't understand. I'm a killer. I'd dedicated myself to destroying life because mine had been stolen from me. And I enjoyed taking life. Doing it for something as cheap as money made it all the better. I wanted to burn down the world for what it did to me and my family."

"I know the feeling."

"If things had gone a little differently years ago, I might have become someone like Madame Cinders. If you hadn't come along on this journey, I would have given her the book. I would have made a deal with the Dominions to bloody the whole world. I still thought about doing it, right up until the end."

"Why didn't you?"

"What do you think? I used you that first night because I wanted sex, so I gave you drugged wine. I needed someone to stand next to me at Madame Cinders', so I lied and told you she'd fix you. I needed someone who knew Hell, so I dragged you into something that could have killed you a thousand times. And I wouldn't have blinked if it had. Every time you gave me something I needed, I wanted to get rid of you. I strung you along because I knew how."

"If you came back to call me a sucker to my face, why don't you put it in a postcard and stick it up your ass?"

Shrike came closer, resting a hand on the bike's throttle, not touching him.

"I kept waiting for you to bolt. I kept waiting for you to catch on and betray me. But you wouldn't. At first I thought you were playing a game, waiting to get the book for yourself. Then, I decided it was simple self-preservation. You wanted to get out alive and get the magic to restore your precious ignorance. But you kept not betraying me. You kept..." She hesitated.

"Caring about you?"

"I told myself you were trying to manipulate me, but when you destroyed the book, I knew you'd never deceived me. I would have killed anyone to have the power in that book. You had it in your hands and you threw it away to save me."

"You know I did."

She looked away and frowned. "I couldn't bear that. Being with you brought back all these feelings I'd thought I'd burned up years ago. Then, I had my father and I knew he was dying and it was all too much. I had to run away. Can you forgive me?"

"Consider yourself forgiven," he said, putting the key in the bike's ignition.

"No," she said, holding onto his coat sleeve. "Not like that. Don't forgive me like you forgive some street urchin who picks your pocket. Save me one more time, that's all I want. Forgive me from that other part of you that refused to betray me or leave me."

Spyder tossed his cigarette, looked at the crowd milling in front of the theater. "I can. I do. For a long time I wanted to strangle you for that Houdini in the tunnel, but I knew you must have had a good reason. And I always knew I'd see you again."

"Really?"

"No. That was me being gallant. I didn't know what the hell to think when you took off. I was going out of my mind and I fucking hated you." He turned and looked at her. She was beautiful in the drifting fog. "But you didn't lift my wallet, which is more than I can say for most girls you meet in alleys."

Shrike smiled and leaned against him.

"Maybe we can go to your place and try that first meeting again."

"On one condition."

"What?"

"Teach me magic. I'm going out of my mind. I can't control it. I dreamed about my younger self the other night and in the morning the street outside was full of all the cars I'd ever stolen."

Shrike stroked his hair and nodded.

"I can only teach you the little I know. But there are others who can teach you more." She shrugged. "I'm going to take back my kingdom from the brigands who now hold it. If you come along, learn to control your power, we can figure out a way to drive the Dominions back into the oblivion where they belong."

Spyder ran his hands down Shrike's back, thrilling to her warmth and smell, the reality of her presence.

"It's sweet, how you have no ambition," he said.

"I'll have to leave this Sphere to get ready. You'll come with me?"

"There's not much holding me here," he said. "I can't go without telling Lulu."

"In the morning," said Shrike. "In the morning."

Shrike climbed onto the back of Spyder's bike and wrapped her arms around him. Spyder kicked over the motor and gunned the engine. They shot off and the fog closed in behind them, swallowing the tail lights and even the engine noise.

They were gone.

RICHARD KADREY IS A FREELANCE WRITER LIVING IN San Francisco. He has written about art, culture and technology for *Wired, The San Francisco Chronicle, Discovery Online, The Site* and *Wired For Sex* on the G4 cable network.

He is also the author of three other novels: *Metrophage, Kamikaze L'Amour,* and *Angel Scene.*

Along with the Pander Brothers, he developed the original comic, *Accelerate,* for DC/Vertigo, which will be reprinted as a graphic novel in Fall 2007 by Image Comics. His short fiction has appeared in *Isaac Asimov's Science Fiction Magazine, Interzone,* Rudy Rucker's *Flurb, InfiniteMatrix.net,* as well as a number of anthologies. His story, "Goodbye Houston Street, Goodbye," was nominated for the British Science Fiction Association Best Short Story award.

In 2001, Haft Entertainment turned his story "Carbon Copy" into the truly awful film, *No Ordinary Baby,* starring Bridget Fonda.

Kadrey is currently working on a new novel and continuing his photographic side project, KaosBeautyKlinik.